COME
A LITTLE
CLOSER
Rachel Abbott

black dot
publishing

Published in 2018 by Black Dot Publishing Ltd

ISBN 978-1-9999437-0-7

British Library Cataloguing in Publication Data
A CIP catalogue record for this book is available from
the British Library

Page design and typesetting by SilverWood Books
Printed in the UK by TJ International on responsibly sourced paper

Find out more about the author and her other books at
www.rachel-abbott.com

Prologue

I don't know myself any more. My life is unrecognisable – severed into two distinct periods: before – when I could feel the wind on my skin, watch the sky turn from blue to black, hear the birds singing in the morning, smell the earth, damp with rain; and after – the life I am in now, where I cannot tell if it is night or day and the only sound I hear is the slap, slap of bare feet on a linoleum floor.

I sit on my narrow bed, staring at the bare wall opposite, wondering how I came to be here. But I can find no answers. All I know for certain is that they are coming. They come every night.

I didn't understand how easy it could be to lose a life. To lose myself. But now I am not me any more. I'm someone else. Someone I don't recognise.

My name is Judith. And I killed a man.

Four Weeks Earlier

1

'Night, everyone,' Sharon shouted over her shoulder.

'You going already, Shaz?' she heard. She didn't know which of her friends it was, and she didn't respond. With her back to them all she raised her hand in the air and waved as she reached the exit. She didn't want them to see her face – to see the guilt in her eyes and the hot flush of her cheeks.

Sharon was looking forward to being married to Jez – he was the best – but somehow the pressure of it all, the *finality*, maybe even the predictability, had got to her, and she had persuaded her friends to meet at the club in town. Jez had gone out too, staying with his brother for the night, so there was no one to rush home to.

She had expected to be dancing until dawn with her friends, but when Sharon went to get a drink there was a good-looking bloke she had never seen before leaning against the bar, watching her, and there was no denying that the attention felt good. Usually she would have told him to get lost, but tonight everything seemed different. The music was loud, the beat making her body throb, and the flashing multicoloured lights made the most mundane seem extraordinary. Maybe it was the thought of doing something that she knew was wrong, but she had felt a pulse of excitement as the man's hand rested on her lower back, hidden from view, and then slowly started to move south.

When she turned to face him he had such hot eyes, asking her an unspoken question. It got a bit heavy – and public – as he moved his head towards hers, his hand behind her neck. But instead of kissing her, he whispered in her ear that they should get away from prying eyes, drive somewhere they could be alone, and a thrill shivered up and down her spine. Sharon agreed, suggesting a local beauty spot – Pennington Flash. There would be no one there at this time of night, and if they went separately nobody need ever know.

There had been weather warnings all day about significant snow overnight followed by a period of sub-zero temperatures. But it hadn't started yet, so Sharon wasn't worried as she fumbled around in her bag for her car keys. She had intended to have only a couple of drinks – that was why she had taken the car. Maybe she had gone over a bit, but it would be fine. She felt okay.

On the third attempt Sharon got her key into the ignition, starting the car with a roar, her foot too hard on the accelerator.

I'll drive slowly, she thought.

Sharon had been on family outings to the Flash throughout her childhood and knew the way backwards, so almost as if on autopilot she managed to negotiate the streets until finally turning off the main road towards the entrance. The first car park would be closed by now, but the main one by the lake didn't have a gate, and that's where they had agreed to meet.

The inky darkness of the car park gave Sharon goosebumps, and she took one hand from the steering wheel to rub her other arm briskly. The place was deserted, and if there was a moon it was hidden behind clouds heavy with the promised snow. The bloke hadn't arrived, but he had said he would give it five minutes after she left so no one would suspect. It only occurred to her briefly that she didn't know his name. It wasn't a relationship she was interested in, though, so it hardly mattered.

Driving to the far end of the car park where overhanging trees increased the blackness of the night, she turned her car to face the entrance. She wanted to make sure she would see him before he saw her.

She opened her window a fraction. The night was silent. She

closed her eyes and tried to block out images of Jez's smiling face.

A sound – a rattling noise – startled her. *What was that?* She switched on her headlights briefly and let out a long breath of relief. The wind had caught a discarded Coke can and was rolling it across the tarmac. She turned her lights off again, but the icy blast of air on her face and the pump of adrenaline seemed to have knocked some sense into her. What the hell was she doing? This was madness. She needed to go, to get out of there.

She reached for the ignition key, but it was too late. There was a new sound – a car engine.

Shit. It's him.

What if she told him it had been a stupid idea? But what if he didn't take it well? What if he raped her? She'd heard stories of girls being forced when they realised too late that they had made a mistake. She had to get away before he saw her.

Thanking God that her crappy car had a broken interior light, she quietly opened the door and slithered out, sliding the key into the lock with shaking fingers and turning it quickly. Bending double, Sharon scurried along the path by the edge of the still, black water, out of sight of the approaching car, and crouched behind a low shrub.

It wasn't until the car turned into the car park that she realised its headlights weren't on. *Why would he do that?*

The car circled the tarmac as if the driver was looking for someone, and she knew it could only be her. But then she looked again. The guy had told her to look out for his silver Golf. This car was dark, possibly even black, and much bigger than a Golf. It was someone else.

It didn't matter who it was. She realised how vulnerable she was – a young woman alone in the early hours of the morning in the middle of nowhere. *What an idiot.* She had to stay hidden.

The car pulled to a stop directly in front of her old Toyota, and someone got out. She couldn't make out much because the person was on the far side. Then she saw the beam from a torch. He was approaching her car, the beam searching its interior.

Oh God. Was this some kind of a set-up? Had the man in the club lured her to a deserted location for someone else – maybe more than one?

When he realises the car's empty, he's going to come hunting for me.

The man tried the door – thank God she'd locked it – and flashed the light around a bit more. He went back to the front of the car and shone the torch on the number plate. He was noting down her number! *Why would he do that?*

He walked away from the car and she thought he was leaving, but then he stepped onto the path, shining the torch first away from her and then the other way – towards her.

Sharon crouched as low as she could, dipping her head so her white face wouldn't show in the beam of light, praying her black coat would keep her hidden. She slipped off her high-heeled shoes and hid them under the bush in case she had to make a run for it.

She heard the crunch of his feet on the gravel.

He was coming.

2

As I wake up, I wonder for a moment where I am. I didn't think I would sleep – my internal clock is totally confused by travelling so far east – but maybe it is relief at all I have left behind.

I nearly didn't come, and had Ian had his way I would still be at home tending to his every need.

I'm here because of my grandfather, who for over seventy years had wanted to return to a place that was close to his heart – Burma, or Myanmar as it is now known – where he was stationed during the war. He never made it, but he bought me a ticket and asked me to promise to make the trip for him – to be his eyes and ears.

Pops died before my trip began, so he was never going to hear about the places I'm visiting, but in those last days as I sat by his sickbed he still begged me to go.

'Take a break, love,' he said, his voice breathy and faint. 'Get away from here and give yourself some space to think about your future – the kind of life you deserve. I only want you to be happy, you know that. And I don't think you are.'

It was as if he was shining a bright light on my life, especially on my relationship with Ian.

When Pops died I tried to hide my tears from Ian, but he saw me crying and told me to get over myself and move on. 'He was an old man, for God's sake. At least you don't have to take that ridiculous trip now,' he said, folding his arms as if to signify the matter was settled.

I felt a pulse of dread. I knew what was coming. 'What do you mean?' I said, hating myself for the quiver in my voice.

'You're not going all that way on your own. You don't have to now.'

He had always hated the thought of me taking the trip. It was, and always had been, a ticket for one.

Ian tried everything to sway me – from refusing to acknowledge my presence by ignoring every word I said, to blaming me for his inability to get a job. I was making him miserable, dragging him down. He wanted me to cash in the ticket so he could have a share of the refund.

'You only ever think of yourself,' he repeated over and over again.

I came close to giving in, as I had done so many times before, but I thought of Pops and how much he had wanted me to go. So I refused to be swayed by Ian's accusations that I was self-centred, thoughtless, inconsiderate; his threats to somehow hijack the holiday; his almost deranged bouts of anger as he paced the living room.

The arguments left me weak, exposed and increasingly aware of the number of times I had backed down during the year that Ian and I have been together, feeling I was the one in the wrong, the one who didn't understand how difficult I made life for the two of us. This time it was different. I saw Pops' face, his eyes telling me to be brave, to stand up for myself, to break the pattern.

I waited until the day before I was due to leave. I had been practising my lines for days, but I still stumbled over the words as I told Ian it was over between us. I wanted him to move out of my house while I was away. As I spoke I felt a shiver of fear. I couldn't meet his eyes, scared of what I would see there, and by the time I boarded the plane I felt battered and bruised by all that had happened.

I didn't realise how vulnerable I was. Maybe that was my mistake.

❖

I need to forget Ian and focus on how lucky I am to be here.

I've never stayed in such a luxurious hotel, and while there is a huge temptation to burrow back under the crisp white sheets, I need to get up and face the day. I'm half excited, half anxious. Travelling alone is a first for me, and I'm in a strange country with different customs, smells, sounds. And my confidence levels aren't where they should be right now.

In spite of the constant whisper of anxiety that haunts me, I can't wait to look out of my bedroom window and see the sights that we missed last night by arriving after dark. The streets of Yangon outside the hotel are crowded, chaotic and colourful. Street vendors have set up their stalls with bright parasols to protect their wares from the sun, and the driver of every bus, car and scooter seems to feel the need to sound his horn.

It feels odd to be somewhere so hot after leaving a Manchester landscape covered in thick snow. I had worried that the flight would be cancelled and I would have to return home, tail between my legs. Wouldn't Ian have enjoyed that? But the journey had gone like clockwork, although there had been a strange and slightly uncomfortable moment when we arrived.

We had all crowded into the lobby for our keys, anxious to get to our rooms after the long flight. I was tired, needed a shower and wasn't feeling very chatty, so I stood, head bent, staring blindly at my suitcase, listening for my name to be called. I could feel a pair of eyes watching me, burning a hole in my skin – and I lifted my head. Over by the reception desk a man was looking at me. He was on his own, and as my eyes met his I expected his attention to shift – to move on – but he didn't flinch and showed no embarrassment, continuing to stare straight into my eyes as if asking me a question. Was he single? As I am possibly the only unattached woman under sixty on the trip, did he think I might be a likely bet? I should have looked away, but I raised my eyebrows and tipped my head to one side to show that I wasn't impressed. Then my name was called, and I took my key and escaped to my room.

That was last night, and now it is a whole new day with so much to look forward to. Soon we will join the chaos below and make our way by coach to where we will board the boat and begin the journey up the Irrawaddy River.

For a second I wish I was half of a couple. Having another person by my side would be so much more comfortable than having to eat, sleep and travel alone. Then I imagine that the other half is Ian and I shudder. I can hear his voice in my head, moaning about the coach journey, telling me what to wear, mocking our fellow travellers behind their backs and expecting me to laugh with him.

I thought I needed him once. But I don't need him now.

As I board the coach I dive into the first available empty seat. Everyone is smiling and nodding at me. I can hear a lot of American accents as they shout their hellos with that relentless enthusiasm peculiar to their culture, and they all seem to know each other already. *Of course.* There was the traditional 'meet and greet' cocktail party last night, and it seems I was the only one who didn't go.

I turn my attention to the view out of the window, to the teeming mass of people going about their daily lives, both men and women wearing the colourful long skirts that I read in my travel guide are called *longyi*. As we slowly weave our way through the traffic and leave the city, passing roadside stalls showing off their goods – spices, fruit, vegetables – I notice that everyone is smiling. I wonder about their lives, and how different they might be from my own.

My thoughts are interrupted as someone plonks himself down in the seat beside me. I turn, smiling, before realising it's the man from the lobby last night.

'Hi, I'm Paul,' he says. It's a friendly greeting, but his eyes are blank, expressionless, and I feel he's weighing me up in some way that I don't understand.

I can't deal with him right now. What does he want? Is he going to hit on me? If so it's going to be very embarrassing, so I give him an apologetic smile and close my eyes, explaining that the jet lag is getting to me. He stays for a while, then I feel movement and realise he has gone to sit with more amiable people.

Now that I'm alone, I can open my eyes and start enjoying the view again. I pull out my phone to take a few photographs, grateful that I won't get a mobile signal while I'm in Myanmar unless I buy a local SIM card. And I have no intention of doing that. I feel safe, protected from Ian's rancour.

My phone's been off since I boarded the plane in Manchester, and as I turn it on I'm horrified to see that I have messages. They must have come through before I left, but the airport was noisy and I didn't check before switching it off. They've been sitting there, waiting to be discovered, ready to spew their malice when I am least expecting it.

There are at least ten texts, and I know who they are all from. I glance at the first one and I don't want to look at any more. The language is foul and I almost gasp at the vitriol. My eyes flood with tears. I realise I've been a fool, but I met Ian when I was at a low point in my life. Pops was ill, my dad was refusing to speak to me, and I was about to move to a new city where I knew no one.

Now it seems Ian is hell-bent on destroying me.

3

The two women sat at either end of a small pine table, both staring at the bowls of soup in front of them. As if by some unspoken command, they picked up their spoons at the same time and slowly started to scoop the dark brown liquid into their mouths.

A single low-wattage bulb dangled above them, creating a pool of light in the centre of the table, leaving the rest of the room in shadow. The only sound was the clink of metal spoons on earthenware bowls.

For a few moments neither of them spoke.

'She's gone, then,' the younger of the two finally said, pushing her straggly hair behind her ears. The other one grunted in agreement and carried on eating. 'She was ready, I think.'

Another grunt was all she got by way of response. The woman opposite was next in line. She had been there the longest, and was preparing herself for the day when she would leave, when her time and her usefulness were done.

'At least we get a break now,' the young woman said, trying once more to start a conversation.

There was no answer, but slowly the other woman lifted hollow eyes to look at her.

'I'm ready to go,' she said finally. 'I don't want to wait any longer.'

They rarely spoke. At times they weren't allowed to, but when they were down here, alone, they could – if they wanted to. Usually they were too tired, too lethargic, and there was always so much to do.

The young woman felt as if every bone in her body had turned to jelly. It was hard to find the strength to get through the day, and she had to force herself to get out of bed each morning.

In spite of the listlessness that she seemed unable to shake, she still sometimes tried to fight against what was happening to her. But as she kept being told, she was safe here. She was fed, warm and only had to do the tasks she was set each day to pay for her keep. The alternative was far, far worse.

But then there was the other question. How long could it last? How long before she went the way of the woman who had left two, or was it three, days earlier? That one had barely spoken a word to either of them for weeks, and had seemed relieved when her moment of release came.

'I think someone else must be coming to join us,' the older woman said, her voice flat, expressionless.

'Do you?'

'It's always the same. One out, one in.'

Somewhere in the back of the younger woman's mind, that didn't make sense. But she couldn't quite figure out why it felt wrong. It was too complicated, and it didn't matter really. It didn't change anything.

Finally they both pushed back their chairs and walked to the sink, deep in the shadows of the kitchen. It didn't matter that they could barely see there. They knew their way around in the dark. It was the same, night and day. Without another word, one rinsed the dishes, the other dried and put them away.

The young woman didn't want to go to bed, even though she was exhausted. Sometimes the dreams came: vivid, gaudy images that frightened her with the stories they told. Other times the sensations assaulted her when she was awake – leaving her feeling out of control, disconnected from her body. But the hours of sleep were the worst. The dreams were so clear – so graphic and colourful – and when she woke it was hard to convince herself that nothing she had experienced was real.

Maybe the dreams were better than the memories, which seemed hazy, fuzzy, as if she couldn't quite grasp them. Mostly she didn't want to because they just served to remind her of everything she had lost.

Her thoughts started to fall away before they had concluded – she couldn't keep hold of them. Her head was swimming, and if she didn't go to bed soon she would drift off, standing in the corner of the kitchen.

The other woman stood motionless by the sink, staring at nothing, the tea towel in her hand.

'I'm going to bed,' the young woman said softly, touching the other woman on the arm. 'Goodnight, Judith.'

There was no response.

4

The only word I can think of to describe my cabin on board the riverboat is sumptuous. The rich-coloured cushions and dark wooden furniture add to the sense that I'm now inhabiting a different world – and I'm glad of it. I walk out onto the small balcony and breathe in the humid air, thick with the musty smell of the river as we head upstream, listening to the strange sounds of a foreign country: the shouts of children playing in the muddy brown water and the chanting of Buddhists as we pass spectacular temples apparently situated in the middle of nowhere.

I can already feel the tension ebbing slightly, the tightness in my chest and shortness of breath slackening. I move back inside, closing the sliding glass door to keep the mosquitoes at bay, and sit down to apply some make-up before dinner. I look at my pale face in the mirror, the dark circles under my eyes, and rest my chin in upturned palms, wondering how best to add some colour to my cheeks.

My laptop is charging on the dressing table in front of me, and I am about to move it out of the way when it pings to tell me there's an email. The Wi-Fi signal is intermittent, as it depends where we are on the river, so clearly we're in a good position right now.

I glance at the screen and my heart plummets. The email is from Ian. I don't know whether to open it or not, and I am furious that my hand shakes as I reach forward to touch the trackpad.

He's failed to get a response to his texts – I deleted them all, and couldn't have answered even if I had wanted to – so now he is resorting to email.

The subject line might seem innocuous to anybody else – 'I will be waiting when you come home' – but it chills me. I don't want to open the email, but if I don't its malevolent presence will haunt me.

The tone has changed. He's no longer ranting about what a bitch I am. He knows, I'm sure, that while his insults may shock they are easy to deflect.

> I know I've been angry with you, but I've decided I'm prepared to forgive you. It has taken a lot of soul-searching on my part, but I understand you were upset. Deep down, you know you need me – and what will you do if I go? Remember how difficult it was for us to find each other. Do you really want to be alone for the rest of your life? I don't think so.

He even suggests I try to get an early flight back, and I realise he's not going to give up. Why would he? I could kid myself that he loves me, but I know that is not the reason. He was living in a horrible little bedsit with a bathroom shared by about ten other people when we met, and now he lives in a decent house and has me to wait on him hand and foot. He's not going to walk away from that life in a hurry, especially as until now I have always given in to his demands. For him it is – or has been – a stress-free existence.

I have been an idiot, and it is a hard thing to admit to myself. Ian and I met online. I know lots of people have forged successful relationships over the Internet, but when you meet someone through a dating site all you know about them is what they choose to tell you. They can say anything they like, and with no friends or colleagues in common to tell you anything different, you believe every word. At least, I did.

Will I ever be rid of him?

After a few minutes I take some deep breaths, and with renewed determination I jump up from the chair. I can't let him ruin this holiday, and dinner started ten minutes ago.

Locking the cabin door behind me, I make my way along the wood-panelled corridor and push open the door to the dining room, hoping I can slip quietly into a seat. The sound of excited chatter hits me, and long before I reach the small empty table I have spotted in a corner I realise I am not going to be able to escape so easily.

A loud, jarring American voice hails me: 'Hey, young lady! Don't sit on your own. Come and join us – we have a spare place. Harry, move round here and give the girl a seat.'

I look towards the strident voice and see a plump woman with yellow-blonde backcombed hair and perfect make-up sitting at a table for eight. She is waving her arms at me, and Harry, a balding man in his mid-fifties with a florid face, dutifully jumps up and goes to the spare chair on the other side of the table. Short of being downright rude, I have no option but to take a seat. I smile tentatively at everyone as they introduce themselves.

The questions start to fly. 'Where are you from?' 'Have you been on a trip like this before?' 'What brings you to Burma?'

I answer to the best of my ability, until the woman who told Harry to move asks, 'Are you travelling alone?'

'Yes,' is all I can muster. I get a sympathetic smile from an older lady with beautiful long silver hair who is sitting further along the table.

I relax a bit as the attention moves away from me, but as I turn to thank the waiter for the plate of food he has placed in front of me I catch the eye of a man sitting alone at a table on the other side of the dining room.

It's him again. Paul. He has clearly escaped the waving arms of the American woman, whose name I now know to be Donna. It's definitely him. His eyes are small, sharp, perched over a hooked nose. He has the look of an eagle and seems to be weighing me up again. He neither smiles nor averts his eyes when I return his gaze. Just like last night.

I lift my chin and turn back to the table.

Donna is in full flow, requiring no input from anyone else, and this gives me time to study her and my fellow diners. Down the table to my right sit an older couple, probably in their early seventies. She is the one who smiled kindly at me earlier, and is called Thea, but I have no idea what her husband's name is because she always calls him 'dear' or refers to him as 'the doctor'.

'The doctor and I have been to some beautiful places in the past few years, haven't we, dear? I think Vietnam was our favourite.'

The doctor, a striking man with the unusual combination of black eyebrows, white beard and an almost bald skull, merely looks up and nods. His brows point down towards his nose as if in a permanent scowl, and he seems content to leave his wife to do all the talking.

Strangely, I am grateful to Donna for asking me to join them. Chatting with them over dinner has forced me to think about something other than Ian and the situation I'm going to have to face when I return home. The thought never entirely leaves me, though. It has settled like a heavy stone in a dark corner of my mind.

5

As DCI Tom Douglas walked down the long corridor back to his office from a particularly tedious meeting, he smiled at the message on his phone. Louisa was cooking dinner that night and wanted to know what he fancied eating. He was so engrossed in her message that he didn't realise for a moment that Becky Robinson was approaching. He glanced up at the sound of footsteps and immediately flattened himself against the wall, arms outstretched to either side of him, palms and fingers splayed against the grey partition.

'Ha, bloody ha,' Becky said. 'I'm not *that* big.'

Tom grinned, and they both moved towards his office door at the same time, Tom standing back to let her through.

'What are you so chipper about, anyway?' she asked as he pulled out a chair for her. 'And stop treating me as if I'm made of glass, will you please.'

'I'm feeling quite good about life, that's all.' Tom walked round the back of his desk and indicated the facing chair to Becky. 'Sit.'

'No time, I'm afraid. We've got a body out at Pennington Flash Country Park. Suspicious death.'

Tom raised his eyebrows. 'Okay, what do we know?'

'Not much. A woman, probably around thirty. Found inside one of the birdwatching hides by some poor guy out to do a bit of twitching. The local DI says he doesn't want to cloud our judgement by giving his take on things, so was reluctant to say much.'

Tom picked up his keys from the desk. 'Right. Let's go and find Keith. He can come with me.'

Becky put her hands on her hips and glared at Tom. 'Why are you taking DS Sims? Why am I not coming?' Tom's eyes travelled to her middle. 'Oh for God's sake, Tom. I'm seven months pregnant. I'm not incapacitated.'

'Yes, but it's bloody freezing out there and treacherous underfoot. Why risk it?'

'If I lived in some remote part of the world I would probably be out in the fields working until the baby pops out. I'm *fine*. Stop mollycoddling me.'

Tom looked at Becky's face, her mouth tense and her eyes firing shots at him. He knew he'd been overprotective of her since she nearly died diving into a river to save someone, but that was a while ago now and he had to get over it.

'Okay, on your head be it.'

'Thank you, boss,' she said, her tone sarcastic.

Tom might be her boss, but he was well aware that she knew more about him than most people, and in the years they had worked together they had become close. She behaved impeccably when other members of the team were around, but that didn't stop her from speaking her mind when they were alone. He didn't know how he was going to manage without her when she went on maternity leave.

'Shall we take the newbie with us, do you think, for a bit of experience?' Becky asked. 'Just as an observer.'

'Good idea. Let her know, will you, and I'll meet you in the car park. We can brief her on what to expect as we go. What's her name again?'

'Lynsey. She's mad keen, bright as a button, and terrified of you.'

'Excellent. Let's hope she stays that way. It would be nice to have some respect round here.'

Becky snorted and made her way out of the door. 'See you downstairs in five minutes.'

❖

The local police had given concise instructions on how to get to the Flash, and as Tom pulled into the snow-covered car park a young officer walked towards them, his arms flying out sideways as his legs nearly went from under him. It was treacherous out there.

'What is a flash, anyway?' Becky asked, staring at the expanse of water ahead of them.

Tom was about to answer when Lynsey's quiet voice came from behind: 'There's more than one here, although the one you can see is the biggest. I believe the lakes, or flashes, were formed as a result of mining subsidence.'

Tom saw Becky smile. He could see how much she liked this girl.

'Thanks for that, Lynsey. I'm glad one of us knows,' Tom said.

'Sorry, sir, I'm not being a smart-arse. I looked it up on my phone while you were talking to Inspector Robinson.'

'Don't apologise; it shows initiative,' Becky said. 'Come on, let's go and see what we've got.'

Tom looked around at the view. Such an attractive place, and undoubtedly popular. Apparently it had been cut off by the heavy snow for days, and only the most intrepid of folk were likely to venture here today, even though the access road had now been cleared. The weather was wicked with a fierce wind blowing the snow around in little flurries, and it was with some reluctance that Tom stepped out of the warm car.

The young police officer, walking more carefully now, approached them.

'Sir, it's a bit of a walk to the hide. It doesn't overlook the main lake, so we need to take the path from the end of the car park and then turn off to the right, down a bit of a hill. It's not too good underfoot,' he said, staring pointedly at Becky's middle.

Tom almost smiled as he heard a tut of irritation.

Becky took Lynsey's arm. 'We'll hold each other up. Okay?'

'Is this the closest car park to the hide?' Tom asked.

'Yes, it's the one used most by visitors. We've laid an approach path nearer to the hide, sir, so if you would just follow me...'

Tom stood back to allow the women to go first, turning up his collar against the biting wind. From the car park they walked along a wide track, but within a few metres the constable veered off to the right where the path was sealed off with crime-scene tape. Becky gave their names to the officer at the head of the approach path, and they stopped to don protective suits.

'It doesn't look like there's much space in there,' Becky said. 'Maybe you should go first, boss, and we'll follow if there's room.'

Tom nodded and started to make his way along the narrow path, bordered on both sides by a wooden fence, his feet crunching on the icy snow underfoot. It appeared the hide had no door, and as he got closer the bulky figure of Jumoke Osoba filled the entrance, a wide white smile splitting his black face. This was one figure that Tom was always relieved to see at a crime scene.

'Morning, Jumbo,' Tom said. 'I didn't expect to see you here, but I'm delighted you are.'

'It's not usually my patch, that's true. I'm covering for Saul Newton, but glad to help. The first officers on the scene assumed it was an overdose or death from exposure. But I'm not sure that's the right call. That's why I'm pleased to see you and Becky.'

Tom nodded. Jumbo was an excellent crime-scene manager – the best – and if he thought something was up, Tom believed him. He also knew Jumbo wouldn't divulge his suspicions until Tom had formed his own opinion. Signalling Becky and Lynsey to follow, Tom moved into the confined space.

He stopped and took in the scene. Daylight spilled into the hide through a wide viewing window, but the floor was in deep shadow. In spite of that, he could clearly see the body of a young woman at the far end, sitting on the ground propped up against the wooden slats of the hide wall, her face peaceful, her eyes closed. A bitterly cold wind was blowing through the unglazed opening, and Tom crouched down on a level with the woman's face. She looked to be in her early thirties, small and slim, and her clothes – while not stylish for someone of her age – didn't look either old or tatty. She certainly didn't have the appearance of someone living rough who might have taken shelter in the hide from the icy weather.

No matter how many dead bodies he saw, Tom always felt a stab of sorrow that a life had ended, especially when the deceased was so young, and he paused for a moment before pulling a torch from his pocket to flick its beam over the woman. There was no sign of trauma – no blood that he could see – and her hands were placed neatly in her lap with no obvious signs of a struggle. It looked to all the world as if she had wandered in, sat down, closed her eyes and died. There was only one point arguing against that: she wasn't wearing any shoes.

Her feet were stretched out in front of her, and Tom could see that the soles were dirty but the tops weren't. It didn't look as if she habitually walked outdoors without shoes; the skin appeared too soft for that. She had no bag and was wearing nothing more than a long cardigan over a pair of jeans a couple of sizes too large. Tom wondered if maybe she had lost weight recently – maybe been ill – or whether the clothes belonged to someone else.

What had happened to this poor woman?

'Boss,' Becky said, interrupting his thoughts. 'Do you need me to call the Home Office pathologist? I could have a word with the man who found her too?'

'Yes please, that would be good.' Tom turned his attention back to the dead woman.

Jumbo was right. There was something wrong here, something that didn't tally.

6

Becky had been glad to make her escape from the hide, ashamed to admit that the sight of the body in the confined space had made her constantly queasy tummy turn over. Although she was sure she wasn't feeling anywhere near as bad as the poor man she could see just beyond the perimeter of the crime scene, sitting on a log that had been dusted clear of snow.

She made a quick call, relieved to hear that the pathologist would be with them soon, and inched her way gingerly along the icy path towards the man.

'Mr Denshaw?'

The man looked up, nodded and started to push himself to his feet. He seemed to be in his early sixties, with a wiry body and a full head of grey hair – which more or less matched the colour of his cheeks.

'Sorry,' he said, pointing at the log as if he shouldn't have been sitting down. 'It was a bit of a shock. I thought she was just having a rest, you see. I hunkered down and spoke to her quietly, not wanting to frighten her. She looks such a little thing – in the gloom I thought at first that she was a child.'

Becky nodded at the log. 'Sit down again, Mr Denshaw. I'll join you.' She lowered herself gingerly onto the smooth surface of the wood.

Knowing that the local police would already have asked him some questions and noted his responses, Becky decided to let him talk without prompting.

'I come here all the time,' he said. 'You can often see kingfishers from this hide, and I worry about them when it's as cold as this. They're vulnerable in hard winters, so as soon as I thought I might be able to make it through the snow I came to see how they were getting on.'

'When did you last come to check on them?' she asked.

'More than a week ago.' He pulled the satchel looped across his chest to rest on his lap and rummaged inside it, finally pulling out a small notebook. Opening it, he ran his finger down the page. 'It was ten days ago. I don't normally leave it that long, but with the weather and everything…'

His voice trailed off, and Becky got the impression he felt guilty about not visiting as often as he should. She could see something that looked like tinfoil in his satchel. 'If that's a sandwich you have in there, you might want to eat it,' she said. 'Might make you feel a bit better.'

Mr Denshaw looked at her and pulled one corner of his mouth down. 'Not sure I could eat right now,' he said.

'Do you know any other people who come here?' Becky asked, trying to move his mind away from the body.

'Not so much to this hide. It's a bit off the beaten track. Most of the hides are padlocked overnight, but not this one. I suppose that's how she got in. But how do you think she got here? The place has been cut off for days. Do you think she's been in there a while?'

Becky shook her head. 'It's hard to say. When it's this cold—' She had been about to say that the body didn't seem to have decomposed much, but thought better of it. 'I don't suppose you have the names of other people who come here regularly, do you?'

'No, I only know them to nod to. There are some online forums, though. People often chat on there about what they've seen.'

Becky noted down the web addresses Mr Denshaw gave her and pushed herself up from the log. He looked up at her.

'She wasn't wearing any shoes. Did you notice that? Of course you did. Sorry. But what do you think happened to her shoes?'

Becky shrugged. 'I'm sorry, but at the moment we don't have any answers. We're going to need to take a formal statement from you, and I'll get someone to arrange that. I'll organise a lift home for you as well.'

Thanking Mr Denshaw for his help, Becky shook his hand and walked over to Tom, who was talking quietly to Jumbo by the entrance to the hide.

'So what's up with our victim, then?' she asked. 'I can see from your faces that you think she *is* a victim and not just some young woman who wandered in and died.'

Tom shook his head. 'Jumbo's not entirely happy with the overall picture, and I agree with him. She doesn't look like a vagrant who decided to shelter overnight in the hide. If that were the case, we might assume she died of hypothermia. But she's too clean for someone who sleeps rough, so how did she get here? She isn't wearing a coat, and it's been too bloody cold to be out without one. Her feet are a bit grubby, but if she had walked here after the snow started she would almost certainly have frostbite. So that suggests she drove here. And yet there's no abandoned car in the car park.'

'Or she walked through the snow and threw her shoes in the water,' Becky said.

Jumbo nodded. 'Possible, although quite why she would do that I can't imagine.'

'She has no identification on her,' Tom continued, 'and there's no sign of what might have killed her. The most obvious possibility is an overdose, but there's no evidence in the hide that she took anything – no debris – pill bottle, blister pack, water, needles.'

'She could have taken a lethal dose and then come – or been brought – here to die,' Becky suggested. 'Or she could have died somewhere else and been brought here by a third party – removed from the place of death to avoid incriminating them.'

Tom nodded. 'The pathologist might be able to tell us whether she died here, and we'll have to wait for the post-mortem for the cause of death. Drugs were the first thing that came to mind, but Jumbo pointed out that there is the faintest hint of cyanosis in her face. I know it's not a sure thing, but that would normally indicate hypoxia. If so, how?'

Lynsey had joined them as Tom spoke, and Becky could see the confusion in her face.

'Cyanosis is when the skin takes on a bluish colour, which is usually associated with a lack of oxygen, Lynsey,' Becky explained. 'This is normally due to being asphyxiated – smothered, strangled, drowned – but she doesn't look like she's been in the water, and if she'd been strangled we would expect to see petechial haemorrhaging – small red dots on the skin.'

At the crunch of footsteps on frozen snow, Jumbo looked up and jerked his head towards the new arrival.

'Here's someone I suspect might have the answers,' he said. 'Amelia Sanders – likes to be called Amy. She's the new Home Office pathologist for this area, and I think you'll both like her.'

Becky turned towards the path. A small, thin woman with cropped black hair was striding towards them.

'You must be DCI Douglas,' she said to Tom. 'Amy Sanders.' She nodded briskly to Becky and Lynsey. 'Right, Jumbo. Let the dog see the rabbit then.'

Jumbo stood back to let Amy and Tom go ahead, turning to wink at Becky before he disappeared into the hide.

7

I think it's raining outside. I don't know for sure because I can't hear it and there are no windows in the room. But the air smells different. There is a mustiness creeping through small gaps under the locked doors and through the air bricks that at least allow me to breathe. I realise how much I have begun to rely on all my senses. Perhaps because for a while they were dulled, damaged, deadened.

I know the others have finished eating. I can't hear them because they rarely speak, but the squeak of chair legs against the old linoleum floor tells me they are moving to the sink to wash their pots.

I'm very careful now about what I put in my mouth. I'm hungry, but tonight's meal would have been a thin broth, and there is no way to avoid what I know is hidden in there. I wait for the one meal each day that may include a few whole vegetables, and eat nothing that has been mixed with another substance. Even mashed potatoes seem dangerous to me. The others think I'm ill, but they know better than to ask questions or to tell tales.

I don't know what's going to happen to me. I can see no way out – no end in sight that would give me hope. Perhaps the others have got it right – maybe I should give in and be who I'm expected to be, who they tell me I am. But I'm not ready to do that yet.

Suddenly the silence is pierced by the sound of the buzzer, and I know what this means. I hear the slap, slap of bare feet against lino and the clicks of doors closing as the others obey the rules and return to their rooms. I know my door should be closed too, but it's slightly ajar. For a moment I consider leaving it open as a gesture of defiance, but that would give my game away. I push myself up and quietly close it.

There is a wide gap below the door, and I can hear what is happening. I hear the clunk as the bolts go back on the door at the top of the stairs. A minute later, the door bangs shut, the locks automatically engaging, but then it is silent.

I know that someone is coming down the stairs and along the corridor, because each night it's the same. I don't hear footsteps, because our visitor's feet are covered in soft slippers that are soundless on the shiny, slippery floor. There is a sliver of light spilling into my room from the gap below the door, and a shadow passes. I think – hope – that perhaps I'm not the chosen one tonight, and I start to relax.

But I don't hear another door open, and my heart begins to thump. And then the shadow comes back, the light under the door blocked by two feet, heels together, toes splayed.

The handle is slowly pressed down, and I know this is my moment. I need to pretend. I need to remember everything I have seen the others do, how they react, from the lethargic lifting of their heads to the time it takes to focus their eyes, and I force my tense limbs to relax. I need to be as floppy as possible, and I half close my eyes, trying not to stare at the doorway and who is about to walk through it.

The door opens slowly, silently, and I look beyond the figure blocking the light as if I have not quite noticed they are there.

When the voice comes, I know what the words will be, and I wonder if I can continue to be who I am expected to be. Will I give myself away?

But I have no time to wonder any more. The words I have been dreading are spoken in a low voice.

'Are you ready, Judith?'

8

I've been on the boat for five days now, and I'm beginning to feel settled. Thea, the older lady who smiled at me so kindly on the first night, has been keeping an eye on me. She makes sure I'm not left floundering and is adept at changing the subject when she sees that I'm uncomfortable with Donna's nosiness. We always share a look of understanding as the heat is drawn away from me.

Paul – or Eagle-Eye, as I've come to think of him – is the one person who still bothers me. We all gathered on deck last night for a pre-dinner drink and he was there, talking to Thea. He kept glancing over, and I could see he wanted to speak to me, so it came as no surprise when, after five minutes, he wandered across.

'Have you been on any other interesting holidays recently?' he asked. His voice was clipped, almost as if he was challenging me.

'No, I'm afraid not. I've been a bit boring until now. It's the first trip of this kind that I've taken.'

'What about other types of holiday – in the UK, maybe? Lots of women your age seem to like going on retreats – yoga, well-being, that sort of thing. Have you ever done anything like that?'

His gaze was intense, as if he was trying to catch me in a lie. It felt more like an inquisition than a casual conversation, and Thea must have sensed my discomfort. She was watching me, and I saw her brow furrow for a moment. She strolled over and tapped Paul on the forearm. 'Paul, I was meaning to ask if you've been to China. It would be wonderful to speak to someone who knew something about the country.'

Paul gave me one final hard look and then turned towards Thea. I was able to relax again.

I'm hoping I don't end up alone with him at any point, although I don't know why he bothers me so much. Maybe I just don't feel at ease around men right now.

The rest of the evening passed without event, and I woke this morning to another bright, sunny day. I'm excited that we are off to visit the stupas at Bagan this afternoon – one of the highlights of the trip – and I grab a window seat on the coach, relieved when Thea slips into the place next to me. She's a tall, slim woman with wonderful bone structure that has lost nothing of its beauty as she has aged. Her long silver hair is swept back into a low ponytail during the day, but in the evening it sits resplendent on her shoulders. Some of the passengers come to dinner in shorts, but Thea always wears something in silk, with modern chunky jewellery at her neck. I can't help thinking that this is how I would like to look when I'm older – elegant but a bit funky.

As the coach pulls away from the river, I fiddle with my bag, making sure it's firmly closed and attached to some part of my body so it can't be stolen.

Thea looks at the bag and laughs. 'Why on earth have you brought that enormous bag with you, dear?'

'I don't have a pocket big enough for my key,' I say. I have wondered a couple of times why the management of the boat has chosen to use such a heavy metal ball as a key ring. It weighs a ton.

She pats me on the leg. 'There's no need to bring it with you. We're stuck with each other for the whole trip, so if anything goes missing the crew will search everyone's room or call the police.'

'My laptop's in there, though.'

'A little secret, dear: probably every cabin on board has a laptop or an iPad lurking inside. Except ours, of course. People these days seem compelled to share their every waking moment on a blog or on social media, an obsession I fail to understand.'

She gives a little shudder, and I want to ask if she and the doctor have any children. I know people of Thea's age often use Facebook to keep in touch with their kids. But for some reason it seems intrusive to enquire.

'Can I ask if there's something worrying you, dear?' she asks in a hushed voice.

'No, I'm fine,' I answer, but even I can hear the lie in my voice.

'I don't mean to pry, but I've noticed that sometimes your eyes glaze over as if you're thinking of something or someone else. And I get the feeling they're not good thoughts. Am I right?'

What do I say? Do I tell her that each time the boat picks up an Internet signal I get another stream of emails? I had managed to convince myself after the first one that I could resist looking, but in the middle of last night when I couldn't sleep I knew it wasn't going to work. I had to find out what Ian had to say, what he's threatening, what he's planning for my return. I only read one message, but it was enough.

I've had a great idea! I know it irritates you when I play games on the telly and it stops you from watching those crap American dramas that you appear to enjoy for some reason, so when I saw there was an offer on TVs I decided to shift things round in the spare room and make it into my man den. I've applied for interest-free credit on the telly, so it should all be sorted by the time you're back.

He's ignoring everything I said before I came on holiday. He thinks he has me beaten and if he pretends it never happened, I will give in.

'It's just man trouble,' I tell Thea.

'Ah. That can be the worst, because logic may say one thing while emotion says another. Do you love him?'

And to think I considered it intrusive to ask her about children!

There is something compelling about her voice, though, and maybe it is the extra couple of glasses of wine I had with lunch, but I find myself almost eager to unburden myself.

'I have a boyfriend. Or had. I don't love him, but I did rely on him when I was going through a bad time.'

I don't want to admit that I made such a terrible choice of partner, but I find myself blurting out the whole story, the words tumbling from my lips unrestrained. I know I'm going to regret this later, but I don't seem able to stop.

'The house we live in is mine – well, mine and the building society's, I suppose. My grandfather gave me some money – an advance on my inheritance, he called it. I have a job which I love, but since moving to Manchester my boyfriend hasn't managed to find anything that suits someone of his calibre.' I try, and fail, to keep the sarcastic tone from my voice. 'He just sits around drinking and listening to music all day.'

'You mean he lives off you,' Thea says, tucking her chin into her chest and raising her eyebrows as if to underline my naivety.

'I suppose so. Before I came away I told him that we're finished, but he won't accept it. I can't stay with him. And I think he's lost it completely.'

It's a strange experience telling this kind elderly woman my story, but I can sense that she's listening carefully and not judging me.

'That's not good, is it?' Thea says. 'Remember you can talk to me any time you like. I'm used to listening.' She leans towards me slightly, as if about to share a secret. 'The doctor is a psychiatrist, you know.' She looks at my face and sees something there. 'Oh, don't worry. I'm not suggesting you need his help, but I often used to speak to his patients when they were in the waiting room, so their barriers were well and truly down before they went in for their consultations. He's helped many people find the right way as a result of the cutting-edge techniques he pioneered. I'm so proud of him.'

Thea glances at where her husband is sitting across the aisle, his head resting against the window, eyes closed. I can feel how much she loves him and I'm envious. But Ian is now back in my head, and as I turn away to take in the sight of the first of over two thousand stupas and pagodas on the plains of Bagan, I wonder what I'm going to have to do to get rid of him.

Maybe it's the sight of all those shrines, or maybe it's the wine, but the words are out of my mouth before I've had time to consider what I'm about to say.

'I'm beginning to feel I'll never be rid of him. Sometimes I wish he was dead.'

Thea pats my leg again, displaying not a hint of surprise. 'Might be best for everyone,' is all she says.

9

One of Tom's least favourite tasks was attending a post-mortem, particularly when the body was that of someone so young. But he was hoping Amy Sanders would be able to give him something – anything – to work with, because in the case of the woman found at Pennington Flash they had nothing to go on at all.

They still had no idea who she was, and nobody who fitted her description had been reported missing in the last few weeks. The team had started the laborious task of checking through older missing-persons records, both locally and from further afield, but it felt as if they were looking for a needle in a haystack. Given that across the country more than three hundred thousand people were reported missing each year and the authorities were often not informed if they returned home safely, it was a mammoth undertaking. Without having something to help them narrow their search down, it was likely to be a long job unless they struck lucky.

The only clue to the cause of death was the slight cyanosis that Jumbo had spotted, which indicated a lack of oxygen, and Tom was hoping Amy could give them something more concrete to focus on so he could stop his endless hypothesising. Had she been drugged and then smothered? Had she died somewhere else and then been brought to the Flash? If she had come alone, how had she got there? There were no cars unaccounted for, and she had no coat, not to mention no shoes. And where *were* her shoes? Although they were searching for them, everywhere was still covered in snow, and they were unlikely to be found until it melted.

As well as cause of death, he needed the pathologist to give him a time frame so they could review CCTV footage. There were no cameras in the country park itself, but they could access those on the roads close to the entrance on the off chance that their victim had caught a bus and walked the rest of the way, despite the lack of a coat. Maybe her coat was with the shoes.

On top of everything else, the toxicology results were likely to take days, and it felt to Tom as if the investigation had no direction. They were thrashing about in the dark. They didn't even know yet if this was murder, suicide or accidental death.

He pushed open the door to the mortuary suite, trying to curb his irritation at their lack of progress. 'I hope you have some news for me, Amy,' he said to the pathologist, earning himself a pair of raised eyebrows above her mask.

'Yes, I may well have,' she said, in the brisk voice that Tom had become accustomed to over the previous twenty-four hours. 'I'm as certain as I can be that she died exactly where she was found. Look here,' she said, pointing to an area of lividity. 'This is where she was sitting, the lowest point in her body. If she had been moved – unless she was in exactly the same position where she died – the pattern would be different. Do you understand what I'm saying?'

Tom resisted the temptation to mention that he had been to one or two post-mortems in his time, and smiled at her instead. 'I get that, thanks.'

'Good. I thought you would. So there's no sign of any physical trauma, and all her organs seem to be in reasonable order, although I would say she was slightly undernourished. But nothing too serious. She was possibly of quite a nervous disposition – her nails are badly bitten – but she was clean and unlikely to have been a vagrant.'

Tom nodded, appreciating her staccato presentation of the facts. 'Do you have any idea of the time of death?'

'That's a bit more tricky. The outside temperature was sub-zero – I understand it hit minus ten on a couple of nights – and it was only marginally warmer inside the hut, which gave minimal protection from the extreme cold. She was very close to being frozen, although not enough to stop all decomposition. Based on those factors, I've tried to come up with a timescale, but there are so many variables that could affect it. On balance, I would say she died either immediately before the freeze or within the first two to three days of it. Had it been earlier, more decomposition would have taken place. Sorry – that's as precise as I can make it.'

'She died in the hide, you believe, so that's a help.' Tom mulled over the options, speaking them out loud to try to make sense of them. 'If she arrived after the start of the freeze, it had to have been on foot, given that the park area was closed to traffic. Even if we ignore the lack of shoes and coat, both of which could have been discarded, it would have been a difficult walk in those conditions. On the other hand, if someone took her there by car and left her, whether to die or not we don't know, then it has to have been in the few hours before the freeze set in.'

'That just about sums it up,' Amy said. 'There's something else I would like to run by you, though.' She beckoned him a little closer. 'You mentioned slight cyanosis, and you were right, but as you and Jumbo noted there is no sign of any violent act. Even if she had been smothered with a cushion you would have expected her to put up a fight – unless she was drugged, and we won't know that until we get the tox results. But possibly more relevant is the fact that there weren't any fibres in her mouth or her nostrils.'

Amy pointed to the woman's neck. 'She wasn't strangled, but if you look very closely, there is evidence that something was tied around her neck. Not tight enough to asphyxiate her, but tight enough, and there are one or two places that look as if something was rubbing on the skin before death. See here…and here.'

Tom looked at the marks and then back at Amy. He had no idea where she was going with this.

And then she told him.

❖

Becky looked around the incident room. Everyone seemed to be slouching in their seats, and she understood why. They had nothing to work with. They had no realistic timescale to investigate yet; they didn't know how the woman got to the Flash, or even who she was. It was difficult to know where to start. Tom was due to give a statement to the press later that day in the hope that someone had seen something – anything – but they were clutching at straws.

Just as she decided she should stand up and give a rallying speech to the team, Tom strode into the room and passed a number of photographs to Keith Sims to pin on the board. He was wearing what Becky referred to as his 'important meeting' suit. The very dark navy looked good on him and hung well on his broad shoulders. As Keith organised the pictures, Tom slipped off his jacket to reveal a powder-blue shirt and a tie which Becky couldn't help thinking was unnecessarily cheerful. He unbuttoned his cuffs and rolled back the sleeves to halfway up his forearms.

Becky sat a little straighter. Something was firing Tom up. Her reaction must have caught his eye, as he looked across and raised his eyebrows a fraction. Becky had seen that expression before and she felt a tingle of anticipation.

Tom started to speak, and the room fell silent. He explained that the post-mortem had been completed and he wanted to talk the team through the findings. All eyes were on him.

'Due to the fact that access to the Flash was very limited once the snow came, Dr Sanders believes we should focus on those hours of the night before the freeze started eight days ago. It was zero degrees by midnight, and the park was still accessible then, but by six the next morning the snow was thick and heavy. And it got colder. If our victim was driven there, our window is that night until the early hours, and it's our starting point for checking CCTV. However, we can't rule out the possibility that she walked there. Don't be distracted by the lack of shoes, which might be irrelevant. We're still looking for them. Realistically we need to expand the dates of interest for people walking into the park by three days.'

There was a general groan at the thought of the extra footage they would have to look at, but Becky's eyes were on Tom. She had a feeling he was holding something back – she was sure of it – something that would revitalise the investigation and get the best from the team.

'As to cause of death, we won't know for sure that it wasn't an overdose until we get the tox results, but Dr Sanders has made another observation which is interesting, although it's little more than an idea at the moment. She has confirmed that the woman died of oxygen starvation – hypoxia – but how that happened is far from clear.' Tom pointed to the whiteboard, where a close-up image of the woman's neck was visible. 'During the post-mortem Dr Sanders found the marks you can see here. She believes they were made by something tied securely around our victim's neck. She wasn't strangled – the marks are far too faint for that and there is no damage to her throat – so our pathologist believes there is a possibility that a plastic bag was placed over her head and secured.'

DS Keith Sims, who had joined the team when Becky was on prolonged sick leave and had stayed ever since, raised a hand.

'Yes, Keith,' Tom said.

'It's my understanding that the build-up of carbon dioxide and lack of oxygen resulting from this type of suffocation induces a feeling of panic. Surely the victim would have attempted to rip the bag off her head?'

'DS Sims is correct,' Tom said, addressing the room. 'But our victim doesn't appear to have put up any fight at all, which could suggest that she had been drugged and was already asleep when the bag was placed over her head. However, Dr Sanders has another theory.' Tom pointed to an image on the screen.

Becky peered at it, wondering what it could be. It showed a small depressed circle in the dirt-covered boards on the floor of the hide, as if something had been placed there.

'This picture came from Dr Osoba, the crime-scene manager. He and Dr Sanders believe that her findings, together with this photograph and a very small piece of parcel tape found at the scene, suggest one way in which our victim may have died.'

Becky had no idea where this was going, but there was a briskness in Tom's voice that confirmed she had been right about his expression. She leaned forward, all her attention focused on him.

'We believe that death may have been via what is commonly called an exit bag.' There was a murmur around the room and people shifted in their seats. 'I called our newest team member, Lynsey, from the mortuary and asked her to find a suitable explanation for you. Over to you, Lynsey.'

Lynsey got to her feet and glanced at Becky, her eyes wide. Becky gave her an encouraging smile, and the young detective picked up her notes.

'An exit bag, also known as a suicide bag, usually consists of a large plastic bag with a draw cord – which can be something as simple as an elastic band slipped over the head or a piece of string – to close the bag. A pipe is inserted into the bag and sealed in place using something like parcel tape. This pipe is connected to a cylinder containing helium or nitrogen, both of which are readily available – particularly helium – and the gas is fed into the bag. For the victim, it's a painless death. They breathe normally and comfortably and are unconscious through lack of oxygen in a few seconds. Death takes a little longer – maybe ten minutes – but the victim feels nothing.'

There was a buzz in the room, and Becky nodded to Lynsey. She had done well, and had it not been for the telltale flush that seemed to plague her, Becky would have thought she had all the confidence in the world.

'Thanks, Lynsey,' Tom said. 'That's a perfect description of what has become something of a favoured suicide method. As you probably know, helium can be bought from shops that sell balloons for parties. If nitrogen was used though, it will be difficult to prove. There will be no trace of it in the body because the air we breathe is over seventy per cent nitrogen. Either way, we think the circular marking on the floor might indicate where the cylinder was placed.'

Becky looked around at the team. People weren't slouching now. They were turning to each other and talking in low voices. This was new. They hadn't had a case like this before, and Tom's eyes briefly met Becky's again.

'There was no cylinder at the scene, no plastic bag, and nothing but a tiny scrap of parcel tape. So if this really is how she died, she had help. Someone went with her to that place, and whether she willingly submitted to having the bag placed over her head or was incapacitated before she died, at best this is a case of assisted suicide, which is a crime. Alternatively, this has all the hallmarks of a very clever murder.'

10

Time is passing too quickly on this holiday. I feel as if I'm racing towards the moment when I will have to return home and face reality, and I can't bear the thought. I struggle to focus on conversations and find myself tuning out whenever I'm in a group, letting others speak.

It is as if Thea has read my mind and come to my rescue, because earlier she took me to one side. 'We're going to get a separate table for dinner tonight,' she said. 'Would you like to join us?'

It was kind of her to ask. I do feel safe in their company, and I'm sure Thea wants someone to talk to. The doctor – whose name I have discovered is Garrick – doesn't say much. Thea says he's a thoughtful man who likes to focus on subjects rather more significant than who has the biggest pool in Louisiana, a not-so-subtle dig at Donna.

At dinner we talk about the day, what we've seen, what we love about the place, and it's not until we are on to the main course that things become more intense, and I start to feel slightly uncomfortable. Thea asks me to tell her about my life.

I have no intention of mentioning Ian again, but do I want to tell her about my dysfunctional family? I don't want to talk about my dad. I haven't spoken to him for months – not since he and my stepmother, Annabel, gave Pops hell for giving me some money to help me buy my house. Apparently they thought everything should go to them, and things turned very nasty. Instead, I plump for a safe conversation about my job.

'I work as part of the events team at Manchester Central – the convention complex. I was so lucky to get the job; there aren't many opportunities like that in and around Manchester.'

Thea gives me a wide smile. 'How lovely! We go into Manchester quite regularly. It's become such a pleasant city. We live just on the border with Cheshire. Do you enjoy your work?'

I answer honestly. 'I love it, but it can be pretty full on and it's a huge responsibility logistically. My boss, Tim, is a bit of an idiot, which is unfortunate.'

Thea and Garrick are facing me, and on the table behind them sits Paul. He has kept to himself most of the time, although I often look up and find his eyes on me. Tonight he has his back to us, but I notice he's leaning back in his chair, and I get the impression he's trying to hear what I'm saying. Why would he care about my work?

I've felt even more ill at ease around him since Donna leaned across one day when we were at lunch, signalling with her scarlet-painted talons for us to come closer. 'I heard an odd thing today about that man, Paul,' she said, whispering and glancing around to see if anyone was listening. 'The steward told me that he's taken every trip on this boat since the end of December. He'll have done three trips before he goes home.' Donna nodded her head once, as if this was very telling. 'He's staying on board until early February. What do you think *that's* about, then?'

None of us had an answer, but I couldn't help wishing that I too could stay on board and not have to face what I knew was waiting for me at home.

Thea has just asked me another question about my job when the cruise director, Joel, approaches our table. 'Excuse me,' he says, leaning down to speak to me quietly. 'I'm so sorry to disturb you, but we have an urgent call for you. Can you come with me, please?'

I look blankly at him for a second, thinking that he must have got the wrong person. I know the number on the boat is only to be used in an emergency, and as I rise slightly unsteadily to my feet, my shaking legs knock against the table.

I turn and scurry after Joel. His tiny office is next to the dining room, and he tells me kindly that the call has been put through there. He shows me in, hands me the phone and then quietly leaves.

'Hello?' I say, my voice hesitant, uncertain of what on earth could have happened.

'You're a bitch, you know that, don't you?'

'*Ian!*' I whisper his name fiercely into the phone, my heart pumping. 'What the hell are you doing calling the emergency number?'

'You won't answer my texts, calls or emails, so what the fuck do you expect me to do?'

I feel myself about to apologise, to make excuses, but I swallow the words.

'I can't get a mobile signal here and there's no Wi-Fi.'

'Liar,' he spits down the phone. 'I read the brochure. It says there *is* Wi-Fi.'

'Yes, Ian. Wi-Fi can be transmitted through the ship, but only when there's a signal *into* the ship – which is practically never. It's the truth, honestly.'

It's almost the truth. I don't want him to know that I've read his emails.

'Did you tell them there's an emergency at home?' I ask, certain there isn't. I can feel myself shaking. I want to scream – to let out the tension that is gripping me at the sound of his voice. Why is he doing this?

'I told them your mother was dead.'

The words make me gasp. For a moment neither of us speaks. I want to cut him off, but if I hang up he will just call back.

'But the real reason I called was to ask what the hell you thought you were doing emptying the joint account. I went to pick up the new telly – the one I told you about in one of the emails you claim you can't get – and they said my application for credit had been denied, so I checked the account. There's nothing left. You took it all, didn't you? *Bitch*.'

He's right. It was the last thing I did before I left. I was scared he would empty the account. I didn't trust him. And let's face it, I'm the only one who puts money into the account. Every penny of it. His benefit is paid into his own account, not the joint one. So I knew he wouldn't starve.

How did it become so ugly? Why didn't I notice that his interest in me ratcheted up a few notches when he discovered that Pops had helped me to buy the house? Pops lived in the north, and when I told Ian that I planned to move away from London to be near him, he suggested that he should come with me. It seemed a good idea at the time – if only so that I wouldn't be alone in a city where I knew no one.

Right now, though, I can't find any words.

Ian breaks the silence. 'So, the reason for this call is to give you notice. I'm going to start selling things to get my share of that money back. I'm starting with your jewellery box – all those ugly things of your mum's that you so cherish. And when you get back, we'll sort this out once and for all.'

The line goes dead.

❖

I don't think Joel is in any doubt that there has been a death in the family when he comes back into his office to find me, head down on folded arms, sobbing uncontrollably. Why hadn't I thought about the jewellery? The clearing of the account had been a last-minute panic, and I hadn't thought it through.

'I'm sorry, Mum,' I mumble, wishing she was here to tell me what to do.

A box of tissues is pushed towards me, and I can feel Joel's discomfort. He doesn't seem sure whether he should sit down and talk to me or leave me alone. I take a deep breath and raise my head.

'Sorry,' I say.

'You've nothing to apologise for. What can I do to help?'

I want to ask him not to allow any more calls to be put through to me, but that will make no sense at all if my mother has died. *I* know my tears are those of frustration and anger, but he doesn't.

He talks to me about whether I want to be taken back to Yangon and asks if they can organise a flight back to the UK for me. What am I supposed to say? I wipe my eyes and mutter something about the funeral not being for two weeks so I'm okay to stay and please don't mention it to anybody.

Joel is silent, and I sense that he's embarrassed.

'What?' I ask.

'I'm so sorry, but the lady you were eating with – Thea, I believe she's called – asked me if you were okay, and I told her that we understood you'd had some very sad news. I didn't say more than that. I assumed she was a friend and it would be easier if you didn't have to tell her yourself.'

He looks mortified, and I realise he's younger than me – probably in his late twenties – and has possibly never had to deal with anything like this before.

'It's okay,' I say, pushing myself up and out of the chair. 'I'll just go back to my cabin now.'

'Can I get you anything – a drink of some description? A brandy, a cup of tea? Let me know if there's anything at all we can do for you, won't you?'

I nod my thanks and he opens the door to let me through.

I slowly climb the stairs to the top deck, where my cabin is situated, thinking of what I can do to stop Ian – to get him out of my life – but my attention is diverted because as I make my way along the corridor, I can see that my cabin door is standing ajar. I know I closed it.

I walk quietly towards it, wondering who is inside. I don't know why I feel scared – surely no one on this boat wants to hurt me? I reach the door and push it gently. It swings silently open. The room is empty. The bed has been turned down ready for the night and I let out the breath I didn't know I was holding. The maid must have forgotten to close the door properly.

Ian is making me into a nervous wreck, and I lower myself onto the bed and drop my head, the sobs building again. I fall to the side and curl up, my arms tightly hugging my body.

The sound of a tentative knock silences my sobs and I open my puffy eyes to stare as the door opens. It's Thea.

'I don't mean to intrude, dear, but Joel said you'd had some bad news. Would you like me to go, or can I help?'

I push myself upright, embarrassed that anyone should see me like this.

'Thanks, but there's nothing you can do. It was Ian – my boyfriend.' I end the sentence on a weak laugh that holds not a trace of amusement. 'He told Joel he was phoning to say my mother had died.'

'Oh, I'm so sorry, my dear.' She walks towards me and reaches out a hand, but I lean away. It isn't her fault, but I'm not sure I can cope with kindness just now.

'It would be tragic news if it were true.' I don't try to hide the bitterness in my voice, and I see the puzzled look on Thea's face. 'Thea, my mother has been dead for ten years, and now Joel is trying to rush me back to Manchester. If I go, my trip is ruined. If I stay, I'm going to get sympathy from every person on this boat, and I don't deserve any of it. I deserve their ridicule for being so easily manipulated.'

I rest my elbows on my thighs, dropping my head.

'Please, Thea, say nothing to anyone. I've got to decide how to handle this, and right now I don't have a clue.'

11

'Boss!' Becky called across the incident room to where Tom was standing talking to Keith Sims. 'Local officer has found a pair of shoes,' she said as they both approached her desk. 'He's going to send me a picture he's taken with his phone, but he's not sure it's going to be helpful.'

'Why not?' Tom asked, clearly hoping this was going to be the breakthrough they needed.

'They were found under a shrub quite a distance from where Penny was found.'

Penny was the name the team had adopted for their victim, which Becky thought was as good a name as any, and infinitely better than Jane Doe. Just then her mobile pinged and she opened the message.

'Bloody hell, I can see what he means,' she said.

She turned the screen to face Tom and Keith. Penny's clothes had appeared plain and old-fashioned for a woman of her age, but the shoes were something else.

'Surely they can't be hers,' Becky said. 'Penny was wearing baggy jeans and a long cardigan, and these are party shoes. She couldn't have walked far in these.'

They were, in fact, just the type of shoes that Becky would have chosen until her pregnancy forced her into something a lot more comfortable. Pale pink, with peep toes and a thick wedge heel, they looked like shoes a girl might wear for a night out on the town.

'No accounting for taste. Can we see the size?'

'Yes, he's sent an image of the sole too. They look very new from the lack of wear and tear. Continental size forty-one.'

'Bugger,' Tom said, his shoulders slumping. They knew that Penny's feet were a UK size 5, which he had been reliably informed was a continental 38.

They stared silently at Becky's screen for another moment.

'If we are saying they belong to someone else, how likely is it that we find a body without shoes and then discover a relatively new pair of shoes abandoned in the snow in the same area?' Tom asked.

He didn't look like he was expecting an answer, and it didn't make any sense to Becky either.

Before they had time to voice any alternative theories, a PC approached Tom with an envelope. 'Tox results,' he said, his eyes lighting up. They were praying these might give them something to work with, and they had been rushed through the system.

But Tom didn't have time to look at them. His phone rang. 'Tom Douglas,' he answered. 'Yes indeed, ma'am. I'll come right away.'

He rolled his eyes so that only Becky could see, and she tried to hide her smile. Tom had been summoned from on high, which probably meant his boss had something to say about their current investigation.

❖

Tom's frustration at the lack of progress on the case was echoed by Detective Superintendent Philippa Stanley in what he considered to be an unnecessarily long meeting. She was scathing about Tom's attempts to solve the case and left him feeling disgruntled with himself for not having better answers to her criticisms.

'With the increased threat of terrorism hanging over our heads here in Manchester and more than one gang-related murder on your files that remains unsolved, I'm not sure I understand your obsession with this particular case.' Tom opened his mouth to speak, but Philippa continued: 'And don't tell me it's your famous gut at work again. That *is* what you were going to say, isn't it?'

Tom looked at the woman with whom he had worked for several years and remembered how well she knew him. As a new detective – like Lynsey was now – Philippa had reported to Tom, but she had risen rapidly and determinedly through the ranks until the tables had turned, and she was now Tom's superior officer. Only once, on their very first case together, had Tom seen a chink in her armour. Since then she had cultivated the air of a perfectly poised professional in her ubiquitous navy-blue suit and white blouse, with her hair in a dark bob that never seemed to get any longer or shorter.

Despite her cold, aloof manner, Tom knew another side of her. But sadly she knew another side of him as well, and she had guessed right – he had been about to claim that he had a feeling about this case.

'It's an unusual case, Philippa. We don't know who she is or precisely how she died, but if Amy Sanders and Jumbo Osoba are right about the exit bag and the fact that she had help, we need to find out if she was murdered. If so, who by? If it was assisted suicide, who helped her? The tox results came in just before I got your call. I haven't had a chance to analyse them in detail, but I had a quick scan in the lift and read them a bit more thoroughly while I was waiting outside your door.'

Tom didn't mention that despite the fact she had summoned him, Philippa had kept him waiting for ten minutes.

'The gas analysis shows no sign of helium, but obviously we can't rule out nitrogen, although it's impossible to prove. The blood and urine results were confusing. There were traces of sedatives, maybe enough to make her compliant while she was killed, but insufficient to render her unconscious and definitely not enough to kill her. We don't know what we're looking at here, Philippa, and if Jumbo and Amy—'

Philippa held up her hand.

'I know. They did a good job. I'm not saying stop investigating it, of course. What I'm saying is that I don't think it should be your focus. Give it to DI Robinson and move on to some of the other cases.'

The subtext to this was that Philippa thought gang-related murders were more important than the death of a young woman who as yet had not been identified, suggesting she wasn't missed. It had been several days now, and appeals for information were yielding nothing.

'Just before we give up on this altogether, I want to delve a bit more deeply into the drugs,' Tom said. 'I haven't had a chance to share this with Becky or the team yet, but the hair analysis shows that during the ninety-day window they were able to test she'd taken a very strange concoction – PCP, psilocybin and MDPV. That's a weird mix of hallucinogens, dissociatives and synthetics.'

Even Philippa looked shocked. MDPV, commonly known as 'bath salts', could result in aggressive behaviour, while the other two were known to induce confusion, impair memory and cause no end of visual distortion. They needed to look at the results in far more detail before they could get close to drawing any conclusions.

'Do you think she might have been trafficked? If she was being used in the sex trade, that might explain the mix of drugs.'

'Dr Sanders said there were no signs of recent sexual activity – at least in the hours before she died – but it's certainly something we should consider. There were traces of scopolamine too, but taken at the start of the ninety-day period, and it may well have been legit. Perhaps she'd been on a trip and it had been prescribed for motion sickness. Until we know who she is, it's impossible to say.'

By the end of the meeting Tom had managed to convince Philippa that he needed to continue to treat the case as one of his many priorities, but it was a hard-won battle, and as it was after six he decided to take the unusual step of going home before the rest of his team. They were avidly studying CCTV footage from the main roads leading to the Flash, but he had a feeling they were clutching at straws. He felt a momentary pang of guilt at leaving them to it, but an evening with Louisa would relax him, and hopefully he could return the next day with a clear mind.

As he drove home through the dark winter streets he thought back to when he had first met Louisa. It seemed so long ago now, although it wasn't really. She had been a friend and colleague of one of the victims of a particularly horrific crime, and in her role as an anaesthetist had been involved in the care of Tom's ex-girlfriend, Leo. With the trauma of all that had happened during those weeks, he hadn't made a move to get to know her better, and it had taken Becky to engineer a meeting between the two of them. Since then they had spent as much time together as their work schedules permitted.

As he pulled into the drive, Tom was delighted to see that Louisa's car was already there.

'Hi,' he shouted as he pushed open the front door. He knew she would be in the kitchen, probably poring over something work-related on her laptop. She was as much of a workaholic as he was.

She turned her head as he walked through the door, her shoulder-length auburn hair shimmering in the spotlight above the table. 'You're home early,' she said, giving him a beaming smile. 'That's nice.'

Tom walked over and wrapped his arms around her from behind, bending down to kiss the back of her neck.

'Get off,' she said with a laugh. 'You'll make me lose my concentration.'

'Would that be such a bad thing?' he asked, not moving.

'Have patience, man! We have the whole evening – and the night.'

He was pleased to hear she would be staying, because she didn't always and he wanted to change that. Louisa had now met his daughter, Lucy, several times, and from the start they had been comfortable in each other's company. Lucy liked her, which was the main thing and a huge relief to Tom, and Louisa seemed to enjoy watching Tom's affectionate relationship with his child, who was fast becoming an opinionated teenager.

He let his arms drop and walked over to the central island to pour himself a glass of wine, leaving Louisa to turn back to her work.

'Need a top-up?' he asked, seeing she had a glass next to her on the table.

'Not just now, thanks. Maybe later when we eat. I'm starving.'

She was always starving, and he loved seeing her here in his home, eating, drinking, laughing. It was a life he could get used to.

'Have you thought any more about what I said last week?' Tom intentionally kept his tone light. He didn't want her to feel any pressure, and with her back to him it gave her somewhere to hide.

'Of course I have,' she said, turning to face him. 'It's still no, Tom. But it doesn't mean never.'

Her brown eyes didn't waver as they looked into his, and Tom returned her gaze.

'Is it because I bought this place when I was with Leo?' he asked. He knew some people would find it difficult to move into a house that had been shared with a former lover, but it came as no surprise to him when Louisa laughed.

'Of course not. That is truly unimportant to me. We both have pasts, and we've both loved other people. I would find it a bit sad if you *hadn't*, to be honest. But I was badly burned, as you well know, and after that relationship I decided to give myself at least a year with any new man before making a forever commitment. In my mind, moving in with you would be that kind of commitment.'

Tom smiled. 'I'll go with that,' he said. 'What is it you're looking to prove during those twelve months? What is it that you don't already know?'

'I need – no, I demand – total honesty. My ex lied to me about everything, and I only discovered that when we split up. I don't ever want to feel that stupid again, so I reckon that if I haven't found any skeletons within a year, I might be safe. I just don't want to go through all that pain again.'

Louisa stood up and walked towards Tom, and this time it was her turn to wrap her arms around him. She rested her head on his shoulder. 'I don't see you as a cheat and a liar, Tom. But I have to be sure.'

Tom felt torn in two. He had never lied to her, but he had intentionally misled her about one thing right at the start of their relationship. His reasons were identical to those she had given for not moving in with him. It was simply a matter of trust. Would it be safe to trust Louisa with the one secret he had, knowing the repercussions could be devastating for so many people? Or should he wait until she believed in him enough to stay?

It wasn't just his secret, though. It could end Tom's career, even send him to prison. And Philippa Stanley, who knew exactly what Tom had done, could suffer a similar fate. Worse still, it could result in an evil bastard, who was currently rotting in jail, getting the revenge he so badly sought.

12

I only have a couple of days left on the boat, but my cabin no longer feels like a place of escape, and when I'm in there I can't think straight. I am always conscious of my laptop. I feel as if it's watching me, daring me to open it. I have to get away to somewhere I can't see it.

On the top level of the boat is a rarely used sun deck. It's too hot to lie out for long, but one of the loungers is shaded from the burning rays by the roof of the adjoining open-air bar, so I sink down onto the comfortable mattress. The bar area is bordered by a half-height wall with an intricately designed wooden screen above it. No one will know I'm here.

I close my eyes and try to drive all worries and concerns from my mind, and it is a while before I realise there are people sitting on the other side of the divider from me. There is a bit of shuffling, as if someone is trying to get comfortable, and then I hear a couple of tiny sniffs and a strangled sob.

Just as I contemplate moving away from such a private moment I hear a deep, gravelly voice. 'For God's sake, Thea. People will see.'

I have never heard Garrick speak harshly to Thea before, and now I feel as if I can't show myself. I'm sure she would be embarrassed, so I lie perfectly still. *What on earth can be wrong?* I hear Thea blow her nose, and for once Garrick is the one to order the drinks.

'A sweet sherry and a large brandy, please,' he says.

I imagine him glaring at Thea as the waiter retreats, ashamed of her display of emotion.

'I'm sorry,' Thea says quietly and clears her throat. There's a minute or so of silence, and when her voice comes again, it shakes with suppressed tears. 'I know I'm making you uncomfortable. I miss her. That's all.'

Garrick grunts but doesn't respond for a few moments. 'I know you do,' he says finally, his voice less abrupt. 'We both do, but I don't want that Donna woman rushing over to ask what's the matter. She keeps glancing across, and I don't like people knowing our business. I didn't mean to be sharp.'

Thea's voice is little more than a whisper. 'Could we have done things differently, do you think?'

I hear a sigh, and I'm sure it's Garrick.

'No, Thea. You did everything you could. We both did.'

What on earth can they be talking about? Thea has never given me any indication that life is anything short of perfect for them both, but something has obviously hurt her – someone important in her life has gone.

They are quiet again, and I hear the sound of glasses being placed on the table and a muttered 'Thank you' from Garrick. They give the waiter time to move away.

I would really like to roll off this sun lounger and crawl away from here on my hands and knees. I don't want to listen to Thea's unhappiness or Garrick's rather uncomfortable response to whatever is causing her so much grief, but I am sure they would hear me if I were to move. All I can do is lie here and wish I was somewhere else.

They are quiet for a few minutes. I know they are still there, though, because I hear the pages of a magazine being turned rather too quickly for them to have been read and glasses being placed, more gently now, on the table.

'Another?' Garrick asks after a while.

'Yes please.'

I imagine him signalling the waiter and hear him place another order.

'I'm sorry about my little outburst, dear,' Thea says. 'I'm okay most of the time. I just had a tiny wobble.'

Garrick grunts in his usual way. 'The girl seems to be making things easier for you,' he says.

The girl? Could he mean me? I can't see who else it could be, and if spending time with me has helped Thea forget some sadness in her life, I'm delighted. She has saved me from losing my sanity on this holiday, and quite honestly I don't know what I would have done without her.

'She is, and I'll be sorry to say goodbye to her. Focusing on someone else's problems always makes one's own slightly less all-consuming.' It's definitely me she's talking about. She waits a beat. 'Don't you think she looks like—'

'Of course I do,' Garrick answers quickly. His voice softens again. 'And I'm glad it's helping.'

I hear some shuffling, a creak from the rattan chair, and I realise one of them is getting up.

'I'm going to the room. I think I'll have a lie-down. Are you coming, Thea?'

There is no response, but I know they have gone. I don't need to lift my head to check. I can feel their absence.

Thank God they don't know I heard them.

13

It was nearly two weeks since Sharon Carter's terrifying night at Pennington Flash, and she had lived every day in fear of Jez finding out how stupid she had been. Just as she was beginning to feel safe, confident there was nothing to worry about, she had turned on the news two nights ago. Since then the same story had been on every bulletin, and each time she saw it her whole body shook.

She stared at the television screen as a police detective made a plea for witnesses. A body had been found at the Flash, and Sharon knew she should call and tell them what she had seen. But by talking to the police she could land herself in a whole heap of trouble. They might come to the house, and then Jez would find out where she'd been. She would have to explain to him why she had gone there at that time of night. On the other hand, what if a killer was on the loose and she said nothing? What if he killed someone else? Oh God, it was such a mess.

She was supposed to be getting married and the wedding was now only a couple of weeks away. If it all came out, Jez might call it off. What had she been thinking?

'Do you want a cup of tea, babe?' Jez shouted. He popped his head round the door to their tiny kitchen and grinned at her. 'Wow, you look a picture of misery. What's up?' He glanced at the TV. 'Oh, don't go worrying about that. One of my mates says he knows a local cop, and they think she killed herself. They're just looking for anyone who knows her.'

That's not what they said on the news report, though. They said the police were treating the death as suspicious, and maybe

Jez's mate had it wrong. No, forget that. Jez's mate *did* have it wrong.

Sharon knew.

Because Sharon had been there.

She remembered slipping off her shoes, her heart thumping so loud that she was sure the man walking slowly towards her, shining the torch into the bushes, would hear it. She'd been terrified of making a sound, but she had to get away from the path. Moving as silently as she could, her feet like blocks of ice on the slowly freezing ground, she had crept to a denser patch of shrubs.

She could barely make out the man on the footpath. Why was he trying to find her? Why did it matter that she was there – somewhere – having apparently abandoned her car? She knew it wasn't the man from the club, so what did he want with her?

The torch flashed around, searching the area where just moments before she had been hiding, and she ducked her head.

The light had moved on, and when she risked peeping – still petrified that the torch would pick out the whites of her eyes – she saw the beam retreating back along the path towards the car.

Thank God. He's leaving.

But Sharon was wrong. The man got back into the car, but instead of driving towards the exit he pulled onto one of the footpaths that led to the smaller lakes and ponds. All she wanted to do was leave as quickly as she could, but getting to her own car could be dangerous. He might see her and come after her.

Sharon pushed herself up from where she was crouching, feeling nauseous as the tequila shots she had knocked back sloshed around in her gut, not helped by the hard knot of fear gripping her throat. Despite the freezing air, her clothes were clinging damply to her back. She made her way on bare feet to where the car had disappeared and peered around a tree trunk. It was parked no more than ten metres away. The door on the driver's side was open, and the man was walking towards the boot. He pulled out a long thin bag, which looked heavy. *What was he doing?*

Then the rear door behind the front passenger seat opened and another figure got out. Against the black sky it was hard to see much, but this person was a lot shorter, and Sharon felt sure it was either a woman or a child. Neither person spoke, and the shorter of the two waited patiently at the side of the car. Then the boot lid was slammed shut, and they started to walk down the lane together, turning off down a narrow path without a word spoken.

For a moment Sharon thought this was her chance to escape. But what if they were just going down there to dump the bag? They could be back before she was halfway across the car park. Whatever they were up to, it didn't look good. Why else would the man have checked her car so thoroughly and come looking for her? Why else drive without lights?

There was nothing for it. She had to hide, and wait.

It was hard to find the perfect spot. A lot of the shrubs had lost their leaves, and yet she wanted to keep the car in sight – to know when it left. The bloke from the club was obviously not coming, and although she was relieved, part of her would have been pleased to see him – or anyone else. Safety in numbers. For now though, she needed to find a place where the cover was good enough. Huddled into her black coat, she reasoned that if she kept her head down she wouldn't be seen.

The wait seemed endless. She didn't think she had ever been so cold, and her bare feet had lost all feeling, but she wasn't going back for her shoes. After about twenty minutes the driver returned, still carrying the bag. But he was alone – the person with him, whether woman, girl or child, wasn't there. *Where was she?*

He opened the car door, but in the brief flash of the interior light Sharon couldn't make out any features. He had his back to her. She heard the purr of an expensive engine, but no headlights came on. Suddenly the area where she was hiding felt exposed, illuminated by the car's reversing lights as he backed along the lane. Sharon stayed perfectly still. Sudden movement would be easy to detect, so she slowly dropped her head again, hoping her dark hair would blend in with her black coat. Her heart was pounding as the car reversed past her.

That would have been her chance to look at the driver's face, possibly glowing green from the instrument panel. But it would have been his chance to see her too, so she kept her head down, hoping and praying he wouldn't stop.

For a moment she thought he had as the car drew to a halt. But she breathed again when she realised he was putting it in gear to go forward. She lifted her head as the sound of the car moved away.

He had gone.

Sharon heard herself whimper as the fear that had been clutching her started to fade.

But where was the other person? Was there still a danger?

Sharon felt the first thick flakes of snow on her face and realised she needed to go. But where was the girl?

She couldn't wait to find out. If she stayed much longer and the promised heavy snowfall came she would be trapped, and there would be no explaining that away to Jez.

She ran as if the devil was chasing her and leaped into her car. This time her key went straight into the ignition, and she was out of the car park and on her way home within minutes. Her breath was coming in gasps, and her teeth clattered together as shivers racked her body.

Then the questions started, flitting round and round in her head.

What had he been doing? But more to the point, why did he want her car registration number? Was he going to hunt her down, to check what she'd seen?

She was so stupid. She didn't deserve Jez, and he must never know about this.

She should go to the police. But how could she keep it from Jez? How could she stop him from discovering what she so very nearly had done?

14

As my plane begins its descent into Manchester, I look out of the window at the snow-covered landscape and whisper an apology to Pops for the ruined holiday. I haven't been able to force the uncertainty of all that is waiting for me at home from my head, and after the word spread around the boat that my mother had died, the other passengers had treated me with sympathy. It made me uncomfortable and drove me back into the shell from which I had slowly been emerging since the start of the trip.

The tension gripping me increased with each passing day, and I found myself distrustful of everyone. More than once I returned to my cabin, convinced that someone had been in there, and when Paul spoke to me to say how sorry he was for my loss, I had the uncomfortable feeling that those beady eyes of his were looking straight through me. How could he know it wasn't true?

The ten-minute warning sounds, and we are told to fasten our seat belts for landing.

As we taxi to the gate I feel more lonely than I have ever felt in my life. I had hoped that Thea and Garrick would be travelling back on the same flight as they live so close to Manchester, but my flight was via Dubai and theirs via Singapore. Thea became my protector in the last few days of the holiday, and when Paul suggested one evening that maybe I would like to join him for dinner for a change, she was up in arms.

'Excuse me,' she said. 'This young lady is having a very hard time coming to terms with the loss of her mother. Right now she needs the support of those closest to her.'

Paul looked at me, raising his eyebrows as if in challenge, and once again I had the feeling that not only did he see right through me, but that there was something he wanted to say. I didn't like the questions he kept asking me about my life in Manchester, the holidays I had taken, the people I had met. He made me nervous.

After that he didn't speak to me again until we were leaving the boat. He leaned in close, and for a moment I thought he was going to kiss me goodbye. I could smell the soap he must have used to wash his face and feel his breath on my cheek. I pulled back sharply, alarmed at the thought of his skin touching mine.

I was wrong. He didn't want to kiss me.

'I'm watching you,' he said softly.

❖

I disembark and make the trek through the endless corridors of the airport to pick up my luggage. I don't mind if it's the usual long wait. I'm in no rush to get home, but it's the end of January and the airport isn't very busy, so the bags are with us within fifteen minutes. I heave my suitcase off the conveyor belt and head for the taxi rank.

I'm halfway to the door when I hear my name being called, and I stop dead. This can't be right, surely? I turn slowly, and there he is.

Ian.

Clutching a bunch of supermarket flowers and holding them out towards me, he smiles as if nothing has happened, but I can see his eyes are narrow, calculating.

'You didn't think I would leave you to get a taxi home, did you?' he asks. 'Here, let me take your case. You have these. Sorry they're not more exciting but it's the most I could afford.'

'Why are you here?' I stutter. But I know why. It's another of his games to put me on the back foot.

'Why wouldn't I be?' He reaches out his spare arm to touch

my shoulder, and I flinch. *Is he insane?* 'Oh, I get it. You think I'm still mad at you,' he says.

He laughs then, the harsh note piercing the racket of the airport. I want to shout at him, to tell him how he ruined my holiday, to ask him why he hasn't moved out of my house. But he is behaving as if none of it ever happened.

'Look, you're right: I was pissed off with you,' he says. 'But everybody has rows. We were fine until you insisted on going on that stupid holiday. You were just being obstinate, but I'm over it. Come on, let's get you home.'

I know exactly how his mind is working. He thinks I'm too weak to put up a fight, and if he acts as if everything is normal I will probably accept it. I don't know how to react. I don't want to get in the car with him, but I need to go home – to *my* home. Taking the bus or a taxi isn't going to make any difference. He will get back before me – in *my* car – and will be sitting in *my* chair, waiting for me.

'We'll talk in the car,' is all I can bring myself to say.

I hear him sigh. 'Oh, don't look like that,' he says, a hint of irritation in his voice. 'It's over now. I've forgiven you, so let's move on.'

At that moment the only thing I want to do is slap him. I'm not given to violence, but somehow everything has become my fault. I'm the one who is apparently behaving badly, and I know with certainty that this is how it's always been, but I was too blind to notice.

He takes my arm as we cross the road to the car park, and I can feel his fingers pinching my flesh. It seems that my refusal to cancel the holiday and my insistence that our relationship is over has unleashed something beyond the bitter words that spilled from his mouth before I left. I expected savage arguments, but not this. He is playing a game and I don't know the rules.

15

Sharon had been glued to the news every night for the past week. The police were still asking questions about the woman's body at Pennington Flash; even after all this time they didn't know who she was. Every time Sharon closed her eyes she saw the man shining his torch at her car, taking down her number. What if she was the only witness – the only person who could point the finger? What if the man was looking for her right now?

Sharon had tried to convince herself that any statement from her wasn't worth having, that she knew nothing. Two people had got out of a car and only one had got back in. There could be a hundred reasons for what she had seen, and it might have nothing to do with this woman's death.

The trouble was, Sharon couldn't think of a single reason other than the obvious one. It was making her irritable and edgy, and Jez kept asking what was wrong. She blamed it on pre-wedding nerves, and he liked that, saying she had seemed blasé about their big day up until now, so he was glad she was feeling a buzz of excitement. The stress was stopping her from thinking clearly about the wedding, though. Her mum had called her at work to ask if she was away with the fairies for some reason, because she'd forgotten to order the cake.

She pulled her feet up onto the sofa and cuddled up to Jez. He felt lovely and warm, just as he always did. She was the one who was cold, with chills of fear running through her day and night.

The phone rang – their landline, which practically nobody used these days.

'Bugger,' Jez said. 'Who the hell is that?'

She had no idea but knew he would get up to answer it. She would probably have let the answerphone take it.

She heard him say his name to the caller, but one of her favourite soaps was about to start so she wasn't focused on what else he was saying until she heard, 'Yeah, that's right. It's registered to this address.' A pause. 'Yeah, that's Sharon. My girlfriend. It's her car.'

Sharon jumped off the sofa just as she heard him saying, 'I don't think she was out that night. Hang on, I'll ask her.'

She snatched the phone out of his hand and pressed the button to end the call.

'What the hell did you do that for?' Jez asked.

'Who was it? Who wanted to know about my car?'

'Jesus, Shaz, what's got into you? It was the police, okay?'

She shook her head, gripping both of Jez's upper arms tightly and giving him a small shake.

'It wasn't the police. If it rings again, don't answer it, okay?'

'What the hell are you talking about? You're behaving like a loony. He said he was calling from Greater Manchester Police. He was a detective.' He shook himself free of her grasp.

'No, he wasn't. He was lying.'

Jez grabbed hold of Sharon's hands. 'Come and sit down. Talk to me.'

Just then the phone started to ring again. He reached for it.

'No!' she shouted.

Jez shook his head and cancelled the call. 'I wasn't going to take it, babe. Not until you've told me what on earth's wound you up.'

She had no idea what to say. How was she going to get out of this? She had the few seconds it took them to return to the sofa to come up with something plausible and as close to the truth as possible.

'What night was he asking about?' she said to Jez.

'A couple of weeks ago – that Thursday night when I stayed at Al's. You were in all night, weren't you?'

'No. I forgot to tell you. Some of the girls from work had organised a surprise pre-wedding do for me at that new club in town. I took the car because I didn't want to drink much.'

Jez gave her a puzzled frown. 'Why didn't you tell me?'

'Oh, with everything else in my head, I forgot. You were full of your night out with Al, and we had so much other stuff to talk about that was more important. It was no big deal.'

'Okay, so why do you think someone other than the police would be phoning about your car?'

Now came the difficult bit.

'When I left the club – before all the others, by the way – I got in the car to come home and I felt a bit…I don't know, nostalgic, I suppose. We're getting married soon, and everything will change.'

Jez raised his eyebrows, his face registering his shock. 'What are you talking about? What's going to change apart from your surname? It's you and me, same house, same jobs, same car, same irritating families. What the hell do you mean?'

Oh God, what had she got herself into?

'I know all that. But it will *feel* different. Anyway, whatever the reason, I decided I'd pootle about a bit – go to some of the places I went as a kid, or you and I went to when we first met. So that's what I did.'

'And?'

'I thought I was being followed. I took some odd turns and there was this car. It was always behind me, no matter which way I went. I was scared.'

'So – I repeat – why the hell didn't you tell me about this?'

Sharon looked at his concerned face and felt sick at what she was doing. 'I didn't want to worry you.'

'Shit, Shaz, that's not good enough. We're getting *married*. You should tell me everything!'

Sharon dropped her head and said nothing. She didn't want to make this worse.

'How did you lose him, then?' Jez asked.

'I pulled into a twenty-four-hour petrol station. I was going to talk to the cashier through the speaker and ask him to call the police. The car pulled in but parked on the edge of the forecourt. I looked over and I saw the driver writing something. I thought it might be my number plate. Then he drove off.'

Jez pulled her close and stroked the back of her hair. 'That must have been bloody awful for you. I wish you'd told me. Have you seen him since?'

'No, but it seems that somehow he's traced me, and I'm scared, Jez. Really scared.'

That was no lie. She knew the man must have been involved in the death of that woman at the Flash. And now he was coming for her.

16

It is over for another night. I was subjected to nothing more than an hour of words, but such powerful words. Words chosen intentionally to confuse me.

They must know I'm not eating the food they give me. I pick at it and push it around my plate, trying to look as if I have lost my appetite. I feel ungrateful because they say they only want to help me. But I don't understand what is happening to me.

All I know is that I have done something terrible, something that defies belief. Worse, though, I don't remember a thing about it, and that keeps coming back at me time and time again, hitting me with a force that almost knocks me down. Could I really have done what they tell me I have?

I look at the other two women who are here with me, sitting at the wooden table under the bare light bulb. Both of them seem resigned to their lives and how things have to be. We are here for our late-night cocoa. But I won't let a drop past my lips, however enticing the sweet smell of chocolate.

It's been a hard day for all of us, as is every day. But while the others accept it with resignation, I can't do that. There are things I want to know, to understand. They don't get it. They can't figure out why I have to question everything.

One of them seems a little more focused. She's the younger of the two – even younger than me, I think – and from time to time I see a spark of intelligence in her eyes, as if her real self is trying to battle through the fog.

'Why are you here?' I ask her, keeping my voice low, my mouth

disguised by the mug of cocoa that I'm pretending to drink.

It's not the first time I've asked, but tonight she seems a little more responsive than usual.

The other woman raises her weary eyes. 'You shouldn't ask questions. It's not allowed.'

I want to tell her that I'm an adult, not a child, and I will make my own rules. But I don't want to show my hand. She's more likely than the other to tell tales, I think.

'Sorry,' I say. I have to think of a way of getting the younger woman on her own when she is slightly more alert than usual. In the end, though, the matter is taken out of my hands as the older woman excuses herself and heads towards the bathroom.

The younger woman's head is bowed, staring into her cocoa, but then I realise that without raising her head she has lifted her eyes and is looking at me.

When she starts to speak, her voice is cracked but low so she can't be heard by anyone except me. I move closer. From behind the mug, I whisper one word: 'Careful.'

I think I see a slight nod. Then she puts down her cup and rests her head between her hands, squeezing as if she's trying to force some sense into her brain. She knows we can be seen and heard by others outside the room.

'I don't know why I did it,' she says softly. 'I loved him. Why would I do that?'

I want to ask her what she means, what she did, when it was, how long she has been here, but before I get the chance the buzzer sounds and we push back our chairs to return – as we must – to our rooms. As we shuffle along the corridor, I hear her mumble two words.

'Safe here,' she says with a nod, and I'm not sure if she's trying to convince herself or me.

She may think we're safe, but right now all I can think about is why they are coming back tonight. Only one of us is ever selected each night – and that was me earlier.

They know something is wrong. They have to. That's why they're coming back.

17

The two days since I returned from holiday have been dreadful. Being with Ian in the house is almost more than I can bear, but I have nowhere else to go – no friends who are close enough to welcome me if I turn up on their doorstep asking if I can stay, no family who are interested in my problems.

I have to go back to work today, so I need clean clothes and my work stuff. Everything I own is in my home, so what choice do I have? And besides, it's my house. Ian is the one who has to leave.

The journey home from the airport was driven in silence. With my mouth clamped tightly shut, I gazed out of the window at the winter scene. The streets had all been cleared, but the pavements were a mixture of packed snow and filthy water washed up from the gritted roads. I could sense Ian getting more and more furious with me for not talking to him – not that he wanted to hear anything about Myanmar or the people I had met, of course. But like all bullies he thought he could back me into a corner and I would give in under pressure. My lack of response to his 'forgiveness', though, was telling him that something in me had changed.

As Ian drove – rather faster than was entirely necessary – I decided it was better not to speak at all than to start a battle of words that would end badly. I knew I had it all to come and by letting him fester I was possibly making everything worse, but his driving was erratic enough without risking him speeding even more just to scare me.

I was relieved to get home safely, but when I walked into the house it didn't welcome me. It felt alien, cold, and there was a cloying smell of cheap rose-scented air freshener trying to disguise the stink of stale beer. The sitting room was littered with newspapers, the waste-paper basket overflowing with empty cans. I turned to look at Ian. My face must have shown what I thought, but he ignored it.

'Glad to be home?' he asked. 'The weather's been shite while you were away – I barely made it out of the door.'

He was smiling, but it was a fixed smile that didn't reach his granite-like eyes, and his actions were exaggerated – throwing the door open a little too hard, kicking off his shoes so they banged against the wall. I could feel his fury, but he was waiting for me to do something, say something, that would allow him to vent his anger on me.

In the end my silence became too much for him. He flung himself into an armchair. 'Spit it out, then,' he said. 'I've told you that you're forgiven, but you're still behaving as if you've got something to say. Sorry might be a good place to start.'

I took a deep breath. I knew what had to be said, but I had no idea how he would react.

'Ian, I told you before I went away that we are done. I'm sorry it hasn't worked out, and for my part I can only apologise. But I would appreciate it if you would find somewhere else to live.'

He laughed. He actually laughed. 'I'm going nowhere. If we're done, you're the one that's going to have to go. This is my home too, and I'm not the one ending things. I said I'd forgiven you. I even bought you fucking flowers to show there were no hard feelings, *and* I had a clean-up to welcome you home. As I said, I know you've been upset and maybe that's an excuse for your behaviour, but with a little effort from you we can go back to how things were before.'

I stared at him. Putting used cans into the bin and giving each room a quick squirt of crappy air freshener was, I knew, Ian's idea of a clean-up, but I couldn't get the smell out of my nostrils, the taste out of my throat, and it made me nauseous.

'It's my house, Ian. You know that. I paid the deposit, and I pay the mortgage. It doesn't matter whose fault it is. It's time to go our separate ways.'

'You invited me to share your home,' he said, a hard, knowing smile on his face that chilled me. 'I left my roots because you promised we would be a couple for life. I've supported you emotionally, moved to the other side of the country to be with you, shopped, cooked and cleaned so that you have the freedom to do your job. I've been the main carer.' I glanced around the room at the mess, but he just laughed. 'That means I have what is known as a beneficial interest in the property. It's the law. I bet you didn't know that, did you? This is my home, and I'm going nowhere.' He folded his arms and sat back.

'That can't be right,' I told him, my voice rising. I tried to bring it down a notch, but I struggled. 'You *know* it's not. I've paid for absolutely everything while you've sat on your backside and done nothing.'

He couldn't wipe the smirk off his face. It was clear that he genuinely believed he had some rights, and I felt my eyes fill with tears of frustration. How do you handle someone who is so unreasonable, irrational and deluded? I didn't know, and the only thing I could think of was to run from the room before one of us said or did something from which there could be no coming back.

I heard Ian's voice, laced with derision, calling after me, but I couldn't hear the words over the thundering of my feet on the stairs. I fled to the bathroom, locked the door and leaned against it, my breath coming in gasps. But in moments they had turned to sobs, and I slid down the door until I was on the floor, knees pulled up to my chest.

I don't know how long I sat there. I never heard him creep upstairs, but I knew he was outside the door. I could hear him breathing. He was waiting for me to come out.

'Go away, Ian,' I said, keeping my voice level.

'You're going to have to come out of there some time, and I'll be waiting,' he replied, his speech slow, sinister. 'It's time you learned that you can't have everything your own way.'

It was a clear warning, and there was a sense of inevitability about what would happen the minute I stepped out of the room.

I had never been afraid that Ian would turn violent before, but I had been wrong about so much. I couldn't risk it, so I pulled my phone out of the back pocket of my jeans and dialled three numbers.

'Police, please,' I said as quietly as possible, my voice shaking.

'What the fuck are you doing?' I heard him shout.

'I'm calling the police,' I yelled. 'I'm scared to come out of my own bathroom and you won't leave my house. What do you expect me to do?'

I heard the calm voice of the operator, asking for my name and address. Biting back a sob, I told her.

'I'm not going to hurt you,' Ian screamed. 'For Christ's sake, hang up the phone. Tell them it's all a mistake. It's just a disagreement. Please, we don't want this, do we?'

All of a sudden I felt stupid. Surely Ian wouldn't hurt me, especially now he knew I had called the police? Maybe I had overreacted. The operator was still talking, but I couldn't do this. It was going too far, and as the fear abated it was replaced with shame. How had I ended up like this, in a relationship that needed intervention from the police?

I apologised to the operator and told her it was just a row, that I had panicked unnecessarily, and asked her to please forget it. I had to reassure her that I really was okay, but eventually she believed me and I hung up.

'Ian,' I shouted, my lie prepared. 'The police want me to call them in an hour to tell them I'm okay. Now move away from the door, please.'

That did it. He looked at me warily as I inched open the door, but he backed away and didn't threaten me physically.

The potential for violence was only part of the problem, though. Nothing seemed to shake Ian's conviction that he deserved to be in my house, and those first hours at home set the tone for the weekend. I did my best to keep out of his way, but I knew I wasn't going to be able to change his mind.

❖

Today I'm relieved to be going back to work, out of the stifling atmosphere of the house. I need to work out how to reclaim my home, and I don't think Ian has a case based on what I have read online, but I have no idea how long it might take me to prove it, and I can't go on living with him.

I can feel the frown on my face as I walk into the office, and assume that is why I'm getting some strange looks. I expected people to smile and ask me about my holiday, but nobody does. I look around the room, trying to plaster a grin on my face to show that all is well, but nobody will meet my eyes. Instead, they look at their computer screens or their phones. *What's going on?*

I plug my laptop in, but before I can open it, the internal phone on my desk rings.

'My office, please.'

It's my boss, Tim, and he doesn't sound happy either. It's strange because I checked over the weekend to see if there were any emergency emails – anything that I might have missed with regard to the event I've been helping to manage. But I hadn't received one single message, so I assumed everything was going to plan. Maybe I was wrong.

I walk into Tim's office and smile. 'Hi,' I say and stop dead. Heather from HR is with him, and I look from one to the other in surprise. 'Is everything okay?' I ask.

'I presume you're here to hand in your laptop,' Tim says, and there's not a trace of a smile on his face.

'What do you mean? Have I done something wrong?' My eyes flick to each of them in turn. 'What is it?'

Heather picks up a sheet of paper. 'Have you forgotten your Facebook post?' she asks.

I've no idea what she means. I had intended to do a bit of posting when I was away, but I'm not addicted to social media and after the first couple of days I decided not to bother any more. I was too worried about seeing something derogatory that Ian might have posted.

Heather reads from the paper in front of her.

'"Can't believe I'm going to have to leave this beautiful country to return to my lousy job, made all the more lousy by my idiot boss, who cocks up everything and is a bit too free with his hands, if you get me. He should be sacked. Our clients get such a bum deal." What do you have to say to that?' Heather adds, putting the sheet of paper back down on the desk.

My heart pounds. *What is she talking about?*

'I didn't post that!' I know full well that I have been known to say that Tim's an idiot, but I'd never be stupid enough to post it on social media. And he might make the odd sexist remark, but he's not a groper.

Tim jumps up from his chair, pushing it back on its wheels, and stomps out of the door. I can see through the glass that everybody is trying hard not to look at what he's doing. He is at my desk, where I put my laptop just moments before, yanking the lead out. Then he marches back into his office, slamming the door behind him.

'Log in to your Facebook account,' he demands.

I shrug and click on the link, knowing my password is stored so it will log in automatically, but confident he's not going to find anything in my posts other than a couple of early pictures from Myanmar. He pulls the screen round to face him and Heather, and I begin to feel slightly sick. All of Ian's emails are on my laptop, and I pray they don't go searching through those as they hunt for further evidence of my misconduct.

There's a click on the trackpad, and Tim sits back in his chair, shaking his head, his mouth in a tight line. He's a big man with a florid face, and his lips almost disappear into his jowls. Heather spins the computer back to me.

'Does anyone else know your Facebook password?'

I look from one frowning face to the other, speechless, and shake my head.

Tim and Heather can see my confusion, but they're not backing down.

'That's being disrespectful, and as if that weren't bad enough you are bringing the company into disrepute,' Heather says, leaning towards me as if being empathetic rather than dealing me a death blow. 'As I'm sure you know, that is an offence that results in immediate dismissal, and you should think yourself lucky that Tim isn't going to sue you for defamation of character.'

I barely listen as they talk through the details of when and how I must leave. I want to shout out a denial, but I've already told them it wasn't me and I have no way to prove my innocence. I know I won't be allowed to work out my notice, and I'm not going to be able to say goodbye to the rest of the team. I thought they were my friends, but from their behaviour this morning maybe I was wrong. Or perhaps they're just scared of the repercussions. I want to go out there and deny it all to them too, but they won't believe me because it seems like the only possible truth.

A million thoughts flood my mind. I'm not going to be able to pay the mortgage, let alone afford to move out of the house while I find a way to get rid of Ian. I thought my life was a mess when I arrived at work this morning, but now it's ten times worse.

I walk back through the office towards the main door. The phones continue to ring, my colleagues take the calls, tap on their keyboards, sip from their coffee cups, shuffle papers on their desks. And not one of them looks up.

18

After I leave the silent office I'm not sure what to do, but I'm not ready to go home to face Ian. I walk aimlessly along the street until I find myself in Saint Peter's Square, where I park myself on a bench. It's freezing, and I pull my coat tightly across my chest and huddle on the seat, pretending to watch the world go by but actually seeing nothing. Everyone has their head down into the wind, racing towards somewhere, someone. I'm alone on the bench.

I try to tie in the date of the Facebook post with my trip, to decide which day it was and what I was doing, and it comes as no surprise when I realise it was the night Ian called with the lie that my mother had died. Surely he didn't hack into my account somehow and post those words? Maybe he didn't need to hack in. I can't remember if I logged out of Facebook on our home computer the last time I used it. I should have thought about that and told Tim and Heather. But I doubt they would have believed me.

I have been known to say that Tim is an idiot; I even mentioned him during the holiday. I remember Paul leaning back in his seat to listen to the conversation, but what would he have to gain by sneaking into my cabin to post something on Facebook about someone he didn't even know? On the other hand, I can't believe that at any point I was sufficiently drunk to write those words for the whole world to read and not remember I'd done it. So who else could it have been?

It had to be Ian. It would be just his style. Anything to undermine me, to weaken me. I can picture him after our phone conversation had ended with so much vitriol, thumping upstairs in a rage to the spare room where we keep the desktop computer and hammering out something he knew would get me into trouble.

I start to shiver, and I'm not sure if it is the weather or my fear of the hours, days and weeks ahead. The world around me looks grey – the sky, the buildings, the dirty wet pavements. I know I need to go home, to get out of this wicked wind, but Ian will be there and I'm sure he will laugh at my predicament, particularly if he was its architect.

I can feel tears running down my cheeks and lift my hand to wipe them away with the backs of my fingers. I push myself up from the bench and head towards the tram stop.

It is only a five-minute walk from my stop to the house, and I find myself dawdling, not wanting to get there, not wanting to tell Ian what has happened. But I can't go in looking defeated. I take a deep breath and lift my head.

As I turn the last corner I'm surprised to see a woman in a long royal-blue coat walking up our path towards the door. I'm even more startled when I recognise the silver hair and realise that it's Thea.

'Hello,' I say, unable to disguise my relief at seeing a friendly and supportive face.

'Hello, dear,' she says, a smile lighting up her eyes. 'How lovely to see you. I thought you'd be at work. I popped round with a card with our address on in case you ever fancied a visit.' She waves a piece of cream-coloured card in the air. 'I've been to see an old friend in hospital, and as I was on this side of town I thought I'd kill two birds with one stone.'

'I didn't know you had my address,' I say. 'I meant to give it to you, but I think my worries about coming home drove all the sense out of me.'

Thea nods. 'I know. I didn't want to bother you with trivia when you were so concerned. I looked you up in the electoral register. Anyway, I hope things have turned out better than you expected. If not, the doctor and I are here, if you ever need us.'

She smiles at me kindly and reaches out to touch my arm. It's enough to set me off and the tears start to fall, the words tumbling out: how I've lost my job; how hateful Ian is being; how I don't know what to do.

She stands in the street and listens, appearing unconcerned that people are walking past and giving us inquisitive glances. Eventually the tears dry up.

'I'm sorry,' I say. 'I'd better get inside. I'm sure Ian will be watching and wondering what's going on.'

'If he cared about you, he would have come to find out, don't you think?' She pauses and frowns. 'I have an idea. Why don't you go into the house and tell him what's happened? See how he reacts. If he's helpful and positive, that's fine. Great news, and you can work things out.'

I snort unattractively at the very thought that Ian could be helpful.

'I see,' she says. 'It's every bit as bad as you thought, then. Why don't I wait in my car? If he's a total nightmare and you need to get out, you must come to stay with the doctor and me. You would be very welcome, you know. We have a huge house so you could be totally independent. No pressure. Whatever works for you. Even if it's just for a couple of days until you get your head straight, it might be useful. We're on completely the opposite side of Manchester, but it's only about eight minutes' walk from a tram stop, so you wouldn't be cut off, and you can always borrow one of our cars.'

I can't accept this. I've only known Thea for a couple of weeks, and while it is such a generous offer, it doesn't feel right to simply run away from my problems.

'I can see you hesitating, dear, and I understand. I'll leave you to it. The invitation is there, if ever you need it.' Thea gives my arm another squeeze and turns away.

I suddenly panic. I have no doubt at all how awful it is going to be when I go inside, and Ian and I will have to live there, together for twenty-four hours a day, while we work out the future. I know that nothing will be resolved if we're in the same house. And I need to look for a job, but I will be in no frame of mind with him undermining my last ounce of confidence.

'Wait,' I call before I can change my mind. 'I'm sorry, Thea. It's a wonderful offer. Do you mind hanging on for a few minutes? I would ask you in, but…'

'You take as much time as you need.'

I lean forward and give her a hug. 'You are so kind,' I say. 'I promise I won't keep you waiting long.'

Thea shrugs. 'I'm not doing anything else and I've got some music to listen to. Pack enough for a couple of nights. You can always come back for more.'

I suddenly feel so much better, and there is a slight spring in my step as I walk up the path to the front door.

My moment of positivity is soon crushed.

'Who was that old bag you were talking to?' Ian says, without looking up from his newspaper. 'And what the fuck are you doing home at this hour?'

I look around the room. Although I tidied it and cleaned over the weekend, it's back to looking a tip with two coffee mugs and a plate of half-eaten toast on the floor.

'I'm here because I've been sacked.'

That gets Ian's attention and his head jerks up. 'What?' There is a trace of a smile on his face, and I can't decide whether it is because he is enjoying my pain, or whether it is pleasure that his plan has come to fruition, or both.

'There was a Facebook post about Tim apparently made by me, but I've no idea how that happened. Anyway, the details don't matter.'

Ian throws his head back and laughs. 'How the mighty are

fallen! This is priceless. You do know that if you're sacked you can't claim benefit for three months, don't you? Maybe you'll realise it's not so easy to get a job now, after nagging me for all this time.'

I'm almost certain now that it was him.

'I will get a job, Ian, whatever it takes. It doesn't have to be an office job. I'll work in a bar, as a cleaner. I don't care. But I'll have to cancel the lease on the car.'

Ian crumples the newspaper and throws it on the floor. 'Don't be fucking ridiculous. I need a car.'

'Fine, you pay for it,' I tell him, walking towards the door.

He leaps up from his chair. 'Where do you think you're going?' he asks, storming across the room and blocking my way.

'I'm going to stay with a friend for a while. I need to work out what to do.'

'Which friend? You don't have any.'

I have no intention of telling him where I'm going. Not that I know any details.

'And how am I supposed to eat now that you've cleared out the bank account?' he says, a whine of self-pity in his voice.

I want to tell him he should have thought of that before he started messing with my Facebook account. He probably thought I would just get a warning, a telling-off, and now it has backfired. But I feel so tired I want to drop to the floor where I'm standing. I can't cope with this. There must be something of the hopelessness I'm feeling in my expression because Ian drops the arm that barred the doorway.

'Do what you want,' he says. 'You always do.'

No, Ian, I think to myself. *What I would really like to do right now is see you disappear off the face of the earth – disintegrate in front of my eyes.*

But I say nothing and trudge upstairs to get a bag, thinking only about the minimum I can pack to get out of there as quickly as possible.

19

It was ten days since the body of the woman, 'Penny', had been found at Pennington Flash, and well over two weeks since she had died. And yet they still didn't appear to have made any real progress in finding out who she was or where she had come from. The shoes that had caused a flutter of excitement had definitely not belonged to Penny. As well as being the wrong size, the DNA wasn't a match.

The tox results had confounded them all, with no reasonable explanation for such a weird mix of drugs. Although it was clear from the hair analysis that Penny had been taking some of them for months, they were not the direct cause of her death. Despite forming all kinds of hypotheses about why she had taken this strange concoction, they still had nothing concrete. Tom was hoping that an investigation into the source of the drugs might help them identify Penny, but as yet they hadn't found anything of use.

Becky rested her chin on her fist. At this rate they wouldn't solve the case before she went on maternity leave, and that thought was driving her mad. Her frustration was making her irritable, and her partner, Mark, had raised his eyebrows a couple of times when she snapped at something trivial. But he said nothing. It was amazing what you could get away with when you were pregnant.

Becky glanced across at Lynsey. She had settled in well and her confidence was growing, but she was clearly picking up the vibes from the rest of the team. From where Becky sat in the incident room she could see the girl trying to concentrate on the latest reports, but judging by her lack of enthusiasm as she flipped the pages, it was doubtful that they revealed much.

Becky's phone rang. 'DI Robinson.'

'Hello.' The voice was quiet, hesitant, female. 'I don't know if I'm speaking to the right person, but I'm ringing because I think I might have some information.'

'Well thanks for calling. Can you tell me your name?'

'What? Do I have to?' she asked, the pitch of her voice rising.

For a moment Becky thought the caller might hang up, so she hurried to reassure her. 'No, no, not if you don't want to. But it might be easier for me if you did. I'm Becky.'

'Will my first name do? It's Sharon.'

'Hello, Sharon. How can I help you?' Becky said in her friendliest voice.

'I was told this was the number for anyone with information about Pennington Flash.'

Becky immediately sat up straight. Several members of the team saw her reaction and the general hubbub in the room died down as eyes turned towards her.

'That's right. We're investigating the discovery of a woman's body, found there ten days ago.'

'Oh,' Sharon said, her voice dropping with a hint of relief. 'It said on the news that it was longer ago than that. Sorry. I'm probably wasting your time, then.'

Becky spoke quickly: 'The news reports were right, Sharon. We found the woman ten days ago, but we think she had been there for longer. Perhaps from when the freeze began more than two weeks ago. Whatever you were going to tell me might be more useful than you think. Shall we give it a try?'

There was a moment's silence, as if Sharon was gathering her nerve.

'Right.' Sharon took an audible deep breath. 'Well, I've been away, see, and only just got back – that's why I haven't called till now.'

From the way Sharon spoke, Becky suspected she was reading from some notes she had prepared before calling, which suggested she could be lying. Combined with the reluctance to give her name, Becky surmised that Sharon had been trying to decide whether to talk to the police or not.

'That's okay. It's good of you to call now,' Becky said. 'Why don't you tell me what you're thinking? Don't worry about whether it's relevant. It's our job to make that decision.'

'Okay.' There was another pause. 'I might have seen something. I was there – at the Flash. Look, I don't want my boyfriend to know any of this, okay? He'd call the wedding off, and that would be a disaster...'

Becky thought Sharon was about to cry, and realised that whatever she had been doing at the Flash, she was regretting it now.

'Don't worry. Just tell me what you saw, heard or think you know. Take your time.'

'It was Thursday night – as I said – just over two weeks ago. I thought I'd like a bit of space – do a bit of thinking, you know? So I thought of the Flash. It's a lovely spot, and I was sure it would be deserted at that time of night. It was well after midnight.'

Becky desperately wanted to interrupt to ask her what the hell she thought she was doing – a girl alone – driving to an isolated spot in the middle of the bloody night! But she didn't. She would save that for later, and anyway, she had a sneaking suspicion the girl might not have been alone.

'Go on,' she said, keeping the sense of rising excitement from her voice.

'I'd been there for about fifteen minutes when I saw a car coming. It didn't have its lights on.'

Becky listened in silence as Sharon told her everything that had happened: where the car had gone, who had got out, and the woman or child who had not returned.

'When they got out of the car together, did you get the impression the man was forcing the woman to go with him?' Becky asked.

'No. If I'd thought that I would have found a way to call you lot. She didn't appear to be struggling or anything and could easily have legged it when she first got out. And I don't know for certain that the driver was a man – I never saw his face, so I suppose I just assumed it was.'

'Do you have any idea about the car – make, model, colour? I suppose the registration number would be going too far?'

'I'm not much into cars. I was more worried about getting away myself, to be honest. The car was a dark colour, not a hatchback – you know, it had a proper boot and everything, big but not massive. Sounded expensive, though. It kind of purred, if you know what I mean.'

'Sharon, I'm sorry to ask you this, but were you definitely on your own? Because if someone was with you we could talk to him or her privately to see if they could add anything.'

Sharon gave a small gasp. 'Gosh, you're not a police officer for nothing, are you? I *was* on my own, as it happens. But... Oh, never mind the rest of it. Honestly, there was nobody else there. Just me. But there was something else. He took down my number plate, and I think he's trying to find me, maybe to find out what I know.'

There was no mistaking the note of panic in Sharon's voice.

Becky tried to reassure her. 'It's quite hard for a member of the public to track down anyone by their car registration number, unless they can provide a good reason for doing that. What makes you think he's trying to find you?'

'Someone called the house. Said he was a detective. My boyfriend spoke to him. It was him, I'm sure.'

Becky thought for a moment. 'Can you hang on for a minute or two, Sharon? I'm going to make a couple of enquiries to see if we can put your mind at rest.'

She turned and called to Lynsey: 'Can you ask round quickly to see if anyone was tracking a car that belonged to someone called Sharon?'

A few minutes later Lynsey stuck a yellow Post-it under Becky's nose.

Becky scanned it quickly. 'Sharon, can I check if your surname is Carter? Because if it is, you really were called by a detective from this office.'

There was a gasp from the other end of the phone. 'What?'

'There are no CCTV cameras at the Flash, so we've been looking at footage from nearby pub and petrol-station cameras, identifying cars with female drivers or passengers. Your car showed up about half a mile away. I gather it was weaving around a little.'

'Oh shit. Am I going to be done for drunk driving now?' she asked, her voice cracking.

'No, we can't prove that from CCTV. But you've been incredibly helpful. We know what time you passed, and you said it was about fifteen minutes after that when the other car appeared in the car park. Thanks to you we now know it was a larger than average saloon, and that a woman was in the back. That is a huge help. I'd like you to come down to the station, if you would. If you could look at the CCTV footage, you might be able to help us identify the car.'

'But what'll I tell Jez?'

'Jez is your fiancé, I assume? It's up to you how you handle it, but you might be able to help us catch this man.'

Becky tried to convince her that it was the right thing to do, but Sharon wanted to think about it. She gave Becky her mobile number, though, so at least they could call her without Jez answering.

For the first time Becky felt a slight glimmer of hope. It wasn't much, but they could check the CCTV footage again in the vicinity for any dark saloons within a much narrower timescale, and then she would call Sharon back and persuade her to come and view the options. Maybe, just maybe, they were finally getting somewhere.

20

As I reach Thea's car – something small, sensible and white – I see her sitting with her head back, eyes closed, and through a window that has been left open half an inch I can hear the strains of classical piano music. I am almost too embarrassed to disturb her, but she seems to sense me standing by the door.

Her eyes open slowly and she turns to me with a sad smile. 'Didn't go well then,' she says, and it's not a question 'Stick your bag in the boot and hop in. We'll soon get you home, and we can have a glass of something to brighten the end of a dreadful day.'

Tempting as that sounds, the idea of making polite conversation suddenly seems too much, and I wonder if I've made the right decision.

'I expect you'd like to be on your own, really, but sometimes that bit of effort you don't want to make can take the edge off your unhappiness,' she says, and not for the first time I am amazed at her understanding.

We set off. Thea's driving is calm and unhurried, if maybe a little too slow for the good folk of Manchester, and she gets more than one angry glare as someone overtakes, engine roaring. She is unruffled and I gradually feel some of the tension ease, although the ache of unhappiness is just as uncomfortable. Neither of us speaks for the first ten minutes, and I'm beginning to wonder if I'm being rude when Thea breaks the silence.

'Did you tell Ian where you were going?' she asks.

'No. I don't actually know, so it would have been difficult. But I could barely bring myself to speak to him.'

'Well, that's a good thing. At least he can't come looking for you. Actually, dear, I'd be grateful if you wouldn't tell anybody you're staying with us. We had a bit of bother when we took in another young woman not too long ago. She had some problems, and we gave her a temporary home – a bit like you, really. A dreadful little tax man came round asking why we hadn't declared any rental income. We told him she wasn't paying us – and of course we don't expect you to either – but he didn't believe us. So he started an investigation. It cost us thousands in accountancy fees to demonstrate that we didn't have a secret account we were hiding money in.' Thea gives a little laugh, but I can see she's not amused.

'I've got nobody to tell, so don't worry about that,' I say.

She glances at me, and the car momentarily strays towards the centre of the road. 'Friends?'

'I thought I had, but based on their behaviour today in the office, I would say not.' The thought is horrendous. I still have friends in London, and maybe I should think about moving back there. But for now I just need to get my head together. 'Let's see if any of them call and apologise for ignoring me,' I say, with neither hope nor expectation.

'That might be a problem, dear. We don't get a mobile signal in the house or the garden. I hope that's not going to be an issue for you?'

I think about it for all of two seconds. 'Not at all. Ian can't pester me, and that has to be a good thing.' I stay quiet for a few minutes. 'He wasn't always so awful, you know,' I say, as if to excuse my appalling taste in men.

'Don't worry. People can hide their true selves until the chips are down, and then we get to see the ugly side. Nobody's nice when a relationship is ending. There's a desire to hurt as much as you've been hurt yourself, and only the strongest behave with dignity.' She indicates right without, as far as I can tell, checking her mirror. 'Having said that, it sounds to me as if Ian is a special case who's occupying more space in this world than he warrants.'

I'm not sure what she means, but right now any criticism of Ian sounds good to me.

Thea turns and gives me a brief smile. 'Not far now,' she says as we turn off onto a wide, leafy road that has been cleared of snow.

It looks as if someone has been out with a shovel in front of each property and everywhere is pristine – a far cry from the slushy mess on the streets close to my home. Some of the houses are impressive in this obviously wealthy area. I should have known that Thea and Garrick were well off, given the way Thea dresses and the wonderful jewellery she always wore at dinner, but I hadn't imagined anything in this league, and as she turns into a narrow lane I realise that I haven't seen anything yet. The hedges are high with tall overhanging trees, and the houses I glimpse briefly are set well back from the road. Each and every one of them is amazing.

Thea then turns onto a well maintained but unmade track, and after about half a mile swings onto a gravel driveway. Finally I see the house. It is all I can do not to gasp at the enormous, sprawling white building with black-timbered gable ends, surrounded by undulating snow-covered lawns and neatly trimmed shrubberies. There is no defined shape to the property; it has at least four different roof heights, each with a gable facing in a different direction. The external walls are mainly rendered and painted, although parts of the ground floor are finished in stone, and there are a number of bay windows. It looks as if it may have once been symmetrical, but over the years wings have been added haphazardly. It shouldn't work, but it does.

'Wow,' is the best I am able to offer.

'We like it,' Thea says with a hint of pride. I'm not surprised.

I notice there is a garage that will hold about four cars, but its doors are closed and Thea pulls up by what I assume is the main entrance to the house. As I open the car door I am surprised by the silence. We can't be far from major roads, but there isn't a sound. I guess the tall trees must act as natural barriers, and after everything I've been through, it is incredibly soothing. It is as if all noise has been deadened by giant earmuffs.

I think Thea can sense I'm slightly overawed, and she becomes brisk and businesslike. 'Right, we'll get you inside and I'll show you where you'll be living, then we can have that drink.'

I grab my bag from the boot and follow her. There is quite a grand stone portico to our right, but Thea walks around to the left where I see another door, which I presume is the one they usually use.

'Boots off, please, dear,' she says as we walk into a narrow entrance hall. There is a shoe rack to the left with nothing on it. I kick my boots off and put them on the rack, cross with myself that the only footwear I have brought is the pair of ankle boots with heels that I was wearing. I'll just have to go barefoot in the house.

Thea leaves her sensible shoes by the door, slides her feet into a pair of slippers, and I follow her through into a dark, narrow passageway. There are no windows, the only light coming from dim wall lamps, and to my right I see three doors, all closed. To my left is a staircase, and Thea heads for it. At the top of the first flight another door faces us, but we turn away and keep climbing, finally coming out onto a small landing with a tiny window. There are doors everywhere, but Thea moves straight ahead into another long, windowless corridor towards the last room on the left.

'Here you are,' she says, flinging the door open and standing back. She's waiting for my response, and she won't be disappointed. I look into a beautiful large bedroom with a wide bay window and a fireplace on the opposite wall. Despite the overwhelming use of pink, it is stunning, and I turn to her and shake my head.

'Am I really sleeping here?' I ask, and she laughs.

'Come on, I'll show you the rest of this floor. You've got it all to yourself.'

I dump my suitcase and follow her out. There's another smaller bedroom next door, then an amazing bathroom with an old fashioned roll-top bath in the centre.

'This is the snug,' Thea says as she shows me a small alcove off the hall. 'Nice and cosy, but you can use this sitting room if you prefer,' she says, opening the door to another huge room decorated with wallpaper covered in more huge pink roses. It's a bit flowery for my taste, but so much more than I expected. 'And finally, the kitchen.'

I've got my own kitchen. I can't believe it. I noticed this top level when we arrived. It only extends over about half of the floor below, and yet it is bigger than the whole of my house, and the kitchen is so well equipped. I have no idea what to say.

'Make yourself at home, won't you?' Thea says with a smile. 'There's just one thing. I mentioned to you that we don't want people to know you're staying, if you remember – we don't want another inspection.' She shudders dramatically. 'The cleaning staff come in each morning, but they're not allowed up here. I'm sure you don't mind keeping this part of the house tidy, do you?'

'Of course not. I'll do any cleaning here – or in the rest of the house – or cooking, or anything I can do to help.'

Thea smiles. 'It's very kind of you, but that won't be necessary. We must make sure the cleaners aren't aware that you're here, though, so I hope you don't mind if I lock the door at the bottom of the stairs in case you forget that you're not supposed to come down. I think it's for the best.'

21

I know that locking the door at the bottom of the stairs makes some sort of sense, but what would happen if there was a fire? I was about to ask if she would consider leaving it unlocked and I would pin a note on it to remind me not to go down, but she turned to leave.

'You settle yourself in. I'll come back up and collect you in about an hour and take you to see the doctor. He keeps to himself a lot of the time, although he still sees a few patients in his study so you might hear some talking. Obviously his study is out of bounds. Help yourself to anything you want in the kitchen. It's all there for you.'

Before I could thank her and ask about the door, she was gone. Since then I've been trying to take it all in. She was right about the phone – there's no signal, and no Wi-Fi either, but as I'm not working and nobody seems to want to speak to me, I can't see that it matters much.

Unpacking takes about five minutes, and then I wander from room to room. I haven't brought any books with me, but in the area Thea called the snug there is a bookcase full of all kinds of paperbacks, and I select one at random. The sitting room has a TV, but it doesn't seem to be working and I can't possibly ask them to get it fixed. I managed without TV on a cruise up the Irrawaddy for a couple of weeks, so I'm sure I can cope here.

There is something soporific about this place, with its silence and isolation, and when I have run out of places to explore and things to do I decide to curl up on a sofa, not expecting to fall asleep – I have too much on my mind – but I feel an overpowering need to close my eyes.

I am woken by the sound of footsteps in the corridor. Thea has come back to take me downstairs for that promised glass of something. I do hope it's not sweet sherry, which seemed to be her drink of choice on the boat, but to be honest I would drink neat rum if they asked me to, given all they're doing for me.

'Are you settling in?' Thea asks, her head on one side as if there might be some doubt.

'I don't know what to say. I'm blown away by the whole place and your kindness and generosity. I promise to sort myself in a couple of days and be out of your hair. I don't want to take advantage.'

'Oh nonsense. I like having you here. As I said, we've helped other people before. The doctor says I'm always on the lookout for waifs and strays, and it will be good to have you around. Come on. Let's get you downstairs.'

I know my way back to the staircase by now, but I take a step back to allow Thea to take the lead. We go down to the first floor, where the door is still closed.

'These rooms are our private sleeping quarters. So I would be grateful if you would respect our privacy. I'm not going to give you a tour of that area.'

'Of *course*! I wouldn't dream of invading your space.'

Thea smiles. 'Well, it's a big enough house for us all to have plenty of room to ourselves, and we have no expectations of you. We're very happy for you to stay in your rooms or join us for the occasional meal.'

That has clarified things for me. They are being more than generous, but I'm not a house guest in the normal way. I won't be eating every meal with them, which I suspect means I will have to work out where to shop for my food.

Once more, it is as if Thea has read my mind.

'We put in a regular order for shopping and get it delivered. I have long ago given up any desire to stand in supermarket queues, so if you give me a list of what you'd like, I'll order it for you. I normally cook too much for us, so I can let you have something to heat up every now and again.'

'That's so kind of you, but not necessary. I don't mind cooking. I'll cook for you, if you like?'

I am not entirely sure how I'm going to pay for food from the kind of supermarket that I suspect Thea uses, and I ponder this as we make our way down to the ground floor. She hasn't responded to my offer to cook, probably assuming I'm as useless at that as I seem to be at everything else in my life. We walk back past the entrance, where my boots still sit in the shoe rack, and along another narrow corridor. I don't think I have ever seen so many doors in a house, and every one of them is closed.

'This door on the left leads to our kitchen. The doctor's study is accessed via a separate corridor leading from there, and it has its own outside entrance. I don't think there will be any need for you to go into the kitchen, but if there is I'd be grateful if you resisted the temptation to explore further.'

I am beginning to feel slightly uncomfortable about all these instructions. I would never dream of poking my nose in where it isn't wanted, but maybe they have had guests before who didn't know how they should behave.

All other thoughts are driven from my mind as we walk into a huge reception hall, obviously accessed from the main entrance. I can see the solid-wood front door to my right, and the space is flooded with light, in stark contrast to the hallways. To the left is a semicircular bay window looking out over a lovely rose garden. There's nothing in bloom at this time of year, and the bushes are no more than bare, spiky branches, but I can only imagine how it will look in late May or early June.

'It's beautiful, isn't it?' Thea says, her voice soft. She sounds almost sad, and I turn towards her. 'It's new. We only planted it a few months ago, and I can't wait to see it in full bloom in the summer. It has special significance to us. It looks so forlorn at this time of year, though.'

It must have been planted to celebrate some major event in their lives – perhaps an anniversary – and I give Thea a gentle smile and turn back towards an open doorway leading into what I imagine they would call the drawing room. I can see the doctor, sitting on a dark red leather chesterfield, nursing what appears to be a large brandy.

Thea walks into the room ahead of me. 'Look who I've brought to see you, dear.'

He looks up, and I notice that his eyes are slightly vacant, as if his mind was somewhere else, but like the gentleman he undoubtedly is, he pushes himself to his feet to take my hand. 'Welcome, Judith. It's good to have you with us.'

For a moment I'm taken aback by his greeting, and I'm about to open my mouth to speak when I see Thea give me a hard stare and a quick shake of the head, so I hold my tongue.

The doctor is still speaking. 'Come and take a seat, my dear. Thea, would you like your usual?' he asks, walking towards a silver drinks tray holding various decanters, each of which contains a dark brown liquid. He pours her a drink and hands it to her. 'What about you, Judith? What will you have?'

He indicates the array of decanters in front of him, but I don't know what to say. I glance at Thea again, and she's watching me. I have a funny feeling it's a test.

Before I get the chance to answer, the doctor speaks for me. 'A sweet sherry?' he asks, a decanter already in his hand.

'Thank you,' I answer, my voice so quiet it's almost inaudible. 'That would be lovely.'

It seems like the only possible response.

But what I really want to say is, 'My name is not Judith.'

22

'Becky, you're with me,' Tom called across the incident room. He knew she was as frustrated at the lack of progress with the Pennington Flash case as he was. Maybe it would do her good to get out for a while, and he needed some inspiration.

They were still no closer to identifying the woman the team had nicknamed Penny. The missing-persons' database had revealed nothing of note, and although they had tried to match her DNA to any samples held on file, they had drawn a blank.

A search of similar cases had revealed that a woman's body had been found on a golf course some months ago. Just like Penny, she appeared to have died as a result of hypoxia with no explanation for how that had happened. Without knowing Penny's identity, though, it was impossible to look for connections between the two women that might give them the answers they were so desperate for.

Although Becky had finally managed to persuade Sharon Carter to come in and take a look at the CCTV footage to see if she recognised the car she had seen, sadly she had been unable to narrow the search down by much. It didn't help that the roads had been gritted on the night Sharon went to the Flash, and black muddy water was splattered over so many number plates that most of them were illegible. In addition, it was a busy stretch of road even in the early hours of the morning, and they didn't know which direction the car had come from.

Becky pushed herself to her feet. 'Where are we off to?'

'I want to go back to Pennington Flash. We focused on the

location of the body last time. I know the local officers are very familiar with the area, but I'm not getting any sense of why the girl went, or was taken, there to die. I've no idea if it will help, but maybe I'll be hit by some sort of revelation. Come on. We'll take my car.'

Becky's driving had become considerably calmer since she had nearly drowned all those months ago, but Tom still found it erratic, slightly disconcerting and not conducive to logical thinking. And that was what they needed – cold, hard analysis mixed with some brainstorming that might initially seem wide of the mark but would stop them becoming too entrenched in any one explanation.

Tom asked himself what they knew, and it wasn't much. Sharon Carter had seen two people, one of whom was almost certainly Penny, heading towards the hide. The other person – presumed male – very probably either assisted Penny's suicide or murdered her. It seemed she had gone with him willingly, but had she known she was going to die? Was she complicit? Maybe some form of depression would account for the cocktail of drugs she had been taking. But the suggestion that it was an assisted suicide seemed to have dampened the enthusiasm of the team a little. The energy generated by a straightforward case of murder just wasn't there. Tom needed some ideas to rejuvenate the investigation, and there was no one better than Becky to help him voice his occasionally wild theories. Right now, though, he didn't have any theories – wild or otherwise.

The road to the Flash had been blocked by snow for days before the woman was found, but Tom was fairly certain that some die-hard twitchers would have made their way through to check out the birds. Somehow they needed to reach these people and find out what they had seen. Either the dead woman or the person who helped her had to have known that this hide wasn't locked, and perhaps they had paid the location a visit in the days immediately before she died.

'Sharon said the driver had a good look around the car park and then drove down the footpath, but only for a short distance, is that right?' Tom asked.

Becky nodded. 'I brought her out here to show me exactly where the car was parked, where they went. She finally admitted that she had arranged to meet someone here, but we haven't managed to trace him. She didn't know his name, and she's adamant he didn't turn up. We can't rule him out, though, so we're still looking.'

'She should have come forward the minute she heard what happened,' Tom said.

He felt a flash of irritation. Did she not appreciate that someone had died? But the fear of destroying her future husband's trust in her before their wedding day must have been immense. Trust was such a huge issue in any relationship, and Tom couldn't help thinking about Louisa. At what point could he risk telling her all that he had been keeping from her? Something he had read years ago sprang into his mind: *Trust takes years to build, seconds to break, and forever to repair.*

If Louisa found out he had been hiding the truth, she might never trust him again.

As he drove into the car park he could feel Becky's eyes on him. 'What's up?' she asked.

'Nothing.' He pulled the car to a stop. 'Come on, let's go for a walk.'

They followed the route Sharon said the car had taken along the footpath, then walked down the path to the hide. It was no longer a crime scene, and without the bustle of an active investigation it had a very different feel to it. The gloomy weather would keep all but the most enthusiastic of twitchers away from the place, and inside the hide it felt more dank and chilly than ever. There was no sound other than the rasping call of a mallard, and Tom gazed out of the viewing window at the water beyond. Brooding grey clouds reflected off the water, and the skeletal branches of leafless trees did nothing to cheer him.

He turned and looked towards the place where the dead woman had been sitting. There was no sign she had ever been there now, but the image was fixed in his mind. Had he missed anything? He closed his eyes for a moment, but nothing filtered through.

Why here?

Penny wasn't the first person to die at the Flash. Tom hadn't remembered the incidents, but the team's research had uncovered two previous deaths – one a prostitute who was dismembered, her body parts placed into bags and thrown into the water over twenty-five years ago, the other a young man who had committed suicide more recently. They had looked into both to try to find a link, but had failed, not helped by the fact that they still didn't know the identity of their victim.

He sensed that Becky was feeling the bleakness of the place too and felt devoid of inspiration. He was about to suggest they head out of the hide when he heard the sound of approaching footsteps on the wooden walkway leading to the entrance. Two men who, judging by their identical mops of ginger hair, were father and son, walked in and stopped. They gave Tom and Becky a puzzled glance. Clearly they weren't used to seeing men in business suits and women who were nearly eight months pregnant in the hide.

Tom fished in his pocket for his warrant card.

'Good afternoon. I'm Detective Chief Inspector Tom Douglas, and this is Detective Inspector Becky Robinson. We're investigating a recent incident here at the Flash.' He pulled a picture of Penny, drawn by a police artist, from his jacket. 'Have either of you seen this woman around here?'

'Sorry, mate,' the younger one said, earning himself a slightly startled look from his father, who clearly didn't think it appropriate to call a police officer 'mate'. 'We've seen her picture all over the park here, but nobody we've spoken to has ever clapped eyes on her.'

'Shame when someone so young has to die,' the older man said. 'And worse when it happens in such a beautiful place, somehow.'

'Do you come here regularly to watch the birds?' Tom asked.

'When we can, but we missed the worst of the weather, thank God. We were in Australia visiting my daughter, so we've only just found out about that poor lass. I was here when the last one tried it, though. I got a bit caught up in it myself, that time.'

Tom knew he was unlikely to mean the prostitute, given how long ago that was. 'You mean the man who committed suicide here?'

'No, I don't know anything about a man. I mean the girl – the one who tried and failed.'

'I'm sorry?' Tom said. 'I don't think I know about that.'

'No, well like as not you wouldn't, because I don't think it was ever reported. Me and a mate pulled her out of the water. I think she thought she could drown herself, but however bad she was feeling, the instinct to save herself kicked in.'

'What happened to her?'

'We called her parents and they came to get her.'

Tom's mind immediately flashed to Penny. Could this be the same person? Maybe she had tried here before. Perhaps the place was significant to her, so she had come back to try again – this time with more success.

'Not that saving the poor lass did a lot of good,' the man said. 'We heard two weeks later that she'd taken herself off somewhere else and done the job properly. Me and my mate went to the funeral – to pay our respects, you know. Dreadful affair. The family were in pieces. Her sister was a complete wreck and had to be carried out of the service by her dad.'

❖

Tom and Becky made their way slowly back to the car. The man had given them all the information he could remember about the attempted suicide, and Becky had taken his contact details. He said he had written the girl's name down – it was somewhere at home – and he promised to find it and give Becky a call. Tom wasn't hopeful it would be of any use, but he couldn't afford to ignore any possible leads.

They got into the car, but instead of driving away Tom sat and looked out of the windscreen, not really taking in the view. They were both silent for a few moments.

'You spoke to the management of the park, didn't you?' Tom asked.

'Yes, and to the volunteers who help maintain it. They confirmed what we already know. The hide where Penny was found is the only one without a padlock. This wasn't a random choice, Tom. She, or whoever took her there, had to know that fact in advance, and as far as we can tell it isn't publicised anywhere.'

'It's such a popular beauty spot, though, so even if the hide had been checked out in advance I don't suppose we'll ever know when, or by whom. Let's give the locals a call and see what, if anything, they have on the girl who tried to kill herself here. It may not have been reported, but I bet they know about it nevertheless. It would be easier with her name, but I'm not inclined to wait. You phone them; I'll drive.'

He was about to switch on the engine when his mobile rang. He could see from the caller ID that it was Keith.

'Yes, Keith. What can I do for you?' Tom asked.

'There's a gentleman here who says he'd like a word with you, sir. I told him you were out, but he said he would wait. Says his name's Nathan Gardner.'

Tom was silent for a moment. Nathan had been a friend of his brother Jack for many years, at a time when Jack was at his most disruptive. Tom and his parents had blamed Nathan for Jack's behaviour, but as the years passed Tom had begun to understand Jack better and knew it was no one else's fault. School had frustrated him, and he had always been in trouble. He was a genius in one field and one field only. Give him a computer and he could make it sing, but ask him to conjugate verbs in French and his resentment at being holed up in a classroom would kick in. He had gone on to make a fortune, but that was before the speedboat accident that changed everything.

Did Tom want to see Nathan? He wasn't sure. Even though he couldn't be blamed for Jack's poor behaviour, Tom had always thought Nathan was a bit of a tosser.

'Did he say what he wanted to talk to me about?' Tom asked.

'No, sir. I did ask, but he said it was a private matter.'

Tom sighed. 'Okay, we'll be about forty minutes or so. He can either wait or leave his number and I'll call him. Thanks, Keith.'

Tom rang off.

'You didn't seem too happy about that,' Becky said. 'Not somebody you want to see?'

'He was a friend of Jack's, and every bit as bad – if not worse – than my brother.'

'Ah,' Becky said, and left it at that. She knew talking about Jack was usually off-limits.

As Tom pulled out of the car park, he realised there was something he needed to ask Becky and thought carefully about his choice of words.

'I'm not quite sure how to put this, Becky, so forgive me if it sounds offensive, but did you ever tell Mark what happened to Jack?'

He wished now that he had asked the question when they were parked, so he could have looked at Becky's face.

'No. He believes what everybody else believes. Why are you asking me?' There was a slight note of indignation in Becky's voice, as if Tom were testing her loyalty to him against hers for Mark.

'I know you well enough to understand that you believe in total honesty, that's all. So I wondered how you squared it.'

'Well that's an easy one. I'd never withhold anything from Mark that impacted on our relationship – never lie about anything I've done – but Jack isn't my secret, Tom. If Mark ever found out, he would understand perfectly that it wasn't my story to tell.'

Tom was quiet for a moment.

'Have you told Louisa?' Becky asked.

Tom's usual response to any questions about his private life was 'Mind your own business' but that didn't seem appropriate right now.

'No. Not yet.'

'Ah,' Becky said again. 'And at a guess you worry that if you *do* tell her and your relationship doesn't work out, she will have a significant hold over you.'

'I don't think she's that kind of person, but let's face it, Becky – we see so many people who have trusted others and it's all gone pear-shaped.'

'Does she need to know?' Becky asked.

Tom wasn't sure. By not telling Louisa he had been lying by omission, but if she asked questions he would have to lie outright, and he wasn't happy with that either.

'Enough,' Tom said. 'I shouldn't have brought it up. Inappropriate to say the least.'

Becky grunted. 'Here we go. Barriers firmly back in place. Listen, Tom, on the basis that the only two people you can talk to about Jack are me and Detective Superintendent Philippa Bloody Stanley, I would guess I'm the better bet when it comes to anything to do with relationships, wouldn't you?'

Becky was right, of course, but nobody could make this decision for him. Should he tell Louisa?

23

I've been here for several days now, in this vast house that always seems to be totally silent. I'm even getting used to being called Judith. According to Thea, the doctor gets confused with names because over the years they have taken in a few of what Thea calls her 'waifs and strays', and he can't remember who's who. The first one was called Judith, and I suspect he doesn't think I'll be here for long, so it's not worth his trouble to try to remember my name.

I've tried to suggest going out to look for a job – in fact, I've mentioned it every day – but I don't get very far with Thea. 'Why not take it easy for a few more days? You need time to recover from all that's happened.'

I can't believe I'm being so laid-back. I should be out there, finding a way forward. Instead I feel bizarrely content to let everything wash over me. I spend a lot of time alone. I didn't hear or see the cleaners arrive that first day, but the drone of the vacuum cleaner penetrates the closed door of my rooms from time to time. I am quiet as a mouse for those few hours and usually stay snuggled up in bed with one of the books that are lying around. I feel so sleepy. Thea says it's a reaction to all that has happened, and I should talk to the doctor about it, but I don't really want to take up his time.

I don't eat with them, but each evening Thea comes up and escorts me back down to the drawing room for a drink. The doctor has decided since that first night that sherry is my drink of choice, so it's always there, ready and waiting for me. Strangely I'm growing to like it, and I certainly sleep well later. Even though

I don't share their dinner table, Thea usually gives me a portion of whatever she has cooked for them for me to reheat and she's provided me with everything from homemade bread to her own marmalade. I'm being spoilt, and I should be getting on with my life, I think. No, I don't just think it, I *know* it. I somehow have to work up the energy.

I'm going to mention it tonight when we have drinks, and now I can hear Thea's feet coming up the stairs to collect me. I know the way, but I think she's uncomfortable with me wandering around the house. Maybe she thinks I'll get lost.

'Have you had a good day, dear?' she asks me.

What can I answer? I've done nothing but read and gaze into space.

'I have, but it's time I made some effort to get out and find a job, Thea. I have to go and see Ian and work out what I'm going to do about the house. It's so kind of you to shelter me here, but it's not a long-term solution. I need to sort myself out.'

'Do you think you're ready to see Ian?' she asks, narrowing her eyes. 'I tell you what. Why don't you have a little session with the doctor? I think you'll find he will know what's best.'

I want to say that *I* know what's best, but it would sound rude and so I find myself agreeing.

As we walk into the drawing room the doctor gets to his feet, as he always does. 'I've poured you a small sherry, Judith,' he says, his voice slightly hoarse as if he doesn't use it much.

'Judith would like to have a chat with you, my dear,' Thea says. 'Do you want to go to your study, or shall I leave you both in peace here for half an hour?'

'Oh, here's fine, I think. Don't you, Judith?'

The urge to correct him – and now Thea – has waned over the last few days. What does it matter, really?

I take a seat opposite him, sitting right on the edge of the chair, my hands clasped on my knees.

'Come a little closer,' he urges. I move to the space next to him on the sofa, and he turns sideways to smile at me. He doesn't often smile, and when he does, those black eyebrows rise up at the outer corners and form a deeper V, pointing down towards his nose. 'Now, sit back and relax. This is just a chat to establish a degree of trust between us. Maybe you could start by telling me a bit about yourself – your family, friends and so on.'

I feel a faint wobble of tension. I don't want to talk about my parents, my upbringing, the stepmother I despise. Strangely I've thought about my dad and his wife quite a bit in the last few days, about the argument when Pops gave me the money and how much their anger hurt me. It feels distant, though. Remote. I wonder if the doctor is trying to find out if there is anyone else I can turn to. Perhaps he thinks I have been here long enough. Somehow, I manage to stutter out the story of my dysfunctional family, avoiding his eyes. I don't want to see pity there.

'And friends?'

'We moved up here to be close to my grandfather, so I could be with him for those last few months. I thought I'd make new friends here. It didn't quite work out like that though.'

'Judith, people travel to their jobs from every corner of the city. At the end of the day they go home to their own friends and family. It's not the way it's painted on TV, you know. Work is not all fun, laughter and forming new and exciting relationships.'

I think that is the longest speech I have ever heard from the doctor, who is leaning back and no longer looking at me. Sipping his brandy, his naturally vacant scowl melts into something a little more benevolent as he turns his head back towards me.

'So what value do you think you bring to the world, Judith?' he asks.

'I'm sorry?'

What sort of a question is that? My brain feels muddled, and I take another sip of the sherry.

112

'We all need to leave something of value behind,' he carries on. 'What do you hope your contribution will be?'

I have no idea. I've never thought of life like that. I've thought it was something to be endured or enjoyed – depending on the circumstances. What value am I to anybody?

'I'm not sure I have any value,' I find myself saying, realising I have nobody to love, nobody whose life is made better by my presence.

'Thea tells me there's a man involved, and that he's making your life miserable. Is that true?'

'Yes. I want him gone, but he won't move out,' I answer, almost sobbing at the thought. I've been managing to suppress all thoughts of Ian for the last day or so, but now they burst to the surface with renewed pain. I take another gulp of the sweet sherry. It must be going to my head because I start to feel slightly woozy. The doctor's black eyebrows seem to be zooming in and out of focus. I shake my head in an effort to see clearly.

'Is he worth anything?'

'What do you mean?' I have to concentrate really hard to answer. 'Financially he's not worth a penny, but that never bothered me.'

'No, is he worth anything as a person? If he were to die today, would anybody miss him? Would he leave a hole in this world?'

I feel I should be shocked at such a terrible question, but I'm not. I'm struggling for an answer when the doctor speaks again: 'If he is of no value, he's taking up unnecessary space. You have to find a way to rid yourself of him.' He downs the rest of his brandy and smiles.

❖

The session with the doctor has left me feeling completely disorientated. After his initial comments I just wanted to get out of there, but as I sipped my sherry and listened to him talk, I found myself mesmerised by the deep, rasping tone of his voice, although I am embarrassed to find myself unable to remember much of what he said.

Thea was waiting outside the door when I left. 'Was that helpful, dear?'

'I don't know,' I said, trying to be honest. 'It's left me feeling a bit disturbed about who I am and where I'm going, but more convinced than ever that Ian needs to somehow be eradicated from my life. I just don't know how.'

Thea's eyes glowed. 'You'll work it out. The doctor's so clever, isn't he?'

I'm not sure what to think. I don't feel capable of coherent thought, and everything seems muddy and confused. I need to get some direction back into my life, and I don't believe I'll be able to do that while I'm staying here, lulled into a false sense of security. For all its beauty and comfort, there is something oppressive about this house, and when I go back upstairs after my session with the doctor, I force myself to think. My mind keeps wandering, so I grab a pen and paper to capture any constructive ideas I have.

I decide to go into Manchester tomorrow morning and explain my situation to the mortgage company. I might have enough money in the bank to meet this month's payment, but after that I'll be in trouble. And after sorting – or trying to sort – my finances, I might brave a trip to see Ian. We have to agree a way forward, and perhaps he will have calmed down by now. I need more clothes too. I brought the bare minimum with me – the things I was wearing plus another pair of jeans, a pile of underwear and two jumpers.

Then a thought hits me: *How am I going to get out in the morning?* I'm confined to my floor until the cleaners have gone, and the door isn't unlocked until they leave. I've still never seen them, and I never hear footsteps or the sound of talking, laughter or singing. Maybe they are told to be quiet. There's only one thing to do: I need to find Thea and ask her how I can go out without the cleaners seeing me. I also need to say that it's probably time

I left, although I may have to ask if I can stay for a while longer – at least until either Ian moves out or I manage to get a job so I can afford to rent a room in a house somewhere.

I've never been down to the lower floors of the house without Thea to escort me, other than to go out of the side door if I feel like a short stroll. She normally pops up in the afternoon with a dish of something she thinks I might like for dinner – stew or soup – ready to be reheated, and often suggests I have a walk around the garden. But most of the time I can't be bothered. The only part of the grounds I'm not supposed to walk in is the rose garden. That seems to be a special place for Thea, and from my window I have seen her sitting out there, hunched in a thick coat. I made a token effort to go outside earlier and had a short stroll around the lawn, but I really don't have the energy for anything more strenuous.

With renewed determination to beat the lethargy that's plaguing me, I push open the door to the staircase and start to make my way down. For some reason I feel I have to walk on tiptoe, but as I'm only wearing socks I'm unlikely to be heard. When I reach the first-floor landing I don't stop. I know this is where Thea and Garrick sleep and I wouldn't dream of going into that part of the house, so I head down to the ground floor.

I have no idea where they will be. I've been given the impression that they only use the drawing room for pre-dinner drinks, but there are so many doors and corridors that I don't have a clue. Thea did mention the kitchen to me on the first day, but I can't remember which closed door it hides behind. I listen for voices, but everywhere is silent, all sound deadened by the thick walls and solid oak doors. I pause at each one in turn, listening. If I hear talking, I'll knock and ask to have a word. It's not until I get to the third door on the left that I hear a murmur. It's hard to make out what Garrick is saying, as his voice is so deep, but I can hear Thea plainly.

'I think she's ready to move on, my dear. Do you?'

I have no idea who she's talking about. It could be a relative – I still don't know if they have children of their own – or it could be one of the cleaners. But I have a horrible, sneaking suspicion that they might be talking about me. What does she mean, *move on*? She wants me to leave, that's all I can think.

I don't want to interrupt them in case they *are* talking about me, so I creep back along the corridor, grateful now that I walked on tiptoe. I feel the need to hurry in case they catch me, but I'm being ridiculous.

I don't know what time the cleaners arrive, but if I get up early enough I might be able to get out before Thea locks the door at the bottom of the stairs to my room. The only obstacle then might be the side door, the one I always use to go out into the garden.

I make my way towards the narrow passage and the small lobby that leads to the door, and I'm relieved when I see it has a Yale lock with bolts at the top and bottom, all of which can be opened from the inside. Making my escape in the morning won't be a problem as long as the door to the stairs isn't locked when I come down. Sighing with relief, I turn, but out of the corner of my eye I see the shoe rack. And that's when I realise I won't be going anywhere.

The shoe rack is empty. I wore my boots earlier in the garden, and I know I left them here, but they've gone.

24

Despite the fact that Jack's old friend Nathan Gardner was waiting back at headquarters, Tom decided to delay his return. Becky had spoken briefly to a sergeant at the local police station who remembered the attempted suicide at the Flash, and it seemed an opportune moment to look into the incident, although Tom had neither hope nor expectation that it would lead them to the identity of Penny.

'It wasn't reported,' the ruddy-faced sergeant told them, 'but everyone knew about it. The poor kid was obviously determined to kill herself, and managed it in the end. The sister – the one you were told had to be carried out of church – was actually the girl's twin.'

Tom knew only too well how devastating it was to hear that a sibling had died, and he could only imagine how much worse it might be if it was both a twin and suicide.

'Do you know anything about the family – where they are now, how they coped?' Tom asked.

'There was quite a fuss because the surviving twin blamed her parents. She said they had made no effort to understand the one who died – Esme, she was called. The other one, whose name I can't remember, by all accounts walked out of the house without a backward glance. One of my colleagues lives not far away, and it was the talk of the area. Eventually the parents upped and moved to Scotland.'

They tested the sergeant's memory for a little longer but finally accepted that there was no more to learn. Tom asked him to get in touch if anything else sprang to mind, and in the meantime to check the details of the girl's family, including the name of the surviving twin. The twitcher at the Flash who had attended the funeral might well call in with it, but Tom preferred to have the facts confirmed by the sergeant.

Tom had felt a tingle at the back of his neck as they discussed the twins. There had to be some reason why Penny, as they continued to call her, had chosen to die where she had, assuming it was her choice. The Flash may have had some significance for the girls. On the other hand, the prickling feeling could be because Nathan Gardner was waiting to see him. Was it something to do with Jack? Why else would Nathan want to talk to Tom after all these years?

Tom had called Keith Sims to say he was delayed and he was hoping that Jack's old friend would have gone by the time they finally arrived back. But as he and Becky made their way into the office, Nathan was still sitting there.

Tom felt unaccountably irritated. He wanted time to process all they had learned that day, and he could really have done without talking to this man right now. Given how long he'd been waiting, though, Tom didn't really have much choice.

'Nathan,' he said, holding out his hand. 'I'm sorry you've had to wait.'

Nathan stood up and shook Tom's hand, both men quietly weighing each other up. It was at least twenty years since they had seen each other, and Nathan was almost unrecognisable. When he and Jack were friends they had both had long, wild hair – in Jack's case dark, in Nathan's a mousy colour. Now he was almost bald, and what hair he had was neatly cut. But the nose and eyes hadn't changed.

'Tom, I'm sorry to barge in on you like this, but I need to talk to someone and you were the first person I thought of.'

'Let's go to my office. Do you want a coffee or anything?'

Nathan shook his head. 'Your guys have looked after me well, thanks. I'm just about coffeed out.'

As they walked along the corridor, Nathan briefly touched Tom's arm. 'I was sorry to hear about Jack. He'd done so well, and then to die in a crazy speedboat accident. To be honest, I couldn't believe it. He was always reckless, but he wasn't stupid.'

Tom said nothing until they were through his office door. 'Thanks, Nathan. It was a shock to us all.' He felt uncomfortable. Any mention of his brother automatically put Tom on edge.

'I don't suppose Jack ever told you that we stayed in touch right up until he died,' Nathan said. 'I know when we were kids I was wild and probably wasn't a particularly good influence on him, but he was his own guy, you know. He did what he wanted, and I don't think being friends with me was as bad for him as you thought.'

'It's all so long ago now, Nathan. We're both very different people. What have you been doing with yourself?'

Nathan sat back in his chair and folded his arms. He looked Tom straight in the eye. 'I'm a professional gambler. I've lived in the States for many years now, mainly Atlanta, but as you can hear I've kept my Manc accent. They think I'm some hick with no idea half the time, and that suits me.'

Tom looked at Nathan's clothes and shoes, and surmised that gambling must be a profitable business for him. 'What's your game?'

'Poker. I don't play the tables, or rarely. Maybe a bit of blackjack, but never roulette. I like to feel at least an element of control. It seems to have worked for me, and I like living over there. It's a long time since I've been back to Manchester.'

'So what brings you here now?'

Nathan leaned forward, his expression hardening. 'Do you remember that I had a kid sister?' he asked. 'She was a lot younger than us – fifteen years younger, in fact. She was a baby when I knew Jack.'

'Sorry, Nathan. That detail escaped me. I remember your parents, though.'

Nathan barked out a laugh. 'I bet you do. They were always round seeing your mum and dad to see what could be done to curb the excesses of their boys, weren't they? But Jack did brilliantly, and although you might not think much of gambling as a profession, I do well enough.'

'So this is about your sister, is it?' Tom wasn't interested in comparing success stories; he wanted to get back to the job and then go home.

'Yes, it is. I've been a crap brother on the whole. She was just a tiny thing when I left home, and my parents were glad to see the back of me. Then they fell apart too and ended up divorcing. Anyway, I heard from her – she's called Hannah – completely out of the blue. She wrote to me while she was away on holiday. Things hadn't been going too well for her, and I think I was a last resort. I was at a poker event in Vegas when the letter arrived, and by the time I got back to Atlanta I wasn't sure what to do.'

'Why not?' Tom couldn't imagine a time when he would have turned down an opportunity to get in touch with his brother.

'I don't know. Guilt, I suppose. She had a tough time when my parents split, and I'd already moved out by then. I should have been more supportive. In the end, though, I decided not to write but to come over and surprise her.' Nathan leaned forward and rested his forearms on his thighs. 'But here's the thing, Tom. She seems to have disappeared. No one knows where she is.'

❖

Tom asked Nathan a few more questions about his sister and then excused himself, ostensibly to make a cup of tea but in reality he wanted to think carefully about what to say. Was there a chance it was Hannah's body that had been found at the Flash? She was the right age, and Nathan had confirmed that he hadn't reported her missing yet.

'She's an adult,' he had said. 'As far as I know she's not vulnerable in any way, so she'd just get added to a long list of non-urgent cases. I couldn't see the point. I thought I'd ask you what I should do.'

Tom was torn between hoping for Nathan's sake that Hannah was alive and well, and wanting a name for their victim.

He brought his mug of tea back into the office and sat down behind his desk. 'Can you describe Hannah to me? Height, weight, hair colour, that kind of thing?'

'Why do you want to know all that stuff if you're not in charge of missing persons?' There was a puzzled tone to Nathan's voice, as if he suspected Tom of keeping something from him, which indeed he was.

'We've had an incident recently, and I'd like to rule out any connection with Hannah.'

'What sort of an incident? Don't bullshit me, Tom. Just tell me.'

Tom sighed. 'Have you seen the news since you've been back?'

'No, I just got back from following what I thought was a good lead but was probably a wild-goose chase. I decided to come straight to see you. Anyway, I don't watch the news if I can help it. What have I missed?'

There was little choice but to tell him. 'We found the body of a young woman at Pennington Flash. Do you know where that is?'

'Course I do. Do you think it's Hannah?' Nathan might be good at controlling his facial expressions, but his voice had risen in pitch.

Tom shook his head. 'I don't want you to worry. There's no reason at all to think it's Hannah. Thousands of people go missing every week, but I'd like to rule her out. What can you tell me about her?'

'That's a bit of a hard question, given what a crap brother I've been. I couldn't tell you if she's fat or thin, or whether her hair is long or short. I told you – I haven't seen her for years. Her hair is naturally very dark, but if you're going to ask me about tattoos or scars, I don't have the first idea. Sorry.'

'Don't you have any pictures?'

Nathan sighed. 'I know it sounds pathetic, but no, nothing recent. I might have been able to dig out something from when she was about ten if I was back home in Atlanta. She has a Facebook page, but the privacy settings are high. Her cover image is of the sea, for some obscure reason, and her profile picture is a girl in a Halloween mask. I presume it's her, but it's no help.'

Tom managed to draw out everything Nathan did know about his sister, which was essentially confirmation of her age, height and the natural colour of her hair, and he felt a pang of concern for the man. The scant description matched Penny's.

'I may not have seen her in a while, Tom, but I would recognise my sister. I'm sure of that. So why are we faffing around guessing? I want to know for sure if it's her. You'd better let me take a look.'

25

Tom had informed the mortuary that he was bringing someone to possibly identify Penny and suggested that Nathan travel with him in his car. They hadn't spoken on the journey, Tom leaving Nathan to his own thoughts, but as they stepped out of the car Tom felt a familiar tension. Although he had never been a fan of Nathan's pugnacious character, he knew how difficult the next few minutes were going to be for him. Being asked to identify someone close was a dreadful experience, and he remembered having to do it himself not long ago when a woman very closely resembling his ex-girlfriend Leo had been found.

He would never forget how it had felt: the sick dread that he was going to see the face of someone who mattered to him lying lifeless, the colour drained from her cheeks. At least Penny, as he continued to think of her until proven otherwise, didn't have any damage to her face. There were no visible signs of trauma.

He had suggested looking at photographs first, but Nathan didn't feel that would be conclusive. Had he seen Hannah recently, he would have felt more comfortable with the idea, but he wasn't confident that it would be enough.

'If you're still unsure after you've seen her, we can do a DNA analysis, so please do say if you have any doubts, one way or another.'

Nathan nodded, his eyes staring straight ahead as they entered the mortuary where Penny's body was being held. Forensic evidence had already been taken, but Tom advised Nathan that he wouldn't be able to touch her.

Tom couldn't tell from his face or his demeanour how Nathan

was feeling. His eyes were fixed, his mouth a straight line, and he walked with his hands by his sides. Only one aspect of his behaviour suggested that there was more than ice water running through Nathan's veins: when they reached the trolley he seemed unable to look at the face of the woman lying on it. He gazed above her at the wall, psyching himself up for the moment when he would see what might be his sister's body.

Tom looked down at her, not for the first time. She looked serene, at peace, and he knew that her appearance in itself wouldn't be the cause of any distress. He waited, looking away from Nathan to take away any pressure. He felt, rather than saw, Nathan lower his head.

'No.' The voice was loud, decisive. Nathan turned away, heading towards the door.

'Hang on,' Tom said. 'Speak to me, Nathan.'

'It's not her.'

'You're sure?'

'Of course. The face shape is wrong. The nose is too big. She was the lucky one; she didn't inherit the family's worst feature like I did. I'm glad I saw her. It's not Hannah.'

Tom let out a long breath. He was relieved for Nathan, but it meant their search for Penny's identity was not over yet.

❖

As Tom pulled into the drive of his Edwardian semi, his thoughts were of Nathan Gardner's sister. Where could she be? Nathan had given him details of everything he had done to try to find her and in the end had agreed to report her to the missing-persons team, after considerable persuasion. He was right: she wouldn't be a priority, but if she turned up they would at least know who to contact.

Nathan's appearance had inevitably filled Tom's head with thoughts of Jack. Not a day went by when he didn't think of him, although usually it was a fleeting memory. The earlier conversation with Becky and the unexpected appearance of Nathan Gardner, however, had left him with memories tumbling over each other to get to the surface.

Jack had been a wild kid who had given up on school at an early age. His brain seemed to be hard-wired for technology, and he had built his first computer before most people had even seen one. Tom had been in awe of his brother, with his intense pale blue eyes, as if the brain behind them never rested. Jack had gone on to make a fortune in Internet security, but try as he might, Tom couldn't block out thoughts of his brother's less than honest methods. He had built his business by hacking into the computer systems of large corporations and then going to them as a legitimate expert to sell his security services. His justification was that if he could hack their systems, so could somebody else – he was actually doing his clients a favour. But Tom seriously doubted many people had the skills Jack had, and the systems were probably safe enough.

However he made his money, he was still Tom's brother, and the intense pain Tom felt when he learned that Jack had been in a speedboat accident and was missing, presumed dead, was almost matched by his anger, confusion and joy six years later when his world had been tipped upside down again.

Because Jack wasn't dead at all.

His accident had been a set-up to protect the people he loved from some of the most evil criminals in the north of England. The world had to believe that Jack Douglas was dead, including those closest to him, and even now only a handful of people knew the truth.

Tom would never forget the moment when he had seen Jack with his own eyes on a monitor in the police control room. One of the most dangerous operations Tom had ever been involved in was under way, and right there, in the middle of it all, was the man he had been mourning for years. The pain and pleasure had hit him with equal force.

Now he felt an overwhelming need to speak to his brother, but he couldn't. Tom hadn't spoken to him face to face since the day he had hurled insults and recriminations at him for causing them all so much pain, but he knew Jack had hacked his home computer. He could tell Jack was watching, listening, because folders were sometimes moved on his desktop. It was Jack's way of letting Tom know that he was still there. So tonight, as Louisa was working, Tom was going to get a message to him, something he did infrequently and at irregular intervals because, although he didn't believe anyone could detect how they were communicating, it wasn't a good idea to make a habit of it. Better just to know that Jack was alive than to risk everything for the pleasure of this one-sided communication.

He had a folder called 'Jack' on his desktop, filled with images of the two of them over the years. Tonight he would create a document in that folder telling Jack all that had happened recently – perhaps about Louisa and his dilemma but also about Nathan's visit. He always wrote as if it were a personal diary. 'A friend of Jack's came to see me today,' or, 'Something happened today that I think Jack would have enjoyed,' rather than addressing the content directly to his brother. It was better to be safe.

As he walked into the house, he felt his spirits lift a little. He would give anything to get together with Jack for a few beers to argue about music, politics and the difference between right and wrong, as they always used to. That wasn't possible, but although he might not be able to see or talk to him, it would feel good to know that his brother was listening.

26

I'm going nowhere this morning.

Much as I had wanted to go into town to try to restore some kind of order to my life, I can't bring myself to get out of bed. I'm lying here shivering, even though the room is warm. I don't know what happened to me last night. From the moment I discovered my boots had disappeared, everything seemed to collapse.

I felt trapped. I didn't know whether to run along the corridor and barge into the room where I had heard Thea and the doctor talking, or to hunt around for my boots, but it felt so wrong to be sneaking around this massive house with its unlit corridors. I felt like a burglar, and my panic was out of all proportion to what was happening. I tried to explain away the empty shoe rack, but I couldn't get away from the fact that I was sure Thea had been talking about me earlier, and I began to feel as if the dark walls of the house were crowding in on me. I slumped onto the bottom stair, trying to get a grip, trying to work out what on earth I was going to do. I felt trapped. A prisoner.

I didn't hear Thea approaching. The first I knew she was there was when a hand came down on my shoulder.

'Thea,' I squealed. 'You frightened me.'

I looked up into her kind face and realised what an idiot I was being. I was making things up – weaving all kinds of evil thoughts around these people who had only shown me kindness. Admittedly the doctor can be a bit strange, but maybe all psychiatrists are. I don't know.

'What on earth's the matter?' Thea asked, briskly rubbing the top of my arm.

'I wanted some fresh air. But my boots have gone, and I didn't bring any other shoes with me.'

She gave a light tinkling laugh. 'They've not gone, dear; they're in the utility room. They were muddy after your walk today, and I was sure you were going to want to go into town soon. I was going to suggest a trip tomorrow, so I thought I would give them a quick clean for you.'

I felt such a fool. She was being kind, and I was being an idiot. 'I'm sorry,' I said. 'I was thinking of going in the morning, before the cleaners arrive. You said there's a tram stop nearby, didn't you?'

'There is, but you don't need to worry about that. You can take my car any time you like. Come with me, and I'll show you where the keys are kept. If I need a car, I'll take the doctor's. He doesn't go out much on his own. Come on. Get up off that cold step and come into the kitchen.'

Not only was I clearly not a prisoner, but she was giving me free access to her car. I felt my cheeks flush with embarrassment.

As we walked along the corridor Thea pointed to a board on the wall on which hung all kinds of keys. 'The bottom left key is the one to my car. The garage isn't locked, and the car's always full of fuel. No need to ask, dear. Just help yourself.'

She was so kind. All I wanted to do was crawl back up to my room and be ashamed of myself in private, but Thea was having none of that. 'Come and sit with me. The doctor is in his study so we won't be disturbed.'

I followed her into a huge kitchen with units along two walls, an Aga under a wooden mantelpiece and a dresser stretching the length of the third wall. The fourth wall consisted of windows looking out over the garden. A long table filled the central space. It felt warm and more than a little disorganised.

'Sit down. I'm going to make you one of my special teas.'

'There's no need, Thea,' I said. 'I'm happy to go back up and make my own.'

On my first day Thea had presented me with a tin of home-filled tea bags. 'These are my own brew,' she had said. 'They're comforting and warming – perfect for just before bed. You'll have a wonderful night's sleep.' And she was right. I always made a cup before bed and was out like a light every night.

'I'm going to make you an extra-special version tonight,' she said. 'It'll calm you, and if you're going to be sorting things out tomorrow, you need to be calm, don't you?'

I couldn't argue with that, so I sat with her and chatted about nothing very much – I seem to remember she told me about some of the foibles of her car – while I sipped her delicious tea. It certainly did the trick because by the time I went upstairs to bed I was feeling much more settled.

But all that was to change.

I went straight to bed and fell into a deep sleep. Later I vaguely remember waking up feeling hot – too hot. I'm sure I threw off the bedclothes and then sat up. I was confused, I think, but I'm not sure why.

That is the last thing I remember until I woke up back in Thea's kitchen, a blanket around my shoulders, shivering. She was in her dressing gown, rubbing my feet with a warm towel, and my chair was pulled close to the Aga.

I don't know how I got there. One minute I was in bed, the next I was in the kitchen, cold, disorientated, with Thea in her nightclothes trying to warm me up.

'Oh, my dear, I didn't know you were a sleepwalker,' she said, concern in her voice.

'What?' I said, struggling to make sense of her words. I'm not a sleepwalker, or at least I'm not aware of being one. And I didn't understand how I had come to be in her kitchen with her fussing over me. I could see how dark it was outside, but it was only when I looked at the clock that I realised it was 2 a.m.

Thea pulled a chair close to mine and reached for my hand.

'I found you outside, Judith. You were by the garage. I woke up because the security lights came on. I'm usually a heavy sleeper, so it's lucky my knees were playing me up and I was awake. Don't you remember?'

Thea seemed as baffled as I was, and hard as I have tried, I can remember nothing.

When she thought I had warmed up enough, Thea helped me upstairs and into bed, but although I've been curled up here ever since, I haven't slept. I dread to think what might have happened if she hadn't found me. Thea says I had her car keys in my hand. I must have been intending to go somewhere. *What was I doing?* It could have been a disaster.

I feel dreadful – nauseous, achy, my head is sore, even to touch. *What happened to me?* Have I got some kind of fever?

I don't know, but all I can think is, thank God Thea found me.

❖

I've finally managed to force myself to leave the safe haven of my bed. I had to get up because in reality it's not my bed, it's Thea and Garrick's, and I need to find a way of getting my own bed – and house – back.

I'm getting the events of last night completely out of proportion. Yes, it was a shock to learn that I had nearly driven off in a comatose state, but I didn't. It has never happened before, and I'm sure it will never happen again. I need to snap out of it.

After a shower I begin to feel human again, and I know I must start planning my future. I'll ask Thea if I can borrow the car tomorrow to go into town for some legal and financial advice, and then I'll go to see Ian. There's so much to sort out, and I've been languishing here for far too long.

I've just finished dressing when I hear footsteps, and the door at the top of the stairs opens.

'Hello, dear. How are you feeling?' Thea asks. She is carrying what looks like a wide-necked Thermos flask.

'Cross with myself,' I say. 'I shouldn't have made such a meal of what happened. It was strange, and I felt weird, but I've got to get a grip. Do you think it would be possible to borrow the car tomorrow, please?'

'Actually, I came up to suggest that we go this afternoon. I can come with you, do some shopping in town while you deal with the building society, and then I can wait while you go and see how things stand with Ian. How does that sound?'

'You're too kind,' I say. 'But you don't have to trail in with me. I'm sure you have things you would rather be doing.'

Thea gives me a smile. 'It's no trouble. I'd like to come with you, and you might be feeling a bit shaky after last night.'

I'm beginning to get irritated with my indecision and how passive I seem to have become. I'm thirty-two years old. I shouldn't be so pathetic, but I'm struggling to battle my way out of this indolence.

'I'm fine to drive, thanks, but if you need something from town and you really don't mind waiting while I try to talk to Ian, it would be good to have your company.'

Thea nods and turns towards my kitchen, beckoning me to follow her.

'I thought you might need a bit of a pick-me-up after last night, so I've brought you some lovely home-made soup. I don't suppose you've eaten today, have you?'

She's right, of course. I haven't. It seemed like too much effort, and although I'm hungry I prefer hunger to going to the trouble of making something to eat. I realised today that I have been losing weight. I don't have much to lose, but my jeans seem loose.

'Sit down, dear.' She grabs a bowl from the shelf and a spoon from the drawer and then opens the Thermos and tips the contents out. The soup smells wonderful. It's a deep orange colour and I presume it's carrot soup, but Thea tells me it's roasted butternut squash.

'Roasted with onions and garlic, then blended with stock and a hint of curry powder.'

My mouth is watering, and I take my first spoonful. It's delicious – packed with flavour – and I begin to feel better. Thea sits and watches me eat, telling me in a jokey voice that I have to be a good girl and eat it all up or we won't be going out today.

I know she's teasing me, treating me like a child, but somehow I get the sense that she might mean it. So I eat every spoonful, and she's right. I feel so much better – energised and raring to go.

'Come on then,' Thea says. 'Let's seize the moment while you're feeling so positive.'

I grab my bag and jacket and follow her downstairs. My boots are looking very clean and I feel another pang of guilt for my suspicions the day before. How could I have imagined even for a moment that my boots had been taken?

We walk out to the garage. The doors stand open, and I can see Thea's car parked next to a Land Rover.

'We use that if we get snowed in,' she says, 'but we don't need it today. We can take my car. The doctor's is a bit big to park in town.' She points to a black Mercedes on the other side of the Land Rover.

The lethargy has dropped away, and suddenly I feel I could take Ian on and win. I don't realise I am driving too fast until Thea touches my arm and points to the speedometer.

'Oh gosh, I'm so sorry. I was miles away, thinking of all the damage I would like to do to Ian.' I take my foot off the accelerator and slow the car down to a respectable speed.

Thea laughs. 'What do you think he deserves for everything he's done?'

People say all the time, 'I could kill him,' but I don't want to because I know it would hold a ring of truth.

27

Tom was no longer concentrating most of his energy on the Pennington Flash case. Philippa was right: there were other cases that demanded more of his time, and each member of his team needed a fair share of his attention. He hadn't been ignoring them, of course, but he had been preoccupied with Penny and he needed to give the other crimes more focus. But Penny kept intruding into his thoughts simply because hers was the most intriguing case. All murders had to be solved and the perpetrators brought to justice, but most were relatively straightforward. His team often had an immediate idea where the guilt lay, and it was just a matter of amassing the evidence. But Penny was unique, and try as he might to focus elsewhere, she kept forcing her way into his head.

There was a knock on his open door, and Tom looked up to see Lynsey standing in the doorway.

'Excuse me, sir. Do you have a moment?' she asked, flushing as she always did when she spoke to him. 'DI Robinson said I should come and have a word with you.'

'Come in, Lynsey. Have a seat.' She hurried forward and sat down, a bundle of papers held tightly in her hands. 'What can I do for you?'

'It's about the drugs that were found in Penny's tox analysis, sir. I know they have already been flagged as an unusual combination, but I've been looking into ways in which she might have obtained them, and when I wrote down the order in which the hair sample tells us they were taken, it seemed a bit strange.'

Tom looked at her anxious face. It was always difficult to be a novice detective desperate to make the grade, and he wanted to put her at ease. 'That sounds interesting. What are you thinking, Lynsey?'

'As you know, hair grows around a centimetre every thirty days, and the sample from Penny has been analysed for the last ninety days. I've made a note of all the possible effects of each drug, and I've also looked into where she might have bought them. A couple of them could have come through legitimate prescriptions, although they're also available on the street – or online of course – so that's inconclusive. But when we look at the sequence, it raises a few questions about her state of mind.'

Tom had already indicated to Philippa that the mixture of drugs would have conflicting impacts on the mind, so he was keen to hear what Lynsey had to say, but through the open door he heard the squeak of rubber on vinyl flooring that indicated the arrival of Becky, who had taken to wearing trainers around the office as she had grown larger. And they were moving at a faster than normal pace.

'Hold that thought, Lynsey. If Becky's moving that quickly, something must be up.'

Becky's face appeared around the door, beaming from ear to ear.

'We've got her! We know who Penny is.'

Tom and Lynsey followed Becky back to the incident room, where Keith was pinning photographs on the board. He turned as Tom entered the room, his back straightening ever so slightly. Even after all these months working in the team, he seemed to find it necessary to stand to attention when a senior officer walked into the room.

'Okay, Keith, what have we got?'

'We've been looking into the girl who tried and failed to kill herself at the Flash – the one who was rescued from the water but who subsequently succeeded in committing suicide elsewhere. She was Esme DuPont. Her twin was Jasmine, more commonly known as Jaz.'

Tom was hit by conflicting emotions: relief at the possibility that they knew who their victim was, and dismay at the thought that Keith was about to tell him their Penny – now dead – had been Esme's surviving twin, Jasmine. How horrific for both sisters to die so young.

'We managed to get photos of the girls. It's only just over two years since Esme committed suicide, and the twins were both Facebook users. A lot of their pictures are of the two of them together.'

Tom walked towards the board, not sure what he was hoping to find. His eyes were drawn to the girl on the right of each picture, who he knew instinctively was Jasmine. She was happy, smiling, laughing in every one. He glanced at the girl on the left. There were clear similarities between the two of them, but he could sense that this girl was more troubled. This one had to be Esme. Her smile looked forced and her eyes seemed to be unnaturally wide, as if she was doing her best to look happy. He looked back at the first girl, the one that Keith was irritatingly tapping with his telescopic pointer pen. Could this cheerful, lively-looking girl really be Penny?

'What makes you so convinced it's her, Keith?'

The sergeant moved his pointer to the photo of the body they had found at the Flash, taken as she sat against the wall of the hide. 'Tiny scar above the left eyebrow, sir, and a small mole to the left of her chin.'

Tom stepped closer and peered at the image. Keith was right. It was hard to compare photos of a laughing smiling woman of around thirty years of age to one of a body that had been dead for days, but in addition to similarities in general facial structure, Keith was right about the marks of identification.

'So our Penny is actually Jasmine DuPont. What else do we know about her?' Tom asked, staring at the two beautiful young women, both of whom were now dead. Maybe life without her twin had proved unbearable for Jasmine and drained the joy from her, to the point where she had asked someone to help her die. It was a heartbreaking thought.

'Not a huge amount yet, sir. We're gathering information as quickly as we can. We've sent someone round to her last known address and we're waiting to hear back. Jasmine hadn't used social media since about three months after her sister died, although in the period immediately after Esme's death she used Facebook as a platform to denigrate her own parents, and anyone with children who refused to listen to their problems or told them to "get a grip", as she put it. She didn't have any privacy settings – it was as if she wanted the world to find her posts. There were several with links to sites that deal with depression, and towards the end even more that deal with suicide.'

Tom let out a long breath. 'Okay. Well done, everyone. Now that we have a name, we can start to make some progress. But to be clear, just because she was posting links to suicide sites it doesn't mean we can ignore other possibilities. Keep your minds open and use each bit of new evidence to form a picture – one that right now we don't know either the shape or colour of. No preconceived ideas, please.'

He saw a few heads nodding and turned to leave the room, stopping for a quick chat with Lynsey.

'We need to prioritise, Lynsey. As we already know, the tox results proved conclusively that the drugs didn't kill Penny – or Jasmine, as we must now call her. But when we have more of a picture of her life we might be able to make sense of her medications, prescribed or otherwise. That's when your work will come into its own, so make sure you've got it all written up, and then we can see how it fits into Jasmine's story.'

Thank goodness they had a name at last. The investigation should begin to move forward at a pace now, and the team would be re-energised.

Tom couldn't help thinking about the girls' parents, though. They might have lost contact with Jasmine, but it would still break their hearts. To lose both daughters at such a young age would be devastating.

28

The meeting with the building society didn't go well. I had to admit to the girl sent to talk to me – who looked about twelve – that I had been fired from my job. I asked for a few months to get back on my feet and she said they might be able to allow me some leeway, but I found myself getting angry with her when she tried to explain the limitations imposed by their procedures.

'You don't understand,' I said, leaning across the desk towards her. 'I was sacked for something I didn't bloody well do! None of this is my fault. All I'm asking for is time to sort myself out, and no, of course I can't commit to resolving the situation in the next four weeks. My boyfriend won't move out, so I can't even rent rooms out to cover the cost.'

I could hear my voice rising, and the girl's head shot backwards as if she was scared I was going to punch her. I sat back, ashamed of myself for a moment, but there was a huge ball of anger building inside me, spinning, growing, wanting to burst out and spill over everything and everybody in its way. No one wanted to listen to me; they all thought I was every bit as bad as my idiot ex-boss said I was. In the end I jumped up and stormed out of the door, shouting that they could stuff their mortgage.

Now, as I sit outside my house in Thea's car, I take a deep breath to try to calm myself.

'I know you're trying to be cool,' Thea says, 'but it might not do Ian any harm to see how angry you are. If you're always pleasant and balanced about things, he's never going to take you seriously, is he?'

She's right, of course, but I need to feel in control, and I've never believed that shouting was the answer to anything.

I lean over to the back seat to grab the house keys from my handbag. 'I'm sorry, Thea. You shouldn't have to be involved in all this. Why don't you go home? I can get the tram.'

'Don't be silly, dear. It's no problem to wait. It's quite soothing just sitting here, watching the world go by while I listen to some lovely music. Take all the time you need. I promise that if I get fed up, I'll go home. So don't worry. You've got enough to think about with that madman in there trying to control your life. He's taking everything from you, and you mustn't let him.'

I nod once, open the door and get out. I can feel my heart pounding, and I lean back against the car for a moment, closing my eyes, trying to calm down. But the backs of my eyelids seem to be painted with multicoloured fractured images, and I quickly open them again. With both hands I push myself away from the car and march towards the front door, key at the ready. Shoving the key into the lock I try to turn it, but nothing happens. I pull it out and try again, but it still won't turn. With mounting fury I realise he's put the catch on, and I can't get in. *The bastard!* I pound on the door with the side of my fist and open the letterbox to yell through it.

'Open the fucking door, Ian. *Now*, or I'll break a window.'

I think of all the times I have meekly stood by while Ian has hurled abuse at me, intimidated and controlled me, and for the first time I don't care if my behaviour angers him. I'm so tightly wound I know I will give every bit as good as I get.

He still hasn't opened the door. The garage is open, though, and I'm about to march through to the back of the house when I hear Ian fumbling about behind the front door. There is a click as he releases the lock. He pulls open the door, and I'm horrified at the sight of him. In my absence it looks as if he hasn't shaved for a week, and his hair is greasy and flattened to his skull. I always thought he was quite good-looking, but not now. I never realised how high his forehead is. With so much facial hair, he looks as if all his features have been squashed into the lower half of his face, and my head jerks back.

'Don't look at me like that.' His voice is harsh, abrasive. 'If I'd known you were coming, I might have had a shave. But then again, probably not. You're not worth the trouble.'

I take a step towards him, and he must see something in my expression because he moves back. I give him a shove anyway, just because it makes me feel better. I see the shock register in his eyes.

'What's the matter with you?' he says, his voice sounding squeaky to my ears. 'Have you lost the plot completely?'

I throw my keys on the hall table and storm into the sitting room, which is looking just as hovel-like as I expected. But I almost don't care. It's him – every bit of him suddenly seems repulsive, hideous, and I bend down and pick up a slice of toast from a plate on the floor and fling it towards him, Frisbee style, so it spins through the air. It hits him in the middle of his T-shirt.

'You're disgusting.' I hear the sneer in my voice. I pick up the detritus from the floor and head to the kitchen. Flicking the lid of the bin open, the smell hits me before I realise that it is full to overflowing. He can't have emptied it since I left, and I wrinkle my nose in disgust, reaching in to push everything down.

'*Shit!*' I scream as my hand hits something sharp. I pull it out quickly, but blood is pumping freely from where a piece of broken glass has pierced my palm.

Ian says nothing.

I grab a tea towel, but that is filthy too, so holding my hand above my head I march back through the sitting room and up the stairs, dripping blood in my wake, but I don't care. The whole place will have to be scrubbed before it's fit for anyone else to live in. In the bathroom I find the last of the clean towels and push it against my hand, but the blood is still coming. This is all I need.

Ian has followed me upstairs, looking defiant, waiting for the moment when he can tell me that none of this is his fault. It will be all down to me – for going away without him, for asking him to leave, for dragging him away from his life in London. I don't want to hear a word of it, and I round on him, still pressing the towel hard against my hand.

'I'll tell you what's going to happen, shall I? You are leaving this house. I'm moving back in and renting out the spare bedroom to make some money to put towards the mortgage. If you don't do as I say, I will default on the mortgage and tell the building society I'm not going to make any more payments. They will repossess and throw you out anyway. I'll tell them to do it sooner rather than later.'

'You can't do that!' Ian's voice sounds uncertain though. He's never seen me like this, but the rage is building nicely inside me and suddenly I feel capable of anything.

'I can, and I will. The house is in my name only, so when it's sold – and it will no doubt go for a ridiculously low price so they get their money back quickly – the balance, the fat deposit that I put down, will all be repaid. To me. Not you. Now, if you think you're going to get any of that, you can whistle for it or sue me. Whichever takes your fancy. Have you got all that, Ian?'

I realise I must look like a fishwife. My head is thrust forward towards him.

He looks shocked. 'Jesus, what a bitch you are.' He spits out the words. 'You can't make me do anything.'

'Watch me,' I snarl.

I push past him again and march into the bedroom to collect some more of my things, and Ian returns to the sitting room, no doubt hoping that if he doesn't argue I might leave as soon as I've packed.

The bedroom is a tip too, Ian's clothes all over the floor, most of them dirty. I slept in the spare room when I got back from holiday, and the bed in here smells as if it hasn't been changed since before I went to Myanmar. I feel my nostrils flare with disgust. And something snaps.

I thrust open the window, initially to let in some air. Then I eye the clothes on the floor and scoop them up, an armful at a time, and chuck them out of the window, my blood all over them. I rip the sweaty bedding off the mattress and that follows. I hear a thundering of feet up the stairs.

'What the fuck are you doing?' Ian yells.

'Giving your clothes an airing, you slob,' I scream back at him.

I glance towards the window. A couple are walking past, staring up at us, and I glimpse a look of concern on the woman's face.

I spin back towards Ian. 'Get out of my way.'

I reach under the bed and grab a soft case, randomly flinging in underwear, tops, jumpers and jeans, ramming them into every corner.

'You're a mad bitch, you know that, don't you?'

I advance on Ian until my nose is inches from his. 'If you call me a bitch again, I will punch your sad, squashed-up face. Understood?'

Ian raises a hand, and for a moment I think he's going to hit me, but he just rubs the top of his head as if he's totally confused by the person in front of him.

Good.

I snatch the case from the bare mattress and stomp towards the door, elbowing Ian in the guts as I pass for good measure. He grabs my arm and spins me round.

'What's happened to you?' he says, genuine bafflement in his tone and on what I can see of his face.

'I've realised what a wanker you are,' I spit as I yank my arm free. I push him away with my bloodied hand and pound down the stairs and out through the front door, heading towards my car, which is parked on the drive. I open the boot and reach in for the flat shoes that I wear when I go for a walk. I can't see them and push Ian's never-used fishing gear to one side.

He is hard on my heels, and I just want to get out of here. I can live without the shoes.

'Come back and talk to me,' he pleads. 'We can sort something.'

I hide a smile of satisfaction. *Now* he wants to talk, when his back's against the wall and he has lost. I spin round. 'I would rather slit my throat than spend another sixty seconds in your company. No, scratch that. I would rather slit *your* throat. Don't push me, Ian. What have I got to lose?'

Another passerby – a middle-aged man – peers at me nervously and crosses to the other side of the street, but I don't care who sees me or what they think. All I want is for Ian to be out of my life, one way or another.

29

I return to Thea's car and throw myself into the passenger seat. Without a word I grab my seat belt, buckle up and fling my house keys onto the back seat.

'I thought you might be upset, so it seemed a good idea for me to drive,' Thea says.

The journey passes in silence, with me staring sightlessly out of the window, my lips clamped tight together, my body rigid. Slowly I try to calm my breathing and let my blood pressure fall to a reasonable level, muttering nothing more than 'Thanks' to Thea.

She doesn't speak, giving me time to calm down. I always thought the anger I had felt when I rowed with my father and Annabel over Pops' early inheritance would be impossible to beat, but that was tame in comparison to my feelings during the confrontation with Ian. Anger has always reduced me to tears in the past, but not today. I don't for a single moment feel like crying. I am beyond frustration; I am a boiling cauldron of rage.

I don't realise we are home until Thea speaks. 'Is your hand okay? Do you want me to look at it for you?'

'No, thanks. It'll be fine. I think it's stopped bleeding now.'

'You should go straight up and have a lie-down,' she says, her voice low and even as she pulls the car to a halt outside the door. 'You'll find some plasters and ointment in your kitchen. I'm going to make you one of my infusions to relax you. I'll be up in a few minutes.'

I kick my boots off at the door, and Thea bends to pick them up and put them on the shoe rack. I am still totally wired, and

I charge up the stairs to my room, thrusting the door open with such force that it crashes into the wall. Flinging myself on the bed, I lie with my hands behind my head and gaze at the ceiling. Ian is a bastard. How could I have ever thought I loved someone as mean and lazy as him?

I can't settle and jump back off the bed and stride to the window. It is dark outside now, and all I can make out is the black shape of the trees that border the vast garden. Suddenly, they make me feel hemmed in. I want to get out of here. I want to sort my life out once and for all.

The bag that I brought with me is sitting on the floor where I threw it, and I pick it up and up-end the contents onto the bed. I stare at the flimsy lace knickers and bras, the low-cut tops and the short-sleeved T-shirts – ridiculous clothes, not at all practical. At least I thought to push in a couple of jumpers and some clean jeans. I bundle everything into drawers and then I don't know what to do. I can't lie down, or even sit down. I'm so tightly wound I think I'm going to snap.

There's a tap at the open door, and I swivel towards it.

'Sit down for a moment, dear,' Thea says calmly. 'Drink this. I find it does the trick when I'm a bit worked up.'

I want to tell her that I'm more than a bit worked up, but even in the state I'm in I know none of this is Thea's fault, so I do as she asks. She perches herself on the edge of the bed and pushes her hands under her thighs as she watches me sip her infusion. It tastes good – I can taste lemons, but other herbs too. For a moment my mind is distracted as I try to identify the ingredients, and as always Thea seems able to read my mind.

'It's got some camomile in it,' she says, 'but I like lemon balm for stress, and a bit of sage too, not forgetting the valerian. Oh, and a bit of passion flower. All designed to make you feel better.'

It seems to be working, but maybe it's the comfort of a hot

drink and my hands cupped around a warm mug. 'I lost it, Thea. I really lost it with him.'

She smiles. 'Good. From all that you've told me, it sounds as if he deserves everything you threw at him. Do you have a plan?'

'I told him to get out because I want to let the spare room. If he's not gone in two days, I'm going to tell that snotty kid at the building society to repossess the house and throw him out on the street. At least I'll get my deposit back.' I can hear my voice getting a little calmer and my breathing has steadied. I feel a pang of guilt about the way I spoke to the girl, who was only trying to do her job.

'Would you like to have a chat with the doctor? He is so good at helping people see things as they are.'

I don't want to be rude, but I remember the last session. 'What value do you bring to the world?' he had asked. I have thought of those words often since, and on top of everything else I don't think I could cope with feeling worthless right now.

'It's kind of you,' I answer, relieved that my manners seem to be returning, 'but for now I think I'm fine. I've expended so much energy over the last few hours that I think I might have a bath and go to bed. Is that okay?'

Thea pushes herself to her feet. 'Of course, dear. But you need to eat something. I made us some soup for lunch – how about that? I'll go down and get you some now.'

'No, Thea. It's fine, honestly,' I say, embarrassed about all she is doing for me.

'I'm not taking no for an answer,' she says. 'Back in a moment.'

I give in. I am starting to feel lethargic and I imagine it's the adrenaline seeping from my system. I'll probably just do as I'm told.

I don't know how long it is between Thea going and coming back, but she returns with a bowl of soup, some bread and butter and a glass of wine on a tray. She puts it on the table beside me and

I lean forward and start to eat. She's talking to me in a low voice, and gradually I begin to feel numb.

I feel Thea's hand under my armpit. She's lifting me from the chair and helping me towards the bed. There's a mist over my eyes, and it's getting darker by the second.

30

Tom Douglas leaned back in his chair and pondered the case at Pennington Flash. Information was coming in thick and fast about Jasmine DuPont, the woman found in the bird hide. They now knew that her deceased twin sister, Esme, had been troubled for years. She had suffered from depression since her early teens and had been bulimic for a while. Jasmine, it seemed, had always been the cheerful one, supporting her sister through her illness, desperate to protect her from the worst of the demons that had haunted her.

In spite of Jasmine's insistence that her parents could have done more for her twin, Tom could only imagine how difficult it must be to deal with a child who was suffering from any kind of mental health issue. However much you might want to help, it would be so easy to take the wrong step. But Jasmine clearly felt they should have done better with Esme.

He thought back to the night when, as far as they could determine, Jasmine had died at the Flash. The witness, Sharon Carter, had seen two people get out of a car and only one get back in, so it seemed certain that Jasmine had been driven to the place of her death on the night the big freeze began. The driver appeared to go with her into the hide, carrying a bag which must have contained the cylinder of gas, although it was impossible to tell for sure. The post-mortem and the routine toxicology analysis revealed plenty about the drugs that Jasmine had been taking around the time of her death, but they didn't kill her. Amy Sanders had been unable to find any other cause of death, so the only logical conclusion, given the lack of helium found in the gas analysis of her lungs, was that an exit bag filled with nitrogen was used.

It seemed that Jasmine had voluntarily got out of the car and gone with the man – if it was a man. Maybe after all those months of missing her twin it had seemed to her that she had nothing left to live for, and so she had sought the help of a person she could trust. Maybe she felt that dying at the place where her sister had originally tried to kill herself would bring them closer together in death.

Tom recalled the case they had discovered with similarities to Jasmine's death – the young woman who had been found dead on a golf course, hidden from passing view in a deep bunker. Another team had investigated her death but found nothing to indicate how she had died. Just like Jasmine, she appeared to have died as a result of hypoxia, but there was no explanation as to how this had occurred. They had assumed the woman had gone there on her own. Her footsteps were clear in the sand of the bunker, but the area around her was raked to perfection, so due to a lack of any other evidence it had been assumed that the woman had walked in alone, sat down and died.

Perhaps now they knew the identity of their hide victim – Jasmine – they could find a tangible link to the other woman. Maybe the woman on the golf course had been helped too. It could have been the same modus operandi, the evidence of the cylinder and another person's footprints having been removed by raking the sand.

He would get Becky on to checking it out the next day, because if Jasmine was the second person to suffer death with help from an unknown third party, it suggested a pattern. And Tom had to ask himself if that meant more women were destined to die the same way.

31

I gradually become aware of myself. I can feel my arms, my legs, and they are warm, relaxed. I don't want to open my eyes – it seems like too much effort. I just want to enjoy the calming sensations. I can hear the sloshing of water, and I feel its heat on my chest. Something is rubbing gently on my hands, up both arms and along my shoulders. It feels wonderful, and I hear myself sigh and settle back further. I'm in water. It's up to my neck and it's soft and soothing.

I must be in the bath.

Vaguely I sense movement and maybe the sound of a door closing quietly, and it takes a moment for me to realise that someone is here with me, holding my arm with one hand, rubbing it with the other. I slowly open my eyes. The room is dark, lit only by two candles placed on a low stool at the end of the bath I am lying in. I look at the hand holding the flannel, and I know it belongs to Thea.

The calm evaporates in an instant.

Why is Thea bathing me? This isn't right. I struggle to sit up, covering my breasts with my arms.

'What are you doing?' I mumble, my words sounding jumbled as if my mouth is full of cotton wool.

'Shh. It's okay, Judith. We'll look after you.'

I don't know what she means.

The candles flicker as if a gust of wind has hit the wicks, and light momentarily flashes onto the water. I stare in horror, unsure for a moment what I am seeing.

The bath water is red. Blood-red. I glance to where my clothes are piled on the floor. My cream-coloured jumper seems to be covered in something dark. It looks black in this light, but I know what it is. Blood.

I lift my arms clear of the water. There's not a mark on me, apart from the cut on my hand from earlier. But the plaster is holding firm, and I'm sure it can't be that. One by one I lift my legs, exploring my body for signs of injury, but I can find none. So where am I hurt? I rub my fingers over my scalp, but I feel no pain. *Where has all this blood come from?*

I look at Thea. 'What's happened?'

She tries to shush me again, but I need to know.

'Tell me, please, Thea.'

I realise she's kneeling on the floor, and that can't be comfortable for a woman of her age. She struggles to her feet, using the lip of the old-fashioned bathtub for help, then goes to sit on a chair. Her face is in shadow. I can't see her. I can only hear her words.

'I found you outside again, my dear. You took my car, and we didn't know you'd gone. It was only when you came back that I woke up, and I found you like this.'

'Am I hurt?'

'Not that I can see, no. But there was a lot of blood on your clothes and on you. It had soaked right through.'

'I don't remember. Thea, *I don't remember!*' I realise I'm starting to panic. *What have I done? Where have I been?*

There is a gentle knock on the door, and I hear the doctor's voice. 'Thea, a word, please,' he says softly, as if there is someone in the house that he is scared of waking.

'I'll be back in a moment. You just relax,' Thea says as she slips out of the door.

I hear frantic whispering. I can't make out what they are saying, but I can tell by the inflection in Thea's voice that she's asking questions. After no more than two or three minutes, she comes back into the bathroom.

'What?' I ask rudely.

She comes over to the bath, and I feel self-conscious again, although given that she obviously stripped me it's a bit late for modesty. Thea is looking down at me, the candlelight casting strange shadows on her face. Her eyes seem lost in sunken hollows, and I can't guess what she is thinking.

'I'm not quite sure how to tell you this, my dear, but the doctor was listening to the radio. He does that sometimes when he can't sleep.'

I wish she would get to the point, and I lean towards her, my hands gripping the edge of the bath.

'I'm afraid they're saying that a man has been killed in Crumpsall. They're not giving any more details until his next of kin has been traced, of course, but we thought you should know.'

I wonder what that has to do with me. Yes, my house is in Crumpsall, but I don't know many people – only Ian. I feel my eyes opening wide. Surely that can't be what she means?

'Ian?' I ask, the word almost choking me.

'We don't know, Judith. They're saying that the man was attacked and suffered multiple skull fractures. They won't say any more. I'm so sorry to have to ask you, but do you know where you were tonight?'

I can feel myself staring blankly at her. I don't know what she is talking about. The last thing I can remember is climbing into bed. I don't know why I was outside, but if I was then surely I couldn't have driven anywhere? I give a tiny shake of the head.

Thea purses her lips and nods. 'When I found you, you had rather a lot of blood on your clothes. You seemed dazed by whatever had happened to you – you couldn't speak.'

I feel tears spring to my eyes. What's going on? Surely I can't have hurt Ian? That must be wrong. I know I was furious this afternoon, but he was fine when I left. Thea was *there*. She knows he was okay. But she's saying I went out later, after everyone was in bed.

My gaze returns to the blood-drenched clothing on the floor, and I can't tear my eyes from it. Thea reaches into the shadows for a towel and lifts it to shakes out its folds. The candlelight flickers and grows stronger for a moment.

I gasp. Protruding from under my jumper is a rubber-covered handle. It too is covered in blood, and I recognise it. I remember buying it weeks ago. I keep it on a shelf in the garage.

I don't have to see its split, curved, stainless-steel head to know that it is a claw hammer.

32

I'm still shaking, and it's hours since I woke up in the bath. However tightly I curl myself up in the bed, I can't get warm, and the tears won't stop.

Thea left me last night after she showed me the hammer. She took everything with her – my clothes, the flannels she had used to wash the remnants of blood from both me and the floor, and the claw hammer. I never asked what she intended to do with any of it, I only know that I felt totally dazed. And I was so cold. The bath water was warm, but my whole body was covered in goosebumps, and however much I rubbed my arms, they wouldn't go away. They still won't, even now.

I forced myself to get out of the bath and dried myself quickly, wrapping the towel around me to run to my bedroom. Thea said she would be back with something to help me sleep, but I didn't want to sleep. I wanted to lie there – awake – wondering whether I had done something terrible. I couldn't believe it. I still can't. I know that my behaviour yesterday was aggressive, but not *violent*, never violent. Just words and a few gestures to demonstrate my anger and frustration.

I have to be rational. The dead man was probably some random bloke in Crumpsall. It might have nothing to do with Ian at all. But what if it does? I can't wipe from my mind the people who had seen me yelling at him, throwing his clothes out of the window.

I'm being ridiculous. Surely there is a perfectly reasonable explanation. But where did the hammer come from, and why was

I covered in blood? Did I go to see Ian and then someone came in while I was there and attacked him? Did I try to defend us both?

My mind is spinning round and round, thinking of every single possibility. Because none of it makes sense.

It's light now, so I know it's morning, but I haven't slept. Thea's infusion is still sitting next to the bed. I wish the television in here worked so I could find out what was happening, but I have no access to the Internet, television or radio. I feel blind and deaf.

Someone is coming along the corridor. I don't know if I'm ready to speak to anyone, but I don't suppose I have a choice.

Thea knocks briefly on the door and pushes it open. She is frowning, the corners of her mouth turned down and deep worry lines between her eyebrows.

'What is it?' I ask, sitting up in bed and leaning eagerly forward. Perhaps she has discovered that the victim is some unknown vagrant and there's a perfectly sensible explanation for the blood.

She walks over to the bed and sits down.

'I'm so sorry, my dear. They have announced the name of the victim on the news. Is Ian's surname Fullerton?'

I nod, speechless.

'Then I'm afraid he's been murdered. They must have informed his next of kin, otherwise they wouldn't have released his details. Does he have family?'

I nod again, staring blankly ahead of me. Ian's parents will be devastated. *Oh God, what is happening to me?*

'The situation is rather worse than I had hoped,' Thea continued, her voice sombre. 'They have named the person they are looking for in connection with his murder.' She paused. 'I'm sorry, Judith, but I'm afraid it's you.'

I turn towards her and shake my head slowly from side to side. 'I didn't do anything, Thea. I would have remembered if I had. I need to go to the police and tell them.'

Thea nods. 'If that's what you want. But I will have to give them the hammer and tell them about the blood. You do realise that, don't you?'

I thrust the bedclothes away from my legs and jump out of bed. 'Can I see what they're saying on the television?'

'I'm so sorry, we don't have a television. And the radio will only confirm what I'm telling you.'

I pace backwards and forwards, my hands clasped at the back of my neck. This is madness. I wouldn't kill anyone, not even Ian. They must have got it wrong.

'You were very angry yesterday, Judith, and you told the doctor that Ian had no place on this earth. Don't forget that you wished him dead on more than one occasion.'

I stare at her, horrified. 'That doesn't mean that I would have actually *killed* him!' I cry.

Thea says nothing and puts her head on one side as if asking a question.

I haven't got a clue what to do. Not only am I appalled by what's happened to Ian, I feel guilty about bringing all of this down on Thea and Garrick. What the hell must they think of me? I spin round and face her.

'I'm so very sorry that this has happened while I'm staying with you. Obviously I'll get out of here. I can't get you involved. Please give me the clothes and the hammer. I'm going to have to talk to the police.'

Thea's brow wrinkles. She looks at me then glances at the full mug of tea, now stone cold. 'You didn't drink your tea. Have you slept at all?'

'No. I didn't want to sleep. I wanted to think.'

She makes an irritated tutting sound, the only sign of disapproval I have ever had from her. 'You're not thinking straight. You should have done what I said.'

Her voice is harsh, and I can tell she is really quite cross with me, but given everything else that is in my head I don't give it much thought. She jumps up off the bed with far more energy than one might expect from a woman of her age.

'Right. I'm going to get you something to eat, and please don't argue. We need to work out what is for the best, bearing in mind that we are implicated in this too. It was my car, and it's probably caught on CCTV somewhere, and you're in my house. So I would be grateful if you would accede to my requests until we are able to come up with a solution that causes the least damage to all of us.'

I stare at her back as she marches out of the door.

When Thea returns with a big bowl of porridge I can't bear the thought of eating it, or of drinking the herbal brew sitting alongside it on the tray. I just want to throw up. But Thea's mouth is set in a hard line; it's unlike any expression I have seen before on her face. She seems angry with me, and who can blame her?

I start to get out of bed again. 'I should go, Thea. None of this has anything to do with you. I'll tell the police that I honestly don't remember what I did, but I'll take my punishment if I have to.'

Only part of me believes this. I don't want to go to prison, but I can't stay here either.

'Will you please sit down, Judith.'

'My name's not Judith,' I say, with a flash of defiance.

'Eat this now,' she says, ignoring my remark. 'Nobody thinks well on an empty stomach.'

I will try to eat it to please her, but I'm not sure I can swallow.

I take a mouthful of the hot tea and manage to get it down my throat, so I pray that I can swallow the porridge, which sits like a grey puddle in the bowl, swimming in honey and cream. I take a spoonful, the sickly sweet honey masking all other tastes. The porridge feels thick and claggy and seems to grow to fill my mouth so that I can barely find the saliva to swallow it. I gulp, and Thea nods.

'More,' she says, staring at me fiercely. I do as she says.

Gradually it becomes easier, and I feel myself start to relax. Thea was right – hunger was making me incapable of coherent thought. She stands over me until every scrap has gone and the mug is completely empty. I begin to feel the tension slipping away.

Thea is talking to me, but her words are washing over me, her voice hollow in my ears. She is holding her hand out, and I realise she wants me to take it. I feel her gentle pull and know I have to get off the bed and stand up, but for a moment my legs feel too weak to support me.

Words are echoing in my head. 'Come with me,' Thea seems to be saying, over and over again. I hear the word 'safe' and find myself walking towards the door, her arm around my waist.

Slowly, slowly, we make our way along the corridor and down the stairs. I'm not taking much notice of where we're going, so when she opens a door on the ground floor that I don't think I've been through before, I think we must have become lost in the maze that is her home. Her grip on me has become so familiar that I almost don't notice she's there.

There is a wall straight ahead. Thea opens a small cupboard and presses a series of numbers on a keypad. There is a loud *clunk*. A question slithers through the fog in my head and then away again. The wall seems to open, and I realise it is a door without a handle. I think I hear the sound of other doors closing somewhere.

After a few seconds Thea pushes the door fully open and I see we are at the top of another staircase, which leads steeply down into a gloomy space below. I'm not sure I can manage the stairs – the treads beneath my feet swim in and out of focus – but Thea helps me reach the bottom. The corners of the space we are in hide in deep shadows, and I squint towards a single light bulb, suspended above a small table, creating a puddle of yellow light on its surface. Thea coaxes me past the table and along a narrow corridor. There seem to be a lot of doors, and all I want to do is lie down.

Without knowing entirely how I got here, I find myself in a small room with a bed and not much else.

Thea is speaking, and I try hard to catch her words, but they come and go – closer, then further away. I latch on to one word. *Safe*. She seems to be repeating it, and it's all I need to know. Thea says I'm safe, and that must be right.

I tumble onto the bed and curl into a tight ball. Thea may say I'm safe, but I seem to be in some sort of hell and I've no idea how I got here.

33

Becky waddled along the corridor as fast as she could. She needed to talk to Tom about Jasmine and wanted to catch him before the end of the day. Now that they knew who their victim was, they finally had lines of enquiry to pursue.

She tapped on Tom's open door.

'Come in, Becky,' he said, without lifting his eyes from the screen of his computer. She didn't bother to ask how he knew it was her.

'These trainers give a bit of an advanced warning of my arrival, don't they,' she said, sitting down and stretching her feet out in front of her, frowning at them. 'But I do have some news, and it's looking interesting.'

Tom clicked his mouse, presumably to close whatever he had been looking at, and lifted his eyes.

'Ooh, you don't look too happy. What's up?' Becky asked.

'Just looking at some figures for a meeting. We've got too many unsolved crimes. The trouble is, we know exactly who did what, but everyone is covering for everyone else. It's a nightmare. Anyway, you didn't come in here to listen to me moan. What's up?'

Becky sat up straight.

'It turns out that Jasmine DuPont had been going to a bereavement support group here in Manchester. According to the few people who knew her, she was constantly in search of an explanation for why her sister had taken her own life. Jasmine didn't have a regular job – she took bar work to pay her way – and she tended to live in flat shares and even the odd squat. It's made it really hard to check her movements, but it seems that nobody had seen her for months – at least eight, from what we can work out.'

'If she moved around, is that so unusual?'

'Yes, because one thing she always did without fail was visit her sister's grave every Friday. The man who tends the graveyard says she never missed. She used to sit on a plastic bag with her legs crossed and talk to her sister. But suddenly she stopped coming, and she didn't turn up at the bar where she'd been working for a few weeks.'

Tom lifted clasped hands and put them behind his head. 'What was the feedback from the people where she worked? Did they think she was flaky?'

'That's the point. They said it was obvious she had issues and seemed to struggle hugely with her sister's death, but in spite of that she was reliable. In the short time she was employed there she'd only failed to turn up for her shift once, and she called to let them know she wasn't feeling well. They thought she was troubled but reliable, and were surprised when she stopped showing up for work. They never heard from her again.'

Becky could see Tom's mind ticking over, and she stayed quiet to let him think.

'What about the bereavement group? Did you manage to get any information from them?'

Becky sighed. 'Yes and no. I've only managed to speak to the woman who runs the group, and it took a bit of persuading to get her to tell me anything. When I explained that Jasmine was dead and that we are treating her death as suspicious, she opened up a bit. She said Jasmine seemed to blame herself for Esme's death but wouldn't admit why she felt that way. This woman had a theory, though, based on little nuggets of information that Jasmine shared in the sessions.'

'And that theory was…'

'Jasmine knew how ill Esme was and had bought drugs for her sister on the street – ones she thought might lift her spirits. When Esme died, Jasmine not only blamed herself but was terrified that maybe she would be accused of killing her sister because of the drugs in her system, most of which Jasmine had acquired for her.'

'So why would Jasmine take such a weird cocktail of drugs herself?'

'I looked at the drug report that Lynsey wrote to see if there was any correlation – maybe Jasmine was trying the same combination as her sister to see if the drugs she procured had been the indirect cause of her death. There were overlaps but lots of discrepancies too. Lynsey was right about the pattern being weird – drugs that fire you up followed by those that calm you down. We'd ruled out any concerns about the scopolamine she'd taken, partly because she took it too long ago for it to be related to her death, but also because it's used in legal drugs – for motion sickness, among other things. But taken in high doses it makes you lose your memory, and I don't know if that's relevant.'

Tom got up from behind his desk and paced the floor as if it might help him think; Becky just wished he would sit down so she didn't have to keep swivelling her head to look at him.

'You know it's used a lot in South America – Colombia in particular – don't you?' she asked. 'The favourite trick is to dope victims and then coerce them into emptying their bank accounts.'

Tom spun round and looked at her. 'Devil's Breath,' he said, nodding. 'It can turn you into a compliant zombie. A nasty beast and highly dangerous. It could suggest that she was being controlled. Philippa and I talked about whether she might have been involved in either the sex or drugs trade, but we have no evidence to that effect, so I'm not sure it gets us anywhere unless we can find her dealer.'

'No luck on that yet, but we're going to go back to the

bereavement group to see if we can find any other members who might talk to us.'

Tom started pacing again and Becky fell silent.

'Was there anyone she was close to in the group – someone she might have turned to for help?' he asked, turning to face her.

Becky shook her head. 'Not really. The group leader said that on a couple of occasions she saw her heading towards the tram stop with one of the other members. But she didn't get the feeling they were going anywhere in particular, just home.'

'Did she know who the person was?'

'No. Like Jasmine, the woman doesn't go any more.'

'So Jasmine disappeared and nobody reported her missing.'

'That's right. Not a soul.'

Tom pulled back his chair and sat down. 'How awful that someone so young wasn't missed by anyone. Do you remember I had a visit from one of Jack's old friends the other day? His sister Hannah is missing too. Nobody reported that either, until Nathan showed up to surprise her.'

'Do you think her disappearance is related?'

'I doubt it. So many people go missing it would be absurd to assume there's any connection without more evidence. I just hope for Nathan's sake that she turns up.'

Becky sensed that the meeting was over and was about to stand up and leave when Tom spoke again.

'Do you remember the woman who was found on the golf course? Now we've identified Jasmine we might be able to find some connections – anywhere their paths may have crossed, people they knew in common. Do you know the case I mean?'

Becky nodded. 'I do, yes. We couldn't make any links other than the hypoxia because we didn't have any background for Jasmine. I'll dig out the file. I can't remember her name, but I'll look it up.' She pushed herself out of the chair and headed for the door. 'I'm on it.'

'Hang on a minute, Becky. I think her name was Williams. That might speed up the search. And her first name was…' Tom looked up at the ceiling as if for inspiration. 'Julia, or maybe Judith? Something like that, anyway.'

34

For a moment, as I struggle my way out of a deep sleep, I wonder where I am. I remember nothing, but as my eyes flutter open and I see the stark, bare walls of the room in which I am lying, I am assaulted by flashes of memory, none of which make sense.

I have no time to think though, because someone is sitting on the end of the bed, someone I've never seen before.

I sit up too quickly, and for a moment the room spins as I push myself back as far as I can against the wall to get away from the dark silhouette. The memories begin to solidify and I want to scream that it can't be true. Have I dreamed the whole thing, or am I really hiding in Thea's cellar because I killed Ian? I groan out loud and lift my hands to cover my face. I want to cry, to beg someone to believe that I can't have murdered him. Whatever they think, it wasn't me.

But I had the hammer, the blood, the anger.

I want to return to who I was *before*, when I still believed I had a chance at a normal life.

The person on the end of the bed watches me quietly, saying nothing. I can see now that it's a woman, but I don't know who she is or why she is here. Does she know what I've done?

I hardly remember how I got to this room. I have no more than a vague sense of Thea guiding me and helping me walk down some stairs; the feel of her hand gripping my arm harder than was necessary; a snapshot of a single light bulb casting a dull, yellow glow. It seems like it was hours ago, but I don't know whether it is day or night because the room has no windows.

'Drink this,' the young woman perched on the edge of my bed finally says as she holds out a cup. My vision seems to have recovered a little, but there isn't much light. All I can make out is a slight figure with tied-back dark hair and the biggest pair of brown eyes I have ever seen.

I look at the cup she is thrusting towards me and shake my head frantically. 'I don't want it. I think I'm going to be sick.' My throat is dry and my voice croaky, as if I've been crying.

'You have to drink it. Thea will blame me if you don't.'

'Who are you? What are you doing here?'

She says nothing, and pushes the cup a little closer.

'Give it to me, then. I'll tip it down the toilet,' I say, although I have no idea where the toilet is.

The woman's eyes grow even larger at what I have said. 'She'll know,' she says, her voice dropping to a hoarse whisper. She glances over her shoulder as if Thea is going to materialise through the gloom.

My head is aching and I feel vaguely as if I have a hangover, but I only had a single glass of wine with the soup that Thea brought me. I don't know if that was yesterday or the day before, but I know I'm in her cellar. Why is this other woman here? Now that I'm used to her presence she no longer seems threatening.

'Do you have any paracetamol?' I ask.

She furrows her brow and shakes her head as if I've said something ridiculous.

'If you have a headache, this will make you feel better,' she says, trying to force the cup into my hands.

I ignore her and rub my eyes. They feel sticky, gummy, and I wonder how long I slept. The horror of the last twenty-four hours comes racing towards me again, out of nowhere, threatening to knock me down. I gasp out loud. Will it always be like this – thoughts of what I have done retreating into a background ache, only to gather steam to punch me in the gut again?

'Are you okay?' the woman asks.

I don't know what to say to her. How can I tell her that I've killed someone but don't remember anything about it? I shake my head.

'Thea said you'd be confused. That's why you have to drink this. I have to go in a minute. I've got to finish the ironing. Please take the cup. I've got to stay until it's all gone, and I'm going to be late if you don't hurry. We all have to drink our tea and eat our food. It's one of the rules.'

I have no idea what she's talking about, but she looks concerned and I know I'm being obstinate, so I hold out my hand. The hot sweet liquid tastes good, and I don't know why I was being so difficult. The slight nausea abates, and I feel the panic attack that was about to engulf me retreat as my breathing slows.

'Thea says you don't have to do anything right now, so you can stay in here. There's a bathroom across the hall, but if you hear the buzzer you have to come straight back here and close the door until it sounds again.'

I barely take in what she's saying, but there is something slightly vacant in her expression and I don't know what she means about the buzzer. I'm sure if I can find Thea she will tell me what's going on and how long she thinks I need to stay here. But then it hits me. If I don't stay here, where will I go? To the police – to prison?

I struggle not to cry out as a memory of the last time I saw Ian leaps into my mind. At least, it's the last time I *remember* seeing him. We were in our bedroom and I threw his clothes out of the window. But I have no memory of going back there, of hurting him. Have I erased it from my mind?

I want to do something decisive that will clear my name, but my eyelids start to feel heavy, and the woman takes the cup from my hand and walks towards the door.

'What's your name?' I mumble as she reaches the door.

She stops with one hand on the jamb, and my heart jumps as she answers.

'It's Judith, of course,' she says.

35

I can't believe that I slept again. It's so quiet down here, but after I drank Thea's brew I settled back and my worries seemed to float away.

They're back now, though.

I remember Thea telling me that I was safe, but for how long? What's going to happen? When can I leave? Is Thea planning to help me flee the country? I'm so confused and I'm desperate to talk to her. My eyes flood with tears. How did I get myself in this mess? What did I do? I just want to go back in time to before the nightmare began.

I turn my head and see another mug of something sitting by me. I'm thirsty, and I know that Thea's herbal remedies always make me feel so much better, but right now I don't want to feel better. I don't want to forget, and that's what will happen if I drink the contents of that mug. I want to force myself to remember.

No matter how hard I push my thoughts, to dredge deep down for a glimpse of what happened, all I get in my head is the afternoon when I visited Ian and lost my temper. Nothing more.

'Come on,' I moan, beating the heels of my hands against the side of my head. But there's nothing. Only a blank.

I reach for the mug, suddenly eager to sip its delicious contents and sink slowly back into oblivion. But at the last moment I change my mind. I push myself off the bed. Maybe a cool shower will drive the fog from my brain and allow me to focus.

I turn the handle on the door, for some strange reason expecting it to be locked. It isn't, and I tiptoe into a dim corridor, scared that I shouldn't be out here.

'Hello?' I call softly. There is no response.

I turn to my left and after a few hesitant steps realise that I am in a kitchen area, a place I vaguely remember from when Thea brought me down here. It is tidy, but the single bulb casts very little light. The walls seem to be a dingy cream colour and the tops of the cabinets hide in deep shadow.

I know Thea helped me down some stairs, so I creep silently along until I see them on my right. I'll go up and find her. She'll know what to do. There is clearly no one else here, so I tell myself there is nothing to be afraid of.

Wearily I climb the stairs, holding on to the banister for support. There is no handle on the door, so I push against it. It doesn't move. To my right is a keypad. I remember Thea pressing some keys to gain entry when she brought me down here, but I have no idea which ones or the sequence.

For a moment I consider banging on the door to attract attention, but the bathroom is calling. I feel sure that once I'm showered and dressed my head will be clearer. I look down at myself, suddenly aware that I'm still wearing the nightdress Thea left in the bathroom for me after she washed the blood from my body. I shudder with horror at the thought, and my stomach heaves, but nothing comes up.

I stumble back down the stairs. I have to get out of this night-dress with all its memories and I need to find some clothes. But all I find in my room is some underwear that seems clean – but isn't mine – some baggy tracksuit bottoms and a couple of T-shirts. My clothes aren't here.

I pull what I need from the cupboard and wander back out into the hallway. It's an effort to put one foot in front of the other, and for a moment I look back at the bed, wanting to once again crawl beneath its covers and shut out the world. But I mustn't do that. A shower will make me feel more alive, even if it won't stop abhorrent images of Ian's death bursting into my thoughts every few moments.

I'm not sure which door hides the bathroom, so I open them one after the other. There are three bedrooms exactly like mine. They are identical in every way, and I find this slightly unnerving. There are signs that two of them are in use, but the third one only has a bare mattress. Does this mean that there are three of us living down here?

The thought makes me uneasy. But they're not here now, and I'm sure I will hear if anyone is coming, so I creep over to the wardrobe in the first room and look inside. Whoever is sleeping here appears to have no more clothes than I do.

I tiptoe back into the corridor to check there really is no one around and go into the other room that seems to be occupied. I pull out drawers at random, hoping to find something – anything – that will tell me who lives here. I remember the girl from earlier and wonder if this is her room.

The drawers reveal nothing personal until I open the one in the bedside cabinet. Inside is a notebook, and when I flick it open I realise that it is some kind of diary. I read the first page.

I brought Albie to meet Thea today. He is usually such a good baby, but today he was a bit grumpy. I really wanted Thea to like him because sometimes I don't know what to do with him for a full day and it would be a break every now and then to come here. But I don't want his crying to upset Thea and the doctor. She said it was no trouble at all, and Albie was probably teething. She said I could bring him any time I like and she made him a drink of squash. I didn't like to tell her that he's not allowed that because of the sugar. He seemed to like it, though, and he settled a bit afterwards.

I am about to turn the page to read more when I hear the buzzer – the one that tells me I'm supposed to go to my room and close the door. I don't know why there is this rule, but I don't want to be found in here. I hastily flip the diary closed, and a photograph falls out onto the floor. I don't have time to put it back, so I pick it up and run into my room, sticking the picture under my pillow.

A few seconds later my door is pushed open. Thea stands in the doorway and I have a flashback of the first time I saw her. She was smiling at me from the far end of the long dinner table on the boat as Donna from Louisiana quizzed me about why I was travelling alone. I remember thinking how kind and gentle her expression was, how beautiful she looked with her long silver hair resting on her shoulders. Today the woman I see seems so different from the one I thought I knew, and I feel a heavy sensation in my chest, as if the air is being forced from my lungs.

'You shouldn't be up,' she says, her eyes narrowing as she looks at me, her mouth a thin, straight line. Her hair is scraped back into a tight ponytail, and it seems more of a pewter colour than silver down here in the gloomy cellar. The cheekbones that I always admired catch what little light there is, giving the contours of her face an angular look. Her gaze moves to the full mug next to the bed. 'And why haven't you drunk your tea?'

I'm not sure how to respond. I feel I am on a knife edge here. Will Thea hand me over to the police? Is she angry with me for bringing so much trouble to her home? I can hardly blame her if she is.

'Thea, I'm so very sorry for this…mess!' I say, knowing that such a trivial word doesn't come close to describing the catastrophic quagmire I have landed her and Garrick in. I feel a sob building, but I swallow hard and pray that I can control it. I'm sure I would get little sympathy.

Thea gazes back at me, and I can see she's thinking, but I have no idea what is going on in her head.

'We will protect you,' she says finally. 'We've helped others who have found themselves in a difficult position, and the doctor will talk to you about what brought you to this situation. That is non-negotiable, Judith. If we are going to keep you safe, sessions with the doctor will be part of your treatment. We need to understand what demons are lurking within your psyche – whether you can be cured or whether you have no hope.'

What does she mean, 'treatment'? I've already had a session with the doctor, and I didn't enjoy it at all. It left me confused and anxious. And what happens if he decides I have 'no hope'?

'While the doctor is making his assessment, you will help around the house but live down here, where you'll be hidden from the outside world. The police won't find you here.'

'Of course I'll help,' I say, only too happy to do something to pay my way. 'What would you like me to do?'

She still hasn't moved from the door, and I wonder – now she knows I can be violent – if she doesn't trust me.

'The other girls will explain your duties. They have a rota of tasks – cleaning, cooking, ironing. It's a big house and it takes a lot of looking after. You are not allowed into our private rooms on the first floor. One of the other girls has that task. You will be allocated jobs downstairs.'

I blink when she mentions 'other girls'. How many of us are there? Do we all live down here, behind a locked door? I knew there was one other, of course. I've met her, and I noticed there were two occupied rooms, but are there others?

For some reason I don't feel able to ask, although it seems obvious that these girls – and I include myself in that number – are the cleaners, the women she didn't want to know about my existence.

'That's not a problem,' I say, eager to please.

She spins on her heel as if to go, but turns back and glares at me, her face a hard mask. 'Oh, and Judith – you will eat and drink whatever is put in front of you. If you don't – and trust me, I will know if you don't – we will call the police and tell them where to find you. We can't afford for you to be ill. How would we explain who you are and why you're here if you need medical treatment? Now drink your tea.'

I am so stunned by this new version of Thea that I say nothing. She goes out of the room and closes the door.

I sit down on the bed. My legs are trembling and I am no longer sure they will hold me up. *What is going on?*

I get a sudden glimpse of my future – living down here, cleaning for Thea and the doctor, being told what I can do, what I should eat, when I must sleep. And then I think of why I'm here. It's because I'm a killer.

It's not until I decide to stir myself from the confusion Thea has left in her wake that I consider drinking the tea. Almost as an act of defiance, I decide to have the shower I've been promising myself and then maybe come back and take a few sips. I pick up the clothes that I discarded when I rushed back in here and take a towel from the foot of the bed.

That's when I remember the photo under my pillow. I must return it to its hiding place.

I pull it out and look at the image for the first time. I see the small eyes, the hooked nose, the face that looks like an eagle. He looks much younger, but I know this man.

I swallow and reach for the mug, taking a swig as if the tea will drive his image from my mind.

I have to get it back to its hiding place – I must – but I can't move.

The face staring at me is the one that disturbed me from the first day of my trip to Myanmar.

It's Paul, the man from the boat. The man who said he was watching me.

36

Tom wasn't given to delving deeply into his emotions. He had always thought that too much introspection wasn't good for the soul, and on the whole he took things as they came. But as he sat opposite Louisa in their favourite Indian restaurant, watching her scoop up chicken tarkari onto a torn piece of paratha and pop it into her mouth as she rolled her eyes in ecstasy, he knew this was how being in love should feel. With Louisa everything was a pleasure. She enjoyed life and did nothing merely for effect, nor did she pretend to be anyone other than the person she was.

Tom had been in love before, but it had never felt as easy as this. Behind him was a failed marriage and a relationship he'd had great hopes for which never quite made it. He had begun to feel that he was destined to be alone, but then, with Becky's help, he had started seeing Louisa. It had been so easy since their very first date.

There was only one dark cloud hanging over Tom's head, and that was Jack.

As he smiled at Louisa, both of them with mouths too full to speak, he decided that tonight he was going to tell her about his brother. He would wait until they were in bed, facing each other, lips inches apart, the cool, soft skin of her body lying against his. She would lift one leg and wrap it around him, as she always did, smiling at the thought of what was to come, and then he would tell her.

It was time to show her that she meant everything to him. The burden of carrying his secret alone would be gone, and he felt a flood of relief.

❖

They left the restaurant earlier than usual, and Louisa seemed to have sensed a difference in Tom's mood. She had given him a few puzzled looks but said nothing until they were nearly home.

'I enjoyed that,' she said, reaching out to touch his thigh.

'I could tell.' He smiled as he drove, grateful that he had drunk no more than one glass of wine so they didn't have to bother with a taxi. He needed to think about the words he was going to use to explain all that he had been holding back for months.

'You're quiet,' she said. 'But you're smiling, so I guess you're not unhappy about anything.'

'Not in the slightest.' He glanced sideways at her. 'But I do have something to talk to you about.'

'Ooh, that sounds interesting,' she said.

That was typical of Louisa. So many women would have assumed it was something they didn't want to hear, or would demand to know immediately what he was thinking. Louisa was content to wait until he was ready to tell her.

'Is this a chat over a glass of wine in the kitchen, or a chat in bed?'

Tom laughed. 'Shall we go straight to bed?'

'Sounds like a plan.' She gave his thigh a gentle squeeze as he parked the car on the drive.

Tom draped his arm around Louisa's shoulders as they walked towards the door. As he put his key in the lock, he could hear the answerphone pinging and hoped it wasn't anything that was going to ruin his plans for the night.

'Sorry, but I'm going to have to check that isn't something important,' he said. 'Nobody's tried my mobile, though, so that's a good sign.'

'It's okay. I'll get a glass of water to take up. Do you want anything?'

He shook his head and Louisa walked towards the kitchen.

'Did you leave the light on, Tom?' she shouted over her shoulder.

'Doubt it,' he said, pressing 'Play' on the phone. He listened for a moment to some salesman suggesting that Tom change his energy supplier and then hung up. As he put the handset down he thought he heard a faint gasp.

'You okay, darling?' he called. There was no response.

Tom hurried down the corridor towards the kitchen. The door was open. Louisa was just inside. She was standing perfectly still and Tom couldn't see beyond her into the room.

'Louisa?'

She didn't turn, but moved one step to the side. Tom took a pace forward and froze. In his kitchen, sitting at his table, was a man with a scruffy beard and wild black hair held back loosely in an elastic band, a laptop computer open in front of him. He looked up and smiled.

'Sorry if I gave you a fright,' he said.

Tom knew he should say something, but he couldn't speak.

'Lost for words, little brother?' the man said.

37

I haven't drunk my tea yet. I know I'm being ungrateful, and I can see why Thea wants to keep me well, but I need to organise my thoughts and I have learned that her tea doesn't help; it makes me groggy, sleepy.

A foggy recollection of the woman sitting on my bed insisting I drink my tea nags at me, and I suddenly recall what she said as she walked out of the room.

She said her name was Judith. *Did I imagine that?*

I don't think I did, so is she the original Judith, the first of what Thea called her 'waifs and strays'? I got the impression that the first Judith was long gone, but if that's who the woman is, why is she still here? And why do they call me Judith too? Weird as I've always found it, it now seems twice as weird, and I feel a shudder run through my body.

The shower beats down on my head, and I lift my face to the water, feeling hot spikes prick my skin. I want to release the tight knot of tension that is gripping me, and I feel a stab of nausea every few minutes at the thought of Ian's body, the blood gushing from the wounds where I must have hit him with the claw hammer. Each time I visualise the scene it is different. I know I'm imagining how it must have been, painting a picture of what I did, but I have to invent the images because I can't remember.

Before another thought can hit me, I switch the shower to cold. I want to suffer, and I hold my breath as the icy water stings my flesh. For the first time in days I begin to feel alive, and I know that for my own sanity I need to focus – to plan what I am going to do. I stand under the freezing water for as long as I can bear it, and then step out and rub my skin vigorously with the thin towel.

Within seconds, though, my determination crumbles as I see a future ahead of me that holds no hope. I feel the tears welling up again and hurry back towards my room. But before I get there I see Judith and another woman walking towards me from the bottom of the stairs that lead up into the house. Both of them are moving slowly, lethargically, their heads bowed. This must be the woman who occupies the other room, but why do they live down here too?

I don't know which of them the photo of Paul belongs to, but I'm relieved I managed to return it to its hiding place. If I am to find out anything, I mustn't antagonise either of them. I brush away the tears with the heel of my hand.

'Hi,' I say, doing my best to offer a friendly smile but knowing it's a poor, shaky effort.

They raise their heads slowly and gaze at me. The younger of the two – Judith – looks slightly puzzled, as if she has forgotten I'm here, but finally nods her head in acknowledgement. I turn my attention to the other woman. Her shoulders are hunched, her eyes red-rimmed, and there is not a flicker of interest in her gaze as she shuffles to the kitchen and starts laying out bowls and spoons.

There is so much I want to ask them, so much I'm confused about. Do they know what I've done? But I stand, saying nothing, watching while Judith heats a pan of soup and the other woman pours glasses of water from a jug.

I'm stunned by their lack of interest in my presence. They don't look at me or at each other as they go quietly about their tasks, and suddenly I see the same scene but with me at its centre – perhaps slicing some bread, dressed in the same clothes with the same level of apathy. It's a terrifying image.

As Judith turns to the table with the soup, I look once more at her huge eyes and notice that each pupil, black and shiny as coal, almost obscures the brown iris. She looks dazed, and I want to ask which is her room. Is the photograph of Paul hers? How does she know him? I have a feeling she will simply look puzzled, and of course she will know that I've been through her belongings.

The older woman, who carries herself like someone in her seventies although I'm sure she's probably only a few years older than me, comes to the table with the water and a plate of bread, and we all sit down. For the first time, she meets my eyes. I can just tell that her eyes are blue – almost all I can see are twin black orbs reflecting the yellow light of the single hanging bulb.

Finally I have to face something I have suspected for a while. I have been so grateful for the oblivion that I have chosen to ignore the truth. It is time to accept that there are far more than a few harmless herbs in Thea's infusions, and possibly in all the food that I have eaten since I have been in this house.

For a moment I feel breathless and I fight to control the panic rising in me. I know very little about drugs, but by the look of the other two women I would guess they are on some kind of tranquilliser. I have been free from Thea's food and drink for a few hours and the effects are fading, but now I crave more, desperate as I am to sink back into a stupor which masks the reality I am struggling to deal with.

A bowl of soup is pushed towards me. 'You have to eat this,' Judith says.

I start to shake my head, but I see her eyes dart sideways and upwards. I want to follow her gaze, but something tells me to be careful. I wait a moment and then casually glance around the small kitchen area, my attention not lingering on any particular spot. The room is poorly lit and the tops of the cupboards are in deep black shadow. In the gloom I spot a tiny pinprick of green light.

They are watching us.

❖

In the end I ate the soup. I didn't have much choice, given what I now know. I don't want to be thrown out of the house, and I need Thea and Garrick's protection, even if I don't like the fact that they are spying on us, drugging us. *Why are they doing this?*

I want to ask the other women why they are here, but neither of them have said anything. Judith doesn't seem quite as institutionalised, and I get the feeling she is more aware that things are not quite right. Because they are not.

Perhaps they are both simply cleaning staff. Maybe they are paid to work here – they know the code to get out and can come and go as they like. Thea is right: this house does take some looking after. Then I risk a quick glance up towards the tiny green light and I know that the others are no more free to leave than I am.

As soon as we have eaten, I excuse myself and make my way to the bathroom, checking around, hoping that they wouldn't stoop so low as to hide a camera in there. I turn off the light to look for a telltale glow, but there is nothing and nowhere to hide a camera. I kneel down by the toilet bowl. I have never done this before, and I'm not looking forward to it, but I close my eyes, count to ten and then push my fingers down my throat.

It's awful. It's the most dreadful feeling, and the temptation to give in and let the soup perform its magic is massive. But I feel my stomach heave, and finally the contents of my meagre supper spew out of me, leaving my throat sore and burning with acid. God help me if I'm going to have to do this after every meal. I could have trusted the bread, I think, but that has all come back too. I rinse my mouth out, gargle with cold water and, feeling far worse than if I had left well alone, I stagger back to my room.

There is a mug of tea by the bed, steam rising from it. Once more I cast my eyes around, searching every corner, but there is nowhere to hide a camera as far as I can tell. The one in the kitchen isn't well disguised. It's as if they want us to know that we are being watched. I sit down on the bed and rest my head in my hands.

I don't realise anyone has come into the room until I hear a small cough.

'You need to drink your tea, Judith,' a quiet voice says. It's the same woman again, the one who says she is called Judith too.

I look up. 'Why do you call me Judith?' I ask. I know I have never given her any name at all.

'We're all called Judith. It makes it easier.'

'Who for?' I say, my voice rising in shock at her words. She takes a step back, obviously uneasy at my refusal to conform.

'Please, Judith, just drink your tea. Thea will be coming for you soon. She's going to be angry if you've not drunk it, and she might blame me. I can't afford to upset her. *Please*, Judith,' she begs, tears filling her eyes.

'What do you mean, she'll be coming for me?' I ask, my heart once more starting to pound uncomfortably.

'You're due a treatment with the doctor. Honestly, it will be much better for you if you've had your tea.'

Before I can say another word, we hear the buzzer. The woman's eyes go wide and she glances at my mug. She shakes her head frantically as she backs out of the room and scurries away, the door slamming behind her.

So what do I do? Do I drink my tea and conform, or do I risk incurring Thea's wrath? I can hear the *thunk* of the bolts sliding back on the door at the head of the stairs. I only have a moment to decide.

38

'Jack?' There was a question in Tom's voice, one he didn't need to ask. He knew exactly who this was and he couldn't help feeling a leap of pleasure at the unexpected sight. 'You've grown a beard.'

Jack laughed, his intense blue eyes dancing. 'Is that all you've got to say?'

The last time Tom had seen his brother, all hell had broken loose and a man had died. Jack had then tricked him and disappeared into the night before Tom had had the chance to talk to him about anything important. They had spoken just once since that day, and Tom had felt an overwhelming sense of frustration, knowing that his brother was out there somewhere – he had no idea where – but that he was unable to speak to him. His only method of communication was via notes left on his laptop. But it was no substitute for being in the same room with him, talking face to face.

He had never had the chance in all these years to hug his brother and simply rejoice in the fact that he hadn't died, so he walked across the kitchen, reached out his right hand and pulled Jack up off the chair towards him.

'I guess that means I'm forgiven, then,' Jack mumbled into Tom's shoulder.

'No, but it does mean I'm genuinely happy to see you. But why are you here? Isn't it a huge risk?'

'I'll get to that.' Jack looked over Tom's shoulder. 'Sorry about this. You must be Louisa. Tom's told me about you. We're not normally given to displays of brotherly affection, but it's been a while.'

Seeing Jack in his home had momentarily driven everything else from Tom's mind, and he turned slowly to face Louisa, knowing that he had left it hours – minutes – too late to tell her about his brother. She had a faint smile on her face, but her eyes were troubled, and Tom didn't know whether to kick himself or kick Jack for turning up without notice.

'Louisa, I'm sorry for not introducing you. As you've probably gathered, this is Jack. My brother.'

He waited for her response, fully expecting her to say, 'You mean the brother you told me had died in a speedboat accident?' But sarcasm wasn't Louisa's style. 'Good to meet you, Jack.' She paused. 'Look, I think it's best if I leave you guys alone so you can catch up. Tom, I'll let myself out.'

She turned towards the door, but not before Tom had seen the distress in her eyes. And so, it seemed, had Jack, who shot Tom a look of irritation.

'Bloody hell, Tom, you're an idiot,' he said quietly. 'Louisa, please don't go,' he called as she walked out of the kitchen. 'I'll disappear for a while and let you talk to Tom. Please. This is entirely my fault. Whether or not you've realised it yet, my kid brother always tries to do the right thing by everybody – everybody, that is, except himself. Can I ask you to listen to what he has to say? I know how much you mean to him.'

Louisa turned back. 'How do you know that?'

Jack glanced at Tom. 'I'll let him explain that, and everything that's led us to where we are today. He will underplay his role in events, but all I can tell you is that to keep me and three other people alive – two of them children – he took a huge gamble with his career and his freedom. So at least give him the chance to demonstrate that while he might be an idiot, he's an honourable one.'

Tom watched Louisa's face. He could sense the indecision. He had lied to her – the one thing she said she couldn't tolerate – and it hung in the balance whether she would stay or go right now.

Jack sauntered towards the door in that casual way he had. He pulled a key from his pocket and waved it in the air. 'Okay if I keep your spare key for now?'

Tom didn't bother to ask how Jack had found it. A family tradition had been to keep a spare key in a polythene bag buried under a rosemary bush. And even if Tom had set the alarm before he and Louisa had gone out to dinner, he had little doubt Jack would have cracked the code.

For now, though, he had to focus on Louisa. He had hurt her, something he had never intended to do, and he had to hope and pray that she would understand.

Tom poured Louisa a glass of red wine and a whisky for himself.

'Let's go through to the sitting room,' he said. 'It's a long story, and I want to be facing you as I tell it.'

At least she seemed prepared to give him a chance to explain, but he could feel she had emotionally withdrawn. She wouldn't shout and scream at him for lying to her, nor would she storm off in a temper. She would listen, and then she would decide. He needed to tell this story well.

Louisa sat back against the overstuffed cushions of Tom's sofa, and he took a seat opposite her, leaning forward with his forearms resting on his knees, clutching his whisky glass in both hands.

'I think it's best if I give you the abbreviated version of this story – get to the crux of it quickly – and then we can spend as long as you want on the details. Is that okay with you?'

Louisa gave him a small nod.

'Jack was involved with a criminal gang and got in over his head. It started when he was in his teens, and when he wanted to pull out not only was he threatened, but the whole family – his fiancée, me, Lucy, everyone who mattered to him – was in danger. The only way he could see to escape was to fake his own death and make sure nobody knew. Not even me. I mourned my brother for years. I didn't lie to you about that. I was devastated. I knew nothing about the life he had been leading and the events that had driven him to make that decision. All I knew was that he was extremely wealthy as a result of his computer security company. He left most of his money to me.'

Tom took a sip of his whisky. He had noticed Louisa's slight frown when he said how devastated he had been, and hoped this meant that – even for a moment – she understood.

'Jack was – and still is – brilliant. But he lost his way, and it was only when he learned that someone he cared deeply about was in terrible trouble that he came back – returned from the dead, if you like. He pulled off a stunt that saved a young child's life but at the same time he put himself in danger. Everyone had believed he was dead – especially the criminals he was involved with – but he risked exposing the fact that he was alive, and there was every chance he would end up with a bullet in his head.'

Tom looked at Louisa again to see if she appreciated how serious this was.

'He got away, and only a handful of people – good people – knew he was alive. That wasn't the end of it, though. We had to fake the deaths of a woman, a teenage girl and a baby. Jack set it up, and I helped.'

Louisa's eyes opened wide. She would understand the implications of Tom faking a death.

'Jack got them away and I had to tell my superior officer what had happened, expecting her to throw the book at me. She didn't. She covered for me.'

'So if this came out, what would happen?'

'If the enforcer of the gang Jack was involved with knew he was alive, he would use every person in his network to track him down and kill him.'

'And you, Tom? What would happen to you?'

'I would probably end up in prison. My boss, Philippa Stanley, would lose her job at the very least. Becky knows too, although we could probably hide that.'

Tom didn't want to say any more. He could fill in the gaps about what Jack had been doing and how he had been communicating with him some other time. But he wanted to make Louisa understand why he had kept this from her.

He was about to speak when Louisa said, 'You didn't tell me because you thought if things didn't work out for us, I would have some kind of hold over you. Is that it?' He could hear the hurt in her voice.

'Louisa, I never thought for one moment that you would use anything I told you against me. I don't believe you have a malicious bone in your body. If it had been *my* secret and no one else was involved, I would have told you weeks ago. But it wasn't. In the end, I couldn't live with the fact that I was keeping something from you, and that's why I decided to tell you tonight. It was the ultimate sign of my commitment to you.'

Tom waited. He still wasn't sure which way this was going to go. He was tempted to keep adding explanations, but he needed to give her space to think.

Louisa leaned forward slightly and picked up her glass from the table. She put it down again without tasting the wine.

'I understand why you didn't tell me. You didn't trust me enough.' Tom opened his mouth to speak, but Louisa held up a hand to stop him. 'It's the truth. And I didn't trust you enough to agree to move in with you. So in a way we're equal, although bizarrely it feels as if the fact that you hid this from me vindicates my decision. If you had simply lied by omission, it would be one thing. But it was more than that, wasn't it? I asked you how you felt about Jack's death. I held you as you talked about the shock and how much you miss him. I cried, Tom, when I thought of how much you were hurting. I know your feelings were real when you thought Jack was dead, but when you told me about it and I comforted you, you knew he was alive.'

She shook her head slightly and fixed her gaze on the empty space above Tom's head. She might never believe that he had planned to tell her everything. She would think Jack's untimely arrival had precipitated his honesty.

'Here's what I think,' she said, after what seemed like far too long a pause. 'We have a good time together. I believe we care about each other – no, that's undervaluing what we have. I love you, Tom. That hasn't changed. I absolutely understand why you thought you couldn't tell me about Jack. But understanding is a logical acknowledgement of something that makes perfect sense. There's an emotional response too – one that doesn't seem to want to recognise reason, however hard I try to force it. I am struggling to forget those moments when I thought I was sharing your pain, and yet all the time you knew you were deceiving me.'

Tom could sense where this was going, but he wasn't going to put up a fight. He knew Louisa well enough to realise she would make her own decision and was just as likely to back away if she felt he was pressurising her.

'Whatever you decide, I won't argue with you. Nothing that's happened has changed the way I feel about you,' he said. 'I know you have to decide if I'm the kind of man who has a shedload of skeletons lurking in his cupboard, and I can't prove otherwise. I'm thrilled Jack is here, but I wish he'd left it a couple of hours before showing up. By then you would have known everything. All I can say is that I'm truly sorry. I didn't fake the emotions. I remember clearly how I felt when I thought Jack was dead, and at the time we had that conversation I was really missing him. None of that was untrue. And I can't help but be glad to see him.'

Tom risked a smile, and Louisa responded.

'I'm not running out on you,' she said. 'But you need to spend some time with your brother. And I need to sort my head out. Is that okay?'

'Of course. I take it that means you want to go home tonight?'

Louisa nodded slowly. 'I'll get a cab.'

'No, you won't. I'll take you.'

Louisa nodded at the whisky in his hand, the glass now almost empty. 'Shit,' he said. 'Sorry.'

She stood up and reached out a hand to pull him to his feet, wrapping her arms around his waist.

'I know I'm probably being unfair, Tom, and I'm sorry.'

'I need you to be happy,' he said, drawing her closer. 'I don't want there to be a single barrier between us – no doubts, no hesitancy, no pretence.'

She lifted her head and kissed him gently on the lips. 'Me too.'

39

I'm not going to drink Thea's tea. I want my wits about me. I need to understand what's going on and what my options are, although I know they're not great.

Thea is an elderly woman. She's going to be slow coming down the stairs, and my room is furthest from the kitchen, round a bend in the corridor. I grab the mug and race barefoot across to the bathroom. I can't hear her slow steps plodding down the stairs in her soft velvet slippers, so I have no idea if she is getting close. The bathroom door is open, and I don't hesitate. I throw the contents of the mug into the washbasin. I fly back to my room and fling myself on the bed.

I realise I haven't shut the door, although I know I'm supposed to when the buzzer sounds, but I can't now – it's too late. I try to control my breathing and lift the mug to my lips as if I am savouring the last few drops as Thea appears in the doorway.

'This door should be closed,' she says, her voice sharp. 'You need to follow the rules.'

I want to ask her why, but I'm supposed to be lethargic and amenable, so I nod my head and don't meet her eyes. I mutter, 'Sorry,' under my breath and I hear her give a small sigh.

'The doctor would like to see you,' she says. 'I'm sure you'll find it helpful in coming to terms with what you've done.'

I close my eyes for a second. Thea is right. I do need to accept my guilt, although I seem to remember her suggesting more than once that it might be better for everyone if Ian were dead. Of course, that was just a figure of speech. I'm sure she never meant it.

'Come along,' she says. 'Follow me.'

The other doors are shut, and I wonder what is going on in the heads of the women hiding behind them. Were they as confused as I am when they first arrived? I have no time to think as we reach the top of the stairs.

'Turn away from the door, please,' Thea says. I realise she doesn't want me to see what number she punches in. Each number has a different tone, and the sequence sounds eerily tuneful.

'Why do you lock us in, Thea?' I ask, realising too late that had I taken my soup, topped up by the drink, I would probably be too doped to ask questions.

Thea turns towards me and narrows her eyes. She's not sure what to make of me, and I lower my head meekly.

'We can't have you – any of you – walking up into the house whenever it suits you. We may have visitors, and I'm sure that by now your face is all over the newspapers. We have to make sure that you're hidden. It's for your own good. Do you not understand that?'

Her voice rises with irritation, but I can't help myself.

'So if I want to leave, I can?' I try hard to keep my voice dull, slow, as if these thoughts are just meandering through my mind rather than being the focus of my attention.

Thea tuts. 'Of course you can. I really don't understand your problem.' I can hear a trace of anger in her voice now, and I am worried that I have gone too far. 'I invited you here because you were in trouble and had nowhere to go. And now you're in far greater trouble, and we're trying our very best to help you. In return, you seem to feel it's acceptable to insinuate that you are here under duress. Would you like me to show you where the key to the front door is? Would you like me to drive you to the police station? It can be arranged, believe me.'

I don't know if I believe her or not. I feel I should be grateful for the fact that they are helping me – hiding me – but why do they have to drug me? I can't ask that question. It might be the last straw. She might throw me out, and I'm not ready for that.

I follow Thea down the hall into a part of the house I haven't visited before. We walk down a short corridor and she knocks on a door.

'Come,' a gruff voice calls.

Thea pushes open the door, and I know where we are. We're in the doctor's private study. It is a parody of every psychiatrist's consulting room ever seen in the movies: dark red walls lined with shelves full of leather-covered tomes, a chaise longue and a comfortable chair for the therapist. I am tempted to laugh, but I realise how inappropriate it would be. Maybe I'm hysterical.

I stand silently, waiting to be told what to do, my hands hanging limply at my sides, my head bent slightly. I can just see the doctor if I lift my eyes.

'Sit,' he says. He glares at Thea as if blaming her for something, then nods his head to dismiss her and she backs out of the door.

I shuffle across the room and sit down nervously on the edge of the leather chaise, tucking my hands under my thighs. I know I'm supposed to be a lot less aware of my surroundings than I am, and although Thea might have noticed, I don't want the doctor to.

He ignores me as he studies a page in one of his books. It's making me even more nervous, and I'm sure he's doing it on purpose. After what seems like ages, he speaks.

'Lie down,' he says. 'Close your eyes.'

I don't want to. I know the idea is that it will make me relax, but it won't. It will make me feel vulnerable. Why would anyone think it a good thing for someone who has been traumatised to be flat on their back with their eyes closed in a dimly lit room with a man they barely know? I can't imagine the doctor has any motive other than to help me sort out my mental state, but I'm not going to close my eyes, no matter what he says.

I hesitate for a moment too long, and under my hooded lids

I see his eyes narrow. I'm giving this simple instruction too much thought for one who should be lightly tranquillised, so I do as he asks, slowly lowering myself, my movements languid. I keep my eyes averted so he can't see my pupils.

'Your clothes are too tight, Judith, and they will impede your progress. You will feel them, be conscious of them instead of listening to the sound of your thoughts. Loosen the knot around your middle so you can no longer feel it restraining you. Insert your fingers into the waistband and pull the fabric free.'

I know that if I was drugged I would do this without question, so I quickly pull one end of the cord to release the bow. It's a small thing and not worth worrying about. I try to settle as if I am relaxing into the session.

And then it begins. The doctor's voice is raspy and low, and I find it hard to listen to him initially. Then I remember the other times he has spoken to me, and how I felt I had fallen under some spell, barely keeping awake. It never occurred to me that I was drugged, but perhaps I was. I had drunk nothing but sherry, and as Thea was drinking it too I assumed it was only the effects of the alcohol and the doctor's mesmerising words that had lulled me into semi-consciousness. But I'm not sure I believe that any longer. And right now I don't want to be soothed by his voice. I need to keep alert.

'Tell me,' the doctor says. 'When did you realise that you were capable of killing a man?'

40

Since the doctor sent my heart into my throat with his opening gambit I have struggled to control the impulse to jump up from the couch and ask him what he knows. I need to hear what is being said on the news, learn what I have done. I so desperately wanted to ask Thea when she came to collect me, but everything happened too quickly – from the moment I heard the buzzer and raced to chuck my drink away, to walking through this door. Without the dulling effect of Thea's magic potions I feel as if my head will explode with all the facts, feelings and fears that I am trying to assimilate.

I'm terrified that if I'm not careful they will throw me out onto the street in the freezing cold with no money, no shoes and no proper clothes, and equally petrified by the fact that there is a warrant out for my arrest for what I did to Ian.

Through my half-closed eyes I am facing the study window and I can see outside for the first time since Thea took me down to the basement. Was that just this morning, or have I lost track of time? The curtains are open even though it is dark outside, but I have no idea whether it is early evening or late at night. I have nothing tying me to the fundamental security of knowing the day of the week or the hour of the day, and I feel detached from reality.

'Before we start your treatment and talk about the impulses that drove you to kill, we need you to understand your options.'

Do I have any? They seem very limited at this moment.

'You can, if you wish, walk out of this door right now. If you implicate us in any way – tell anyone that we tried to protect you – we will deny it. There is no evidence at all of our involvement. We've taken care of that.'

I want to ask what they have done with the claw hammer and my clothes. Maybe if they no longer exist the police will have no evidence to hold me. But Thea has already said that the police have named me as a suspect, and given that I have no idea what happened that night, there may well be other evidence at the house.

'Your second option is to trust us and to stay here under our protection. I think Thea has explained what we would expect in return. We are both getting on in years, and help around the house would be useful. In addition to that help, I would want you to agree to some treatment with me. I am fascinated by the mind of the killer, and as a psychiatrist I would like to leave a legacy of understanding for my colleagues. For as long as evil has existed, people have wondered about its source, and I would like to explore it with you. For that to work, you will have to learn to trust me implicitly.'

He thinks I'm evil. Oh my God! What a dreadful thought. But why he would let me live in his house if he thinks that? I have no answer, but it doesn't matter because he answers my question for me.

'I don't think we're at risk from you. I don't believe you killed for the pleasure of killing, and Ian had pushed you to the edge of sanity. You killed to remove the source of your distress.'

I'm appalled by the idea that I have done something so dreadful to rid myself of a problem, but I have to consider what the doctor said. He has offered me two options, and with every cell in my body I hope he is about to offer me another, more appealing choice. But he is quiet. I feel he is waiting for me to speak.

'I appreciate so much what you are doing for me,' I say quietly. 'But how long can this last? Will there come a time when it will be safe for me to leave?'

'There is no statute of limitations on murder, Judith,' he says.

'Any time you leave here, you are in danger of being arrested.'

I feel a sob building and I don't have the strength to fight it. It's a life sentence, whichever way I look at it. And which is worse? I don't know. I need time to think. I need my head to be clear of the last of the drugs.

'Make no mistake, though. Once you have made the decision to stay, you can't choose to leave in a week, a month, a year. By then we would certainly be guilty of harbouring a criminal. At the moment we could say we didn't know, but that will become increasingly difficult as time goes on. You go now, or you stay.'

I don't know if I am capable of making that decision without time to think, but before the options have sunk in, he starts talking again.

'This needs to be a symbiotic relationship. Do you understand what that means, Judith?'

I nod my head.

'We need to develop a relationship based on trust. We will support and protect you, and slowly I'll help you to relive the impulses that drove you to kill, so that both of us benefit from that knowledge.'

I don't understand how this will work. I don't remember killing Ian, and I tell the doctor that I'm not sure I can help him. He just smiles and nods his head slowly.

'I know. You've blocked it from your mind. Relax now. I'll take you back to the moment so you can be freed of your confusion and doubt. You will once again lift that hammer high, feel the *swish* of air as it swings down. I'll help you to recall the sense of climax as Ian's control over you was relinquished, and the elation you felt as you eradicated him from this world.'

❖

When I go back down to the basement the two women are sitting at the kitchen table, resting their chins on their upturned hands. They must be able to see my confusion. I feel as if the energy has been sapped from my body by the doctor's words, so with little more than a glance in their direction I walk past and go to my room.

I need time to think. I know that I don't want to go to prison. I have always wanted children, and by the time I get out I will be too old. That is only a fraction of my fear, but it is the only part that I can look square in the face. The others are shadows, creeping at the edge of my consciousness – dangers and horrors I don't even want to contemplate.

I jump as the sound of the buzzer breaks the silence. I had assumed nothing more would happen that night, but I was wrong. I hear the scraping of chair legs on the floor as the other two stand up and hurry back to their rooms. Surely she can't be coming for me again? I don't think I can bear it if she is, and childishly I cross my fingers behind my back.

But I am safe. I hear the shuffling of feet in the corridor, and when I think they are safely past I slide the door quietly towards me and peep round the corner. The older woman is meekly following Thea, head bent.

Maybe this is my chance? Maybe I can get the younger woman to talk to me – to tell me her story. I wait until I hear the *clunk* of the locks slipping back into place at the top of the stairs, and I tiptoe across the corridor. I was right about which room she is in. It's the one where I found the photograph of Paul.

I'm not sure how my questions will be received, but I have to try. I knock gently on the door and push it open.

'Can I come in?' I ask, keeping my voice low.

The woman looks up from where she is seated on the bed, her eyes round with fear.

'I just want to chat a bit. Is that okay?'

She glances over my shoulder towards the door. 'They've gone,' I tell her. 'We'll hear them if they come back.'

I move slowly towards her and sit down, leaving plenty of space between us so she doesn't feel I'm crowding her.

'Can you tell me your name?' I ask. She looks even more worried, if that is possible. 'Okay. It doesn't matter.'

I open my mouth to tell her mine, but she shakes her head. 'Judith,' she says. 'You're Judith, I'm Judith.'

I mustn't frighten her any more than she already is, so I nod.

'I understand,' I say. 'Have you lived here for a long time?'

I see her brow furrow. Maybe this isn't a forbidden question and she is trying to sort through her fuddled brain for an answer.

'Since November,' she says eventually.

That is only three months before I arrived and yet she seems to be totally institutionalised. *Is this how I will be in a few months?* The thought terrifies me. I can't let that happen.

'Did you come here for a job – to work for Thea and Garrick?'

She pauses again, each question requiring a huge amount of thought, it would seem. Then she shakes her head. 'They're helping me. I'm in trouble.'

I nod. 'Me too.'

I want to ask her more questions, but she is like a deer – slender, beautiful, with those great big eyes that seem frightened into flight by the slightest movement. So I wait.

'We're not supposed to talk about it.'

'Okay,' I say again. 'But do you want to talk about it?'

She shakes her head fiercely, and I can see that whatever happened, it's tearing her in two.

'I can't believe I did it,' she says. 'I loved him.'

For a moment I think she is going to tell me a story like my own – except I didn't love Ian. Did she kill her partner too? I find that hard to believe.

'I took him. Why would I do that? It doesn't make any sense to me.'

She starts to cry, and I reach out my hand to hold hers, worried that if I move too close I will scare her.

'Was this before you came here?' I ask gently.

'I came to see Thea. I brought him with me. But then I don't know what happened. It was all over the papers and the television. Why did I do it? I just don't know.'

She is sobbing now, and I move a little closer and put my arm around her shoulders.

41

Tom was slouched on the sofa with the same glass of whisky in his hand when Jack returned, letting himself in with the spare key he had found earlier.

'Louisa gone, then?' he asked, looking slightly sheepish. 'Sorry about that. I assumed you would have told her about me, given how serious you seem to be about her. Considering the shock she had, I thought she took it well.'

'Oh, well that's okay then. Especially since she's now gone home to consider whether she wants to be with someone who has been lying to her for months.'

Jack laughed and Tom gave him a dirty look, which he ignored.

'She'll be back. Stop worrying. Where do you hide your whisky?'

Tom pointed towards the kitchen. Tossing the oversized beanie hat he had been wearing – an attempt to disguise his unruly black hair, Tom could only assume – onto the sofa, Jack sauntered off. It seemed weird that they hadn't seen or spoken to each other for so long but had almost immediately reverted to the relationship they'd always had: Jack the cool guy, always in control – or so it seemed – and Tom the one who tried to do the right thing.

'Why are you here, Jack?' he asked as his brother returned with the whisky bottle. 'I'm both delighted and staggered by your presence in my house, but aren't you worried that someone will spot you?'

Jack flopped into an armchair and shrugged. 'Of course, but it's been a while, and everyone believes I'm dead so they're not looking. As long as I keep away from places I might be recognised,

I should be safe enough. The beard's a good disguise, and I wear unremarkable glasses and a variety of hats. I'll probably shave my head again soon. As long as I don't sneak around, hiding behind trees and stuff, no one should even look at me twice.'

Brave talk, but they both knew that if anyone from Jack's past caught sight of him he would be made to suffer for escaping from the clutches of the gang all those years ago. Once you're involved in that kind of life, there is no escape.

Tom waited, wondering if Jack was going to explain his presence, or if he was going to have to force the truth out of him. There had to be a reason he was here.

'Emma's five months pregnant,' he said finally, a beam transforming his usually inscrutable face.

Emma was Jack's partner, the woman with whom he had escaped to the other side of the world eighteen months previously.

Tom was delighted. 'Congratulations, Jack. That's excellent news. But in that case I would have thought Emma would be more inclined than ever to keep you away from the dangers of this part of the world.'

'You'd think so, wouldn't you? But she wants the baby to be born in the UK, and because she's not as young as she was, she wants to be in hospital for the birth. She swears that she only trusts the doctors and midwives here, and I'm not about to argue with her.'

'Isn't that risky?'

'I don't think so. I honestly believe we can avoid any risk by changing our names. We'll go for something pleasant and innocuous that will draw no attention – I'm thinking of Pete Johnson for myself. What do you reckon?'

Jack grinned at Tom, who responded with a non-committal grunt.

'And we'll move somewhere off the beaten track. I was thinking north Wales. Not too far away so that, if we're very careful, the baby might be able to meet his or her Uncle Tom.' Jack raised his eyebrows and gave his brother a half-smile. 'Anyway, that's why I'm here. I'm going to try to sort out the documentation for our new identities, and I'm not saying another word about how I'm doing that.'

'No, please don't.' The less he knew, the better. Jack's methods were unlikely to be ones that Tom would find acceptable, but he couldn't be too high-handed because he understood only too well what would happen if Jack's identity was exposed. He was thrilled at the thought of them being close by, though. Tom had always wanted more children after Lucy, but there had never been the right moment. Now he was going to be surrounded by babies, with both Becky and Emma giving birth in the near future.

'I know you're going to say it's risky, but is it okay if I stay here for a couple of days?' Jack said. 'Nobody's going to be watching your house after all this time, but I'll be careful going in and out and I'll be making a few trips to find the perfect place to live. Do you mind, or does it put you in a difficult position professionally?'

Tom almost laughed. After what he had done to help his brother's family already, having him stay hardly counted. The only problem was that if anyone had any doubt about whether Jack was dead or alive, Tom's home was the obvious place to watch.

'Nobody has the first idea I'm alive, Tom. It's years now – nearly eight, to be precise – since my so-called accident. And nobody from back then has been sniffing around. I'd know if they had, you know that. I have alerts on my name, yours, Emma's, the kids', and all the obvious suspects. Plenty gets said, but nothing we have to worry about. They stopped looking long ago.'

Tom knew that Jack had the tools to check anything that was posted online, especially in the depths of the dark web. He hoped his brother was right.

'Anyway,' Jack said, 'what's all this stuff about my old mate Nathan?'

'Oh, you read that, did you? His sister's missing. Do you remember her?'

'Not really. No trace?'

'Nothing. She'd been on holiday just before she went missing, and I'm guessing she met up with some people and went travelling.'

Jack said nothing and swilled the whisky round in his glass. Tom could almost hear his mind turning things over.

'Have you lot taken it seriously?'

Tom blew out a long breath. 'It's difficult. So many people disappear every year – every day, come to that – and so we have to take a view about their vulnerability. Her risk level is low, so other than some obvious checks, I doubt much has been done.'

'What about her computer, social media, that kind of stuff?'

'Nathan doesn't know the password for her computer. Her social media accounts have been checked as far as possible, but he doesn't know her friends and everything's locked down to outsiders. Because of the low risk level, her laptop won't have been sent for investigation. It's expensive to do and not a priority.'

'You'd better get it to me then,' Jack said, as if that was going to be the easiest thing in the world to do.

'I can't do that, Jack – it's not my case.'

'So phone Nathan and tell him you've got a friend who's a bit of a dab hand at getting into other people's computers.'

Tom laughed. 'Nathan's got plenty of money. I'm sure he'll have hired someone to try to hack her computer.'

'Well, he hasn't employed the best, has he?'

'I see you're as arrogant as ever,' Tom said, raising an eyebrow at his brother.

Jack grinned. 'Come on, Tom. A laptop isn't going to be a problem for me, is it? What have you got to lose?'

'I'll think about it,' he said, staring at the golden liquid in his glass.

The problem with Jack was that he always made Tom question

his own ethics. In his career as a policeman he hadn't always followed the rules, sometimes allowing his belief in justice for the individual to override the laws he was supposed to be upholding. But Jack took this further, arguing that the end often justified the means. It was how he had rationalised some of his past illegal enterprises, which he still maintained had benefited his victims.

Knowing Jack had committed crimes didn't in any way diminish Tom's affection for his brother, which came from the heart, not the head. But sometimes Tom found it difficult to know where to draw the line – when to deny Jack what he asked for. And this was one of those times.

42

Last night Thea came for me again, and I felt myself shaking at the thought that I had to go for another treatment. But I wasn't ushered into the doctor's study. He was waiting in the corridor at the top of the stairs, no more than a silhouette, backlit by the dim wall lights. They demanded to know if I had made a decision. Was I going to stay, or was I going to take my chances and leave?

I had thought of nothing else. Neither option felt good, but it would feel no better if I had another day, a week or even a year to consider it. They weren't prepared to give me any more time. I had to make a decision on the spot, so I told them I would stay. I couldn't see any other option. They seemed pleased, and I felt guilty about not being more grateful.

'You will be a big help to me in the house,' Thea said. 'And the doctor is working on a wonderful research project. You will be able to help with that too.'

I was sure she was referring to the doctor's exploration of the origins of evil, using me as his source material, and I shuddered at the thought. But what choice do I really have?

The two other women were in their rooms when I returned. I wanted to talk to them, to find out whether they too had been forced to make such a difficult decision, but I don't know if I can trust them. I still haven't asked the girl who has the room opposite me why she has a photograph of Paul in her diary.

I was about to go into my room when I heard muffled crying from across the corridor, and I thought maybe I had upset the girl by asking too many questions earlier. I remembered what she had said to me: 'I don't know why I did it.' 'I loved him.' 'I took him.' But I still didn't know what she was talking about, so I knocked softly on her door and pushed it open.

'Are you okay?' I asked – a silly question, given her blotchy cheeks and bloodshot eyes. 'I'm sorry if I made you remember something you would rather forget.'

She gave a choked laugh. 'I can't forget. The problem is, I can't remember either.'

'Do you want to tell me about it?' I asked, not for the first time.

'I've told you,' she said.

'You said you took him and you loved him. But I don't know who you mean.'

'I took the baby – Albie. I *took* him.' She seemed to be getting slightly hysterical so I sat down and put my arm around her again, pulling her close to me.

We talked about it for a long time, and gradually her story came out – how she had been working as a nanny for a couple who had a baby called Albie, a baby she had dearly loved. And then, for some reason that she couldn't explain to herself, she had abducted the child. She had brought him here and asked Thea and the doctor to help her keep him as her own. Thea had immediately taken control of the situation, and the baby had been safely returned to his parents. She didn't explain how, but she was so distressed that I didn't want to make things worse by asking. Thea and Garrick had been sheltering her here ever since, safe from prosecution for what she had done.

Finally, as I rocked her slowly backwards and forwards, she started to drift and I realised she was falling asleep. I helped her into bed and pulled the covers over her, as if tucking in a child.

It was a long time before I got to sleep myself, my heart breaking for both the girl and for the baby's parents. She didn't seem capable of doing anything so shocking, and all I could think was that it had to have been a single moment of madness.

Now it's morning, though, and a working day. Apparently every day is a working day.

I still know nothing about the other woman, the third Judith. She won't talk. If ever I get her alone, she just says that her time is coming, that she will soon be free. I don't know what she means, and I'm not ready to ask yet. She went for a treatment late last night and was gone for a long time. I fell asleep and didn't hear her come back. She is here now, though, and in a few minutes we will be summoned up into the house to clean. My duties are restricted to the ground floor. I don't think they trust me with the bedrooms yet.

I'm playing a game, pretending to be under the influence of Thea's potions. But I've ingested nothing that will affect my conscious mind for a while now, and as my brain starts to function normally I am becoming increasingly anxious. One minute I'm grateful to Thea and Garrick for their help in saving me from arrest. The next, I distrust them completely because of the drugs and the spy cameras. I can't make sense of it.

I hear the buzzer go, and this time I know it's not the signal to return to our rooms. I join the other two as we trudge upstairs to start the morning's cleaning. I have to do the drawing room today, and I lower my head and shuffle slowly along as the others do, making my way towards what always struck me as such a beautiful, restful room. It will be the first time I've been back there since I was moved to the basement. Last time I was there – my life *before*, as I now think of it – I had sherry with Thea and the doctor. Life had seemed dreadful then, but it was nothing compared to this.

The three of us go to a storeroom where there are trays set out with all that we will need – dusters, polish, hand brushes, glass cloths – and the other two head for the stairs. Laden with the tools of what is now my trade, I slowly walk barefoot along the hall towards the drawing room. It is just as beautiful as I remember, and for a moment I wander around, touching some of the lovely items. I can't help being drawn to the decanters and wonder if I could risk sneaking a small sherry. I hated it when I first came here, but after a few days it became something of a lifeline.

There are several decanters, each with a beautifully engraved silver label hanging around its neck. I can see one that says WHISKY, another BRANDY – Garrick's tipple of choice – and third in the group is sherry. It is tempting, but I know Thea would smell it on my breath, so I simply dust the cut glass. There is another decanter, which looks remarkably similar to the sherry one. It has a tag round its neck with just one letter on it: J.

I quickly take the stopper out of the bottle and sniff. Then I do the same with the one labelled SHERRY. They smell identical.

I have the urge to pick up the decanter and hurl it at the window because I suddenly know exactly why it is labelled J. I stand for a full minute, holding it so tightly in my hand that I fear the crystal will shatter. Every woman in the house apart from Thea is known as Judith. I wonder if they have all been dosed with the doctor's sherry before being moved to the depths of the cellar?

I turn away from the decanters and carry on with my tasks, but my anger mounts as I move on to the other rooms in this part of the house. I need to stick to my schedule because when the clock strikes twelve I am supposed to return my cleaning things to the storeroom and trail back downstairs. The door has been left open for this purpose, and the last one through closes it behind them.

Finally, twelve o'clock comes, and I take my materials back to where they belong. I'm first to pack away because I'm the only one working on this floor, and suddenly I have an idea. I have time to carry out my plan, I'm sure, before the others come downstairs, and Thea and Garrick are nowhere to be seen, so I scurry along the corridor back towards the drawing room. I rush over and smile to myself as I swap the labels on the sherry decanters. Let's see how Thea feels about being drugged.

I nearly jump out of my skin as the silence of the house is suddenly shattered by the shrill peal of the doorbell. I have never known there to be a visitor, but I do know that Thea will be coming along the corridor from the kitchen, blocking my escape route. The other girls will be on their way down to the cellar now, but I have no way of getting past Thea.

'*Shit!*' I mutter. What if she brings her visitor in here?

I look around, but there isn't anywhere to hide. I'll just have to brazen it out and hope that if she invites her visitor into this room, he or she won't recognise me from the news. With fumbling fingers, I swap the labels back, terrified Thea will give the drugged sherry to someone else.

I hear footsteps right outside the door, which I left ajar when I came in, and the thud of bolts sliding back on the front door. I crouch down low, in case Thea or her visitor glances in here. There is a brief silence.

'You!' Thea says, anger clear in her voice.

'Yes, Thea. I'm back.' It is a man's voice, thick with a northern accent, and there is nothing friendly in his tone. 'I told you I'm not going to give up – I've been telling you that for a whole year. This time I'm not going to be fobbed off. I'm not going anywhere until I've seen her. Now get out of my way.'

'Are you really going to use force against an old woman, Vincent? Surely not even you would stoop so low.'

I hear an exasperated sigh. 'Not unless you leave me no choice, but you can't stop me shouting for her. Even in this house, if I shout long enough and loud enough she'll come. She'll see me, talk to me.'

'She has no desire to see you – not now, nor ever again.' I hear the fury in Thea's voice. 'She's told me not to let you in. She doesn't want anything from you. It's over, Vincent. You're done.'

The man speaks in a low growl, and I can only just pick up his words, although the tone speaks for itself. 'You're lying. She's my wife. She would never have left me without an explanation.'

There is a bit of a scuffle and Thea gives a small yelp. Should I go to her aid? Is he hurting her?

'Give over. I didn't hurt you.' His voice is closer. He must have got past her.

'Get out of my house,' she says, anger and determination in her voice.

'She's going to have to tell me herself if she wants a divorce. I'm not taking your word for it.' Then the man yells, '*Judith!* It's Vincent! I've come to get you. We're going home. *Judith!*'

43

My thighs are beginning to ache from crouching for so long, but the man who calls himself Vincent has finally left, promising to be back very soon. Which Judith was he searching for? The one I've been speaking to has only been here since November, so it has to be the older woman. Is she the original Judith, and Vincent her husband?

After Thea slammed the door on him, I heard her stomp off to her kitchen, muttering to herself. I could tell the incident had disturbed her, but I'm sure she would be furious if she knew I had heard everything.

All I care about now is whether I will be able to make it back down to the basement unnoticed, so I creep along the corridor on tiptoe, moving as quickly as I can, and push open the door that leads into the small room hiding the entrance to the cellar. In the dim light the door looks as if it is closed, and my heart sinks. I inch towards it, certain that when I push against it I will find it locked and will have to admit to Thea that I have broken her rules. I should be safely back downstairs with the others by now, and I have no idea how she will react. Will she tell me I have to leave?

I nudge the door with my bare toe and sigh with relief. They have left it ajar for me.

Closing the door as softly as I can, I scuttle down the stairs. The women are at the table. The younger one looks up, and I know I am going to have to speak to her again. Something is far from right in this house, and without drugs in my system I am seeing things more clearly every day. The older woman hasn't lifted her eyes.

'Is your husband called Vincent?' I ask her.

She slowly raises her head and looks at me, deep frown lines between her eyes. 'No.' She seems unprepared to offer any more, but if she isn't Vincent's wife, who is?

The younger woman is still looking at me, and I indicate with my head that she should follow me. I don't know if she will or not, but I walk to my room and wait.

I don't hear her approach, her soft bare feet making no sound on the lino, but when I look up she is standing in the doorway. She says nothing, so I pat the bed by my side. She frowns at me, as if I am asking her to do something dreadful, but then her features relax a little and she makes her way towards me.

'What's your name?' I ask her. 'And don't tell me it's Judith. I know you're not Judith.'

She looks perplexed, as if this is all too much for her, and I realise I must try to wean her off the drugs if I am going to get any sense out of her. She doesn't answer, and I reach for her hand.

'Listen, I'm not spying on you, but when I first came down here I had a bit of a look around. I'm sorry, but I found your diary.'

Her eyes open wide. 'I'm not supposed to have that. Thea will take it if she finds it.'

'Well I suggest you find a better place to hide it then. How did you get it down here? They haven't let me have any of my own stuff.'

She drops her head, clearly not wanting to tell me.

'I'm not going to tell tales, you know,' I say softly. 'But I want to understand the whole set-up because at the moment I'm not comfortable with how it all works. Please, trust me?'

She is quiet for a moment longer. 'I went upstairs when they were away.'

I don't speak, scared that anything I say will throw her and stop her talking.

'I learned the combination for the keypad by the door. I've got an ear for a tune – I used to be a pianist, quite a good one. Anyway, they went away for a while just before you came. I worked out which numbers had to be pressed and in which order from the sounds made by the keys. Do you understand what I mean?'

I know exactly what she means.

For a moment I am puzzled about Thea and Garrick going away. Then I realise it must have been when they were with me, in Myanmar. It's hard to believe they left the girls here on their own.

'What did you do about food? Didn't you try to run away?'

For a moment she looks terrified. 'It wasn't a problem. Thea left all the meals in the freezer. They were labelled for each day. And why would I run away? They're helping us. But I was worried there might be a fire or something and we would be trapped, so I wanted to know how to get out if that happened. And then… well, once I was in the house and I knew they wouldn't catch me, I was curious and went snooping. I found where Thea had hidden all of my things. Everything was still there. My phone, my house keys, my credit cards, my cash – even my passport. I only took the diary. I don't suppose she'll ever check.'

'Why would she have your passport?'

The girl shrugged. 'Perhaps it was in my handbag. I don't remember. Maybe I had planned to smuggle the baby out of the country. It all seems so unreal, so impossible.'

This feels so wrong to me.

'Why can't we have our own things – diary, purse, make-up, clothes that fit?' I indicate the baggy tracksuit bottoms and T-shirt I'm wearing.

'It's all part of the doctor's regime of trust,' she says with a shrug. 'We have to trust them, and they us. For that to be effective we need to reject our former life and everything that came with it.'

I don't know what to say to this. The doctor has talked to me about trust, but this is extreme. It doesn't feel like trust; it feels like dependence.

'You'll learn,' she says. 'The doctor has some rituals that help us with trust. They're part of the treatment. He says I remind him of someone. I have her gentle hands.'

A shudder runs through me at her words, but I worry that soon we will be interrupted and there are things I need to know.

'When I found your diary there was a photograph inside. I'm sorry – you'll think I'm really nosy – but I looked at it. I think I know the man in the picture. Will you tell me who he is?'

She leaps up off the bed. 'You're asking too many questions and I'll get in trouble. If they throw me out, I'm going to prison. Or I'll get offered the other option, and I'm not ready.'

'What other option?' I ask, getting up slowly to be sure I don't frighten her any more than I already have.

'The doctor says that when we decide we're no use to the world – when we realise we have nothing left to give – there is only one sensible way to go. He offers us a way out.'

I stare at her.

'We get the choice. Judith, the other Judith, has made her choice. She's just waiting until he's ready. He doesn't make us do it, and he makes sure it doesn't hurt. He says it's the best way to go.'

❖

I'm alone again in my room, my head spinning with everything I have just learned. The meaning of her words about a way out seemed clear, but surely not? I started to ask her, but I must have spooked her because she scurried out like a scared rabbit. I know that any minute now she or the other one will be summoned upstairs to bring down the washing and ironing. There is a rota, apparently, for cleaning all the rooms from top to bottom. The curtains have to be taken down and washed, carpets shampooed, the works. I don't know the sequence yet, so one of the others will do it today.

I feel as if I have missed my chance to find out more, but when the buzzer goes and I peer round my door, it's the older woman who is traipsing upstairs, and I maybe have one more chance to learn the truth. I check there is no one in the corridor, that Thea hasn't crept down here when I wasn't looking, and I make my way to the closed door opposite mine.

I knock softly. 'It's only me. Sorry if I freaked you out before. Can I come in?' I wait for her permission, not wanting to frighten her again.

'Okay,' comes the soft reply. She sounds resigned, as if she knows I'm not about to give up, and I push the door open and walk slowly into the room.

She has a photograph in her hands, and I'm sure it must be the one of Paul, but as I get closer I see it's of a girl and a woman. The picture is old, judging by the clothes they are wearing. I guess it was taken in the late 1960s or '70s based on the short pleated skirt, the over-fussy blouse and the flicked-back fringe of the girl.

'Is one of these women your mum?' I ask, assuming she took this photograph when she stole her diary.

She shakes her head and puts the picture down on the pillow, away from me. I take a seat at the end of the bed.

'And the picture of the man?' I ask.

I sit quietly when she doesn't immediately answer, hoping to gain her trust. I ignore the photo on the pillow; all I care about is the picture of Paul from the boat and why she has it. *How is he involved in all this?* I'm trying to think of how to phrase the question without her feeling that I'm interrogating her, but to my surprise she speaks unprompted.

'Nathan,' she says, and I give her a puzzled glance. 'The photo is of Nathan, he's my brother.'

I don't understand. I'm certain the man in the photo is Paul.

'I'm sorry,' I say. 'He looks like a man I met on a holiday to Myanmar recently – the one where I met Thea and the doctor – but his name was Paul.'

For the first time I get an instant response, and I can see she is trying to fight her way through the fog in her brain. 'Paul? That's Nathan's middle name. Are you sure it was him?'

I nod. I'm as sure as I can be. I would recognise that hooked nose and the beady eyes anywhere. Strange as the arrangement of features sounds, he was oddly attractive – or would have been if he hadn't terrified me with his questions and his staring.

'Why was he on that boat?' she asks. 'Maybe he got my letter.'

I have no idea what she's talking about, but she's shaking her head furiously, her eyes screwed up tightly. For the first time it seems she wants to think clearly, but she can't.

'What's your name?' she asks, mimicking the question I asked her earlier. I'm frustrated by the change of subject, but I answer.

'It's Callie,' I tell her. 'Callie Baldwin. Are you going to tell me yours?'

'Hannah,' she says, so quietly that I have to ask her to repeat it to make sure I heard her correctly.

'You said that your brother may have got your letter. What letter, Hannah?' I ask, and it's almost as if hearing her real name – possibly for the first time in months – shocks her into reality.

'I wrote to him. It's a long story, but among other things I told him I'd met a lovely lady when I was on a retreat, and she was planning a trip to Myanmar. I even told him which boat she was travelling on and said how I would love to go too.'

'Did you tell him the dates of the Myanmar trip?'

'No. I wasn't sure of them. Thea said they were planning to go some time in January. Do you think he was looking for me? No one knows where I am.'

I don't know what to tell her, but before I get a chance to say anything the shutters come down. She turns towards me and glares. 'Why are you asking so many questions? Are you spying on me?'

I can't believe the change in her. 'I don't know what you mean. I'm not spying, I promise you.'

'Are you one of them? Have they sent you to make sure I'm not breaking the rules?'

'Why would you think that?'

She picks up the photo she was looking at when I came into the room and hands it to me, watching my eyes.

'What?' I ask.

'She looks like you,' she says.

I look more closely at the photograph of the two women. Hannah has a point. If you strip away the heavy flicked fringe and the bushy hair of the young girl, she does look a bit like me – similar mouth and nose, for sure. 'Where did you get this?'

'I took it from upstairs this morning. It was in Thea's drawer.'

I gape at her with astonishment. It seems so unlike anything she would do. 'Why?'

'I was putting things away, and it was under a book. Most of it was covered – only the lower half of the face was showing – and I thought it was a picture of you so I pulled it out to look. I know it's not – it's too old – but what are you to them? Are you here to check up on the rest of us?'

I shake my head. 'Of course not. I have no idea who this woman is. I'd never met Thea and the doctor in my life until I went on holiday. I really don't know who she is.'

Hannah raises her huge eyes to mine, and I can see she is wondering whether to believe me.

'I know who she is,' she says finally. 'Turn it over.'

I flip the photo and read the back.

July 1971
Thea and Judith Atwell

44

For Tom the day had dragged. He had heard nothing from Louisa, and Jack had disappeared on some mysterious business of his own, promising to be back that evening.

Tom was torn between wanting to spend time with his brother and desperately needing to know how Louisa was feeling, but just as he was about to leave work for the day he had a call from Philippa Stanley. Ahead of the meeting that she and Tom were required to attend the following day, she wanted an update on all of his cases, particularly the Jasmine DuPont investigation.

'I know I told you to pass it on to someone junior, Tom, but given the fact that you believe at least one other death has strong similarities, it seems some of your instincts may have been correct.'

Tom realised that was probably as close to an apology as he was going to get.

'Becky – if DI Robinson is the "someone junior" you are referring to – has done an excellent job,' he said. 'We've identified a case that has some parallels and we're looking at any commonalities. We've failed to find out where Jasmine got the drugs from, though. She had no fixed address, so even if she managed to get access to a computer to buy them online, it's not clear where she would have had them delivered.'

'So you think she bought them on the street?'

'I doubt it. Unless she was stealing to pay for them, and we have no evidence of either that or prostitution, it's hard to know how she could have afforded them. Some of them are expensive, and PCP – angel dust – isn't easy to find in the UK. The combination of

Jasmine's low income, her lack of a fixed address and the difficulty of obtaining some of these drugs on the street makes me believe that someone was giving them to her – maybe for their own purposes.'

'Well, it's a theory, but it would be useful if we had some idea of what that purpose was.' There was nothing like stating the obvious, but Tom didn't have a chance to respond before Philippa continued: 'It would be particularly helpful if we had a workable theory ahead of the meeting tomorrow. See what you can do.'

Tom felt momentarily frustrated with Philippa. He knew she had to show results, but they couldn't just pluck an idea out of thin air with no evidence to support it.

'I need to go,' she said. 'I have another team to deal with and they have far bigger problems than you right now, one of which I might be passing your way. But more of that later.'

On that cryptic remark, she hung up.

Tom put the phone down and thought about how he was not looking forward to the next day. One of the realities of being a detective chief inspector was that the time he spent doing what he thought of as the real job was often eaten into by the other rubbish that he hated – crime figures, reviews, staffing crises. He had been asked several times why he hadn't applied for promotion, but he shuddered at the thought of even more paperwork and sometimes felt demotion was a more attractive option.

Tomorrow was supposed to be his day off, but like it or not he had to go to a meeting in the morning that was deemed more important than either his free time or dealing with his caseload.

He sighed as he logged out of his computer, but before he had chance to escape, his phone rang again.

'Tom, it's Philippa again. That problem I said I might be passing your way? Consider it passed. I need you to take on another murder case.'

45

I'm sure that tonight it will be my turn for a treatment with the doctor, and I've been dreading the moment Thea appears in my doorway to escort me upstairs. I hate everything about it – the vulnerability of lying on the couch with him sitting next to me – so close, but not touching. I can't believe he would touch me, but I never fully close my eyes, ready at any moment to jump up and run from the room.

My anxiety is enhanced by Hannah's apprehension whenever she thinks it is her turn for a treatment. There is something she won't tell me, something that's expected of her that she is uncomfortable with.

I've no time to panic, though, because now Thea is here, outside my door, and I follow her up the stairs. This time we don't stop at the ground floor; we continue up the stairs towards the first floor, the floor I've not been allowed access to until now. What can there be here that I'm not supposed to see?

When we reach the landing, Thea points me towards a small seating area. There is a side table with a flask and a cup on it. 'Before you see the doctor, I need to speak to you,' she says, her tone gentle. 'You must understand that we have your safety at heart, and all we want is for you to feel part of our little family. You do know that, don't you?'

I no longer know what to think. I need Thea and Garrick's protection, that seems like the only solid fact I can cling to. I constantly try to force a clear memory of what I did to Ian into my head, but it won't come. Instead, my mind is flooded with images of Ian as he was when I first met him – when he was trying to be the perfect boyfriend. I see his mum, smiling at me, telling me how good I am for him and how pleased she is that he found me, and I think of how she must be feeling now that her son is dead. Maybe Ian was right. Maybe he changed because *I* changed.

Thea is waiting for an answer, and I can't risk saying anything to upset her because I still can't see any alternative to staying here.

'You've been very kind, and I can't thank you enough for sheltering me in your home,' I tell her.

'We offered because we don't think you're altogether a wicked person. We trust you, you see. But the doctor and I feel we don't have your absolute trust in return, Judith, and that's a concern to us, particularly to the doctor, who sets such great store by it.'

I'm certain she is alluding to the fact that I'm not taking the drugs. Despite my best efforts, it seems I haven't been fooling them.

'Before I take you to see him, I'd like you to drink this.' She pours some yellow liquid from the flask into the cup. 'It will relax you.'

I'm flustered and I don't know what to do. I don't want their drugs, but if I refuse to do as she asks I have no idea what will happen. Will they decide that my usefulness has expired, as Hannah explained to me? Maybe just this once I will comply. I can float senseless in a sea of calm while the doctor spins his psychological word tricks on me. Maybe it will be easier if I'm not myself.

I take the cup and sip the liquid. It tastes wonderful – passion fruit and mango, I think. But goodness knows what else is in there, and I flinch at the thought of what it is going to do to me.

'You'll start to feel calmer in a few minutes, and you'll realise it's for the best. Come on, let's go and see the doctor. We've put a lot of thought into creating an ambience that will put you at ease, you'll see. This treatment is wonderfully effective, I promise.' She reaches out and gently strokes my upper arm in a rare show of affection. I stifle the urge to pull away.

I don't have time to think about her words, because to my surprise Thea opens the door to a bedroom. A huge bed faces the door, the white covers turned back on both sides as if waiting for its occupants. I feel a tremor of concern, but I look at the bedside tables, and on one side there are Thea's favourite magazines and on the other a couple of textbooks. This is their bed, their room.

To my relief Thea walks past the bed towards another door on the far side of the room. Maybe the doctor has another study up here. I follow, thankful that the bed is nothing to do with me and feeling slightly ashamed of my thoughts.

As we reach the door Thea grasps my hand. 'Remember, my dear, this is about trust. It's about freeing yourself from all those negative thoughts and drawing yourself closer to us. Go with it, Judith. Let down your guard.'

I can hear the words, but her voice sounds hollow. I turn back and glance around their room. Everything seems bigger in the centre of my vision, distorted at the edges, as if I'm looking through a fisheye lens. A huge television hangs on the wall, and its red standby light seems to wobble, moving in and out of focus. For some reason this bothers me, but I can't think why. The drugs must be taking effect already, and I shake my head to clear it. It doesn't work.

Thea opens the door. It's not a study. It's a bathroom. The walls are painted dark green, and a large claw-footed bath takes pride of place in the centre of the floor, steam rising from the surface of the scented water. Candles are positioned round the room, and I shiver as I remember the last time I was in a candlelit bathroom. For a moment I remember the feel of hands washing me as I woke up to see the water stained red. I glance at the bath but the water is clear, with only the reflection of a flickering yellow flame to mar its surface. Music is playing softly in the background. It is a classical piece that I vaguely recognise, the strings melodic and soothing.

The doctor is standing in the centre of the room, his hands

clasped in front of him. He is wearing a white coat as if this is a normal medical appointment, but a pair of pale, hairless legs protrude below the hem, the flesh of his knees wrinkled as if once covered with a layer of fat that is long gone. His feet look huge, his toes misshapen.

'Hello, Judith,' he growls, his voice as gruff as ever. But he's smiling, and even in my confused state that makes me uncomfortable. 'Come in.'

I take a step forward, and I feel the reassuring presence of Thea at my back.

'Thea has explained to you what we hope to gain from this treatment, I believe. Do you understand what she told you?'

I can't speak, but I nod. I know it is what he expects.

'We all put up barriers, you know. We protect ourselves from ridicule, the hurt of a cruel word, the pain of a broken heart. I know you find trust difficult, but Thea and I have helped you, protected you, supported you. We allow you to live in our home, despite the fact that you have killed a man. There are few ways left for us to demonstrate that we're prepared to trust you. But for me to heal you and give you peace after what you have done, we need to knock down your walls, strip away your armour, and expose what lies beneath. For that, you have to trust me.'

The doctor speaks with a passion I have never heard before, and even through the fog of the drugs I feel panic rising up to choke me.

'We even hide behind our clothes, disguising our inadequacies, scared that our less-than-perfect bodies won't be accepted. But we don't need to protect ourselves from those we trust. We need to lay bare our souls, our minds and our bodies.'

His voice has dropped to a steady level that keeps time with the rhythm of the music, and I begin to sway. I feel light-headed, a thin trickle of sweat running down my cheek. I no longer feel in charge of my body or my mind. I hear his words, but they mean nothing. I have become mesmerised by the doctor's eyes – glowing, intense – beneath his thick black eyebrows. I can see the reflection of candlelight in their depths. They are twin luminous magnets drawing me in, and I find myself taking a step closer. I can feel my heart thumping in my chest. I am standing inches from him when he speaks again.

'Tonight I will open myself to you, put myself in your hands,' he says. 'Tomorrow it will be your turn. It's the only way I can help you, my dear.'

I still haven't taken my eyes from his. Everything else in the room has faded into the dark walls. I sense that his hands are moving, undoing the top button of his white coat. I hear a dull *click* behind me as the door closes. Thea has gone.

He still holds my gaze. I can't look away. I don't want to. I hear a whisper of sound as his white coat hits the floor and he steps sideways, his eyes still locked on mine. I hear the water sloshing around as he steps into the bath and my eyes are glued to his as he lowers himself slowly into the water. He leans back.

'Come a little closer, Judith. I'd like you to wash me.'

46

I take a step towards the bath, the music, the candlelight, the perfume rising from the water and those hypnotic eyes dulling all of my senses. I drop to my knees, and the doctor holds out a flannel. My eyes leave his, just for a second, as I reach for it.

No!

The spell is broken, snapped like a dry twig. Feelings, emotions, life – they all come flooding back, releasing me from my catatonic stupor. In my head I am screaming, 'No!' over and over again. But I don't make a sound. My tongue seems glued to the roof of my dry, stale mouth. I can feel the doctor waiting for me to take the flannel, to settle myself on the floor by his side, to listen to him talk as I wash his body, but the moment has gone. The perfume suddenly seems cloying, the music rasping. I might be drugged; I might have to spend years in prison for what I have done, but this is wrong.

I daren't look at his eyes again, knowing he will draw me back in, so I fix my gaze on his chin as I push myself back to my feet and reverse towards the door. I see the hard, angry line of his mouth, but I don't care what he thinks, or Thea either. My vision and hearing have both been distorted by the drugs, but I can still move. Perhaps adrenaline is more potent than their medications.

I reach the door, hoping and praying it's not locked, and fumble behind me for the handle. I yank it open, turn and run. Behind me I hear frantic splashing, and I know that the doctor is getting out of the bath.

Thea is in the bedroom. She is between me and the door to the corridor, and I stop dead when she shouts, 'We're trying to help you, Judith! How can you be so ungrateful? Think of how we washed the blood off you after you had committed such a vile act! We didn't complain. It was our way of showing our faith in you. Why can't you do the same for the doctor?'

As she speaks, a flashback from that night in the bath hits me – the feeling that both of my arms were being held and washed at the same time. But when I opened my eyes Thea had only my right arm in her hands. A vague memory of a gruff voice speaking in a whisper and the click of a door closing comes to me, and I want to heave. He was there, with Thea, washing me.

Oh God, what have I fallen into? What is this?

'Get out of my way, Thea,' I say, and I can hear my voice, shrill and desperate. 'I will hurt you if you don't move.'

I don't know if I can hurt her. I might be a killer, but could I really hit an elderly woman?

The splashing has stopped. The doctor will be in here in seconds, so I rush towards Thea and drag her to the bed, pushing her back onto the mattress. It won't give me much time, but it might be enough. I'm sure I can run faster than either of them.

Thea cries out with shock, but not – I don't think – pain. I glance back towards the bathroom door to see the doctor, water dripping from his naked body.

'Judith, come back! Not again, Judith. Don't leave us again.'

I have no idea what he means, but I reach the door to the corridor and to my surprise and relief I see a key in the lock. I yank it out, open the door and run through, closing and locking it behind me.

I race down the stairs. I can't open the door to the basement to set the other girls free, but maybe I can raise the alarm once I'm out and get help for them. Right now all I want to do is put as much distance between me and the doctor as possible.

I hurry to the back porch in search of shoes, but there are none there.

'Shit!' I can't run round the streets with no shoes on.

I tear back down the corridor, thinking, trying to keep my head clear, although I can feel the grey dullness creeping in, like a sea fret sweeping inland, blanketing all in its path.

Suddenly I find myself standing by the board with the keys on, and I know what I have to do. I'm going to take Thea's car. I've no idea where I'll go, but I have to get away from here.

47

I don't know if Thea and Garrick will come after me. But why would they? They are not physically strong enough to force me to return with them, but they may try to persuade me. Will they call the police – say I've stolen their car? I don't know. All I can think about is making my escape. I wrench open the side door and run towards the garage, almost stumbling as I check repeatedly over my shoulder, expecting to see Thea appear behind me at any moment.

Her car is full of petrol, thank goodness, and I slam it into reverse, tyres spinning on the gravel drive as I change to first gear and put my foot down, anxious to get as far away from the house as I can. I have no money, no proper clothes and no shoes, but at least for now I have transport. What I don't have is a plan.

As soon as I am clear of the track to their home, I open a window to the cold air, hoping it will keep me awake. The drugs weren't intended to make me fall asleep – that would have defeated the purpose. They were to make me compliant, and as I drive I begin to wonder whether I should believe anything Thea and Garrick have told me. I have thought about Hannah's story over and over again, and I don't remember any child abduction being reported on the news in the months leading up to Christmas. I would have reacted emotionally to such a tragic tale and read everything I could find, cursing any woman who would steal a baby. Is there any truth in what they've said?

Thoughts of domestic slavery spring to mind. What a way to capture people and make them do your bidding! Hannah would have felt, as I did, that having committed a terrible crime there was no other choice than to hide in Thea and Garrick's cellar.

Finally I remember why the red light on the television had bothered me. Thea had told me they didn't have a working TV. If that were the case, why would the standby light be on? They are a pair of liars, with motives I can't even begin to guess at.

Perhaps the others had been taken in, but not me. Maybe the reason I can't remember killing Ian is because I didn't do it. Is that possible? Is he still alive, or did someone else kill him?

Thea!

No, surely not. I banish this ridiculous idea from my mind the instant it arrives.

Then I think of the claw hammer, and I know it was mine. I remember buying it and can picture where it sat on the shelf in the garage. How could it have got into Thea's house unless I brought it?

I'm suddenly filled with desperate hope that Ian is alive. Much as I wanted to be rid of him, I would do anything now to walk through my front door and see him sitting in his favourite chair, surrounded by the detritus of the last few days. I still want him gone, but not like that.

As if on autopilot, I find myself turning into my street, praying that I will see the sitting-room lights on. I will know then that the past few days have been nothing more than a terrible nightmare. But as I approach, I see the house is in darkness. There isn't a light showing. It's not late, but if Ian is alive he is unlikely to have ventured out alone. He never does. He always has a pizza or a takeaway delivered – anything for an easy life. So what does it mean? *Is he really dead?*

I pull the car to a halt a few doors further down the street. The street-lights are dim but I can see there is a car parked across the end of our drive. Ian would go insane if he saw it, even if he didn't want to go out. It is just the sort of thing that makes him angry.

He's not there. I know it. I can feel it.

For a moment I wonder if I should try to get into the house. Maybe if I did, I would remember what happened. But I don't have my keys. Thea will have put them with the rest of my belongings – wherever they might be. I am going to have to sit here, hoping with all my heart to see a glimmer of light somewhere in the house that will tell me someone is there – that Ian is home. That he is alive.

I can't leave until I know for sure. I'm scared that Thea and Garrick will suddenly appear at my car window, their faces pressed against the glass, but not as scared as I am of my house standing empty, deserted, its sole occupant lying in a morgue somewhere. So I leave the engine running with the heater on to keep warm.

Despite everything I start to feel sleepy. Perhaps it is the drugs, or maybe it's the adrenaline draining from my system, but I feel myself begin to drift.

I didn't mean to fall asleep, but when I wake up and look at the clock I can see that it is two in the morning. I must have been asleep for about four hours. The house is still in darkness, and I tell myself that Ian may have come home while I was sleeping and gone to bed, even though I don't believe it.

The car parked outside the house hasn't moved, and I realise for the first time that our car isn't on the drive. I don't know why I didn't think of it before, but Ian never puts it in the garage.

Maybe he has simply gone away for a day or two. But I know I'm clutching at straws.

I stare blankly at the house, and then a light comes on inside the car that's blocking the drive. There is someone in there.

For one dreadful moment I think it must be Thea or Garrick. Maybe they have come after me. Maybe they are waiting to see if I come home. But I know that doesn't make sense. They couldn't have got here before me, and the car was here when I arrived.

So why is someone sitting outside my house in a car in the early hours of the morning?

I shiver, even though the heater is still running. There's something very wrong.

I wait. The only sounds are the subdued rumble of the car engine and the gentle hum of the heater fan. Outside, nothing is moving. It is a still, overcast night, and there are no lights showing at any windows along the road, other than the dull glow of what must be a nightlight in a neighbour's house. I know her little boy sleeps in that room, and I wish for a moment that I was in there with him, warm and cosy, curled up in bed with a red spotted toadstool keeping the darkness at bay.

Moments later I hear a different sound. Another car is approaching, and I duck low in my seat, fearing once more that Thea and Garrick are looking for me. But I'm wrong. The car pulls up behind the one at the end of my drive, and a man gets out to go and talk to whoever is in the first car.

I lower my window a fraction in case I can hear what is said, but as the man from the second car bends at the waist to speak through the open window, I realise they are too far away. There is a brief laugh, and the second man bangs his hand lightly on the roof of the car and returns to his own vehicle.

Bright headlights illuminate the street ahead, and the first car pulls away. The second one draws forward to take its place at the end of the drive.

And that's when I see it.

As the car pulls slightly up onto the pavement, it is angled towards the house. And just before the headlights are extinguished I see something blue and white flutter in a rare gust of breeze.

I know what it is.

There is no one in my house. No one is coming home. My last glimmer of hope fades because outside sits a policeman, I'm sure. And across the drive is a strip of police crime-scene tape.

Thea wasn't lying at all.

I killed him.

48

Tom arrived at headquarters just before seven. He hated the fact that he'd had to drag Becky out of bed this early when she was so close to the baby's due date, and he could tell by looking at her that she wasn't sleeping too well. But after Philippa's phone call the evening before, he needed to brief her.

Like the professional she was, Becky was not only there already, but had clearly got in early and made Tom a much-needed cup of coffee.

'Sorry about this, Becky, but Philippa has passed a case over to us. It was with another team, but one of their investigations has blown up in their faces and she wants them to focus, so this one's ours now.'

'Okay, what do we know?'

'Not a lot, and much as it pains me to say this, I'm not going to be able to come to the scene with you. I have to go to a meeting. I thought Philippa might let me off the hook, but I thought wrong. Anyway, you don't need me there. It's in north Manchester and it looks like it started as a domestic and ended in murder.'

Tom handed Becky the details he had received and she quickly scanned them.

'The property is still taped off at the front with surveillance in place in case the woman turns up, unlikely as it seems. But the crime-scene team have finished their work, so I suggest you catch up with the DI who was running the show and get yourself over there. Is that okay?'

'There's no sign of the woman?' Becky asked.

'None. They have started a poster campaign in case anyone's seen her, but there's been nothing up to now, and we're not really expecting there to be. We've had reports that the couple were seen having a violent argument, so I think it's pretty self-explanatory. Names are Ian Fullerton and Caroline Baldwin.'

'No problem. Are you going to be around for the rest of the day after your meeting's finished?'

Tom felt uncomfortable. It was supposed to be his day off, although under the circumstances he wouldn't normally have taken the time. But today he was planning to go home. He had decided there was nothing to be lost by asking Nathan for his sister's computer, and he had arranged for him to drop it off that afternoon.

Hannah's disappearance was too far down the priority list for the laptop to be analysed by the technicians in the missing-persons team, so he had simply told Nathan he had a friend who was quite good at that sort of thing. Nathan had seemed grateful that something was being done, even if it wasn't official, and said he was happy to bring it to Tom's house.

Another good reason to go home was Louisa. Tom had sent her a brief text, telling her to take all the time she needed to come to a decision, but if she wanted to talk more he would be home by lunchtime. He said he would love her to get to know his 'unexpected visitor', as he referred to Jack.

He had heard nothing, but her hectic schedule often meant communication was sketchy, so he wasn't too concerned about her failure to reply. He wanted to be home, though, just in case.

'Sorry, Becky, I won't be coming back to the office, but you can reach me on my mobile if you need to. It sounds pretty clear cut, but let me know how it goes anyway. You should be there by just after eight o'clock, and the DI is happy to meet you at the scene.'

'Okay.' Becky paused, and as he gathered together the paperwork for his meeting, he could feel her looking at him. 'Are you all right, Tom?'

He reached for his briefcase, avoiding her eyes. She could read him so well, and if she thought there was something going on that he wasn't telling her, she would start digging. He couldn't have that.

'Just pissed off that I can't join you, that's all. I'll speak to you later.'

49

I've been driving around since I woke up and saw the policemen outside my house. I don't know what to do, but I feel sick. The momentary glimmer of hope that I had done nothing wrong – that Ian is alive – has been extinguished.

There is still the possibility that Thea has reported her car stolen, and as each vehicle passes I glance anxiously at the driver, certain that it will be either her or the doctor coming to find me. Half of me thinks it would be a relief to see the blue flashing lights of a police car, with a stern officer signalling through his window for me to pull over. It would take away the need to make a decision and I would see it as some kind of divine intervention and hand myself in.

It will be light soon and I have no idea what the day will bring. I can't dump the car – I have no shoes, no coat and nowhere to go. I'm hungry too, but I have no money for food and I desperately need the bathroom.

A thought comes to me, and I immediately dismiss it. But then it creeps back, insidious, not allowing me to think of alternatives. Can I get into the house from the back? If I could, memories of that night might come back to me and maybe I would understand what happened – why I killed Ian. Perhaps he attacked me first. It's no justification of course, but at least it would give me something to cling to.

Access to the back door of my house is through the garage; there is no side path. I can't get in that way because of the car outside the front with a police officer sitting in it. But there is possibly another option.

The house that backs on to ours is owned by an elderly couple who don't get up until quite late in the day. They told me they are a pair of night birds. If I can get into their back garden, I could clamber over the broken-down wall between our properties and into my own. And there is access to their back garden from the road via a path down the side of their house.

I bang the steering wheel with the heel of my hand. That might get me as far as the back door, but how will I get in? I pull into a lay-by and rest my head against the steering wheel. My eyes flood with tears. I'm lost.

The lay-by is obviously a stopping place for people going to the short stretch of shops that line the road, and I glance towards them, wishing more than ever that I could go in and buy something to eat or drink.

My attention is drawn to a poster in the window of the newsagents. I can only read the heading: HAVE YOU SEEN THIS WOMAN? The rest is too small to read from here, but I don't need to. All I need to see is the face in the picture.

My face.

I feel my mouth gape open in horror. *I'm wanted by the police!* But what else could I expect? A passerby glances my way. I spin my head towards the back of the car for fear that he will recognise me, and stare blindly at the seat behind me.

My insides are churning and it takes a second for me to register that I am looking at more than the dark grey upholstery of the seat. Something glints in the orange street-light, and I know instantly what it is. My house keys. I threw them at my bag after my row with Ian – and missed.

Thank God. As long as I'm right about the police only guarding the front of the house, I can get in, take what I need and then run as far away as I can.

I put the car into gear and pull out. Only a few minutes later I reach the street that backs on to ours. As I suspected, the curtains of my elderly neighbours' bedroom are still closed. It's not eight o'clock yet, and at this hour on a gloomy February morning there's very little light. I can see activity in the homes on either side, but hopefully the families will be too busy sorting themselves out for the day to notice me.

I need to be quick. My clothes may not be a total giveaway and with luck I will be mistaken for an early-morning jogger, but bare feet will definitely draw a second glance.

I pull up on the side of the road about twenty metres from the entrance to their drive and look around. There is a group of kids of about twelve years old on their way to school, but they are fooling around and I'm sure they won't look at me. A car goes past, but nothing else is happening, so I open the door, get out and close it quietly. I move quickly along the pavement, but not so hurriedly that people will feel compelled to look, and nip up the drive of the house. The gravel cuts into my feet, but I have to get out of sight of the road. I creep down the side of the house, praying that neither of my neighbours has come down to the kitchen to make a cup of tea.

There is light shining onto the back garden. It has to be spilling from a window, so I approach the corner of the house with caution. Their garden is not well maintained, and even at this time of year is something of a jungle. I'm hoping this will be to my advantage. The branches of a couple of neglected trees hang low over the ground, and if I can duck beneath these I could be at the end of the garden in seconds. But first I need to see where the light is coming from.

Creeping slowly forward, I peer around the corner and sigh with relief. The light is coming from the bathroom, which I know has a frosted-glass window, so moving as quietly as I can I hurry over the weeds and thistles, resisting the urge to cry out as they sting my feet, until I am sheltered by the trees. I stop and turn, knowing that I'm hidden by the gloom from all but the most determined watcher. The light is still on in the bathroom, but suddenly the kitchen light comes on too, and the old lady wanders into the room in her pale blue dressing gown. Thank God I made it.

It's only then that I realise I will have to return this way when I have retrieved my things from the house. I will have to come back over the wall, and by then they are bound to be up. Should I escape now while her back is turned, or carry on with my plan?

I pause for no more than a few seconds. I don't think I have a choice, so I turn away from the house and tread slowly and carefully towards the wall. I want to run, but I'm terrified that any quick movement will attract attention.

Finally, I reach the wall that separates our back gardens. With the help of a rusty old chair I am over the wall in less than thirty seconds and in my own garden, staring at the back of my house.

The house where I killed a man.

50

When Becky arrived at the scene at two minutes past eight, the DI of the team handing over the case was already there, pacing up and down outside the house in the cold February air, looking at his watch.

She struggled her way out of her car and walked up the short drive towards the house.

'Why is it still a crime scene?' she asked after introducing herself. 'Hasn't it been processed yet?'

'Yes, but as it's being passed to you, we thought you might want it preserved as far as possible before we cleared out.'

'Thanks, that's good of you. Shall we get inside out of this miserable weather?'

A uniformed officer unlocked the door and they stepped into the hall.

'I think we should start in the kitchen,' the DI said. 'It looks as if that's where it all began. It's through here.'

He pushed open a door into what appeared to be the living room, with a comfortable-looking sofa and two armchairs, and strode towards a door in the far corner, presumably leading to the kitchen.

Becky took two steps into the room, stopped and looked around. Already the scene wasn't making sense to her. It seemed to be a home that had once been cared for. There were pictures on the walls, books neatly arranged on shelves, an assortment of multicoloured cushions that appeared to have been chosen with care. And yet a smell of unwashed bodies, dirty pots, unemptied kitchen bins and general grubbiness hung over the place. Had they just stopped caring about their home?

❖

I slip my key into the back door and turn it, praying it isn't bolted on the inside. Ian had rarely bothered, saying that no one could get round the back anyway. I sigh with relief as the key turns easily, and within seconds I am in.

The concrete floor of the rear porch is freezing underfoot, and I spot a couple of pairs of boots and some trainers by the door. The boots would be warmer, but the trainers are probably going to be the most practical. There's a coat hanging up too, and I definitely need that. For now, though, the bathroom is calling.

The downstairs toilet was put in at the back of the house by the previous owners, who loved to garden. It saved them trudging through the house all the time, but it is a cold and unloved area. I always intended to decorate it, put something down on the bare floor and change the door so that it closes properly, but I hadn't been able to afford it. For now, though, it is perfect.

Just as I am about to pull the chain of the old-fashioned toilet I hear a noise. I don't move. My hand is still grasping the porcelain handle. Someone is talking. Someone is in my kitchen.

❖

Becky followed the DI into the kitchen, where the smell was worse. The remains of an Indian takeaway, several days old, sat on the table, and the sink was piled high with pots.

'Sorry,' she said. 'This is turning my stomach. Is it okay with you if I open the back door?'

'Of course. Let me,' he said. 'This door leads to the rear porch. There's a toilet there too. I'll open up so we can get some fresh air. It will be cold, though.'

Becky shuddered. 'Rather be cold than sick, if that's okay with you.'

The DI cast her a worried glance as he left the room. She heard him open the back door and he reappeared, rubbing his hands together.

Becky pulled her coat closer around her, but felt much better for the cold blast of fresh air.

'If you don't feel too good, it's okay to use the loo down here. Everything's been processed.'

'No, I'm fine,' she said.

What she didn't want to admit to was that it wasn't just the smell in here that was getting to her; it was the sight of the blood.

❖

I can't move. They are out there, in my kitchen. The tiny room I am standing in is less than three metres away from two police officers and one of them isn't feeling well. I'm going to be caught.

Would it be better to walk out and give myself up? I don't know. All I do know is that my chest feels as if it is in a vice. I gently let go of the handle of the toilet chain and wrap my arms round my waist, trying to hold myself together. They are talking, and I can hear every word.

'There was a massive argument the day before the incident, as we understand it. Caroline – everyone calls her Callie – was screaming at him. Neighbours said she appeared almost deranged.'

I close my eyes. He is right. I had felt as if I was going to explode that day – as if all the blood had literally rushed to my head. I remember catching a brief glimpse of myself in a mirror, my face flushed bright red, my eyes dark, practically demonic.

'What do we know about him – Ian Fullerton?' the woman asks.

'He's got previous. Assault on a woman he lived with a couple of years ago. She withdrew her complaint in the end, but it was nasty.'

I almost make a sound. Ian never told me that. But why would he? Once again the risks of meeting someone with whom you have no shared connections jump out at me.

'He sounds like a charmer,' the woman says. 'Anything else?'

'He'd recently sent her a lot of very abusive emails. Certainly enough to cause a major argument that could have turned nasty.'

'And there's no sign of this Callie? What steps have been taken?'

'Poster campaign, local press. It's not gone national yet. Her passport is still here, and lots of her clothes. She hasn't accessed any bank accounts or used a credit card.'

I hear the woman sigh. 'Okay. So it looks like it's exactly what you said it was. A domestic that turned ugly. Can I have a look at the rest of the house?'

'Sure. There's more blood – it's all still marked up for you.'

There is the sound of the kitchen door opening and then silence.

I don't know what to do. If I try to escape into the garden and back over the wall, they might see me. But if I stay here, they might come back to use the toilet.

They know everything – the emails, the argument, and no doubt they have seen the texts too. Maybe they believe he beat me up and I retaliated, but there isn't any evidence of that. I don't have any bruises.

I know for certain that they're looking for me now, and soon there will be nowhere for me to hide.

I don't know how long I have been here, and I have no idea whether they have gone or not. It is fully light outside, and has been for a while. My calf muscles feel stiff, probably from a combination of being in one position for a long time and the icy cold coming from the floor, creeping up my legs.

There is no safe way for me to find out if the house is empty. I can either make a dash for it and hope they have gone, or I can edge open the door to the kitchen and listen for talking or movement. I won't be able to hear them if they are upstairs, though.

Just as I have decided to risk leaving, I hear the sound of hurrying feet and a muttered expletive. There is a bang as the back door is slammed shut, then heavy footsteps head back to the kitchen, passing within inches of where I am standing. I hear a *click* as the kitchen door closes. The police officer had obviously forgotten the back door was still open. Had he come ten seconds later, he would have caught me.

Suddenly I don't know if I can do this. I feel sick at the thought that I am hiding from the police, but I lean against the wall and take some deep breaths, telling myself that right now the only thing that matters is getting away from here safely.

I will take the trainers and coat from the back porch, but I still won't have money or food and I can't risk going into the main part of the house. How can I go into a shop anyway, with my picture all over the place? My plan had been to walk slowly through the house to see if I could conjure up any memories of what happened that night. But I don't think I'm going to be able to do that. Even if the police have gone, they could come back at any moment.

I give it another fifteen minutes or so and decide that I have to leave before my limbs seize up completely. I edge out of the bathroom and tiptoe towards the kitchen door. I can hear nothing. I want so much to open the door, to go into my house and lie on my bed, to sleep, to have a shower, to find some food. But I can't.

I know I should walk up to one of the policemen outside and say, 'My name is Callie Baldwin and I killed Ian Fullerton,' but I'm not ready. I can't bring myself to admit what I have done.

51

The two women sat at the same table, in the same chairs, as they had done every day for months, the bulb that hung down from above casting its dim yellow light on their faces. The only time they saw daylight was when they went upstairs to clean.

But today was different. This morning Thea hadn't come for them. She hadn't brought down their breakfast, and last night she hadn't come with their flask of cocoa. Hannah felt dreadful. Her muscles were stiff and aching, and she felt a wave of anxiety rising, threatening to engulf her.

The other woman, whom Hannah still thought of as Judith, was irritable and kept rushing to the bathroom. She said she had been sick.

'Where's Thea?' she asked. But Hannah had no answer.

What they both needed was a calming mug of Thea's tea. She craved it and felt certain it was the only thing that would bring back the stability that enabled her to cope.

More worrying was the fact that Callie hadn't come back after her treatment with the doctor. That had never happened before. Hannah knew that he offered an alternative, a way out of life for those who couldn't take it any more. The woman who had left the basement just before Thea and the doctor's holiday had taken that option, and Hannah knew that the other Judith was ready to leave too. But Callie had only been here a few days. Would she have taken that decision so soon?

'Where's Judith?' the older woman asked, and Hannah knew she meant Callie.

She felt a rare burst of anger – at Thea and the doctor, at the other Judith, but most of all at herself.

'She's not called Judith. *I'm* not called Judith. And neither are you. It's so they don't have to remember our bloody names.' Hannah could feel her voice rising. 'My name's Hannah. Don't call me Judith again.'

She felt so ill, and she knew why. She had pretended not to understand that everything was laced with drugs, even when Callie had refused to eat or drink anything that Thea gave her. But Hannah had known. She had become too dependent, but what did it matter? For the last few months Thea's potions had stopped her from falling apart, and now she missed them badly.

The other woman was still looking at her. Her eyes were bloodshot, but perhaps they had always been like that and Hannah hadn't noticed.

'My name is Rosa,' the woman said quietly. 'I'm a nurse. I know what's happening to you – to both of us. It's dangerous.'

Hannah frowned. 'What is?'

Rosa gave a deep sigh, as if the act of speaking took too much effort. 'I think Thea has been giving us some kind of tranquilliser. Coming off any drug in one go can be nasty – that's why you're feeling so dreadful. We haven't had our morning dose, or last night's.'

Hannah's eyes filled with tears. 'Will it get better soon?'

'Not for a while,' Rosa said. 'At worst, one of us could have a seizure. At best, we'll feel increasingly ghastly. You'll probably be sick – I already have been, twice. You'll feel agitated and may start to shake unless she brings us something soon. We're going to have to help each other, Hannah.'

Hannah folded her arms on the table and dropped her head to rest on them. She already felt like death, and it was going to get worse. They were stuck down here, and they didn't know when they would next get food or the drugs they had come to depend on.

A small voice in her head was telling her that she knew the code to get into the main part of the house. But she was confused. She wasn't sure she could remember it. Her head was swimming, and all she wanted was to curl up in a ball and die. Is this how the last woman felt before she took the doctor's alternative way out? The one who had left them just before Callie arrived? Because if he came down here now and offered her the same solution, she would take it without hesitation.

52

Tom wasn't feeling at all comfortable about his offer to help in the search for Hannah Gardner, and wasn't sure why he had given in to Jack's persuasion. He could only hope that his unease wouldn't be too obvious to Nathan. Why was it that whenever his brother was around, Tom ended up circumventing the system – and in some cases, very possibly the law?

Philippa would be furious if she knew he was interfering in a missing-persons case, and his only excuse would be that Nathan was an old friend and he was simply offering a bit of advice. She had been surprised that he was going home on his day off, given the new case they had picked up, but Tom told her he had spoken to Becky and it didn't seem as if he needed to get involved at this stage.

'It's looking like a domestic that went bad,' Becky had told him when she called later that morning. 'There's no sign that anyone else was ever in the house, and Callie Baldwin is nowhere to be found. It adds up, Tom.'

He had agreed and left her to it, telling her they could catch up the next day.

To Tom's surprise, Jack had been home when he arrived back from his tedious meeting, but when the doorbell rang to signal Nathan's arrival he had disappeared into the dining room taking a mug of coffee, a sandwich and his laptop, although he had left the door ajar so he could listen in on the conversation. Tom would have much preferred his brother to be out of the house. He might spill hot coffee in his lap and shout out, or have a coughing fit, alerting Nathan to his presence.

Jack had even tried to provide Tom with a list of questions to ask Nathan, but Tom had merely raised his eyebrows and his brother had laughed. 'Okay, Detective Chief Inspector, but if I'm going to be checking out this computer I'll need some idea of what I'm looking for.'

Reluctantly, Tom went to open his front door to Jack's old friend. 'Come in, Nathan. Let's go through to the kitchen.'

Nathan followed Tom and headed straight for the table, where he sat down and opened Hannah's laptop. He didn't bother with pleasantries and cut straight to the chase.

'I've tried every obvious password, but nothing works. I've written down her full name, mine, our parents' – although I doubt she would use theirs – all our dates of birth, the name of her first dog. The usual stuff. It's all here, if your guy can use it.'

'That's really helpful. Thanks,' Tom said. 'Do you want a cup of coffee? I thought we could talk through what you've been doing up to this point to try to find her.'

'Black, no sugar, thanks,' Nathan said. 'Look, I don't know who this computer expert is, but I've tried a couple of people already without success. Your guy needs to be good.'

'I think he's okay. Better than average, anyway,' Tom said, knowing Jack would be grinning at his almost derisory remarks.

'Pity you can't bring Jack back from the dead. He'd crack it in five minutes.'

Tom was reaching for a couple of mugs, and his hand stopped in mid-air.

'Christ, I'm sorry. That was a bit insensitive. I'm used to dealing with hard-nosed gamblers who don't appear to have much in the way of emotions. At least not visible ones.'

Tom pressed the button on his bean-to-cup machine, and the grinding of the coffee beans covered the awkward moment.

'You need to know, Tom, that although I seem like a cold, unemotional bugger, it's all part of the persona. I've learned to show very little of how I feel – it's something of a requirement in my job. But I do care about Hannah. Rubbish brother that I've been, she's still my little sister, and I'm not giving up until I've found her.'

Tom turned to his visitor. It was a strange moment. He hadn't been facing Nathan as he spoke about his sister, but his voice had been rich with emotion. Now, as Tom looked at him, his face was blank.

'Okay, I get that. Let's make a start, shall we?' he said as he walked towards the table with the two mugs. 'Tell me when she was last seen.'

'She wrote to me after she'd been away somewhere on the south coast. She went on a mindfulness retreat or some such bollocks.'

Tom smiled. He really couldn't imagine Nathan Gardner having a high opinion of an activity that involved any form of soul-searching.

'What made her write to you out of the blue?'

'They told her on the course that she needed to sort out the demons that haunted her, and I guess I was one of them. Well perhaps not me specifically, but our lack of communication could have bothered her.'

'So not all bad then, this mindfulness bollocks?' Tom asked.

'Hmm. Anyway, I've brought you a copy of the letter. It's probably better if you read it yourself.'

Tom realised that Jack needed to hear at least the gist of it.

'Why don't you give me a synopsis, and I'll read it in full later?'

Nathan shrugged. 'She starts with the usual stuff about how we're family and should support each other. She mentions her job, looking after a baby boy she seemed to adore.'

'Did you manage to track down the family she was working for?' Tom asked.

'I did – their details were in her flat – but they gave me short shrift when I called them. They said she had let them down badly.'

'In what way?'

Nathan shrugged. 'They wouldn't say any more than that. It was over three months ago now, but whatever she did, they weren't impressed – angry with her, I would say. I'm surprised, really. She seemed so happy with the job, and there are quite a few pictures of the baby in her flat. She wouldn't have had them all over the place if she hadn't been fond of him, so God knows what she did to piss them off.'

Tom felt a familiar prickle at the back of his neck. When someone did something that seemed out of character, it always made him wonder why. Had there been some traumatic event in Hannah's life? Could it be coercion? For now he wasn't going to mention those thoughts to her brother.

He waved the letter at Nathan. 'She seems to have thought the retreat was good for her. Did she go there before or after she upset her employers?'

'Before. She went at the end of September. As you'll see, she talks about everything she learned about herself – including what a numpty she has for a brother, no doubt. She says the people there were great. One woman in particular had been very supportive. She was planning to see more of her when she got home.'

'And home is Rusholme, didn't you tell me the other day?'

'It is. The heart of curry land. Her flat isn't in such a good area, though. Had I known, paid more attention, I would have given her some money to move. Most of the flats around her are full of students who are years younger than her, and from what I can gather people come and go all the time. No one notices if anyone's there or not.'

'And you've told the missing-persons team all of this?'

'Of course. I know nothing about the woman she met on the retreat, other than the fact that Hannah liked her. I get the feeling from the letter that she thought she'd made a new and important friend. But she doesn't mention her name, and anyway there's no reason to think she'd have any clue where Hannah might be now. Having said that, I've been trying to track her down to at least ask the question.'

Tom was quiet for a moment. Did Hannah's participation in a mindfulness retreat signify that she was struggling with stress or unhappiness? Not necessarily. For some it was apparently about seeing the world with greater clarity, and Tom realised he was in danger of pigeonholing Hannah's mental state to try to align it with Jasmine DuPont's need for the support of the bereavement group. He had to focus on the facts.

'I went to some lengths to try to find the woman,' Nathan continued. 'If you read to the end of the letter, you'll see Hannah wrote that her new friend was planning a holiday in Myanmar. She told me about a boat trip up the river and how much she wished she could go with her. The holiday was planned for January, so when I arrived in Manchester and realised Hannah was missing, I wondered if she might have gone too. There was no sign of her passport in her flat, so I took myself out there and sailed up and down that bloody river three times.'

Tom gave him a puzzled look. 'What do you mean?'

'I knew the name of the boat and that the booking was for January, but it could have been any one of three trips. At the start of each one I waited at the hotel for the group to arrive, expecting Hannah to turn up. It was supposed to be a surprise! But she didn't, obviously. So I tried to work out which of the new arrivals might have been on the retreat with her, thinking if I could find the friend, she might have some idea where Hannah had gone.'

Tom was astonished. Nathan hadn't told him about this when he came to the office. He'd said he had undertaken his own investigations, but then they had been sidetracked by the visit to the mortuary.

'Did you find the friend?'

'I didn't identify anyone, no. She'd talked about a woman, not a couple, so I was specifically looking for single women travelling alone or with friends. There were a few, but the trips attracted mainly older couples, mostly from the States and Australia, so I only had one or two suspects. It was a stupid idea and a bloody waste of time, if I'm honest.'

'Did you ask if any of them knew Hannah?' Tom asked.

'Not outright. I tried to find out a bit about each of the possibles. I don't have a recent photo of Hannah, and given my lack of knowledge about my sister's life I was concerned about asking too many questions. They might have doubted I was her brother – I could have been a stalker or an ex-lover with some other motive – and knowing who I was and what a crap brother I had been might have made them even less likely to tell me anything. So I tried as subtly as possible to identify the friend. I used my middle name, Paul. I hoped if anyone did know Hannah they wouldn't connect her with me, particularly if she had mentioned me in some bloody spill-your-guts group session.'

Tom bit his bottom lip. 'Any good leads?'

'Not really. There was a woman on one of the trips who behaved in a very strange way the whole time, but when I asked her where she was from and tried to get some details of where she worked, I freaked her out. She was hiding something, I'm sure of it, and I had planned to find her when I got back.'

'And did you?' Tom asked.

'No. I didn't know enough about her. People generally don't share their surnames, and I don't know anyone smart enough to hack the travel company's website for more details.'

'Yes, you do.'

The voice came from behind Tom and his heart sank. He closed his eyes for a second. When he opened them he looked at Nathan, whose gaze had travelled to the door to the dining room. His expression hadn't altered, and there was not so much as a flicker of surprise in his eyes. Tom could see why he was such a good poker player.

'Jack,' Nathan said nonchalantly, as if he had been expecting him the whole time.

'Nathan,' Jack replied, and walking over to the table, he sat down.

53

Becky wasn't sure whether to call Tom. She knew he wouldn't mind, but it was his day off after all, and he deserved some time to himself. He seemed to have lost a bit of his usual chirpiness that morning, and she had the feeling there was something more going on than his frustration with a boring meeting. He was always grumpy about what he called a 'gathering of the great and the good', but it was usually little more than a light-hearted moan.

The case they had taken on in Crumpsall was all in hand. Keith was in charge of collating the evidence, and she was confident she could leave it in his hands for now. She was keen to get back to the Jasmine DuPont investigation and would have really appreciated Tom's input on the latest bit of information they had received.

On balance, though, she thought her news could wait until the next day. There wasn't much they would be able to do with so few facts, but at Tom's suggestion they had dug out the file of the woman found on the golf course, and it had proved interesting. She had been missing from home for over eight months before she was found. And prior to that she had been attending a depression support group. It wasn't a bereavement group like Jasmine's, but it was close enough to be interesting.

Lynsey had managed to find and talk to the group leader, and the dead woman's story bore a striking resemblance to Jasmine's. She had been isolated, although her background was totally different. She had been brought up in care and had never managed to establish any close friendships. As an adult she had become depressed and found it difficult to find a steady job. It was her isolation and her mental state that seemed so similar.

The group leader also told Lynsey that there was an older woman at the meetings who had been very supportive. Once again, frustratingly, people didn't have to give their real names, but the leader described her as a woman in her early seventies, quite elegant, with long silver hair. Lynsey had immediately contacted the organiser of the bereavement group that Jasmine had attended and asked if anyone following that description had been a member.

They had. It was a woman fitting that description who had been seen walking to the tram stop with Jasmine.

Could it be that someone was targeting lonely young women with little or no support who were struggling to come to terms with something in their lives? A woman in her seventies, though? Had it been a man then it would have made more sense, or a younger woman possibly working as part of a team. But a female pensioner?

Because it seemed such a ridiculous lead Becky decided to keep it to herself for now. She would think about it overnight and talk to Tom in the morning.

54

Tom swivelled in his chair and stared at his brother. What the hell was he playing at?

'Don't glare at me like that, Tom. I know Nathan well enough to know that he's not got any interest in what happened to me and why I'm supposed to be dead.' Jack turned to his old friend. 'Have you?'

Tom turned back to look at Nathan. The only sign that he was surprised to see Jack was a slight flaring of the nostrils, as if he was trying to suppress a smile.

'Nope. Couldn't care less, but it's bloody good to see you, mate. And don't look so worried, Tom. I'm aware no one needs to know about this, and as I've got no one to tell we don't have a problem as far as I can see.'

Jack looked at Tom again. 'And as you have probably noticed, Nathan is perfectly capable of controlling his facial expressions. If someone mentions my name to him in passing, he's not going to blush and stammer, is he?'

Nathan grinned. '*I'm* not, but *you* want to watch your reactions, Tom. You nearly dropped that bloody mug when I mentioned Jack's name.'

The two other men laughed, but Tom was not amused. Now wasn't the time to read Jack the riot act, but he had made a stupid, irresponsible decision.

'I was fed up with just listening. It's good to be able to have a conversation in something other than Spanish, for one thing,' Jack said, alluding to the fact that he had most probably been living somewhere in South America. 'And for another, I can help you find out where Hannah is. I owe Nathan that, Tom. He's a friend.'

'Fine. But it was one thing asking Nathan to bring Hannah's computer so you could take it away and perform your magic. It's another to expect me to sit here while you illegally hack into various databases right in front of me, because I guess that's what you're going to do, isn't it?' he asked.

'First things first. We need to get into her computer and check her social media and email accounts to see if there's anything interesting that might suggest where she's gone. If they come up blank, we'll check out the people who attended the mindfulness retreat and see if there's any correlation with the passenger list for the boat. I can also see if Hannah's mobile has a signal anywhere, although I would guess that has been tested already?'

Nathan shrugged. 'I don't know if the police have checked it out, but I paid for it to be done. There hasn't been a signal for months – since November. In the couple of days before her phone disappeared off the grid she was all over the place, or at least, her phone was.'

'Okay,' Jack said. 'We can look at that later if we need to. Let's get into her computer first, check out anything she's posted and then see if we can find out what that retreat company was called.'

Tom pushed his chair back. 'I'll let you two get on with it. I'll go and sit on a stool at the island, far enough away so I don't know what you're doing.' He didn't add that he wanted to be close enough to hear what was going on.

He saw Jack pull a lead from his pocket and plug it into Hannah's computer. The other end went into his, and he started tapping on his keyboard. Without asking the question, Tom was sure Jack's computer was communicating with Hannah's in some weird and wonderful way. He gave a small shake of the head and walked out into the hall to grab his briefcase. He might as well look at some of this morning's scintillating reports while he listened with one ear to what was happening at the table.

He was back on his stool and had only read through about half a page – none of which he had taken in – when he heard a mumble from Jack.

'And…we're in,' he said, a small note of triumph in his voice. He spun the laptop back towards Nathan. 'Have a look. Make sure you're okay with me rooting around in all her personal stuff.'

Nathan spun it back to Jack and dragged his chair round so he could look over Jack's shoulder. 'I don't really care what you find on there. All I care about is finding out if she's alive and well and in Honolulu, or some other such place she's got it into her head to visit.'

'Okay, here we go.'

Tom could hear keys tapping, and there were various grunts and murmurs. He had given up pretending to read and was listening to everything the two men said.

It was only a few moments before Jack spoke.

'Right,' he said. 'There's an email here confirming her reservation on the mindfulness retreat. There's nothing of any interest after her return. She hasn't booked anything, hasn't chatted to anyone on Facebook. It could be she preferred to communicate by phone, so we'll have a look at that in a minute. Or it could be in Messenger. Hang on. I'll open that through her Facebook account.'

Jack tapped away again, and Nathan pushed back his chair and stood up, stretching his arms above his head. He walked over to Tom.

'Don't look so worried. Jack is absolutely right to trust me. If he can help me find Hannah, I'll disappear and I'll never mention him to anyone.'

Tom knew he was telling the truth. It wasn't Nathan's responsibility anyway. It was Jack's. He could only hope his brother knew what he was doing.

'Nathan! Come and look at this list.'

Nathan turned. 'What have you got?'

'I've managed to get into the reservations system for the retreat. There were twenty people on the same course as Hannah – most of them women. Have a look and see if any of the names mean anything to you.'

'She didn't mention the woman by name in her letter, but I can check if one of them matches anyone I met on the boat.'

Nathan sat down at the table and read through the list. Both Tom and Jack watched him to see if there was any reaction, although being Nathan, that was unlikely. Finally, he pushed the laptop back towards Jack.

'Nothing. Sorry. I don't recognise any of them.'

'Not to worry,' Jack said. 'It was just a shortcut to save hacking the tour company's database. Give me their name and the dates of the sailings, and let's see what we can find.'

Jack didn't exactly rub his hands together, but Tom could feel his pleasure. He had a puzzle to solve, and he was loving every moment of it. Perhaps he and his brother weren't so different after all. They had a shared obsession with unravelling tangled webs, even if their methodologies were somewhat different.

Tom felt a rising sense of excitement. He knew Jack was going to find something. The only problem was, he didn't know what he would be able to do with it. The information would be illegally obtained. He had no means of passing it on.

Rules were there for a purpose, but sometimes Tom felt the urge to break them.

'Got it!' Jack shouted.

55

The woman Hannah now knew to be Rosa – the woman with whom she had spent the last four months of her life, and about whom she had known nothing until a few hours ago – sat on the end of Hannah's bed, her knees drawn up tight to her chest, her whole body trembling. It had been nearly twenty-four hours since they had been given anything to eat or drink, and they had no idea why they were being left alone.

Since the early bouts of sickness, Rosa's system seemed to be reacting better than Hannah's, although for months she had seemed weak and on the point of giving up.

'They were ready to let me go,' she told Hannah, who was lying down, curled up tightly, trying hard to stop the attacks of nausea. 'Whatever they gave me didn't calm me down, it made me depressed, which meant I was no use to them. The doctor changed my meds – I don't know what to – and I felt more and more as if all I wanted was to die. He said he would help me when the time came, like he'd helped the others before.'

'How many others?

'There have been a couple since I've been here, but the doctor doesn't seem to want to let anyone go until there's a replacement. Who would clean for them then?'

Hannah felt the anxiety well up inside her again, and told herself it was only a withdrawal symptom. 'To think that when they went away on holiday, I was scared they wouldn't come back. I thought I needed them to protect me, to keep me safe. I was *glad* when they came back.'

Rosa gave a shaky laugh. 'Clever Thea, making all our meals in advance. And providing a big supply of her so-called "vitamins" to keep us healthy.'

Hannah realised that Thea and the doctor had been sure they would not escape from the cellar while they were away. Even if she and Rosa hadn't eaten the food or taken the drugs, they would still have been locked in. Nobody knew that Hannah had worked out which keys to press to open the door to their prison.

Oh God, why couldn't she remember the code? She wrapped her arms around her head and sobbed.

Rosa seemed to be trying to control the shaking of her own voice. 'Keep talking to me, Hannah. Distract yourself. It's going to be hell, but you will get through it. *We* will get through it.'

But both of them knew that unless Thea or the doctor came, they would eventually die of starvation. *Why hadn't they come?*

Hannah forced herself to do what Rosa said and began to describe the sequence of events that had brought her here – the mindfulness retreat, the visits to Thea for reassurance, and then the stealing of the baby.

'I brought the baby here. I was going to keep him. It was all over the news that I had stolen Albie, and Thea said she had to prise him from my arms and take him away. She left him outside a hospital so someone would find him and I wouldn't be arrested.'

Her voice caught on a sob of disbelief that she had done something so dreadful.

Rosa was quiet for a moment. 'Do you remember taking him – bringing him here?' she asked finally.

'No. That's what was so awful about it. I've tried and tried to remember, but there's nothing there. What about you?'

'I came here to care for Thea. She'd had a fall and had broken her hip. I felt sorry for her. Her sister had been looking after her, but she had become unwell so I was brought in to take over. I moved in, and it was fine because I'd just split with my husband

and wanted to escape from the world.'

Both women were quiet for a moment, then Hannah lifted her head and groaned. 'I think I'm going to be sick again.'

'Keep talking.'

'I can't.'

Rosa shuffled around, trying to get comfortable. 'Okay, I'll talk then. I'd been here for about a week. I'd never seen the sister, but I thought she was somewhere in the house. I heard someone crying one day. I was going to ask Thea about it, but she wasn't having a good day. That night I was up in my room – I was sleeping in the main part of the house then – when I heard shouting and screaming. I rushed down the stairs, but the door at the bottom was locked. They'd locked me in.'

Hannah gasped. 'What were they saying?'

'A woman whose voice I'd never heard before was shouting, "I need to see him. He wouldn't leave me. Vincent wouldn't do that to me." Or something like that. Anyway, she said she was going home. Then I heard the doctor's voice – very deep. I couldn't hear what he said, just a sort of growl. But she screamed at him. Something about how she didn't need to be given anything to calm herself; she just needed to see Vincent.'

'And you think she was Thea's sister?'

'I assumed so, but I didn't care about their problems. I was so angry about the locked door that I decided to resign the next day. Thea was in a terrible state, though. She was almost hysterical and wouldn't tell me what was the matter.'

Rosa rested her forehead on her raised knees and clasped her hands behind her neck. Hannah could see that the effort of talking was draining her already depleted energy, but after a moment, with a determined groan, she carried on.

'I tried to calm her. She thanked me and said my voice reminded her of her sister's. It made her feel better. Then the doctor came in with a drink. She threw it at him and asked if

263

he was trying to kill her. When he left, I said I would make her a hot drink myself, and she said, "Thank you, Judith." It was the first time she called me that.'

Hannah lifted her hands to wipe the tears from her face. 'I think Judith was her sister's name,' she said, remembering the photograph.

Rosa stared at her. 'Oh God, it all makes sense now. Judith left, so we each in turn became some kind of surrogate. They didn't want her to go; they probably thought she was going to look after them into their old age.'

'And so that became our job,' Hannah whispered. Suddenly her whole body shook violently, and she didn't know if this was a withdrawal symptom or was caused by revulsion at what her life had become.

'I tried to get away,' Rosa said, her voice distant as if she was remembering the pain of that time. 'I told the doctor I was leaving. He begged me to stay until Thea was fully recovered. He said he couldn't manage, but I knew she was nearly better – she was able to walk by then – so I said I was sorry. I had to go. I would leave at the end of the week.' Rosa paused. 'I never made it to the end of the week.'

'What happened?' Hannah asked.

Rosa pulled the blanket she had brought from her own room more tightly around her shoulders, and Hannah could see how much the memory distressed her.

'I had a drink with the doctor the following night. I was sure I'd only had one, but next thing I knew it was morning. Thea was sitting by my bed. She told me I'd run off the night before – packed and left. The doctor had gone after me because I'd had too much to drink and he was worried. He'd found my car in a ditch just down the road. I was slumped over the wheel. He managed to get me out, drove me home and then walked back for my car.'

Hannah could see tears running down Rosa's face. Maybe she

shouldn't ask any more questions, but she was scared of the silence. Without the sound of Rosa's voice, she would be lost to her own thoughts. She was about to ask a question when Rosa started to speak again.

'That morning they learned on the radio that someone – a woman – had been knocked down close to where he'd found me. She was dead, and I had been drinking. The doctor hadn't seen the body, but he was implicated because he'd helped me. They said they would hide me until it all blew over. And they brought me down here.'

Hannah propped herself up on one elbow, the nausea abating a little. 'And you remember nothing?'

Rosa was sobbing now, her thin shoulders shaking. She wiped away the tears with the edge of the blanket.

'No, but that doesn't mean it didn't happen. I can't live like this any more, Hannah. I've been ready to die for weeks now. The doctor was going to help me. I didn't think I had anything left to live for. Do you know how tragic that feels?'

Hannah knew exactly how Rosa felt. 'Maybe the drugs make us do terrible things. Maybe that's why I abducted little Albie.'

Rosa shook her head.

'Maybe. But there's something not right about what Thea told you. She said she'd left the baby outside a hospital, didn't she?'

Hannah nodded, puzzled by why that was bothering Rosa.

'That must be a lie. She would have been caught on CCTV if she was anywhere near a hospital. The police would have traced her.'

'I don't understand what you're saying.' Hannah's heart was pumping and the nausea came rushing back. 'Tell me, Rosa.'

'I'm saying that Thea lied to you. Whether you abducted that child or not, she didn't return him the way she said she did.'

Hannah pushed herself upright and swung her legs over the side of the bed. She was going to be sick. *What had Thea done with Albie?*

56

'I don't remember anyone called that,' Nathan said as he read the name Jack was pointing at on the screen.

By now they were all crowding around the laptop, looking at the list Jack had summoned from somewhere.

'But it's too much of a coincidence that she was in both places,' Jack said. 'She's on the list for the mindfulness retreat, *and* she was on one of the boat trips in Myanmar. Tom doesn't believe in coincidences, do you, Tom?' He didn't respond. 'She has to be the person that Hannah met, surely?'

'But there was only one woman from this part of the world travelling on her own. And she was called Callie. She's the one I told you about,' said Nathan. 'I tried to get to know her, but like I said earlier, there was something odd about her. I think I scared her.'

'Well Dorothea Atwell wasn't on her own, that's true. Are you sure you don't remember her?'

Nathan frowned. 'We didn't share surnames, but wait a minute. When you said the name out loud, it rang a bell that didn't chime when I read it on screen. Dorothea could easily be shortened to Thea, couldn't it? Who was she travelling with?'

'Dr Garrick Atwell. Does that help?'

For once Nathan's face betrayed a flicker of emotion. 'Yes!' But his moment of euphoria didn't last. 'Bloody stupid idea, though. They were both about a hundred and three, and in her letter Hannah was talking about going off on holiday with this woman she'd met. How likely is that!'

'I don't think you should dismiss the idea, Nathan,' Tom said. 'If Hannah was feeling particularly vulnerable, she may have seen this woman as a maternal figure – someone she could trust.'

'If Hannah saw Dorothea as a supportive older woman, she might have at least told her where she was planning on going,' Jack said as Tom walked back towards the kitchen island. 'Can you have someone go out and talk to her, Tom?'

'Not easily, no. How can I say I got her name? She hasn't done anything wrong, and even if I could dream up an excuse, I'm not going to be able to get anyone to go tonight. The problem is that I have no official means of knowing about this woman.'

Both Jack and Nathan were looking at him, clearly waiting for him to come up with a solution.

'Look, there's one thing we could do. If Nathan were to tell me that he had paid someone to check out Hannah's movements, friends, et cetera, and that Dorothea Atwell's name had cropped up as a possible contact, I could register it as intelligence, and it would get into the system officially. Maybe someone from the missing-persons team would then be persuaded to have a word with the Atwells. Would that do?'

Jack stood up abruptly from the table, closed Hannah's laptop and stuck it under his arm. 'And how long is that going to take? Come on, Nathan. We don't need the Greater Manchester Police to do this for us. We can just knock on the door and say that Hannah mentioned this Dorothea woman in a letter to her brother.'

'Jack, you don't even know where she lives,' Tom said, earning himself a derisory look as Jack held up his mobile, which was showing a map that no doubt featured the precise location of Dorothea Atwell's home.

'Come on,' Jack said again. 'Let's go and have a chat with this lady. You drive, Nathan, and I'll continue to search Hannah's computer for information.'

'Hang on, the pair of you,' Tom said, feeling as if he was talking to a couple of teenage boys off on some escapade. 'First of all, she's met you before, Nathan. If she knows anything about Hannah, she's going to find it very odd you turning up on her doorstep if you never mentioned your sister when you met on the boat.'

Nathan looked at Jack and raised his eyebrows. 'He has a point.'

'Okay. I'll ask the questions. You can wait in the car,' Jack said, already walking towards the hall.

Tom threw his papers down on the worktop. 'Listen, you can't go charging in there like Batman and bloody Robin,' he said, the exasperation clear in his voice. 'This is an elderly couple, one of whom very probably met Hannah on the retreat. And if this lady does know anything at all about where she might have gone, you're just going to scare her if you don't ask the right questions. And as for you, Jack, you shouldn't be showing your face anywhere. What happens if they complain about you and there's an investigation? I know you're sick of being dead, but don't blow it now in a burst of ill-conceived enthusiasm.'

Jack looked at Tom for about ten seconds. 'Point taken, little brother. We'll just go and check the place out, shall we, Nathan? And perhaps on the way we can think up a story to get you through the front door. I'll keep to the bushes.' He smiled at Tom, whose heart sank.

He had a feeling this was all going to go horribly wrong.

57

I've spent most of the day in the car park of a cemetery. It seemed appropriate somehow. The day has never grown fully light. Thick dark clouds have been scudding across the sky, the wind scattering dead leaves that scratch against my windscreen. I huddle down in my coat, not wanting to use up all my fuel but for some reason unwilling to drive as far away from Manchester as possible.

One thought keeps jostling its way to the front of my mind. There are still two women in that cellar. They can't be left to the life that Thea and the doctor have planned for them – the domestic slavery, the weird games of trust. I may not have a clue how to solve my own problems, but thinking of them distracts me for a while.

I had persuaded myself that Hannah didn't abduct a baby, but I realise now that my conviction allowed me also to believe that I didn't kill Ian, and I was wrong about that. So if I make an anonymous call to the police about Hannah, will I be committing her to a life in prison for kidnap or will I be freeing her from Thea and Garrick?

And what about the other woman who was in the cellar with us – the one whose name I never discovered? What is her story?

I have a momentary flashback of the man who came to the house – the man called Vincent who shouted at Thea. He had wanted to see Judith. If she wasn't one of the women in the basement with me, then who was she – and more to the point, where was she? I had lived upstairs in that house for days, and I had never seen or heard anyone else.

I know that by thinking of the other women I am merely putting off the moment when I have to make a choice, but I can't run from the police forever. I have nowhere to hide. I haven't eaten and I can't bring myself to steal food.

After a day of hunger, cold, and confusion about what is best for me and for the other women, I know I am out of options. My eyes are dry – there are no more tears – and with a sense of hopelessness I finally accept that I must hand myself in. I am not a hardened criminal and have no idea where to get money, a passport or anything else I would need to start a new life.

I shudder at the thought that if I don't do this, I might reach a point of desperation where I feel I have no alternative but to go back to Thea and the doctor. Then I think of the horror of last night – the setting, the staging, the ritualistic quality of it all. It felt like a seduction scene, but I know it wasn't. It was the request that I should wash him, the suggestion that it was some bizarre act of trust. Most of all, though, it was the doctor's words: 'Tomorrow it will be your turn.'

I put the car into gear. I'm going to drive to the police station, and then I'm going to work up the courage to go in.

58

In the end Becky didn't have to call Tom; he called her.

'It's your day off, boss. You should take it easy. There's nothing that won't keep.'

'I'm sure there's not, but I'm feeling guilty at leaving you to it,' Tom said. 'I wouldn't have come home this afternoon if there hadn't been something personal I needed to deal with.'

Becky knew there was no point asking what it was. He wouldn't tell her.

'All okay now?' she asked instead.

'Not really, no. Tell me what's been going on there.'

She didn't like the sound of that. 'It's nothing to do with Lucy, is it?'

Becky had developed a good relationship with Tom's daughter over the years and had occasionally taken her into Manchester when she wanted female company on a shopping trip. Louisa would no doubt be fulfilling that role now, and Becky missed the girl.

'No, Lucy's fine. She wants to come and see you the minute you've had the baby – so be warned.'

Becky smiled. 'She will be very welcome. Now, a couple of things. I had thought about calling you, but I decided to leave it until tomorrow.'

'Go on,' Tom said. 'I'm not doing anything else useful.'

Becky repeated all she had learned about the woman found on the golf course. 'You were right about her name too. It was Williams.'

'Oh well, good to know I don't have too bad a memory.'

'The thing is, Tom, it sounds like there's quite a bit of similarity between the woman who befriended the golf-course victim and the one our Penny – sorry, Jasmine – was seen with a couple of times.'

'What did she look like?' Tom asked abruptly.

'She was quite an elderly lady, apparently, with long silver-grey hair, sometimes tied back. Quite elegant, they said. Wonderful bone structure, another one said. Why? You sounded almost excited then.'

'Hang on, Becky. I'm going to make a call on my personal mobile. Stay with me.'

Becky could only just hear his voice, but not what he said or who he was talking to. He must have put his phone down and walked away. All she heard was one word.

'Shit.'

❖

As soon as Tom heard Becky's description of the woman who had been seen talking to the two supposed suicide victims, he knew he had to get hold of Jack and Nathan urgently.

Dorothea Atwell had been on the mindfulness retreat with Hannah, and Hannah had said that the wonderful woman she had met was going to be holidaying on a boat on the Irrawaddy in January. Thea Atwell was on that boat, and now a woman of a similar age was linked to both of the dead women. There was nothing to tie her to Hannah's disappearance, so it could be a coincidence, but Jack was right – Tom didn't believe in them. Jack and Nathan could be walking into something they didn't understand.

He called Nathan straight away. 'Did this Dorothea or Thea woman have long silver-grey hair and beautiful bone structure,' he said without preamble.

'Definitely the hair. Can't comment on the bone structure. Why, Tom? What's—'

The phone went dead in Tom's hand. 'Shit!'

He picked up his other phone. 'Becky, I'll call you back. Don't go anywhere. I need to speak to someone.'

He hung up and sat staring at his mobile. Why the hell had his conversation been cut short? He tried again, but it didn't connect.

Tom was about to call Becky back when his personal mobile rang again.

'What happened? Why did we get cut off?'

'I'll put Jack on,' Nathan said.

'Tom, there's something weird going on. We're outside the house. We came up with a plan, and we were heading up the drive while Nathan was talking to you and his mobile went dead. So did mine. I think there's a signal jammer operating.'

'Maybe just a dead patch. Why would you think it's a jammer?'

There was a small sigh. 'I wrote an app for my phone. It pings when there's a sudden loss of signal. It's helpful to know if you're walking into trouble.'

Tom said nothing. There was nothing to say.

'I've tried walking up the drive a couple of times and it pings each time. There's a full signal at the gate and then nothing. It's more than a dead spot – I've moved around a bit to check it out. I'm telling you, it's a jammer. Now why would an elderly couple do that? How would they know *how* to do that?'

'What's the address?'

Jack told him, and Tom scribbled it down while speaking quickly to his brother, hoping that for once he would listen.

'I want you both to stay out of there. Seriously, I think there's more to this than we already know, and if I'm right, I don't want you to alert anyone. Can you do that?'

'I suppose so. The house looks quiet. No lights on anywhere. Even though it's not fully dark yet, I would have expected a few lamps on at least. Maybe they're out.'

'Well keep well away from the entrance, in case they come

back and find you two skulking around in the undergrowth. Understood?'

'Okay, okay. And I promise not to break in.'

Tom sighed with exasperation and Jack laughed.

'Oh, and as we were driving here I accessed iMessage on Hannah's laptop and found an interesting text she'd sent to her employers. I'll forward it to you. Make of it what you will.'

Tom hung up and called Becky. She picked up straight away.

'I want you to find out everything you can about a Dorothea and Garrick Atwell. Husband and wife.' He passed on the address in south Manchester that Jack had given him.

'Okay. Are you going to tell me what's going on?'

'I can't right now. I have to do a bit of thinking about how to deal with this. But there is something about them that warrants a look. And I think Nathan Gardner's sister – the one I told you had gone missing – is involved too. It may all be perfectly innocent, but I need to decide how to play it.'

Tom couldn't tell her everything he knew until he had worked out how to square the fact that some of the information had come via Jack. He didn't want Becky embroiled in this as well.

'I'm on it. Before I go, do you want to know how things are looking with the Callie Baldwin and Ian Fullerton case? She's disappeared without trace – no phone, credit card usage, or cash withdrawals. Everything's been checked, and there's been a press campaign with her face plastered everywhere. But don't worry about that now; it sounds like you have more important things on your plate.'

The forwarded text from Hannah's messages had come through as Becky was speaking, and for a moment Tom was distracted.

'What names did you say?' he asked sharply.

'Just now? Caroline Baldwin and Ian Fullerton.'

'You didn't say Caroline, though, did you?'

'Sorry, boss. She goes by the name of Callie.'

Tom closed his eyes and focused. What had Nathan said? Something about there being only one single woman on the boat from this part of the world. And her name was Callie. He rushed over to Jack's laptop, which was still open at the passenger list. And there it was: Caroline Baldwin, who Becky said was better known as Callie.

And nobody knew where she was.

59

Tom was struggling to get his head round everything that had come to light in the last few hours. More importantly, he was trying to work out whether the information that had come to him legally – via Becky – was sufficient for him to make a move.

Becky had established that an elderly woman with long grey hair was known to both dead girls – Jasmine, and the one found on the golf course. But Tom had only been able to match that description to Dorothea Atwell because of Nathan and the hacked records.

Becky had also confirmed that there was no trace of Callie Baldwin. Once again, if Jack hadn't accessed the passenger list from the boat, there was nothing to link her – officially – to Thea Atwell.

Tom knew what he should do: register Jack's hacked information as intelligence without declaring its source, so it could be checked for reliability. Then an application could be made for a court order so he could officially obtain the information he needed from the travel companies. But it would take too long.

A thought occurred to him. Becky had said there had been extensive press coverage in the attempt to find Callie Baldwin. But Nathan knew her – he had met her.

He quickly dialled Nathan's number again, hoping that he and Jack had stayed outside the Atwells' grounds.

'What can I do for you, Tom?'

'That Callie woman you talked about. Did she have anything to do with Thea or Garrick Atwell when you were all on the boat?'

'Anything to do with them? They practically lived in each other's pockets! I tried to get Callie alone a few times – like I said, I thought she could have been the one who met Hannah and might know where she had taken herself off to – but Thea bit my bloody head off whenever I went near her. She was so protective. I'd have found it claustrophobic if I'd been Callie. Thea seemed to revel in the role of being the understanding older woman, and Callie fell under her spell.'

There might just be a solution here that Tom could work with.

'I can tell you this, Nathan, because it is all over the press in north Manchester. Callie Baldwin is missing.'

'What the *fuck*?'

'There's more to it than that, but I can't talk to you about the rest right now. I'm surprised you've not seen her picture on the news.'

'I told you, I don't watch TV much.'

Tom felt a flash of frustration. Nathan could have helped them solve this days ago.

'Ask Jack to Google her. Check if the girl in the photo is the one who was on the boat and then get back to me. If they are the same, we can say the information that links Thea Atwell, Callie Baldwin and your sister Hannah has all come from you – legitimately.'

Tom hung up and waited, although he knew in advance what the response would be. Now all he had to decide was the most appropriate next step.

60

A few cars have come and gone since I arrived in the police station car park, but no one is taking any notice of me. There are cameras, and I wonder how long it will be before someone comes out and asks me why I'm sitting here. Maybe it would be easier to wait until that happens. It feels like less of a conscious decision.

It's completely dark now, even though I can see from the clock on the dashboard that it is more late afternoon than early evening. The car park is well lit and that makes it worse. If I could have slunk into the station in the dark I would have felt less exposed, less vulnerable.

I'm just procrastinating – putting off the inevitable – and I decide finally that this is the moment. I'm going to get out of the car, go into the police station, tell them who I am and confess to what I have done.

I push open the car door and tell my feet to move. To travel, one in front of the other, to the entrance. It is so hard, and my guts are in knots.

I know that I look grubby and unkempt. I haven't seen a comb or soap and water for a while now, and the police officer on the information desk probably thinks I'm a vagrant.

'Can I help you?' she asks pleasantly enough.

'I think so,' I say. My voice is so quiet that she puts her head on one side as if to hear better. 'My name is Caroline Baldwin. I think you're looking for me.'

Her eyes open slightly wider. 'We are indeed,' she says.

She stands up and turns to the officer on her left, speaking quietly. I can't hear her; the only word I pick up is 'detective' before she turns back to me.

'Would you mind coming with me, please? We'll get you into a private room and someone will be along to speak to you.'

She flashes an access card at a reader on the wall and presses some keys on a silent keypad. I hear the locks go back and I walk through the door. It swings shut behind me with a heavy *clunk*, and I wonder if that is the last time I will walk freely and voluntarily through a door. I feel my body sway, and the police officer grabs my arm.

'Are you okay?' she asks. 'No, clearly not. You're very pale, and I can feel you're shaking. Let's get you sat down.'

She leads me into a small room, and I slump down in the nearest chair.

'I'm going to leave you here for a few minutes while I get you something to drink. Tea, coffee, water?'

I shrug. 'Anything,' I say. It seems too big a decision.

'Are you hungry? It's okay. You don't have to answer. I'll bring you a sandwich.'

I don't know why she is being so nice to me. I want to shout that I'm a murderer and I don't deserve her concern. But walking into the police station has taken every ounce of energy I had, and my limbs feel weak and floppy.

She smiles at me and uses her card to get out of the room. The door closes behind her, and I hear it lock.

Tom had decided he should call Philippa Stanley and lay out the facts as he knew them, making Nathan the source of the information and leaving Jack out of it altogether. He was about to pick up his phone when it rang.

'That was quick, Becky. What have you found out about the Atwells?'

'Nothing yet. That's not why I'm calling. I thought you should know that Callie Baldwin has just walked into divisional HQ.'

'*What?* Bloody hell, that's a turn-up. Right. I guess you're on your way over there now to interview her. I know I've not been involved in the case, but she has links to the Atwell couple. I'm on my way to you, and I'll call when I'm in the car to fill you in on what I know – or suspect.' Tom was rushing around his kitchen, picking up his keys, grabbing his jacket from the back of a chair, pushing his personal mobile into his pocket. 'I've another call to make first. Go and see her, but hang fire on the questioning if you can. Okay?'

Becky agreed, but he could hear the puzzled note in her voice. He didn't have time to explain and needed to speak to Jack.

He ran out to the car, jumped into the driving seat and threw his phones into the well in the central console, where they would automatically connect to the Bluetooth system.

As he reversed his car out of the drive, he tried Nathan's number while at the same time working out the best route at this time of night from his home to divisional HQ on the opposite side of Manchester.

His call went straight to voicemail. For a moment Tom was irritated that Nathan might have switched his phone off; the next second he was furious. He would bet money that Jack and Nathan had ignored him and were somewhere in the grounds of the Atwell property. That was why Nathan wasn't picking up, and he was sure Jack would be behind that decision.

'You stupid, irresponsible idiot.' Tom gripped the steering wheel tightly and fought the temptation to take his irritation out on his accelerator pedal. He was torn. Should he prioritise interviewing Callie Baldwin, who was safe in Becky's hands, or should he stop his reckless brother from being arrested if, as Tom suspected, he would very soon be forced to send a team out to the property where Jack was illegally lurking?

He was about to swing onto the motorway, but at the last

minute he carried on round the roundabout. He was nearer to the Atwell house, so he would have to leave Callie with Becky for now.

He used his work phone to call her. 'Becky, I've been side-tracked so it'll probably be an hour before I get to you. You can't wait for me – you've got a tricky situation there. Are you okay to handle it?'

'Of course, but what's going on, Tom?'

'Nathan Gardner has been doing his own investigating, and I think I know who the woman with the silver hair might be. I think Callie knows her too. So ask her about Thea and Garrick Atwell. That's the priority. Ask what she knows about them; forget about Ian Fullerton for the moment. Call me when you've got anything.'

He cut Becky off and gave in to the temptation to put his foot down.

61

Tom slowed down as he turned into the leafy lane that led to the Atwell home. It wasn't yet six o'clock, but it was pitch dark outside and there was a fine mist in the air that meant he had to switch on the windscreen wipers for a moment, then off again as they dragged across the glass. He wished the weather would make its mind up and rain properly. Perhaps if it tipped down, Jack and Nathan might be less inclined to snoop around in the Atwells' grounds.

The houses on either side of the lane were well back from the road, but Tom could see patches of bright light shining through the hedges and shrubs that bordered each property. He could well afford to live somewhere like this, thanks to the money he had inherited when Jack 'died', but he didn't think he would want to. Each building seemed like an island, self-contained, with no connection to the outside world. He wondered for a moment if any of the residents knew their neighbours.

His satnav was telling him to turn down a narrow track, and he knew he was in the right place when he saw the car that had been parked on his drive a couple of hours ago. Nathan's hire car. As Tom had suspected, though, it was empty.

He pulled up behind it and switched off his headlights. What he really wanted to do was knock on the Atwells' door, announce himself and ask if they knew the whereabouts of Caroline Baldwin. They weren't to know that she had turned up. He could say they had been tracking her movements and understood she had become quite friendly with Thea on the trip to Myanmar.

It was an idea, but he would have a hell of a job justifying his actions later. And it could totally destroy the case against this couple if they had been involved in the assisted suicides of Jasmine DuPont and the woman on the golf course. For now he had to find Jack and get him out of there.

Tom walked to the entrance to the property. The grounds extended into the distance and must have covered at least a couple of acres. His brother could be anywhere.

'Bollocks,' he muttered.

It was too dark to see anything, and there wasn't a sign of life anywhere. He stepped back outside the gates, hoping that if he called Nathan he would get an answer this time, but before he had the chance, his phone vibrated in his hand. It was Becky.

'Any news?' he asked without preamble.

'You could say that! I don't know where you got your information from, Tom, but you're bang on the money. Callie's as nervous as hell and looks like she's going to fall over with exhaustion, but I'll deal with that later. I didn't have to ask her about Thea and Garrick Atwell. I asked her where she had been for the last few days, and she just came out with it. She's been staying with them.'

'Staying with them? What, as a friend? As a paying guest? What, exactly?'

'It's complicated, but she said they were helping her out after the trouble she'd been having with Ian – which is something of an understatement. I obviously need to delve into that a lot more, but you thought the Atwells were a priority, and Callie isn't going anywhere so I let her talk. Tom, it sounds bad. She's been living in their cellar. And not just her. She says there are two other women there too. And one of them is called Hannah.'

'Oh God, I had a feeling this was where it was leading. Okay, we need to get a team here as soon as we can. Did she say if the other girls were safe?'

'She thinks so, but she said there might be a third woman

somewhere in the house too. This woman's husband came looking for her, and Thea Atwell told him she was refusing to see him. Callie says she's never seen the other woman, but she thinks her name is Judith.'

Tom stood still and thought for a moment.

'Isn't that the name of the woman we found on the golf course?'

'No, you were right about the surname, but her first name was Julie. Callie has no idea where this Judith might be, or even if she's definitely there. She says the house is like a rabbit warren, and there are areas she was never allowed to enter, even when she was cleaning.'

Tom had a stream of questions that he wanted to ask. But he didn't have time. He needed to get into that house, and he couldn't do it alone.

'Becky, I need you to be the one to call this in. Would you mind repeating what Callie told you? Use that as the basis for getting the team out here. Let Control know I'm on my way to the scene – not that I'm here already – and I'll meet them outside the property. We may need to force entry, and we'll need a crime-scene manager. See if you can get Jumbo. Oh, and it would be sensible to have an ambulance standing by too. We've no idea what we're going to find. No sirens. I'll brief them when they're en route.'

He could sense the unasked questions coming down the phone line, but there would be time to answer them all later. Right now he didn't want to muddy the waters, and he needed to find Jack and get him well away from the place before anyone else arrived.

62

I look up as the heavily pregnant detective inspector comes back into the room. I don't understand what is going on, because she hasn't spoken to me about Ian at all yet. She only wanted to know where I have been hiding, and then she disappeared, saying she needed to make a call.

I felt a stab of guilt when I told her about Thea and Garrick. Their behaviour since I killed Ian has freaked me out, but before that they were so kind to me, especially Thea. And then I remember the doctor and his 'trust' exercises and I start to shiver again.

The inspector takes a seat.

'Thanks for telling me about Thea and Garrick Atwell. My boss, DCI Douglas, is putting everything together now so we can get into the house and make sure the women you told me about are all okay. As soon as I know anything, I'll tell you. But first, can you explain how you came to be staying with the Atwells?'

I tell my story: how I lost my job and had tried to end my relationship with Ian, and the way Thea had come to my rescue. I don't know how much to say. Should I ask for a solicitor?

'Ian wasn't an easy man,' I say, knowing it is a huge understatement. But I don't want to sound as if I am making excuses for what I did. 'He could be particularly vitriolic.'

The inspector pulls a face. 'Yes, we know that. We read some of the emails.'

I'm shocked by this, although I don't know why. Of course they will have been looking into our history to see what drove me to do what I did.

'I'm sorry, but should I have a solicitor with me? Shouldn't I be cautioned?'

The inspector gives me a puzzled frown. 'Why would you think that?'

I am not sure I'm supposed to say this out loud. I'm fairly certain that I'm not supposed to admit to anything, but as I've no intention of denying it, it doesn't really matter.

'I'm here to hand myself in. I killed Ian. I don't remember doing it, but I've seen the crime-scene tape, and I've seen the posters with my face on. That's why I'm here. I can't hide any longer.'

She's staring at me now as if I have completely lost it.

'Callie, Ian isn't dead. We thought *you* were dead.'

I don't know what to say.

'Ian is being held on remand. He's been charged with your murder.'

❖

Hannah was feeling worse. She and Rosa had run out of words, and the misery had intensified. The pains in her stomach had increased and her muscles kept cramping. With no energy, she lay there alternately shivering and sweating, feeling as if someone was driving a screwdriver into her skull.

Rosa had gone downhill too. She had thought she would be the less affected of the two because the doctor had changed her medication, but half an hour ago she had keeled over and was now lying at the foot of Hannah's bed.

'Rosa,' Hannah mumbled. 'You said we might have seizures. If one happens to you, what can I do?'

'Nothing,' she whispered. 'Don't hold me down. Don't put your fingers in my mouth. Try to get me on my side, if you can. But you can't really do anything.'

We're going to die here, Hannah thought. If Thea didn't come, they would starve.

Slowly, carefully, she twisted her body until she was sitting up on the bed. Rosa opened her eyes and looked at her, but said nothing. It was probably too much effort.

Hannah used the bedside table as support and eased herself to her feet. They needed water. They had to keep drinking, if nothing else. She lurched across the room, grabbing the door frame as she stumbled out into the corridor.

63

Tom's first responsibility was to the women inside this huge house, not to Jack. But there was nothing he could do to help them until the team arrived, and in the meantime he needed to track his brother down before the place was swarming with police. Jack's presence would be impossible to explain. However, Tom knew it would take a while for a team to be assembled – some planning would take place first, and that gave him a bit of time.

He had no idea how far into the grounds he could go before triggering the inevitable security lights, and it would be unprofessional of him to do anything that might compromise the actions of the support team when it finally arrived. He could walk around the perimeter, sticking to the bushes, but that would take too long.

'Bloody hell, Jack,' he hissed.

Suddenly the front of the house was bathed in a bright white light, and Tom saw a tall figure marching up the drive.

'*Shit!*'

Was it Nathan? The man didn't have Jack's relaxed gait, and there was a purpose to his stride that Tom didn't entirely like the look of. He was going to have to go after him. Sticking his redundant phones in the pockets of his jacket, he set off at a run.

Tom had no idea where Jack was but felt sure he would be close by, so as he ran he spoke in a voice that wasn't loud enough to be heard through the closed windows of the house but hopefully it would carry to where his brother was probably skulking in the shadows. 'You have to get out of here, Jack. *Now*. There's a team coming. Get the hell out. You'd better be bloody listening.'

Tom caught up with Nathan at the front door.

'What the fuck do you think you're doing?' He didn't try to hide his anger.

'If my sister's in there, I'm getting her out. It's got nothing to do with you, Tom. If the police can't deal with it, I will.'

'The police *are* dealing with it. We have a team on the way now. You're just buggering it all up.'

'Well, too late now,' Nathan said, raising his fist with the obvious intention of hammering on the door.

Tom grabbed Nathan's forearm. 'You are wilfully obstructing a police officer in the execution of his duty. Do you want me to arrest you?'

'Piss off, Tom. You're being ridiculous.'

'No, Nathan, I'm not. I know far more about what's going on here than you do, because I've been doing my job. And I know that barging in and alerting the Atwells to the fact that there's a problem could be far more dangerous to your sister than waiting for a team of men trained to deal with things like this. Do you want this to become a hostage situation? It's not what you think, Nathan. It's far worse. Come away from that door.'

Tom couldn't help thinking that Nathan was the tosser he had always believed him to be when they were younger, but it wasn't a helpful thought. He just needed to get him clear of the door.

'I've met these two. They're old, Tom. They're harmless.'

Tom wanted to tell him that the Atwells had very probably been involved in the deaths of two young women. Never mind the fact that they had another two women locked in their cellar and possibly a third held somewhere else. But that would be unprofessional and would probably result in Nathan beating the door down to get to Hannah.

'They're not harmless. But as far as we know, Hannah isn't in imminent danger. We need to be sure she stays that way.'

Nathan glared at Tom, his gaze unflinching. 'They'll have seen the security lights.'

'Let's hope not. No lights have come on in the rooms this side of the house. Maybe they live at the back. And I bet the lights trip every time a fox wanders by. If the Atwells are as old and doddery as you say, the worst they could have done is call the police or a security company. We're covered if that happens. You're with me. Come away from the door. Now, Nathan.'

'I'll give it thirty minutes. If your guys are not here by then, I'm kicking that bloody door in whether you like it or not.'

That wasn't going to happen, but Tom knew that to threaten him with arrest again would just wind him up further. So he simply stared back until Nathan turned and started down the path.

Tom caught up with him. 'Where the hell is Jack? He needs to be out of here.'

'He's waiting over there.' Nathan pointed to a thick clump of bushes.

Tom nodded and jogged to where Nathan had indicated. But there was no sign of Jack. He turned and looked at Nathan.

'If he's not there, I don't know where he is. He's your brother, Tom, and you know what he's like. He'll be doing his own thing.'

That was exactly what Tom was worried about.

64

I'm still struggling to take in what the inspector has told me. Ian has been arrested and charged with my murder, although he denies he ever touched me. The poster I saw in the shop was there because they hadn't found my body and were obliged to try to find me in case Ian had been telling the truth.

I didn't kill him. I didn't even hurt him. I didn't go back to the house after the fight. Thea and the doctor had lied to me. But why? And why did the police think Ian had killed me?

'We had a tip-off from a neighbour. She said there was a massive argument, and she saw blood on your clothing. She was sure he'd hurt you. She thought she heard Ian shout that he wanted you dead, so she'd gone round the next day to see if you were okay. Ian told her you'd gone for good and gave her a mouthful of abuse.'

This doesn't surprise me.

'And you had called us only days previously because you had locked yourself in the bathroom, scared he was going to attack you.'

Oh God! I had forgotten about that. I could see how it had all added up in their minds.

I remember a woman walking past as I hurled things out of the window – she must have been the one to call the police. And suddenly there's something else in that image too. Thea wasn't in the car all the time I was in the house; she was on the drive when I started to chuck Ian's clothes out. At the time I had thought she was coming to my rescue, but she had scurried back to her car.

Did she take the claw hammer from the garage then? The door was open, I remember that.

'We found blood at the scene, and it matched yours,' the inspector says.

'I cut my hand,' I say, holding up my damaged palm, which still has a plaster on it.

'There was so much evidence pointing to Ian's guilt,' she says. I can see she is uncomfortable. 'The blood wasn't just in the house, it was on some of his clothes and in the boot of the car. We assumed he had taken your body somewhere.'

I remember seeing the red stains on his grubby T-shirts as I threw them out of the window. And I had rooted around in the car, trying to find my boots.

'My hand bled so much, and I couldn't stop it. My heart was really pumping that day. I have never been in such a rage in my life, so I guess my blood pressure was through the roof.'

The inspector gives me a sympathetic smile. 'They probably laced your food or drink with something designed to fire you up, make you angry. Why did you think you had killed him, though?'

I explain about waking up in the bath and not being able to remember a single thing that had happened.

She shakes her head. 'I suspect they used a drug called sco-polamine on you as well. It makes you compliant, but you forget everything you've done.'

We're both quiet for a moment as I take in the horror of what has been happening to me, and what could have happened had I stayed in that cellar.

The inspector continues: 'The evidence against Ian stacked up further when we found the emails – all of them antagonistic, to say the least. Another neighbour – an older man – came forward to say that he had heard Ian shouting at you and witnessed a seri-ous argument. So we had the blood, the aggression, the shouting, the abusive emails – and you were missing. Your phone hadn't been used; you hadn't withdrawn any money from your personal account or bought anything on a credit card; your car was in the drive, and your passport was in the house. We had to arrest him.'

'What will happen to him now?'

'The CPS will have to be told. We'll need to take a statement from you, saying where you were and why you didn't come forward. Then they will take him to a magistrate to secure his release.'

I shiver at the thought of what Ian has been through. I despise him for the way he treated me, but I know how I felt when I thought I was his murderer and was going to prison for a long time. How much worse to be arrested, knowing that despite all the things you *had* done, this was the one thing that you hadn't.

'So Thea and Garrick wanted me to believe I had killed Ian just so that they could control me?'

'I assume so. If you thought you were wanted for murder you would stay with them – possibly forever. They probably chose you because you were going through a tough time. From what we know of them, that seems to be their modus operandi – to seek out vulnerable young women.'

The thought of the Facebook post that had lost me my job and drove me to staying with them springs into my head.

'I always thought the Facebook post that got me the sack had been written by Ian – an act of revenge because I was going to throw him out. And if it wasn't him, I thought it might have been a man I met on the boat in Myanmar, although I couldn't think why he would do such a thing. It never occurred to me to suspect Thea, even though I found her waiting for me in my cabin more than once. I didn't think she would know how to use Facebook.'

The inspector raises her eyebrows and I realise how naive that thought was.

'I'm sorry, Callie, but I think you were targeted from the start. I can't tell you much about our ongoing investigation, but after they managed to convince you that you had killed Ian, what did your daily life consist of?'

I think back to the brief time I was in the cellar and the devastation I felt. For the first time I begin to imagine how the other two must feel after months of living there, so I tell Becky about the drugs I'm sure we were given, although fortunately for me I wasn't on them long enough to become addicted. I talk about the cleaning, the ironing, taking care of the couple. I don't tell her about the doctor and the treatment sessions, though. Especially the last one. I will have to, I suppose, but I'm not quite ready. Every now and again, through the mist of my anger and revulsion at everything that happened, I see Thea's kind face on the boat as she helped me through such a dreadful time.

And then I think about Hannah and the other woman.

'Can I ask you a question? Do you know if a baby called Albie was kidnapped some time around November last year? That's what they said Hannah had done, but she can't remember.'

The inspector shakes her head. 'Nothing springs to mind, but I'll check it out.' She swivels a laptop to face me. 'DCI Douglas, my boss, asked me to look into Thea and Garrick Atwell. I'm going to share this with you because it's the result of a Google search and not restricted information. Did you know that Garrick was a psychiatrist?'

I nod. 'Retired, I think, but he still liked to practise on all of us women.'

'Not retired, Callie. Struck off. Read this article. It was only written last year, but it exposes malpractice over the last fifteen years. A number of psychiatrists were named. Garrick Atwell is one of them. I'll leave it with you.'

I see sympathy in her eyes as she leaves the room. She must know something about Garrick's methods. I look away from her pity, and I begin to read.

The piece begins with information about his training and

background. It takes a while to get to the meat of the article, which focuses on statements from several patients. Each in turn comments on Dr Atwell's obsession with trust, the treatments that he prescribed and how he encouraged them to loosen or even remove their clothes during a session, to free them from restraint, encourage self-respect and demonstrate their trust.

A shudder runs through my body. I think of myself lying on his couch, listening to his words wash over me, telling me to loosen the cord of my tracksuit bottoms. I want to stop reading, but I can't.

"My actions have been taken totally out of context," Dr Atwell said when interviewed. "Trust is an essential part of any close relationship and all barriers have to be broken down. I am writing a thesis on the subject, and I am confident that I can prove my point. I will continue with my work, using willing volunteers who are happy to put their faith in me."

I wasn't a willing volunteer, though. If I had decided to stay, I would have been forced to become a guinea pig for the good doctor and a servant for his wife. I feel a lurch in my stomach, and for a moment I think I am going to be sick. But then the last sentence catches my eye and drives all other thoughts from my head.

Garrick Atwell lives in south Manchester. He has never married.

65

The track leading to the Atwell house was silent. A breeze rustled the dry leaves of the tall beech hedge that bordered the property. In the distance Tom heard the bark of a fox. Despite the impressive house and its beautiful grounds, it felt like a lonely, isolated place.

Tom had banished Nathan to his hire car, parked at the end of the lane that led to the track and far enough away from the gates not to be seen. He wasn't as far away as Tom would have liked, but Nathan had refused to leave. Only Tom's insistence that he could compromise Hannah's rescue had any impact and had finally persuaded him to keep out of the way.

Tom paced up and down the track. There was no sign of Jack. He didn't know whether his brother was still hiding somewhere or if he had heard Tom's warning and disappeared. He could only hope so, because the grounds of the house would inevitably be searched, and if he was there, he would be found. Jack was good, but the police should – at least in theory – be better.

The lights of several vehicles were approaching. There were no sirens, no flashes of blue to brighten the black sky, but Tom knew the support team had arrived. Following the two lead vans was an ambulance, which he sincerely hoped they weren't going to need. The lights were masked from the house by a thick hedge, and as soon as the vehicles grew close they were switched off and the track was plunged back into darkness, quiet again. Only the soft clicks of van doors being opened and the dull thuds of feet hitting the ground penetrated the silence.

The sergeant heading up the team jumped out of the front of

the van and approached Tom. He had been briefed en route but needed to get the lie of the land.

Keeping his voice low, Tom spoke quickly as the two of them edged towards the entrance to the drive, keeping close to the bushes.

'The crime-scene manager is on his way, but he's a bit behind you. We're expecting there to be two elderly people inside, and I have no reason to suspect they're armed. As you know, we think there are two women in the cellar, probably locked in, and there may be another woman somewhere else in the house, but we don't know where.'

The sergeant nodded. He was listening closely to what Tom was saying, but his eyes were all over the place, taking in access points to the property and looking for any potential hazards.

'We tried to get some details of the layout,' the sergeant said, 'but it seems the Atwell family have owned this property for years, so there are no handy estate agents' plans and we haven't been able to get our hands on anything else that might help.'

'DI Robinson asked Callie Baldwin about the layout. Apparently at this time of night the couple would normally be having a pre-dinner drink in the drawing room, which is the window at the front of the property on the right.' Tom pointed to the room in question. 'There hasn't been a light showing there, although it's possible they have thick curtains. It's equally possible that Baldwin escaping from the house has put the wind up them. They could have absconded, abandoned everything. Callie was inevitably going to discover that she hadn't killed her boyfriend and then it would have been only a matter of time before she reported them.'

The sergeant nodded. 'Anything else we should know?'

'The Atwells' bedroom is on the first floor at the back of the house. The entrance to the cellar is in something that looks like a cupboard, halfway down the long corridor that runs from the side door towards the entrance hall.'

Tom glanced over his shoulder to where the team were silently and efficiently preparing the equipment they would need to enter the premises.

'We need multiple points of entry,' the sergeant said. 'We'll enter via the main door as well as the side and back doors. We need to get up the drive as quickly and quietly as possible, so we'll keep off the gravel until the last moment, and entry through all access points will be simultaneous.'

'Okay. The women are the priority, of course.'

'Absolutely. Some of my men are tasked with locating the cellar and getting the women out. The rest will secure the other rooms and locate any other occupants.'

Tom turned back towards where a group of around ten black-clad men in protective gear waited in silence, several of them carrying forcible-entry tools. They stood straight, legs planted firmly apart, and Tom imagined the adrenaline pumping through their systems, as it was pumping through his.

The sergeant walked back to his men and spoke quietly. Tom saw several nods before the sergeant turned back towards the house. He held out a radio to Tom. 'We'll let you know when we're in.' He signalled to his men, and as a group they disappeared between the gate posts into the dark night. Tom could hear the faint swish of fabric on fabric as their arms and legs pumped them across the grass by the side of the drive, but nothing more.

This was the worst part. Events were out of Tom's hands for now, and all he could do was stand quietly by and wait. The ambulance was waiting too, the paramedics both out of their vehicle and pacing up and down. They, like Tom, wanted things to move. He glanced towards the end of the track and thought about the car parked down the lane. He knew Nathan would be watching, wanting to be there with the team to see if his sister was alive.

Suddenly the security lights came on and illuminated the front of the house. Within seconds there was an explosion of sound – booms, as not just one door, but two or possibly three were smashed open. Loud shouts of 'Police! Police!' ripped through the night air.

Tom didn't need to wait for any radio message to let him know they were in. He set off at a run up the drive. Lights were going on all over the house, and he hoped and prayed that the women were safe.

By the time he reached the side door the noise had died down. Inside, officers were swarming along corridors and running up and down stairs.

'Have we found anyone?' Tom asked the sergeant.

'We've found the door. We're going to have to break it down. They're going in now.'

Tom heard the officers shouting to anyone on the other side of the door to move away, and then there was another loud boom as the door to the cellar was broken down. Tom rushed towards the entrance as two men raced down the stairs.

The sergeant's radio crackled into life. 'Ambulance needed. Woman down, unconscious.'

Tom desperately wanted to get into the cellar, but there were two officers down there and this was a crime scene, so until Jumbo arrived the priority had to be to get the women out.

'Is the other woman okay?' the sergeant said into his radio. There was a crackle before Tom heard the answer: 'There's only one woman here, Sarge. Nobody else.'

66

When Becky returned to the interview room, she wasn't entirely surprised to see Callie with her arms wrapped around herself as if she was trying to keep warm. Her face had a grey, defeated look to it.

'Are you okay, Callie? Are you feeling ill?'

'Yes, mainly because of what I've just read.'

Becky felt a pang of guilt. The article about Garrick was on Google for the world to see, though, and in spite of all that had happened to Callie, Becky felt she was still conflicted. The last few days may have been hell, but prior to that she had seen Thea and Garrick Atwell as her saviours and was struggling to balance the bad against the good. Becky needed her onside – to give them every piece of information they might need to convict the couple for their crimes.

'I'm sorry, but I thought you deserved to know.'

Callie shrugged. 'What a bastard. I never liked his so-called treatment sessions, but I accepted them because I believed I was such an evil person.'

There was nothing that Becky could say to that, so she changed the subject.

'I've found an answer to your question about Albie. There were no babies reported missing in the period you mentioned, but we think we know what happened. DCI Douglas says you met Hannah's brother.'

Callie looked at Becky with startled eyes. 'Yes, he was the man I thought was a bit dodgy on the boat. How did your boss know that?'

'It's a long story. It seems we've managed to access Hannah's texts. One was sent to Albie's parents resigning without notice. They were furious. That was the day she went missing – but she didn't take Albie.'

'*Bastards!*' Callie repeated. 'I bet Thea sent the text to stop them from wondering what had happened to Hannah when she didn't turn up for work.'

Bastards indeed, Becky thought.

'Do you mind if I ask you about the third woman – the one you've never seen, but you think might be somewhere in the house?' Becky asked, trying to move Callie on. 'Judith, you think she is called?'

'I don't know much. Garrick called us all Judith, supposedly because he found it easier, but there was more to it than that. It felt as if we were all somehow stand-ins for the real Judith. Apparently I look a bit like her, although the others don't look at all like me.'

'I doubt any of you were chosen for your looks – your similarity was possibly just a happy coincidence. Now we know a bit more about the Atwells, it's almost certain that the key criterion was vulnerability. Do you think the original Judith could have been Garrick's lover?'

Callie shrugged again. 'I don't know. I think she might be Thea's younger sister, although I don't suppose that rules her out as a lover. It said in the article that Garrick had never married, but he and Thea appeared to share a bed. So I guess she must have been under his spell too.'

Becky was silent as she processed everything Callie had just told her. She knew exactly what the relationship between the Atwells was and had called Tom to share the information. For the moment she thought it better if Callie didn't have any other revelations to contend with.

'Why do you think she was Thea's sister?'

'In the house there was a photograph of two women taken

in the seventies. The names on the back were Thea and Judith Atwell. Not that it proves anything. They could have been cousins, I suppose. Judith looked about fifteen years younger than Thea. I had no idea there was anyone else in the house until Judith's husband came looking for her – Vincent, he was called – but Thea wouldn't let him past the hall.'

Callie explained how Thea had reacted to Vincent's arrival, repeating everything she could remember about the shouting match that had taken place.

If Callie had remembered the conversation correctly and Vincent hadn't seen his wife for a year, Becky realised there was something she needed to do.

'That's really useful, Callie, but I'm afraid it means I'm going to have to leave you again briefly. I'm sorry, but I need to see if we can track Vincent down. While you wait I'm arranging for you to have a bit more than a sandwich to eat. There's a hot meal on its way, and one of my colleagues will sit with you to keep you company. I won't be long.'

❖

Becky lumbered up the stairs, determined not to resort to the lift until she absolutely had to, and sat down at her computer. She was hoping to hear from Tom about progress at the scene and couldn't help wishing she was there by his side, although she wasn't sure how much use she would be with Buster – as her partner Mark had started to call the baby – on board.

Instead of the rush she would be feeling if she was there, she had the joyous task of hunting down Judith's husband, although it wouldn't take long. They knew more about the Atwell family than she had let on to Callie, and it was relatively easy to locate the address and phone number of Vincent.

'Vincent Bickerton? This is Detective Inspector Robinson of the Greater Manchester Police. I wonder if you could give me a little information. It's about your wife, Judith.'

'What's happened to her? Is she okay?' There was no mistaking the panic in his voice.

'Can I ask when you last saw her, Mr Bickerton?'

She heard what sounded almost like a moan from the other end of the line. 'I don't know why you're asking questions unless something's up. It's nearly a year since she went, and I still don't believe it.'

'Went where, sir?'

'Her sister had a fall, and Judith went to help out. I knew it was a mistake and that Thea wanted her to move in with them. She couldn't manage the house any more, you see. She wanted a free housekeeper, and Judith was always so willing, so happy to help.'

'But your wife didn't come home?'

'I *begged* her not to go. I knew that weird bastard Garrick would fill her head with rubbish, make her feel guilty about leaving them. And now she's refusing to see me. Thea says Judith's told her she never wants to see me again.'

Becky heard Vincent Bickerton's voice break.

'Why do you think she won't talk to you, Mr Bickerton?'

'I think they've twisted her mind. They'll have convinced her that their need is greater than mine. I don't know. They're incredibly persuasive. Somehow they have the ability to make you fall under their spell – to make you trust them. And then you learn the truth. They're not who you think, you know.'

67

Tom barely had time to register the fact that only one woman had been found in the cellar when there was a shout from upstairs. An officer was leaning over the balustrade.

'Sir, you need to get up here. Now, sir.'

Tom ran along the corridor to where the staircase curved up towards the first floor, taking the stairs two at a time.

A door part-way along the corridor stood open. Two officers stood by it, their arms hanging by their sides. Whatever lay within clearly offered no danger, and one of them turned to Tom as he approached.

'Ben's gone in, sir. But we thought one of us was enough.'

The men stood to one side so that Tom could see into the room. A large bed stood facing the door. Two people lay on the quilted cover, fully clothed. A thin young woman with long dark hair was standing at the end of the bed, holding on to the brass bedstead with both hands as if she needed the support.

'I remembered the number,' she said. 'I remembered it. We had no food, Thea. You forgot to feed us. We were hungry. We needed a cup of your tea.' She was staring at the people on the bed, rambling – incoherent phrases mingled with short sentences.

Tom spoke quietly to one of the officers. 'Get her out of there, will you? Gently as you can. And get a paramedic up here.'

The officer nodded and approached the girl. 'Come on, love. Let's get you downstairs.'

There was a sudden shout from below and Tom's head whipped round.

'Have you found my sister? *Hannah! Hannah!* She's my sister. Let me through!'

'Bollocks,' Tom said to nobody in particular. 'That's all we need.'

The girl lifted her head, a puzzled frown between her eyes. 'Nathan?' she whispered.

'Take her down, and get that bloody idiot out of here. He must *not* come up here under any circumstances, and if he argues, arrest the stupid bugger.'

Tom wanted to go down and give Nathan Gardner an earful, but he couldn't take his eyes off the two people on the bed. The officer named Ben was crouching by the side of the elderly woman, taking her pulse. He looked at Tom and shook his head.

'Okay,' Tom said. 'Better come out of the room, then. Let's get a paramedic up to confirm it. Both of them, I presume?' The officer nodded. 'Then let's get the crime-scene boys in here.'

'I'm right behind you, Tom.'

For such a big man, Jumbo could move very quietly. Without taking his eyes off the bodies on the bed, Tom spoke. 'Jesus, Jumbo. I've seen some things in my time, but this feels like one of the worst.'

Jumbo stood close to him in the open doorway, their shoulders touching. Neither had anything more to say.

The two elderly people on the bed were holding hands. Matching gas cylinders sat on the floor on either side of the bed, each with a tube leading to a bag firmly fixed in place with parcel tape. The pressure of the gas after all breathing had ceased had caused both bags to split, and Tom could see the features of the man and the woman through the clear plastic, where it had settled onto their faces. The wrinkled polythene clung to the protruding noses, to the lips where they had breathed their last breaths, and to the tears he was certain he could see on the old woman's cheeks.

❖

In the wide corridor behind where Tom and Jumbo were still standing, the crime-scene team were suited up ready to enter the room, waiting for formal confirmation of life extinct, although there was little doubt in anyone's mind.

The young paramedic spoke quietly to Tom, confirming both Thea and Garrick Atwell were dead.

'As I was checking her pulse, I noticed a piece of paper protruding from under the old lady's pillow. Thought you might like to know,' he added, his voice hushed and slightly croaky. For men used to far more bloody scenes, these two deaths seemed to have affected them all with their sense of hopeless surrender.

Tom looked at Jumbo and raised his eyebrows. The big black man nodded and signalled with his eyes for one of his team to retrieve the note. He placed it inside a clear plastic bag and brought it back to Tom.

Tom took it from him. It didn't say much, but it seemed to have been written by Thea.

Please rescue Judith and transfer her remains to their rightful place. Don't think badly of him. He didn't mean to do it. He went too far, but only because he loved her and wanted her to stay.

Tom read it again, out loud, to Jumbo. 'Judith was her sister,' he added for the crime-scene manager's benefit.

'Sounds like we've got a body to find somewhere, that's clear enough. It would have helped if she'd told us where to look. I wonder how he killed her.'

'At least one of them was quite a specialist in drugs,' Tom said. 'I would guess he had the knowledge and she administered them. Maybe that's what she means by "He went too far". We're not going to know until we find her body, I don't suppose.'

'So the husband killed her, and the wife's been living with that dreadful knowledge ever since.'

It said a lot about their lives and their jobs that Jumbo neither blinked nor commented when Tom responded, 'He's not her husband; he's her brother.'

68

Becky was exhausted. All she wanted was to finish processing Callie Baldwin's statement, go home, have a warm bath and go to bed. Mark would fuss over her, making her cocoa and toast, and she would revel in every moment of it.

She had finished preparing the paperwork. She had to get it signed, then they could call it a night. She opened the door to the interview room where Callie was slumped in a chair, looking as if her body had been drained of blood.

'I think we're done, Callie. You've been amazingly helpful, and I'm so sorry that you've had such a terrible time. We can arrange for you to see someone, to help you come to terms with it. Your house is no longer a crime scene, so I can get someone to take you home if you prefer? You can't take Thea Atwell's car. You understand that, don't you?'

'I don't want to touch anything Thea's had her grubby fingers on ever again,' Callie said, a shudder running through her body. 'And I'd prefer to go straight home, please, if that's okay.'

Becky reached out and touched Callie's clenched fist where it lay on the table. There was something else she needed to say, and she wasn't sure how Callie would take it. While Becky had been preparing Callie's statement, she had heard from Tom. He had told her what had happened at the house, and they had decided Callie should know. It would be all over the press tomorrow anyway.

'The good news is that, thanks to you, both the other girls have been rescued. They've been drugged for a lot longer than you, so they're suffering from withdrawal symptoms. But they're on their way to hospital and doing well. Hannah has been reunited with her brother, who sends his apologies for – in his words – "being a dick in Burma".'

That at least brought a brief smile to Callie's lips.

'Did they find Judith?' she asked.

'No. Not yet.' There was no point telling her about Judith until they knew more. A team would be there from first light, complete with cadaver dogs, to see if she was in the grounds somewhere.

'What's going to happen to Thea and Garrick?'

Becky took a deep breath. 'I don't know how you're going to feel about this, Callie. I have to tell you that they're both dead.' For a second Callie stared at her, then her eyes filled with tears. 'I'm sorry. I should have realised it would upset you.'

Callie shook her head. 'I'm not upset. I'm relieved. I'll never have to see them again, and at least they can't hurt anyone else now.' She brushed the tears from her cheeks with the back of her hand. 'Who killed them? That man Vincent?'

'They took their own lives, sadly.'

'It's not sad,' Callie said with conviction. 'They controlled us. The doctor played with our minds and then offered a "solution" to anyone who thought her life had no purpose. I didn't get it to start with. I didn't understand the allusions to an alternative, even though Hannah practically spelled it out to me. The doctor was always talking about whether I was any use to the world, and if I wasn't, then why should I take up space. I think he convinced some women to take the easy way out – a clean and painless death when they ceased to dance to his tune. They could hardly allow them to return to the real world, could they? For some of the poor souls, it was the best option. To be honest, if I'd had to stay there for much longer, I think it might have become my choice too. I wonder how many he helped to die?'

'We know of two, but there may be more from his days as

a practising psychiatrist. We're going to have to go through records from years ago, and that will take time.'

Callie slumped back in the chair, her burst of energy spent.

'It's over now, Callie. You can go home and forget all of this.'

Callie's face closed in. 'Not really. What about Ian? You're going to have to let him out – I get that – but how am I going to get rid of him?'

Becky felt for the girl. This is where it had all begun: Ian refusing to leave, not contributing in any way, threatening Callie and making her life miserable.

'Although his emails were threatening, he didn't actually say he was going to kill you. If he had, we would have been able to charge him with threats to kill, and a judge could issue a restraining order. But without that we can't, I'm afraid. I think you're going to have to get an injunction, but that can take time.'

Callie's eyes flooded with tears. 'I don't want to see him again. Not ever. You don't know him. He'll be the one feeling hard done by. He'll see himself as the victim, and it will all be my fault. He's not going to listen to reason, and if *you* can't stop him from coming back, what chance have I got?'

Becky knew that the hands of the police were tied. All they could do was offer support.

'Okay, so here's what I suggest,' she said. 'Ian's not going to be out until tomorrow. Get your locks changed first thing, and that will keep him out while you get your injunction. In the meantime, we'll have a word with him. We'll advise him to stay away from the house or we might have to arrest him to prevent a breach of the peace. That might make him pause for thought. Hopefully it will be enough to put him off. I'll give you some contact information – people who will help you through the injunction process. Get a good night's sleep and sort it in the morning.'

Becky could see the relief in Callie's eyes and wished they could hold Ian Fullerton on remand for another couple of days to give her time to recover from her ordeal and begin to get her life back on track. But there was no way they could do that. The best thing she could do would be to organise a ride home for Callie and get herself away too.

Tomorrow was likely to be another long day.

69

Tom was beyond tired. He had been at the Atwell house all night, and had spent the morning filling in all the gaps. He needed some sleep and had left the team working at the scene, trying to find Judith's remains. They had called to report that they were now focusing on the rose garden.

Tom thought he had seen Jack briefly, standing at the end of the track as dawn broke, but as he made his way towards the figure, it had disappeared. Maybe Tom had imagined it, or perhaps he had just hoped that Jack was still around. He was relieved that his brother hadn't been picked up lurking in the grounds of the Atwell property, but he was sorry not to have said goodbye.

All he'd had was a text: 'I'm gone. Be seeing you, little brother.'

Tom had cursed Jack for a moment. Why did he always have to slip off into the shadows? Why could he never take his leave face to face? Tom had tried the mobile number the text had come from, but it was dead, so he had no choice but to wait to hear from him. He knew, though, that his brother would be watching, following the case, and would be expecting a message on Tom's computer. And he had a feeling Jack would be back.

Tom had also had heated words with Nathan Gardner before he disappeared in the ambulance with Hannah, berating him for being so irresponsible.

Nathan had looked at him in the usual way, his face devoid of any expression. 'You found my sister, Tom. For that I can't thank you enough. But I don't think I was irresponsible. It's a matter of perspective, and mine is different from yours.'

Tom remembered as a boy how he had occasionally wished he was big enough to punch Nathan for being such a supercilious know-all. Tom was certainly big enough now, but it wasn't in his nature to thump anyone without serious provocation, so he had walked away.

As he arrived home, desperate for a hot shower and to pull the duvet over his head, the last thing he was expecting was to see a familiar car in his drive and the outline of someone sitting in the driver's seat. The engine was running quietly, no doubt to keep the heater going.

He opened the passenger door and crouched down. 'Louisa, why are you sitting out here? You should have let yourself in.'

'I wasn't sure if you would want to see me or if Jack was still here. I didn't want it to be awkward for you.'

'Jack's gone for now, but I think he'll be back, although I've absolutely no idea when. I'm sorry you didn't get the chance to meet him properly, but he's a law unto himself. Always has been. Turn the engine off and come in. Of course I want to see you.'

The tiredness he had been feeling melted away as he wondered whether Louisa's visit was a good sign or a bad one.

He unlocked the door and stood back to let her pass. She headed straight for the kitchen, as he knew she would, but she didn't sit down.

'Would you like a cup of coffee? Something to eat?' Tom asked.

'Coffee would be great. Thank you.' She looked uncomfortable, something that was rare for Louisa. He decided not to rush her. She could say what she needed to in her own time. It was hard to talk over the grinding of the beans anyway.

When the coffee was made, Tom walked over to the island and touched Louisa's arm gently. 'Take a seat. Whatever you've come to say, it'll be okay. You're still allowed to sit down.'

Louisa took a deep breath.

'Tom, you know what I want from a relationship. I've never tried to hide it. Total trust and transparency is something that has come to mean so much to me, and although I realise few people ever experience it, it's always been my aim. Perhaps that's why I'm in my late thirties and still single. Perhaps I'm searching for the impossible.' She shrugged, a look of hopelessness on her lovely face.

There was nothing Tom could say. He had to wait, knowing he had failed to live up to her dreams.

'For someone so pragmatic, so capable of dealing with the horrors of life – and death – in my job, I have a streak of romanticism in me a mile wide. I want to look into my man's eyes and see not one glimmer of opacity. I want to be able to look straight into his heart, without a trace of a shadow between us.'

'I know. I get that.' And he did. He wasn't going to make excuses. He should either have told her everything, or explained that there was one secret in his life that was so big he couldn't share it, that it was nothing to do with her and wouldn't in any way impact on their relationship. Instead, he had allowed her to comfort him about the death of his brother, to speak words of reassurance, saying that although it would always hurt, it would become easier to deal with.

'The thing is, over the last day or so I've been thinking about the eyes I want to gaze into. And I realise that no matter what's happened – and honestly, I understand why you made the decisions you did – the eyes I want to see each morning when I open my own are yours.'

Tom was still for a moment. Louisa was smiling.

'This is where I want to be, Tom. With you. If you'll have me, my bags are in the car.'

He felt a stab of sheer joy. But she hadn't finished.

'I'm not apologising for walking out on you the other night, because I was being true to myself.' Louisa held her hand up, the palm open towards Tom. 'And I don't want you to apologise either. You were doing what you believed to be right.'

'Thank you.'

She leaned towards him. He lifted his arm and slipped it around her shoulders, pulling her closer.

'Just don't do it again,' she whispered into his ear.

Tom laughed and bent his head to kiss her gently. 'I won't.'

70

I can't believe the pleasure I feel at waking up in my own bed. I stretch out, then curl up. Pull the duvet up, wrap it around my body. It feels like heaven, and I start to believe that I will recover from the nightmare of the past few weeks. I have slept for twelve hours. It was midnight when the police dropped me off, and now I can see from the bedside clock that it is nearly noon.

All I remember is stumbling through the front door, kicking it closed behind me and crawling on hands and knees up the stairs, too tired to even walk. I stripped off my clothes and got into bed, filthy but too exhausted to do anything about it. I need a shower, but first I have to have some coffee.

I don't suppose there is any milk in the house, but there is bound to be coffee, and I can cope with drinking it black for once. I decide to get a cup now and think about going shopping and cleaning the house later. I don't care how long it takes. But I'll phone a locksmith before I go out. I suddenly feel empowered, as if I have reclaimed my life.

I know I should feel sorry for Ian. How awful for him to have been accused of killing me. How terrible to be held on remand. But I don't suppose he suffered any more than I did. Both of us believed we were facing a life sentence of one kind or another. I can't help wondering whether he's been released yet. I wonder how he reacted to being warned to stay away from me. Not well, at a guess.

I saunter down the stairs, thinking of what I'm going to do with my time. I need to get another job, of course, and now that it seems clear Thea was responsible for the Facebook post, Tim, my ex-boss, will have to admit that I did nothing wrong. I don't want to go back there, but at least I should get a reference.

I'm about three steps from the bottom of the staircase when I sense that something is wrong. I can neither hear nor smell anything out of the ordinary, and yet there is a sense that the air is thicker, heavier than it should be, as if something is dulling the hollow sound of an empty house.

I stop. The tune I was humming softly comes to an abrupt halt. Every hair on my arms is standing on end, the surface of my skin prickling.

'Don't stay out there,' a voice calls from the living room, a voice I had hoped never to hear again. 'Come in and say hello.' There is a false cheerfulness to his voice that chills me.

I don't know why I thought he wouldn't come back. I had assumed that not only would the warnings of the police be enough to keep him away, but this house must hold the worst possible memories for him – being handcuffed and led out in front of the staring neighbours, as I am sure was the case. Becky had told me to be vigilant and to bolt the door as soon as I got in, but I had thought of nothing apart from falling into bed. I thought he was still safely locked up and I had plenty of time to change the locks before he was released.

I was wrong. He is here now.

I creep down the last three stairs and push open the door to the living room with my toes. He's sitting in his favourite chair. His eyes are black flints, and I know every scrap of his pent-up anger is going to be directed at me. All I can think is that I need to keep the situation as calm as possible until I can get help.

'When did you get out?' I ask, hating myself for the shake in my voice.

'As if you care.'

'Ian, I am genuinely sorry that they thought you'd killed me.

I knew nothing about it because I was locked in a cellar, working as a skivvy in someone else's house.' I'm not intending to tell him that I believed I had killed him. 'As soon as I found out, I went to the police.' This isn't entirely true but close enough.

Ian says nothing. He just scowls.

'Would you like some coffee?' I ask, thinking that the only way to get through this is to try to be civilised until I can get dressed, get out of the house and work out – all over again – what I'm going to do.

'Yes. And make me a sandwich. I haven't eaten – the food in prison is shit.'

'I'll get dressed after my coffee and go shopping.' I'm keeping it normal. I need to be able to walk out of that door and have him believe I'm simply popping out to get him something to eat.

I manage to walk past him without getting close enough for him to touch me. It would be beyond my acting ability not to flinch if he did. The door between the kitchen and the living room stands open, and Ian starts to talk – or rather to shout, as he has his back to me. To my horror he is talking as if we are going to carry on living together – as if the events of the last few weeks have never happened. He's telling me I'd better get myself another job sharpish, and I need to get on to the police to see about getting the car back. He is enjoying the knowledge of what these words will be doing to me.

I switch the kettle on, not responding to a word he says. Then, from nowhere, I hear another voice in my head, one I want to forget.

Some people don't deserve to live, Judith. They occupy space on this earth and give nothing in return. You know who I mean. What does he bring to this world?

I didn't have an answer then, and I have less of one now. But the voice won't be quiet.

How did it feel to kill him, Judith? I imagine it felt good, knowing how much damage he had done to you. And he was waiting to do more. Just waiting – anticipating the moment when you felt the pain.

I want to tell the doctor to shut up and go away, but I'm back in his study, lying on his couch, clothes loosened, listening to his voice.

Talk to me about the moment you hit him, he's saying. *Imagine it again in your mind, knowing that the life of this worthless man is being snuffed out. Does it feel good?*

Even though I now know that I never touched Ian, apart from elbowing him in the stomach when I last visited, it *had* felt good, just for a moment, to think that he had got what he deserved.

I can only imagine the sense of euphoria – of release. With each blow the tentacles he had wrapped around you, growing tighter each and every day, suddenly slackened, loosened, finally fell away, and you were able to walk free. Was it the best moment of your life, Judith? I imagine it was. Trust me, Judith. You have to trust me. You did the right thing.

Ian is still shouting about all the things he has never had a chance to do, and how his short time in prison had shown him how much I owe him, and how he's going to make sure that I pay for what he has been through, because it was all my fault.

I know I should go upstairs, get dressed and call the police. But the doctor is still hissing in my ear.

Relive it, Judith. Lift that hammer high. Feel the swish of the air moving as it swings down, the sense of climax as you are released from Ian's control. The elation you feel as you wipe him out.

I stare at the knife block in front of me. Ian was warned not to come back here, to keep away from me. The police have seen his abusive emails, the threats. And yet here he is. He isn't going to go away. I will never be rid of him.

Do it, Judith. Do it again. Relive it.

I lift the meat cleaver out of the block. I walk back into the living room and stand behind Ian's chair. He hasn't heard me return. He is still shouting about what I am going to have to do, and his words wash over me like angry clouds, blackening the sky and everything beneath. I raise the cleaver in both hands, high above my head.

Then I repeat the words that the doctor made me say over and over again: 'My name is Judith. And I killed a man.'

A Letter to My Readers

Dear Reader

Thank you so much for taking the time to read *Come a Little Closer*. This story has been in my head for several years, and I loved writing it. I do hope you enjoyed reading it too.

The idea came to me on a trip to Myanmar, a wonderful country, although I'm pleased to say I didn't meet anyone like Thea or the doctor on my travels! My father was stationed there during the war. He went when he was just seventeen years old, and I often wonder how it must have felt to be in such an alien place before television had made everywhere seem so familiar. He was the inspiration for Pops.

I was pleased to be able to get my readers closer to Tom in this novel. I love his character more with every book, and I do hope that comes across in my words. His life isn't particularly extraordinary, but there is always something cropping up that lets us see his human side – either through his relationships or through his slightly dodgy but hopefully intriguing brother Jack. I love him too.

Of course the very best thing about publishing a book is getting a response from you – the reader – and I have been delighted by the amazing feedback I've received over the last seven years. I keep in touch with many of you through Facebook, Twitter and a newsletter that I send out regularly, in which I share some of the books I have enjoyed and host other writers talking about their novels. There is occasionally a competition (with, of course, a prize) and I love it when someone offers to be a featured reader and tells me all about where and when they like to immerse themselves in a book.

If you'd like to subscribe or be a featured reader, we'd be pleased to welcome you and keep you up to date with new releases, special offers and other goodies. Just go to www.rachel-abbott.com/contact and submit your details.

If you belong to a book club, I have included some reading group discussion notes on the following pages, or you can print them off online from the website if you would like to share them with your book-lover friends. I hope they get the conversation moving!

I'm going to be out and about at festivals and other events throughout the year – details on the blog and website and in the newsletter – and if you get a chance to get along to any of them, please come and say hello.

Of course, I'd love to know what you think about *Come a Little Closer*, so feel free to tweet me, leave me a message on Facebook or a review on Amazon. Every author loves getting reviews, and I'm no exception.

Thanks again for taking the time to read *Come a Little Closer*.

Best wishes

Rachel

Acknowledgements

My books would never make it into print without the help of so many people, and top of that list has to be my police adviser, Mark Grey. This last year has been particularly tough as I have had two books in development, both of which feature complex police issues, and he has never failed to respond to my questions with so much detail that he inspires me with new ideas. I love to get things right, but occasionally I do stray from reality to improve the story. No mistakes are the fault of Mark – they are all mine!

I also had a stellar team of researchers, who wandered around Pennington Flash taking photographs, drawing on maps and describing the sights, sounds and smells of the location. Judith, Dave, Josh and Alicia provided me with exceptional detail, although once again I may have deviated a little from the truth. So apologies to them and to the management of this beautiful country park for any inaccuracies.

Thanks must also go to Liam Feasey of Lextox in Cardiff for his help in explaining the drug analysis of hair samples. I had no idea it could be so detailed.

My early readers are the best. Not only do they let me know when things aren't as clear as I thought they were, but they make lots of very encouraging noises – just what every writer needs. In particular I would like to thank Maddalena, Harriet, Barbara, Emily, Ann, Kath and Judith.

'Team Abbott', as I call the highly prized group of people who help me to keep my head above water when I'm drowning in all the day-to-day tasks, have been as brilliant as ever. Tish McPhilemy continues to take on so many of the essential aspects of running a business, but perhaps more importantly she brightens my day with her wit and good humour. Molly Maine has joined the team this year, albeit mainly working from Thailand, and her work in marketing has been exceptional. Another year of being guided by publicist Maura Wilding has been as amazing as I knew it would be. The three of you are a joy to work with.

It is interesting to look back over the last seven years and consider the publishing decisions I have made. Without a doubt one of the best has been to sign with my incredible agent, Lizzy Kremer. I am so lucky to have her support and guidance and to be able to draw on the expertise of the whole team at David Higham Associates. Harriet Moore deserves a medal for her patience with this very demanding author, and thanks to the foreign rights team my novels are now available in over twenty languages.

I am blessed with great editors too. Clare Bowron gives superb editorial feedback and makes me realise when I have quite literally lost the plot. Hugh Davis – my copy editor – seems to find so many ways to improve my manuscript, and I always know my books are in good hands with him.

Finally, my thanks to John and the rest of my wonderful family for coping with someone who is only ever half with them, the rest of my mind almost always somewhere else. Your support means everything, and I couldn't do any of it without you all.

Reading Group Questions

Summary

Come a Little Closer tells the story of a young woman who turns to a person she trusts in a moment of need, and finds herself lost in a life she doesn't recognise but from which she can see no escape. But how did she get there?

Believing that she is never going to be able to rid herself of her boyfriend Ian, a man who has become increasingly manipulative in the time they have been together, she seeks refuge with an elderly couple she met on holiday until she can get her life back together again. But when she wakes up in the bath to find blood being washed from her body, she begins to think she is losing her mind. Is it true what they are telling her? Could she really have killed Ian?

As the story unfolds, the reader begins to understand that not only is our protagonist trapped, but there are two other women living down in the cellar where she is sent to hide. And they are both called Judith.

Come a Little Closer is a story about making poor judgements and not knowing who to trust – yourself, or those who are telling you what to do and who you are.

Discussion points

1   At the start of the book, Callie (at that point unnamed) meets Thea and the doctor. Are there any warning signs that they

are not the mild-mannered elderly couple they seem to be?

2   When Callie returns from her holiday and finds that Ian is refusing to move out, what options might she consider at that point, given that he is declaring a beneficial interest in her home? How might you have reacted?

3   When Tom Douglas discovers the body at Pennington Flash, what did you believe had happened to the girl? When you learned how she died, how did you feel about it?

4   When did you first start to be alarmed about Callie living in the house with Thea and Garrick?

5   After Callie returns to see Ian and throws his clothes out of the window, we realise that she has been given a drug designed to make her aggressive. What did you think about her reaction to Ian during that visit?

6   When Callie wakes up in the bath with Thea washing blood from her body, what did you think had happened?

7   Callie finds herself in the cellar with two other women who are both called Judith. What did you think was happening at that point? Why did you think they were they there?

8   Garrick says that trust is important in any relationship, and this is a theme throughout the book. Discuss the trust issues that arise between the various characters and how they might have been resolved.

9   How convinced were you that Callie killed Ian? If you thought that maybe she didn't, what did you think when she saw the crime scene tape?

10 Tom's brother, Jack, makes another appearance in this book. Discuss the dilemma that Tom always seems to find himself in when his brother turns up.

11 When Thea and Garrick stop visiting the women in the cellar what did you think might have happened? Were you surprised at the outcome?

12 Callie returns home, believing that Ian will be safely behind

bars until she can get the locks changed, but Garrick gets inside her head, and she raises a cleaver above Ian's head. Until this point how were you expecting the book to end?

13   What feelings did the book leave you with?

14   If you had the opportunity to ask the author a question about the book, what would it be?

Connect with Rachel Abbott

If you would like to be notified of any new books by
Rachel Abbott in the future, please visit
www.rachel-abbott.com/contact/ and leave your email address.

Twitter: www.twitter.com/RachelAbbott

Facebook: www.facebook.com/RachelAbbott1Writer

Website: www.rachel-abbott.com

Blog: www.rachelabbottwriter.com

The Sixth Window

Every instinct told her to run…

Natalie Gray is living a nightmare. She has discovered a disturbing website link on her new partner's computer and fears he has a dark side and even darker intentions. When her husband died in a hit-and-run accident, Ed had seemed like a safe harbour. Now where can she turn?

Concerned for the safety of her fifteen-year-old daughter Scarlett, she moves them both to a new home beyond his reach, unaware that this apartment holds secrets of its own. Left alone during the long days of the school holiday, Scarlett investigates strange sounds coming from the other side of the wall, never anticipating the danger that awaits her there.

DCI Tom Douglas's investigation into the apparent suicide of a teen-age girl draws him ever closer to Natalie and Scarlett. But will he be too late to protect them from the danger they face, or from the truths that will tear their lives apart?

Will they ever feel safe again?

"*The tension that built throughout this book simply blew me away.*"
– Angela Marsons, author of
Silent Scream

"*Masterly and compelling. I couldn't put it down until its heart-stopping conclusion.*"
– Robert Bryndza, author of
The Girl in the Ice

Also by Rachel Abbott

ONLY THE INNOCENT

A man is dead. The killer is a woman. But what secrets lie beneath the surface – so dark that a man has to die?

"This is an absolutely stunning debut novel from a writer with a gift for telling a tale. I can't wait for more!"
– Amazon Top 500 reviewer

THE BACK ROAD

A girl lies close to death in a dark, deserted lane. A driver drags her body to the side of the road. A shadowy figure hides in the trees, watching and waiting.

"A clever psychological crime and mystery novel."
– Little Reader Library

SLEEP TIGHT

How far would you go to hold on to the people you love…? Sleep Tight – if you can. You never know who's watching.

"Just when you think you've got it sussed, you'll find yourself screeching in frustration at your foolishness."
– Crime Fiction Lover

STRANGER CHILD

They say you should never trust a stranger. Maybe they're right.

"Rachel Abbott will keep you guessing long into the night and just as soon as you've figured it out…think again!"
– Suspense Magazine

NOWHERE CHILD

Someone is looking for Tasha. But does she want to be found? A standalone novella featuring the same characters as *Stranger Child*.

"The tension mounts to a high level as the hunted Tash desperately tries to avoid being captured."
– Cleo Loves Books

KILL ME AGAIN

When your life is a lie, who can you trust? Another woman will die soon, and it might be her.

"This fast paced thriller will have you racing right through to its shocking conclusion."
– Closer